Inheritance

Inheritance

LISA FORREST

ABC
Books

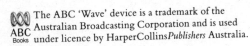 The ABC 'Wave' device is a trademark of the
Australian Broadcasting Corporation and is used
ABC under licence by HarperCollins*Publishers* Australia.
Books

First published in Australia in 2013
by HarperCollins*Publishers* Australia Pty Limited
ABN 36 009 913 517
harpercollins.com.au

HarperCollins*Publishers*
Level 13, 201 Elizabeth Street, Sydney NSW 2000, Australia
Unit D1, 63 Apollo Drive, Rosedale, Auckland 0632, New Zealand
A 53, Sector 57, Noida, UP, India
1 London Bridge Street, London, SE1 9GF, United Kingdom
2 Bloor Street East, 20th floor, Toronto, Ontario M4W 1A8, Canada
195 Broadway, New York, NY 10007, USA

National Library of Australia Cataloguing-in-Publication entry:

Forrest, Lisa.
    Inheritance / Lisa Forrest.
    ISBN: 978 0 7333 2892 3 (pbk.)
    For young adults.
    Clairvoyance–Juvenile fiction.
    Australian Broadcasting Corporation.
A823.4

Cover design by Nada Backovic Designs
Cover images: Girl by shutterstock.com.au; background image © Ann Cutting/
Trevillion Images; all other images by istockphoto.com
Typeset in 11/15.5pt Bembo Std by Kirby Jones

For Indi
and all those who've dreamed of
running away with the circus

PROLOGUE

Constantinople
January, 532AD

The Empress Theodora, eminence of the Cirkulatti, stood trembling in a tunnel beneath Constantinople's hippodrome. Above her were legions of rioters – supporters of Hypatius, unwilling pretender to her husband, Justinian's, throne. Before her stood her people, panting for this opportunity to use the powers ordinarily passed off as circus performers' sleights of hand. Panting too for the opportunity to show her their love and loyalty.

She shifted behind her mask. Made for her predecessor Aspasia of Athens, it silently fed her an echo of the Greek eminence's intelligence. Nefertiti's golden headpiece sent the strength of the Egyptian queen's spirit through Theodora's body like a hot needle of silken thread. Around her neck the arrowed dove of the Assyrian queen Semiramis felt like the wings of peace gently allaying her misgivings. More powerful than any of these, on her right wrist Hecate's topaz torches blazed from the silver cuff of Fulvia, Lioness of Rome, promising the goddess's help in the face of danger to the eminence who wore it. All of these Curios had been bequeathed to her along with

1

the experiences and lessons of those earlier eminences. She drew them all to her now, allowing their strength and wisdom to calm her fears and hone her focus. She turned to her guide, Antonina, who had secured her stilt straps and was standing below her.

The guide indicated the glowing gems on Theodora's wrist. *I don't like this*, she said into her eminence's mind. *You are complacent, my mistress. The gems glow as a warning.*

And a reminder that Hecate is with me, replied Theodora. *Have no fear.* The women looked at each other for a long, silent moment, then Theodora faced her Cirkulatti once more.

She spoke directly to their minds.

We are here to save an emperor. To save an empire. We call on the goddess of magic and the night, the faithful friend of mysteries, Hecate, to walk with the eminence and give the Cirkulatti strength …

The massive doors that led to the hippodrome normally required the strength of many to move them. However, when Theodora gave the word a single man lifted the wooden bolt, thick as a tree trunk, while another on each side pushed the doors out into the arena as if they were mere paper. Immediately the troupe was overwhelmed by the stench and sound of three days of rioting. The sweat of men who'd lost reason and control, the screams of the injured and the smell of blood and excrement were enough to make the eminence's legs buckle before she even took a step. Quickly, she conjured the image of a steel sheet, wrapped tightly into a rod around her backbone, then conveyed that strength to her Cirkulatti as she started them moving towards the seething masses.

Seconds later, she emerged in the hippodrome, high on her stilts, robes whipping behind her, the blackened mask and headdress presenting an ominous visage. The strongmen forged a path for the eminence towards the centre of the stadium floor, through the carnage of dead bodies, broken and twisted limbs and the moans of the not-quite-dead.

The eminence focused on the minds of those in the hippodrome both near and far.

Surrender now while you have the chance.

Their thoughts were not difficult to invade; her voice, so strong and true, echoed through minds across the field and into the high stands until men who had been slashing and thrusting at one another a moment before looked each other in the eye and shook their heads in bewilderment: what was this madness?

You toil in vain. You will not survive the day. Heed what I say.

Theodora waited just a moment for the truth of her words to settle upon them. The vein of doubt had barely wormed its way into their minds when she seized on it, twisted it into a thick whip and tore it from their minds so violently that the rioters in the hippodrome cried out in agony.

The pain will be immense.

She made a slow sweeping turn and raised both arms.

Behold the powers that protect your emperor. Meet the fiery flames of Hecate's torches.

From high up on the stadium walls came a mighty roar. The rioters looked up to see men posted between each of the columns, poised to throw, even though they held no weapon – until flame burst from each of their palms.

With another roar they threw their fire: it leaped and spun from each palm, so that in seconds fireballs rained down from the stadium ramparts.

Arms and weapons flew into the air and men ran pell-mell, looking for some way to escape the scorching. But as the fireballs reached the racetrack they slowed, losing momentum and form until they burst and in a shower of sparks were gone.

The eminence spun on her stilts, quickly scanning the minds of thousands. Could Antonina have been right? There was only one malevolent force with the ability to thwart the firethrowers' attack. She sent a warning to her troupe waiting in the tunnel.

Cirknero.

They acknowledged her caution but it made little difference. As the eminence reached beyond the simple thoughts of those rioters convinced the emperor had lost his way – their frustration and anger were easy to dismiss – and found those with darker motives, thundering horses galloped into the arena and down the long stretch of track on the eastern side of the hippodrome. Standing on the backs of their steeds, the riders were tall and strong. Each held the reins with one hand while the other twirled a thick red ribbon above their head and around their body in a rhythmic display that was totally at odds with a battlefield. With a flick of the riders' wrists, ribbons were charged into javelins, thrown and, like streaks of crimson lightning, they impaled any rioters who stood in their way; others wrapped around the bodies of men and tossed them aside like rag dolls.

Surrender your weapons. See how futile they are against forces unlike any you have seen.

But before the rioters could even think about following her command, an eerie howl like the baying of wild animals rose above the charge of the horses' hooves and echoed around the stadium. And from the shadows of the stands streaked a pack of ...

Theodora could not say what.

Their furred headpieces, black clothing and unnatural four-footed gait gave the impression of a pack of black dogs speeding towards the horses. Not waiting for Theodora's signal, those acrobats who had spotted the aggressors acted: they charged their ribbons into javelins and hurled them at the dog-men, who squealed in pain as the deadly spikes pierced their bodies. From the top of the stadium the firemen rained down another volley of burning orbs, taking out more of the creatures.

But not all. The survivors continued to run at the horses from all angles and leap at the riders on their backs. Some dog-men latched straight onto the acrobats' throats and took them down. Some stood, like men, and caught the javelins then hurled them back at the acrobats. Others went for the horses' rumps. Once on board, the creatures stood, grabbed the acrobats by their throats and drew weapons from the holsters strapped to their backs.

The rioters, scarcely comprehending what they saw, trampled one another in their attempts to get further away from the horses and their monstrous burdens.

There was no time for the eminence to be outraged that Hecate's own beasts were being used against the Cirkulatti. As the acrobats struggled uselessly, the dog-men raised blades so gleaming that the firelight of the stadium was reflected in each metal length. The eminence hissed.

Behind you, watch out.

But the dog-men did not react. She made a grab for their minds, intending to scramble their thoughts and immobilise them, only there was nothing to grab. Their minds were empty.

Before Theodora could form another attack, the dog-men slashed their short swords downwards: screams of agony rent the air and the severed arms of the acrobats fell useless to the floor of the stadium. The dog-men released the acrobats, who fell from their horses and crashed to the ground. So swift were the dog-men's actions that even those acrobats who had not been attacked were unable to rally quickly enough to help.

The eminence ignored the cries of her followers and the rioters and waited fiercely for the moment when the dog-men's taste of blood raised their confidence – and diminished their caution. As the creatures leaped from the horses onto her injured acrobats, helpless prey to be finished off, the moment came. Seizing on the energy in every particle of air around her and drawing on the shared power of the goddesses of magic and nature, on the forces of day and night and on her own considerable magic, the eminence prepared a bolt of energy so blinding that it rocked her own body before she sent the full force of it straight at the dog-men's mental defences. The force of her telepathy flung the dog-men off her acrobats. Before they hit the ground, they had melted from the inside out.

All around the stadium men who had joined up for an ordinary act of rebellion were transfixed, abandoning even their attempt to escape the inexplicable sights. For the first time, the eminence was worried for them. They were caught in a maelstrom with no logical explanation.

Escape while you can. Even now the emperor's army marches towards the hippodrome.

A howl rose from her left. The eminence spun about to see a surviving dog-man loping towards her; behind its mask she could see eyes as wide and wild as a mad animal's. It should not have survived her attack. Now it was the eminence's turn to fight back a surge of doubt. She tried to focus. The armour of its mind was honeycombed by her first charge but had not been completely penetrated. Another would do it. Again she drew on all her magic and this time aimed for the bridge of the nose, right between its eyes.

She grunted – from the force of her throw or the effort to concentrate as more Cirknero-trained warriors stormed the field, she couldn't tell. But instead of striking home, her magic dissipated and flowed past the creature, who barely flinched from the effect.

Theodora stumbled forwards, sideways; in the struggle not to topple, Antonina's warnings echoed through her mind. She *had* been complacent. The Cirknero had returned and was hell-bent on her destruction.

Latching onto the steel rod she'd conjured earlier, she righted herself in time to see the dog-man little more than a leap away. She had one last chance; she would go for its body rather than its mind. As though the physical action might aid her mental forces, the eminence instinctively swung her arms back, determined to fling the creature to the other side of the hippodrome. The dog-man launched itself at her throat, its maw wide. But before she could bring her arms forwards, the trajectory of the creature slowed. The air around it shimmered and warped. Theodora saw the glint of steel as a silver disc spun past her towards the suspended attacker. The steel sliced into the dog-man's skull at his temple. The distortion in the air around him melted and he landed, stumbled and fell face-first into the ground at Theodora's feet. The jugglers who had arrived with Antonina surged around the eminence, firing knives into the fray with pinpoint accuracy, while the eminence reached for the mind of that one who'd saved her life.

Thank you, my friend. But you risk too much with your show of impeccable timing.

Antonina fired off another round of deadly discs before answering. *Then consider my words more carefully next time and I will not have to show anything.*

Her guide had every right to admonish her. This was not just a riot against the emperor: this was a trap to lure the Cirkulatti to its demise. The eminence looked down to the cuff on her right wrist – the gems in Hecate's torch still blazed.

Slowly, Theodora turned and took in the long expanse of the hippodrome, seeking out any minds whose owners thought they could withstand her power. On her next turn, Theodora came to a standstill. She raised her arms in front of her, joined her hands and brought into the stadium the combined presences of the women whose trinkets she wore – Nefertiti of Egypt, Semiramis of Assyria, Aspasia of Greece and Fulvia of Rome – and as they hovered on the edge of her consciousness their individual attributes flowed through her and she heard their whispered assurances.

She put her left hand over the glowing gems in Fulvia's cuff and began to draw slow circles in front of her heart, using her mind to lift the sand from the floor of the hippodrome, sand that had blown across centuries and civilisations, sand that had seen leaders beat back the forces of darkness that surged around the Cirkulatti now. Warning her troupe to protect their eyes and ears as well as their minds, the eminence moved her hand faster and faster, twisting the sand into a hurricane of fury. When she had twirled it as tightly as she could, Theodora flung the sandstorm the length and breadth of the stadium. The rioters cried out in pain and begged for mercy.

But the eminence heard nothing; she focused only on the minds of the Cirknero's agents among the rioters, hunting down the tiniest crack, any hint of weakness.

And then she felt it; like the first buckle in a wall hit by a battering ram. She brought her cuff in front of her, level with her heart, and pushed her left hand onto the gems with all her might. Every atom of Theodora's being screamed with the effort required and her body began to shake. Screams erupted from the men in the hippodrome who were not trained to resist the full force of the eminence. They dropped their weapons in a sign of surrender and crumpled to the ground.

The Cirknero-trained minds pushed back, but resisting even one eminence's powers, let alone those of several combined, was not something they could prepare for. More tiny fractures began to appear in the walls of her attackers' minds and Theodora drove home the advantage.

Behold what will become of you if you continue to betray your one true emperor.

Grunting with pain, she levered those fractures into great chasms and forced a gale of white-hot despair into the Cirknero puppets' minds, so blistering that they disintegrated where they stood or collapsed mid-leap.

Back in the tunnel, with Justinian's army now mopping up in the hippodrome, Theodora faced her troupe.

The Cirknero has shown itself; it has backed those forces ranged against the emperor. Be under no illusion, history has shown us there is only one goal for the Cirknero – banishment or death for the Cirkulatti. You have protected the emperor and the emperor will protect you. You have the word of the eminence.

They kissed the tips of the bunched fingertips of their right hands then used them to draw a circle on their foreheads. 'The eminence,' the Cirkulatti chorused.

CHAPTER ONE

Seacliff, Australia
Monday 13 January

Tallulah Thomson could feel an insistent press on her shoulder but she was too exhausted to move; the muggy warmth that hovered on the edge of her consciousness promised no relief from the battle she'd been caught up in.

She heard a familiar voice speaking through the haze. Despite her weariness, Tallulah forced her eyes open and saw the red-and-white stripes on the ceiling of her circular room: she'd been dreaming. Her dad was trying to wake her up.

'C'mon, Lu, we'll be late.'

Tallulah stifled a groan. First day of real circus school – ever – and she had to wake up feeling shattered. She and Irena had been planning this ever since she could remember, though it had taken the collapse of her father's business for it to happen. As a way of helping Tallulah cope with the upheaval of moving from the city to the coastal town where her parents grew up, they'd finally succumbed to her eight-year campaign to join the circus. She could not afford to stuff up this opportunity.

She shifted her body onto her elbows and tried to remember the details of the dream. She'd been on stilts, surrounded by

11

strongmen and acrobats, striding into an enormous stadium – but rather than an audience, they'd been confronted by chaos and a bloody battle.

'Full on,' she muttered. She lifted her hand to rub the vision from her eyes but an odd heaviness on her right wrist made her stop—

'Aghh!' Tallulah flicked her arm as violently as if she'd found a red-back spider about to sink its venomous fangs into it. The silver cuff flew off her wrist and clattered across the wooden floorboards of her bedroom.

'Hecate's torches,' she exclaimed softly. She had no memory of putting the cuff on the night before – though she *had* been looking at it. Flinging back the sheets, she swung her legs over the edge of the bed, dropped to her knees and, on all fours, crossed the room. She hoped the tiny gems inlaid in the old silver wrist cuff had not dislodged as it bounced.

'Lu?' her dad called from the bathroom. She grabbed the cuff, stood up and quickly tiptoed back to the bed, shoving the cuff under the blue sheets. She grabbed a perfume bottle and necklace from her bedside table as her father appeared in the doorway, toothbrush in hand.

'You all right?'

'Yeah, just knocked some things off as I got up.'

He nodded. 'Well, come on. Shower's free. Mum's already left.'

'Thanks, Dad.'

She waited until she heard him turn the bathroom taps on before throwing the sheets back and staring again at the unusual piece of jewellery, an antique silver wrist cuff that extended to hook over the wearer's thumb. It was covered in engravings of owls and torches and curlicues inlaid with gems.

She rolled it over and back, checking all the gems were in place and she hadn't damaged it. The black-eyed owls that ran along the edge of the cuff seemed to chastise her.

Irena had asked her to keep it safe until she returned. Not wear it. Just keep it safe. To wake up with it on seemed like a betrayal, even though Irena had added, disturbingly, 'And if I don't return, you should be the one to have it.'

Tallulah gave an involuntary shudder. She was missing Irena terribly – her nanny was on her first holiday to Europe in fifty years. Even though Tallulah was now tall enough to have to bend down to farewell her at the airport, it didn't mean she was any less reliant on the woman who had been her closest confidante since she was seven years old.

'Tallulah!' Her father's voice bellowed from the stairs. 'Why aren't you in the shower?'

'Just finishing—'

'*Just* get in the shower, instead of giving me excuses!'

Tallulah grabbed the cuff's dark wood box, put the cuff inside and shoved it under her pillow. She pulled up the sheets and quilt, then headed for the bathroom.

'Wait! Dad! Stop!'

Peter Thomson slammed his foot on the brake; Tallulah's phone flew out of her hand and thudded against the wood panel of the four-wheel drive's glovebox.

'I think it's back there,' she said, spinning around in her seat.

'Tallulah,' he said with a growl, 'we've been around this block a hundred times.'

She looked over at her father and felt her pale cheeks heat up a little. Both of his arms were stretched over the steering wheel, his eyes looking determinedly forwards and she wondered, not for the first time that morning, what was wrong. Even as he'd watched his property business collapse during the recent financial crisis, even as they'd packed up and left the city, his mantras had been, 'it's only money' and 'what goes around comes around'. Tallulah could not remember seeing him this ragged.

'It's just a quiet part of town, Dad, and we arrived before anyone else.' She turned to look out the back window again. 'But others are here now. Look.' She nodded for him to follow her gaze. The roll of his eyes suggested he'd rather do anything else. 'Please,' she added.

He turned around.

'Don't they look like ...' Tallulah faltered. Usually she only had to tread carefully around this topic with her mother, but now it was ticking her father off almost as much.

He finished her sentence anyway. 'Like they belong in the circus?'

Tallulah nodded. Together they watched a young couple emerge from either side of an old black muscle car some fifty metres up the hill behind them. If the guy's frown and the big angry gestures of the girl were any indication, their conversation was more like a fight.

The girl, who Tallulah guessed was hardly older than her, maybe seventeen, looked like she was queen of her domain — and would be queen wherever she went. She seemed impossibly tall, an impression aided by the stacked heel of her black knee-high boots, and the fountain of hair that darted every which way from the crown of her head. At first Tallulah thought the girl's up-do was a mass of dreadlocks, but now she realised it was at least partly a hairpiece of multi-coloured braids. Enormous black sunglasses hid her face and she wore a striped neck-to-knee bodysuit, hot pink and black, and a knee-length cape that billowed behind her as she walked. She looked like a long-legged bird of paradise.

Beside her, the boy – young man, really; he looked about nineteen – had the same olive complexion but needed no assistance to stand as tall as the girl. His face was a little harder, with tight skin over prominent high cheekbones. There was no fat at all on his honed body. His dark hair was long enough to be pulled back into a short ponytail. He clearly preferred to keep his attire simple: a black singlet and loose black yoga pants, which, somehow, did not make him any less exotic.

As they exchanged more harried words, Tallulah was reminded of the gun-grey clouds she'd watched roll in over the Seacliff lighthouse the week before: the cloud formation, a foaming tidal wave ready to obliterate every trace of blue before it, was spectacular, but the harbinger of a storm nevertheless.

'They don't seem too happy with one another,' Tallulah said.

'They're sister and brother, I'll bet.' Peter manoeuvred the car from the middle of the road to the curb. 'She'd spit in his face but take a bullet for him – and vice versa.'

Tallulah wasn't about to contradict him, given the mood he was in. Her father was an orphan and had a tendency to theorise – rightly or wrongly – on family relationships. But it meant he was more understanding of Tallulah's attraction to the circus – to the possibility of a whole troupe of raucous siblings she didn't have either. If her mother had been in the driver's seat this morning they would have given up on Seacliff long ago.

Whoever the duelling couple were, Tallulah decided she needed to speak to them – they, at least, seemed to know where they were going. She'd opened the car door before her father had cut the engine.

The guy's irritation with the girl was so obvious his shoulders were almost squeezed around his ears by the time Tallulah got to them.

'... Yeah, great idea!' he exclaimed. 'Go over untrained. See how far you get then.'

'Excuse me.' Tallulah's interjection was loud and her smile enthusiastic. 'Hi, I'm Tallulah. I'm looking for Cirque d'Avenir and I thought you might be doing the same.'

The girl lifted her sunglasses and looked down at Tallulah. She must have approved of what she saw because her anger evaporated and she perched the glasses on top of her head, revealing eyes so brilliant that Tallulah might have been centre stage, fixed in a golden spotlight.

'I would have been lost too, if I were alone,' she said. 'Luckily, my brother here is the assistant director of Cirque d'Avenir, so he knows where to go. But,' she said with a wink, 'don't be too charmed by his help. He's really very bossy. The new title has gone to his head.'

Her brother sighed. 'It's through there.'

Tallulah followed the wave of his hand to look at a warehouse with a rusty corrugated-iron door. There was a faded street number and the remnants of two words that were the clue to one of the building's past lives: *Stage Door.*

'You should be careful in there. We've fixed it up as well as we can, but—'

'*Should* do this, *should* do that!' The girl linked her arm through Tallulah's and gave an exaggerated sigh. 'See what I'm up against? Sasha, you don't even know the girl and already you've started telling ...' She hesitated. 'I'm so sorry,' she said, 'but I've forgotten your name.'

'Tallulah,' Sasha answered before Tallulah could. She looked at him and found his eyes boring into her: she felt she was being examined from the inside out. When Tallulah was sure her face was the colour of a beetroot, Sasha looked back to his sister. 'Tallulah, with the golden eyes. And this is my sister, Saskia.'

Tallulah shook her head. 'My eyes aren't ... well, only sometimes ... people say ... in the ... sun,' she spluttered.

But the siblings weren't interested in Tallulah's opinion. After giving her brother a curious look, Saskia stooped a little to peer intently into Tallulah's eyes.

Despite the girl's friendly demeanour, Tallulah instinctively took a step back under her scrutiny. A thick drip of doubt seeped into her brain and disseminated along the network of nerves throughout her body. What had she been thinking, that a girl like her could stand next to someone like Saskia, so obviously meant for the circus? Tallulah looked down at her body. Her skin was one of two colours: skim milk or sunburned. Except for her coal-black hair she might have faded into the background completely. What had possessed her to wear shorts over the top of knee-length striped tights; it made her look stupid. No wonder she was never taken seriously; no wonder she was always dismissed as a spoiled rich kid with no talent at all. Tallulah had the overwhelming urge to run back to her father's car, jump in and order him to drive straight home before she could embarrass herself any further. What made her think she was cut out to be a member of Cirque d'Avenir?

'They are intriguing,' said Saskia and Tallulah almost gasped as she was released from the frenzy of doubt.

'Gold flecks in pools of sea green,' the older girl continued conspiratorially. 'Tallulah, I think that your eyes are already having an effect on my brother.'

Tallulah dipped her head as yet another blush rose. She'd quite like to have an effect on Sasha. 'My bag is in—'

'Maybe,' Saskia interrupted, 'your eyes will keep you safe from Sasha's wrath. I think I'll stick with you – safety in numbers, and all that. Watch out, Sash, if you get too uppity it'll be two against one.'

But Sasha had already turned and was headed towards the old door.

'My stuff is still in the car.' A wave of her hand indicated her father, further down the road, removing her bike from the back of the car so she could ride it home when the session was over. More cars and vans had arrived, expelling excited teenagers onto the footpath. 'I'll see you in there,' she told Saskia.

Tallulah trotted back to the car but her thoughts were consumed by what had just happened. For a moment she'd been so overwhelmed by insecurities she thought she'd pass out. She knew she was nervous but that was ridiculous. Before she could contemplate it further, her dad called out.

'Was I right?' He was leaning against the car, arms across his chest.

'What about?'

'Are they brother and sister?'

Tallulah nodded. She stopped in front of him and was surprised to find herself a little out of breath. When she didn't answer immediately, her father pushed off the car so he could properly examine her.

'You all right, Lu? What happened? Did they say something to you?'

'No. They're just kind of ...' She hesitated. 'I don't know. Intense?'

His eyebrows shot skywards. 'Who isn't?'

Tallulah smiled. 'He's the assistant director,' she told him.

'And she doesn't look like the type who enjoys being told what to do. Should be an interesting few weeks for you.'

'I just hope I can keep up,' she confided. 'They look like they were born in the circus.'

'You've done gymnastics and trampolining, and—'

'An acrobatics class at Club Med in France,' Tallulah finished for him. 'I know. Amateur hour, compared to this lot. And I wasn't even the best in those groups.'

'There'll be plenty of beginners like you.' He opened the back of the car and retrieved her bag.

'Thanks,' Tallulah said. 'What did Irena say about this circus?'

'That they were looking for kids from a wide range of disciplines.'

She scoffed. 'I never heard her say that.'

'You were too busy panicking about a grown woman travelling to Europe all by herself to listen.'

Tears pricked Tallulah's eyes as the image of Irena disappearing through the boarding gates shimmered in front of her; she blinked quickly and wondered what was wrong with her. *Enough.* 'Well,' she said stiffly, looking beyond her father, across an ocean roiling with summer king tides, 'she's not a young woman.'

'I'll tell her you said that when I see her.'

'When will that be?' she asked. She had no definite date for Irena's return; it had been two weeks since the last postcard.

'Lu,' her father said with a sigh, 'you've had her devoted attention for eight years; can't you give the woman a few weeks to visit family? She's not backpacking in Uzbekistan, for goodness' sake.'

'Sorry, Dad. I'm just nervous.'

His expression softened and he put both his hands on her shoulders. 'Sweetheart,' he said.

Tallulah shook off her melancholy and brought her attention back to him; the same eyes that the siblings had just been so interested in gazed back at her.

'You know all of this. Irena said that Marie de Clevjard, the director, was a very dear and trusted friend. Their mothers knew one another, so they go way back. Marie is thrilled that you're interested in the circus and she has promised to take great care of you. Irena said that many of the questions you had would be answered at Cirque d'Avenir. Though I'd like to know what questions there are in the world that your dear old dad can't handle.'

Tallulah blanched at his words. She considered asking her father why Irena couldn't have answered her questions and saved her from making a fool of herself. But even if he had understood what was really going on for her, what was the point? He had enough worries of his own at the moment.

'*Do* you have a lot of questions, Lu?'

She arched her eyebrows in imitation of his expression from moments before. 'Who doesn't?' She gave him the most glowing smile she could muster. 'I've got to go.'

He lifted his hands from her shoulders and she stepped away. 'Before you go,' he said, handing her a velvet pouch.

'What is it?' she said, taking the gift.

'Just something I've been mucking around with.'

Tallulah nodded and smiled. She knew what it was before opening the pouch. Her father's hobby was making copies of antique intaglios, tiny pictures carved into small discs of wood or gemstone. Irena had always been more enthusiastic about them than Tallulah, who left them stranded in the bottom of a jewellery drawer. When there was a sufficient number, her nanny had strung the intaglios together and hung them in Tallulah's bedroom window.

But this time her father had outdone himself.

'Wow, Dad. It's very cool.'

A winged woman carved in the style of the Ancient Egyptian hieroglyphs on a black stone disc about the size of a twenty-cent piece, sat in the palm of her hand.

'It's the goddess Isis,' her father said. 'Well, my attempt at the goddess Isis.' He gave a sheepish shrug. 'She brought new life and hope wherever she went: the heavenly scent of spices and flowers to the land, the spring winds to the crops of Egypt, the morning winds to hail the arrival of the sun each day, that sort of thing.' He shrugged. 'She just seemed right for you and the Cirk—' He shook his head. 'Cirque d'Avenir.'

'Oh. Dad.' Tallulah could barely speak she was so touched. She held out her arm while her father tied the intaglio to her wrist using the finely plaited black leather straps he'd wound onto it.

'I thought you'd like it,' he said, obviously pleased by her reaction. 'It's a bit more modern than some of the others I've made. Although I chose the stone, the onyx, specifically.'

'What do you mean?'

Her father grinned. 'Well, it's supposed to cool ardour.' He nodded to the warehouse. 'I've got to protect you from all those admiring circus blokes for as long as I can, or your mother will kill me.'

'Da-ad!' She punched him on the arm. She admired the way the intaglio sat on her pale wrist; it was just the right size. 'Thank you.' She leaned in and put her arms around his shoulders, while he grabbed her waist and held her close.

'It's going to be great.'

When she pulled away from him, he kept his head down and wiped his eyes. Tallulah didn't know what to say – it felt like he was comforting himself more than her. Something was definitely up. Her parents had begrudgingly agreed to circus school and she knew their fears – a dangerous pastime that needed quality instructors because the chances of injury were high, blah di blah. But she didn't think he'd be this weird about it.

'Dad,' she said, with a hand on his shoulder, 'I'll be fine. It's just summer camp – I'm not running away with the circus.'

'Give it time,' he answered, attempting to be jovial.

'Tallulah!'

Tallulah and her father turned to see Sasha holding the old door open, a hand on his hip.

'Can we expect you any time soon?'

Tallulah looked at her father, took a deep breath and gave him a weak grin. 'She said he was bossy.'

'Better stay in his good books, then.' He smiled. 'I suspect the onyx is about to get a workout.'

CHAPTER TWO

'Seacliff has always been very important to the Cirque d'Avenir family. Many of us were based here for some decades after the Second World War, so this is a wonderful place to begin the revival of a circus with a rich and wonderful history. And even though plans are in early stages, we *are* scouting for talent to take to Europe at the beginning of February. That is not our chief purpose, however: here you should simply stretch yourselves and learn from trainers who will have tricks your local teachers perhaps do not!'

Tallulah guided the stage door into the jamb so as not to interrupt the woman on the stage. Inside the theatre were thirty or so teenagers standing in shafts of sunlight slanting through high windows. Two rows of wooden support columns, scratched and graffitied with the messages of time, ran the length of the room.

On a stage at the southern end of the room, a sleek woman dressed in a black fitted tank top and a long black skirt, with a purple flower the size of a saucer pinned behind her left ear, stood in one of the natural spotlights and addressed the assembled group. She spoke English with a French accent. Marie de Clevjard. Many of the students stood listening patiently; a twitchy few on the edge of the group stretched their supple bodies in every direction. Tallulah moved closer to them, put her backpack at her feet and, interlacing her fingers behind her back, lifted her arms, feeling the immediate relief as her own tense muscles and nerves were stretched.

Tallulah peeked through the forest of heads for any sign of Saskia or Sasha. She found Sasha close to the stage, muttering a quiet aside to a girl whose head was slightly bowed as she listened – it was Adelaide Banks. Tallulah might have only been at Seacliff High for a term but that was long enough to know Adelaide – well, know who she was. Adelaide was the quintessential Seacliff surfer girl: a mass of sun-kissed hair, bronze skin, light and lithe and athletic. Tallulah had tried to talk to her once – big mistake! She shook away the memory and forced herself to focus on the stage.

'I look forward to getting to know you over the coming weeks,' the woman told the group, 'and introducing you to the Cirque d'Avenir story. But right now it's time for us to get the first session under way. Sasha Robinson is my assistant, so please follow his instructions. Voila,' the woman said, as Sasha sprang onto the stage in a leap that would not have disgraced a gazelle. Marie embraced him with a light peck on each cheek.

'Thanks, Marie,' he said, then addressed the group. 'It's great you could join us – both new friends and old, from near and far.' Cheers came from a couple of different groups in the room, and then a string of words from Tallulah's right that she guessed was Spanish.

'Thank you, Javier,' Sasha replied with a smile before continuing. 'That you have chosen to spend your holidays being tortured by me means you must be very strange individuals indeed …'

Again the students responded with a variety of hoots and hollers. Adelaide cried in mock outrage, 'I'm not strange.' Goosebumps rippled across Tallulah's shoulders. She recalled her father's words from moments before: Irena said all her questions would be answered at Cirque d'Avenir. That was Tallulah's biggest one: will I ever meet people who are as strange as me?

'Fortunately,' Sasha's voice rose over the hubbub, 'strange is exactly what we're after at Cirque d'Avenir. The stranger the better – my dear sister, Saskia, and I are here, after all.'

'Doesn't get much stranger,' a boy called.

'Cheap shots from the peanut gallery won't get you far,' Saskia retorted from somewhere out of Tallulah's sight.

When the teasing subsided, Sasha said, 'Sparky already, Hui. I like it.' He seemed to search the group near the boy, and finding who he sought, gave a short nod. 'Tom, good to see you here.' There was a distinct formality to his tone.

Tallulah saw collar-length sandy curls bounce as Tom mimicked Sasha's nod. 'Wouldn't miss it, Sasha,' he said in a similar tone.

'We've got an intense few weeks planned for all of you but you will be well compensated for your efforts. Marie mentioned the importance of Seacliff to the Cirque d'Avenir family. And like many extended families that span continents and generations and livelihoods, relatives have come from everywhere, offering more than we could ever need to make this homecoming special. They've set up the camp where many of you are staying, provided and helped transform different venues like this one around town for training and been absolutely fantastic in every way.' He pointed to the ceiling. 'The rooftop of the warehouse has been taken over by an army of abuelitas, nonas and babcias. You can already smell lunch being prepared. The grandpas have been pretty busy up there too. It's like a circus.' He smiled at his own joke. 'It's definitely got the best view in Seacliff and you're going to love hanging out there after our workouts, getting to know each other. So remember that when you're cursing me for expecting another hundred vampire curls.

'But enough chat. We've got a European tour to train for. We'll start by working off some of that holiday cheer.' He patted his stomach as if there was an excess of fat around his middle; the room of students groaned. 'I see many of you are ready to go. For those of you who have just arrived please see Ilya for your Cirque d'Avenir training gear.' Sasha pointed to a bald, thickset man standing behind a trestle table next to the stage. Ilya gave the group a brief wave. 'Get changed as quickly as possible. We're heading to Seacliff baths; it's a good run, very scenic, might make you forget the Ks you're racking up. There are trainers along the route to ensure you don't get lost – or take a short cut. Or maps on Ilya's table, if you'd prefer. It's a gorgeous day, so we need to go before it gets too hot. Let's make some magic, people.'

'The pool?' A student in front of Tallulah muttered to his companion. 'Have you seen the swell? And high tide's still an hour away.'

'I thought we'd joined the circus,' the companion replied.

'Cirque de Surf.'

They both chuckled.

'You know what Sasha is like. It's all about—'

'Anarchy,' they chorused.

'Adelaide still gawping over Sasha, I see.'

'Some things never change.'

The first student clapped his friend on the shoulder. 'The others are heading off. Come on.'

Across the room from Ilya and his table, Saskia, in no obvious hurry to follow her brother's instructions, was talking excitedly to an old woman. Even from a distance, the woman had a powerful presence – a magnetic energy that belied her small stature and drew attention. Her silver hair was in a bun at the nape of her neck, she had a long aquiline nose and her face and neck were creviced with deep lines. She was so craggy that Tallulah was reminded of Baba Yaga, who ate children in the fairy tale Irena used to read to her when she was young.

But then the woman threw her head back in response to something Saskia said and her laughter tinkled through the room. Everyone looked around, the sound was so delicious. Tallulah felt mildly ashamed: she'd been caught judging a woman on age alone – her mother would have her for breakfast. The old woman turned, met Tallulah's gaze and winked.

The shock of the woman's wink – or maybe the brilliance of her golden eyes – made Tallulah start. She gave a weak smile and made a beeline for the uniform table. Had her thoughts leaked into the old woman's mind? Tallulah shook her head as she imagined Irena's look of disapprobation at being caught out. Quickly, she set the barriers around her mind as she'd practised many times, and stood behind the one girl left at the uniform table. The girl was bent to hear Ilya, seated behind the table. Seconds later she stood up straight, folded her arms across her chest and declared, 'No way.'

With most of the students now in the change room, the girl's voice clattered around the old empty theatre.

'You can't wear them to the pool, Mai,' Ilya insisted.

'I wear them everywhere. They have … their value is … they have sentimental value.'

Ilya turned to his left. 'Marie, could you join us, please?'

Marie de Clevjard looked up from where she sat, perusing a stack of forms on her lap. She set the forms down and approached them with such fluidity that Tallulah wondered what her bones were made of.

Arms still across her chest, Mai stepped forwards to meet the woman. 'This was not the deal, Marie. I would not be here if I knew I had to …'

She put her head down, clearly distressed, unable to finish the sentence. She raised her head and showed Marie her shaking forearms. From wrist to elbow, each was wrapped in a red ribbon.

Tallulah gasped; the mental barriers that she had checked all collapsed. Their sudden disintegration was such a shock that her body went rigid. She was powerless to keep the images of howling dog-men from her mind as the hazy remnants of last night's dream re-formed on the edge of her consciousness.

She was so overwhelmed that she didn't see Mai wheel around and rush at her with a guttural cry. She returned to her physical surroundings again in time to see a blur of red hurtling towards her; a split second later she cried out in pain as she was slammed into a wooden pylon so hard that all breath was forced from her body.

'Don't you dare threaten me,' Mai hissed.

Unable to speak, Tallulah shook her head. She couldn't think what the girl meant. What threat? Not only were her dreams coming back to disable her, she was also being pounced on by a possibly unbalanced classmate. Her heart pounded; the effort of sucking breath into her body while pinned to the pylon – the heel of her attacker's left hand pushed against the base of her throat – made Tallulah's head spin. If this was the kind of *strange* Sasha was talking about then maybe it wasn't the place for her. Mai's right hand was raised at shoulder level and the red ribbon curled and uncurled around her arm like a sharp-nosed snake. Despite knowing the full potential of those ribbons, Tallulah forced herself to submit, to let all her muscles go limp, to indicate that she meant no harm. Then Tallulah looked the other girl in the eye and tried to croak an apology.

Mai, we are not your enemies.

For a split second, shock and confusion spiked Mai's fury – and mirrored Tallulah's astonishment. Tallulah had intended to speak her attempted reconciliation aloud despite her mangled throat; every instinct told her that to thought-cast at such a moment would only inflame an already tense situation.

Mai's eyes flicked left and right; she searched Tallulah's face then, coming to a decision, let go of her. Tallulah had to grab the pylon at her back to halt her slide to the ground. Mai pivoted and struck a warrior pose, ready to defend herself against the enemy standing behind her – Saskia.

'It was you,' Mai said.

Saskia, unperturbed, held her arms up in an act of surrender and shook her head. 'Mai, we are not your enemies.'

'Stop saying that,' Mai cried.

'Mai.' Marie stood beside the small girl. Her voice was deep and smooth as dark chocolate. 'Mai, this is Saskia, another student who, like Tallulah a moment ago, is no threat to you. Please, breathe deeply, lower your arms and withdraw your weapons.'

The muscles in Mai's shoulders relaxed a little. She looked at Saskia then at Marie, who nodded. When Mai lowered her arm, the older woman said, 'Mai, we *never* use our gifts on one another.'

Mai baulked. She looked back at Saskia. '*She* did,' she said, pointing at Saskia.

Saskia stood her ground, completely unapologetic.

'Saskia, you should be getting changed,' Marie said firmly.

'I was just trying to tell her—'

'GO. AND. GET. CHANGED.'

The sudden force in the woman's voice was like a torrent of water rushing down a dry riverbed. But Saskia would not be cowed.

She looked at Tallulah. 'You OK?'

'If she isn't, then I will take care of her, Saskia. That is *my* job. Please, go and get ready to do yours.'

Saskia took a series of deep breaths as she stared at Marie. Finally, she turned and strode away.

When Saskia had gone, Marie turned back and looked at Tallulah, still against the pole. 'All right?' Tallulah nodded and, satisfied, Marie looked back to Mai. 'Don't do that again,' she said, her voice shaking, '*ever*. Do you understand? I don't care what happens. And besides there are others. What if Tallulah had been one of the local students whose gifts have not been assessed? As it is, she looks ready to run and who could blame her? You talk of deals. The deal was you wouldn't pull stunts like that. Try that again and I'll kick you out. You can go back to your grandmother. Do you understand?'

Mai's eyes widened and she nodded her head vigorously.

Marie turned back to Ilya and sighed. 'How many students saw that?'

'I think we were lucky this time.'

Marie nodded. 'It was always going to be a risk to come back here for this.' She reached for both of Mai's hands and looked directly into the girl's eyes. 'Now can you see why you must surrender the ribbons when you begin to train?'

'And will you get Saskia to surrender her weapon?' Mai asked defiantly. 'What will she do – hand over her brain?'

'Leave me to deal with Saskia. You have been kept in isolation, Mai, for a very long time, because your grandmother believed it was necessary for your safety.' Marie glanced at Tallulah. 'The two of you have a lot in common,' Marie told them. 'But we on the Cirque d'Avenir team have been dealing with gifted performers for a very long time. You must trust me. Your grandmother does. Oui?'

She dipped her head to look directly into Mai's eyes and the girl nodded again.

'You do not need ribbons to access or to harness your energy.' She moved her open palm to within centimetres of Mai's stomach. 'May I?'

The girl nodded.

Putting her hand in place, Marie said, 'I want you to close your eyes and picture your energy as a perfect round ball right at your core.' Mai's shoulders relaxed as she did what Marie suggested. 'Now, as I unwind the ribbons I want you to see them wrap instead around that ball of energy, just the way you wrap them around your arms, or tape around your hoops.'

Mai concentrated on the instruction as Marie began to unwind the ribbons. 'See them wrapping around your energy core. It's much more effective than keeping them on the edge of your body. Anybody can get them there.'

Tallulah felt a tremor run through her own body again, but this time she recognised what was about to happen and held off the violent image from her dream before it overcame her. She groaned with the effort and Marie looked her way.

'OK, Tallulah?'

Tallulah nodded as she squeezed the image to the edges of her conscious mind. Marie went back to work until the ribbons were unwound and Mai held the end of a ribbon in each hand; a split second later she'd flicked her hands and the ribbons were in tight rolls.

Marie nodded and smiled. 'Bon?'

'Yes.'

'Voila. You'll find a locker in the change room. The most important thing today is to keep focusing on that ball of energy in your tummy. And we will practise it again and again together. OK?'

'Thank you.'

As Mai walked away, Marie's eyes met Tallulah's. She held both arms out and smiled. 'Tallulah, not exactly the welcome to Cirque d'Avenir I planned for you. For anyone.'

Tallulah sagged with relief as she was wrapped in a hug. Then Marie stood back and looked her up and down. 'Just as beautiful as Irena described you.' She gave Tallulah a firm shake but then her eyes darkened. 'But, she did not tell me everything, I think. What do you think you were doing just then?'

'What do you mean?'

Marie tilted her head to one side. 'Tallulah, that was a powerful image you shared. I'm assuming it was you – Saskia is not skilled beyond thought-casting, as far as I know. But, tell me, what did you think you would achieve? Irena did not tell me you were so advanced.'

Tallulah felt her mouth open and close as she attempted to comprehend and answer at the same time. All that fell from her lips were questions. 'Did I …? Did Mai …? Can Saskia …?' She shook her head, until she could form a response. 'Marie, whatever I did, I didn't mean to. I saw the ribbons on Mai's arm and then …'

Marie's brow furrowed as her eyes scanned Tallulah's face, searching for the truth. 'You had no control?'

'No.' Then Tallulah remembered the second wave. 'Well, a few minutes ago, as you were taking the ribbons off, the same image was about to return but I caught it before it caught me.'

Marie's smile was brilliant and full of approval. 'You've set your barriers as Irena taught you?'

'How do you know about …?'

Marie laughed. 'Didn't Irena tell you why you're here?'

Tallulah shook her head.

'She's so used to keeping secrets, our Irena,' Marie mused. 'We'll talk later. In the meantime …'

'Barriers,' they said together.

Tallulah had another thought. If, as she was beginning to understand, she was here with other teenagers like her, why would she need to set barriers?

'So, even here,' she ventured, 'I need to … I mean I tried to set them earlier but then—'

'Even here? Tallulah, set them everywhere and always, from now on.'

'But they're hard to maintain with … everything …'

Marie eyes were piercing. 'All the more reason, I should think, oui?'

Tallulah nodded.

'We will talk more, but not now. You'll be late to the pool.'

She steered Tallulah back to the uniform desk where Ilya had her Cirque d'Avenir backpack waiting for her. Tallulah took the black bag and went in to change. The locker room was surprisingly light due to the many high louvred windows, cream walls and pale yellow wooden benches. Despite the open louvres, the room was stifling.

Mai had changed into her workout gear but was still sitting on the benches with the ribbons in her hands. When Tallulah walked in, she stood up and faced her, soldier-straight. 'I owe you an apology,' she said formally.

Tallulah smiled tentatively. 'We're all nervous, I guess.'

Mai's body relaxed.

Tallulah put her backpack on the pale yellow bench. 'I'm Lu.'

'Mai.' She zipped her bag shut then blurted, 'But I don't think the other one is nervous.'

Tallulah checked to see that the subject of their discussion was not in the change room. 'You mean Saskia?'

'I think she always wants to win.'

Tallulah laughed. 'I think it's too early to tell.'

'And I think you are too nice.'

'Maybe.'

Mai nodded emphatically. But when she sat back down her head dropped and the assured girl from a moment before disappeared. Tallulah crossed the floor and crouched down in front of her. When Mai looked up Tallulah was surprised to see tears spilling from the dark-chocolate eyes. Wiping them away with the back of her hand, Mai said, 'Not so tough now, huh?'

'Oh, you're still pretty scary, don't worry about that.' She held out her hands and said, 'Do you want me to put the ribbons in the locker for you?'

For a moment the other girl's eyes went wide with fright. 'They might—'

Tallulah shook her head. 'I just watched you store all that energy within, didn't I?' Perhaps it was the relief of finding someone more nervous than she was at Cirque d'Avenir – not to mention the relief of having her gift so undramatically *accepted* – that made Tallulah reach out and close her own hands around Mai's fists. When nothing happened she said, 'See? No danger to me.'

Mai's face blossomed with surprise. Slowly she nodded.

Tallulah closed the locker door on the ribbons and then walked back to her own bag as Mai punched in the PIN to secure the lock. A moment later she walked past Tallulah, cap and goggles in hand, and stopped.

'Here we are at Cirque d'Avenir; maybe this is our destiny.'

Tallulah smiled, even though she didn't feel amused. The number of things she didn't know seemed to be mounting by the minute. 'Dunno about that – Sasha's classes should be interesting, though.'

'Do you want me to wait?'

Tallulah shook her head. 'No point us both being late.'

CHAPTER THREE

Tallulah got changed quickly. As she was leaving the dressing room, she heard a voice beyond the entrance that made her stop before she revealed herself.

'I was trying to reassure her, Sash. Compared to the nightmare she was caught in, being hunted down by devil-dogs or whatever they were, a few soothing words should have been nothing.'

Tallulah closed her eyes as she leaned her head back against the wall. How many minds had her images seeped into? She'd really stuffed up.

'So you read her mind and then communicated your own thoughts in the midst of an already stressful situation,' Sasha said, 'and you thought, what? It would make her feel better?'

Tallulah breathed deeply. She should have been delighted to at last have found another thought-caster, but instead she was uneasy. The morning had not been what she expected.

'Mai's not some sort of shrinking violet,' Saskia retorted. 'Unlike Tallulah — so bland she wouldn't say boo to a ghost.'

Tallulah pushed off the wall where she leaned.

'Still waters run deep, Saskia …'

Chuffed by Sasha's defence, Tallulah stopped.

'Oh, puh-lease.'

'Could be Marie's mystery recruit. She has golden eyes.'

'She has green eyes. *I* am the one everyone's been looking for. Marie knows that. She should be happy about me communicating with Mai.' Saskia's final sentence was full of hurt.

'Hecate's torches,' Sasha groaned, 'you sound like your father.'

'*Our* father,' Saskia corrected.

'Who has encouraged your gift, but given you little training in how to earn the respect of others. Understandable, since he has no concept of it himself. But it is what I brought you here to learn.'

'In Seacliff?' Saskia's voice was heavy with derision.

'Seacliff is as good as anywhere to learn about teamwork. Now get your gear on and get to the pool.'

'I won't.'

'Won't?'

'I'm bona fide. I don't need to be tested or assessed or whatever it is you're doing here.'

There was a heavy sigh. 'Fine. Do what you like. I don't know why I ever thought this was a good idea. Go to the station and get on the train to outer Woop-Woop, or wherever the Robinson Family Circus is performing this week, shinny up onto your trapeze and stay there. Forever.'

'Dad won't—'

'Dad won't do anything, Saskia. He's all talk – tolerated but not trusted. You have got to understand that. I'm your only chance of you realising any potential you might have, of you getting any further in this world.'

Silence followed. Tallulah looked around, wondering what to do next. If Saskia came into the room and caught her standing there in the corridor … She backtracked to the lockers, pretending she hadn't heard anything. Then she walked out of the change rooms – as long as she was on the move there was no reason for anyone to believe she'd been eavesdropping.

In one quick glance she took in Saskia sitting on the floor with her head in her hands, and Sasha standing over her like a parent trying to reason with a child. She put her head down and walked past quickly.

'Hey, Tallulah.'

She lifted her head, gave a quick grin, fully intending to keep on moving. 'Hey, Sasha,' she said with a wave.

'I'm sure you're not someone to walk away from a challenge.'

Tallulah hesitated. She'd been expecting something more like, 'Why aren't you down at the pool already?'

Saskia wrenched her head from her hands and eyed her, then looked back to her brother. 'And you're going to do this to her, are you?' Saskia said. 'Look at her, Sasha. She's so pale, she's almost transparent.'

'I'll be fine,' Tallulah said defiantly. In Tallulah's house her complexion was admired, exotic even: 'my little bohemian' her mother had always called her. Yet twice in as many minutes Saskia had dismissed her as weak. Tallulah'd show her just how *bland* she was. 'Do what to me, anyway?'

'She'll burn to a crisp out there,' Saskia continued as if Tallulah had not spoken. 'But don't you go and think about anyone other than yourself, Sasha.'

'The pool has sails over it,' he explained to Tallulah, 'and we have masses of sunscreen.' To Saskia he said, 'If I'd kept you in this warehouse you'd be complaining in about two seconds about its lack of ventilation and air-conditioning.'

'I'm used to looking after myself in this sun. It won't be a problem,' Tallulah replied.

'Of course it won't,' Saskia said mockingly. 'Just like all the minions who'll do anything to impress Sasha — even boot camp in the boiling sun. He'll kill us all.'

'Drama queen,' he said to Tallulah, 'always has been.' Then he turned to Saskia. 'Tallulah's ready to show us what she's got. But you stay here and sulk all by yourself: see if I care.'

Saskia tensed her arms and clenched her fists beside her body, then held out her hand for the unitard Sasha was holding; he threw it to her and Saskia snatched it dramatically before heading into the change room.

'Tallulah will wait for you.' He turned to Tallulah. 'I'm sorry. She's under … well, there are a lot of … expectations.'

Tallulah nodded, mesmerised by the deep dark eyes that promised untold riches if only she would follow him.

'She's lucky to have you, then,' she blurted, and then suddenly wondered how that had sounded to him.

'I don't think she sees it that way,' he said. 'I hope it's OK, though? At least I'll be certain to see her at the pool if she's with you.'

'I'll get her there,' she promised, more than a little giddy at the idea they were co-conspirators.

'There are trainers along the way, so I'll tell them to wait until you guys pass.' He smiled and ran his eyes down her body, slowly, until they rested on her wrist. 'May I?' he asked, indicating her father's intaglio.

Tallulah nodded. The anticipation of the moment when his fingertips touched the soft underside of her wrist was so sweet that she felt her insides dissolve. She pressed her lips together, determined not to reveal any emotion that would embarrass her.

But as his skin touched hers and his fingers wrapped around the onyx intaglio it wasn't desire that consumed her. A hiss of danger snaked through her body and she found herself not in the warehouse but in a dense forest of gnarled roots and twisted vines that were leashing Sasha to something old and heavy. Tallulah sensed she was seeing into his heart or into his mind, and it was weighted with envy and resentment. She heard a cry, an appeal for help so guttural she thought she'd be crushed by it, and she jerked her wrist from his grasp.

Tallulah was inside the warehouse again. Sasha stood a few metres from her, breathing heavily, his right hand cradling the left and a violent expression on his face. 'What did you do?' he hissed. He advanced on her. 'Were you in my mind?'

'You grabbed me,' Tallulah said shakily. 'I didn't do anything.'

'What is that thing?'

Tallulah looked up to find Sasha turned away from her, shoulder hunched as if protecting his heart.

'Look, I'm sorry,' she said. 'I don't know what happened. I would never deliberately ...' She took a step towards him. 'I don't know what's troubling you but ...'

Sasha spun around, suddenly composed. 'You have no idea.'

Before Tallulah could reply, Saskia emerged from the change room, transformed from the tropical bird of paradise into a surly athlete. She took a long look at the two of them and raised her eyebrows suggestively.

'Everything all right?' Saskia asked.

'Yeah,' Sasha answered, quickly. 'Don't dawdle, Saskia, OK?'

He turned and ran off. Saskia gave a petulant sigh to his departing back. 'Yes, sir.'

CHAPTER FOUR

Tallulah would like to have fully revelled in how beautiful the run to the pool was. Seacliff was set against a sandstone escarpment that ran the length of the town and beyond, and this imposing presence loomed on her right as they ran to the pool.

On her left stretched the shimmering blue expanse of the Pacific Ocean, while in front of them was a spectacular coastline: scalloped headlands as far as the eye could see. Pelicans glided high above them, feathers ruffled by the gusting sea breeze.

But Sasha's instruction not to dawdle had been the proverbial red rag to Saskia's bull; she had no intention of running and every intention of making the journey as difficult as possible. She stood still nearly as often as she walked and far more frequently than she actually ran. There were complaints all the way: it was too hot to be out at all and a pool was not a venue for the circus. And she had especially taken offence at being left with a minder – not that she blamed Tallulah for that.

Finally, Tallulah decided this day had its own intentions for her and maybe she would do a lot better if she gave in to it. Nothing was going to plan, but surely it couldn't get any weirder. After everything that had happened so far, Tallulah felt like she was piggy in the middle, with the ball of understanding sailing over her head just out of reach. So much for circus school: she still hadn't so much as spotted a juggling ball.

'Is that it?'

Tallulah glanced left and was surprised to find that Saskia had caught up and was now walking apace. Spread out before them was a grand old fifty-metre pool built out from the rocky headland, skirted by ornate walls complete with corner turrets. Its original form had been updated – as Sasha promised, white sails shaded the entire pool area, giving it the look of a giant marquee. And although the sails stopped the girls getting a full view, a training session – albeit an unusual one – was in progress.

There was a circuit of different stations set up at points around the complex. Ropes and aerial silks, known as tissu, hung like curtains from the same scaffolding that supported the sails, up which the students shinnied and disappeared from view, only to partially reappear as they performed exercises such as vampire curls, coffin-hangs or bow-and-arrows. From one end a group repeated cartwheels from a running start before rounding off into the pool while at the other end, students did pull-ups out of the water from which they pressed into a full handstand before flipping back into the pool and doing it all over again. On the western side of the complex, another group ran the stone grandstand's stairs.

'Well, that's more like it,' Saskia exclaimed.

Tallulah wished she could agree but confronted by the Cirque d'Avenir team in training she'd lost her voice. The troupe she was looking at was no ordinary group of teenage circus performers. She felt a mob of wild brumbies rush through her insides, trampling into oblivion the few pathetic scraps of circus experience she had mustered before this day. She envied the girl who only moments ago had nothing more than the trivial frustrations of a whining Saskia to deal with. She would never make it through the day.

But with their destination – and her brother – in sight, Saskia took off so fast that Tallulah was left in her wake.

'Finally, you grace us with your presence,' Sasha called as Saskia wove her way so regally through the students on the grandstand that she might have been a princess walking down a marble staircase. Tallulah felt like the ungainly lady-in-waiting trying to keep up.

'Well, we wanted to be sure you would really miss us,' Saskia replied, 'didn't we, Tallulah?'

Still panting in an effort to recover from the final sprint to the pool, Tallulah shook her head. 'It wasn't like that,' she told Sasha.

But Sasha refused to look at her. 'You've missed half the session.'

The students had all stopped their workouts to listen to the exchange.

Tallulah waited for Saskia to take her brother on – to scoff at his demands and tell him that he had no right to expect her to run to the pool and that she would take her time whether he liked it or not, especially since he left her with a 'minder': all of the things she'd ranted about for most of the run. But instead she responded with a bewildered expression and said, 'Well, Tallulah and I had a lot to talk about.'

'No! It wasn't like that,' Tallulah repeated, desperately appealing to Sasha for understanding. 'You told me to make sure she got here but she walked and wouldn't hurry—'

She stopped. There were obviously no points to be won by reminding him of his earlier request to get Saskia to the pool. Tallulah's hopes of winning his gratitude by babysitting his difficult sister were dashed.

'We'll be faster next time,' Saskia said.

'You will,' he said. 'Or you will not be very popular here. Because of your lateness the whole class has to start again.'

As the news made its way around the pool, Tallulah could feel the disdain of all the other students. Arms across chests, hands squared on hips, frowns all around her; their angry thoughts invaded her own in a way she'd never experienced. She quailed at the contempt she caught in Adelaide Banks's steely eyes.

'There is a responsibility that we have to others at Cirque d'Avenir,' Sasha said, addressing the team, 'both to fellow students and to the instructors: the responsibility to be where you are supposed to be, when you are supposed to be there. If you don't have that respect naturally then I will find a way to teach it to you. Saskia and Tallulah, eight laps—'

'Eight!' Saskia protested.

'—freestyle or whatever stroke you can do until you get to the thirty-metre mark when you stand and with your hands on your head run the rest of the way. The rest of you back to whatever your first station was. There'll be an extra station when this pair join the group.'

No one moved. Sasha waved his arms at them. 'Come on. The swell is only going to get bigger.'

From the stairs a tall boy with wet curls and a face flushed with the intensity of exercise stepped forwards. 'Sasha, what about a day's grace? We're all here to work hard—'

'Thanks, Tom,' Sasha interrupted. 'I don't need to be told how to run my training sessions. Or how to handle my sister.'

The two young men stared each other down. Was this the same curly-haired guy Sasha had greeted so formally from the stage?

'Well, it's touching you feel the need to argue over me,' Saskia said, breaking the impasse. 'I don't need to be *handled* by anyone. But,' she turned to Tom and her sarcasm dissipated, 'I admire your team spirit, Tom. My brother could learn a lot from you. Thanks.'

Tom gave Saskia a brief nod of acknowledgment without looking her in the eye. He glanced at Tallulah; she hoped her return smile reflected her gratitude. A grin crept across his face as he turned to the team and said, 'Well, where else would we be on a day like this? A beautiful pool. A spectacular day.' It was such a ridiculous suggestion that he won him a few smiles. 'Really, the girls have done us a favour, haven't they?'

'Don't push it,' someone warned, but with good humour.

'As long as there's plenty of food at the end,' another boy called out from the pool. Knowing groans followed.

'There'll be plenty of food, Hui,' Tom yelled back. 'Won't there, Sasha?'

Sasha ignored the question. His attention had been diverted by the arrival of a car. The group followed his gaze to see Marie get out of the driver's side of an SUV. Before she'd made it to the passenger side of the car, the door opened and the old woman from the warehouse emerged.

'Brigitta? In this sun?' Tallulah heard Saskia ask her brother.

Brigitta waved to the group then walked to the top step. Marie brought a cushion from the car and laid it on the concrete; this time Brigitta used Marie's steady arm to lower herself onto the step.

'Could just one thing go the way I—' Then, realising all eyes were upon him, Sasha stopped talking. He clapped twice and the sound bounced off the cement walls around the pool. 'What are we waiting for, people? Don't make me start the session a third time.' He bounded up the steps of the grandstand to meet the women.

Tallulah glanced back to the curly-haired boy. 'The quicker we start the quicker we're done,' he advised quietly.

'OK.' She pulled the swimming cap on her head and tucked her plait into it.

Swimming was easy for Tallulah. She'd trained with her school team back in the city. The only challenge came in standing and running – her lack of height in the deep water especially when a colder ocean wave broke over the pool meant that some of the last twenty metres of each lap was more like treading water. But when she took her hands from her head to steady herself in the wash, Sasha, back on the pool deck again, was on her case. 'There'll be two more laps every time your hands leave your head. This is about holding your position no matter what. I'll give that one to you as a warning.'

'How generous,' Saskia deadpanned from behind. But Sasha's attention was already diverted by another group of students who weren't meeting his standards.

After the warm-up they moved to the silks hanging from the scaffold above the pool – the vertical leap from deep water rolling with the tide to reach the silk was a significant hurdle. 'You're rushing,' a trainer said beside Tallulah. And he was right; she couldn't help it. All around her students moved up and down the silks and along the scaffold like monkeys. Nothing tired or fazed them. Aerials had always appealed to Tallulah but dragging your body weight around with your arms was muscle-shattering work. 'See yourself doing it and you will,' the trainer said. It sounded like a trite line from a sport shoe commercial but one Tallulah would have been willing to try to avoid Sasha's attention. But Saskia, it seemed, couldn't work with it.

'Sasha, you expect the impossible,' she called out from the water as she watched Tallulah make another attempt.

'Legs, Tallulah. Let's see you use them,' he replied. When she failed again Sasha instructed the trainer to aid her jump.

Once up, Tallulah steadied her beating heart and began the climb, wrapping the silk around her foot so as to push as well as pull her way higher; she evaded Sasha's wrath during her set of vampire curls and was halfway across the scaffold without any corrections when Saskia complained again. This time the water was not deep enough for her liking should they fall from the scaffolding.

'That's right, Saskia,' Sasha said. 'Cirque d'Avenir would allow me to put the lives and bodies of thirty handpicked athletes at risk by not following safety standards. Technique, Tallulah. Shoulders away from your ears; use your lats. Don't rely on your rotator cuff.'

Her lats, not to mention her shoulders and arms, were beginning to burn by the time she got to the next silk, which was wetter and heavier to move. 'You can do this,' she told herself, forcefully, as she wrapped the silk around her body. From where she was perched she looked along the coast line and decided she could be on top of the world; she would use the beauty of the setting and the energy of the ocean to aid her. She might not have the other students' skills but she recognised a streak of obsessiveness not unlike her own and used it too. The glide and grace that the water lent her would be available on the silks, she told herself, as she went through the set moves: Rebecca split, coffin-hang and bow-and-arrow. But mind over muscle could only get her so far; by the coffin-hang her muscles began to really shake. She wobbled her way through the final move, caught Sasha watching with a look of shocked despair, and descended the silk with shoulders, arms and core – not to mention dignity – all the worse for wear. The trainer who had been spotting her under the silk complimented her for 'toughing out the set', but it did little to make her feel better.

Saskia straight-up baulked on the next exercise they were assigned: a cartwheel from a running start followed by a round-off into the pool.

'It's suicide on such a slippery surface,' she complained to her brother.

'There's a mat on the ground so it's not slippery.'

Saskia walked along it, sweeping her foot over the mat. 'It's covered in water.'

'Saskia, it's every child's dream to be allowed to do this exercise rather than be warned off by their mother about the supposed dangers.'

'Then that's a sensible mother.'

'Tallulah, show her how it's done,' he said.

Here Tallulah could save face. The setting was as he described: just the place that made you want to run and cartwheel into the pool – if only your mum would let you. And she was good at cartwheels. Maybe not after an aerial workout like she'd just been through, a voice suggested. Not giving herself a chance to think any more, Tallulah walked to the top of the narrow yellow mat that marked the runway, turned and took off; launching into the cartwheel she felt her arms buckle slightly as her legs rotated through the air but she got her body around and sucked on every muscle for the round-off – landing only slightly sideways in the water.

By the time she surfaced, Sasha was already watching his sister come down the runway. Tallulah's mouth dropped as she watched the older girl cartwheel without using her hands and finish with a round-off that was perfect in every way.

'Ten more like that,' were Sasha's only words when Saskia surfaced.

That was the day's game. Saskia started every new exercise complaining that it was an impossible task. 'Tallulah can manage it,' Sasha would say, Tallulah the carrot – or maybe the bunny – to goad his sister with.

And Tallulah did manage it – gallantly if not proficiently – only to face the ignominy of watching Saskia complete the exercise so much better. As the session wore on she felt utter despair about own ability.

The final station was the one Tallulah had dreaded since seeing it from the road above: repeats at the pool-edge of a combined pull-up from the water followed by a press to a handstand – one of the great show-off moves of any circus performer for the simple reason that it was really hard to execute under normal circumstances, let alone when waves were crashing over the metal chains surrounding the pool.

Predictably, Saskia refused. 'It's not possible. This session is too hard. We're exhausted. Tallulah especially.'

'Tallulah's tougher than that, aren't you, Tallulah?'

Tallulah was still recovering from endless running up and down stairs; she had little chance of holding her body weight up by her arms let alone tipping forward and straddle-lifting her legs from the water to meet in a handstand. But she shrugged. 'Sure.'

Set up to be shamed again, Tallulah knew she could blame Irena, not to mention her parents, for her predicament; they'd all agreed on this bizarre circus, hadn't they? She dropped her head and met her own reflection in the water. But if you hadn't been so eager to impress Sasha you would have walked right by them outside the change rooms, she told herself. This is all your own doing.

'Come on; let's show them how it's done.'

Tallulah looked to her right and found the man who'd handed out training gear at the warehouse, the one who'd witnessed the episode with Mai, standing beside her in a wetsuit. The smile she gave him was barely skin-deep but she nodded and moved to the pool edge.

'I'm right behind you,' Ilya told her.

In between waves, the water was up to her hips. She put her palms on the edge, jumped, and pulled her body out of the pool until her arms were straight – which is where she got stuck: her muscles went on strike no matter how much she scolded them. She had no more an idea of how to get to the next step than she did how to fly. But before she fell back in the water, Ilya's hands were under her feet, supporting her. 'Tuck your chin in and hinge at the hips,' he instructed as he lifted her, and she did as she was told. When her upper body was almost vertical she felt a knee in her back as the on-deck trainer grabbed her waist and helped Ilya guide her into position. She now had an upside-down view of Ilya. He smiled. 'Now you're going to suck your legs up with your tummy.' Ilya pushed and she pulled and when her body was finally in a handstand every muscle seemed to scream its protest. Tallulah wasn't sure if she shook with the effort or the humiliation of how many hands it had taken to achieve the exercise. 'Flip back into the water from there,' the on-deck trainer said, taking his supporting hands away. But Tallulah could do little more than crash back into the pool the way she'd come.

'As long as you got the feeling of it,' Ilya told her when she surfaced. She nodded, grateful for the sting of salt in her eyes. 'Once you do it a couple of times you'll be fine.'

Saskia followed – repeating it more often than Tallulah cared to count before Sasha called the session to a halt.

'Everyone found them hard,' whispered a voice behind her. She turned to find Mai grinning. 'Didn't I warn you about that one?' She ducked under the water and kicked away before Tallulah could reply.

At the end of the session, Sasha had the team face each other in two parallel lines on the pool deck – Tallulah the odd number on the end with no partner – and gave the instructions. 'Three balls each,' he said, holding up a trio of multi-coloured balls he'd just grabbed from the bucket resting on his hip. 'We'll work on the run, whatever takes my fancy. You might have to take on an extra item, throw to someone near you or aim for a target. Whoever drops a ball is out.'

As Sasha handed a trio of balls to the students at the other end – Tallulah had discovered that they were from Chile – Mai moved from where she stood in line, opposite Saskia, to partner Tallulah.

'Where are you going?' Sasha demanded.

'I've never juggled. It's better if I'm on the end.'

He shook his head.

But rather than returning to her spot, Mai waved at Guido, the boy now beside her, to shuffle himself and everyone next to him further down the line.

'Mai,' Sasha said sharply. 'Back to where you started.'

'But—'

The angry jerk of his head was enough to convince her she'd lost the battle; with a grimace Tallulah's way, she did as she was told.

When everyone held their quota of coloured balls Sasha put the bucket down and stood in front of Tallulah. She knew it was inevitable but it didn't stop her heart sinking deeper into the pit of her stomach. As others in the line began tossing the balls, Sasha waited for her to start. And waited. She dropped her eyes to the balls in her hands but she could still feel his expectant gaze. Juggling had not attracted her to the circus – if it was any one thing it was the cloud swing and the feeling of flight, of freedom. Somehow she had to channel that passion into the three coloured balls. She gritted her teeth to stop them chattering and silently recalled what she knew: stance relaxed, movement of arms even and steady. The habit of attending chapel at her city school made her think that a prayer might be handy now – if only she knew who the great goddess of juggling might be. From somewhere deep inside, she got a reply.

We call on the goddess of magic and the night ...

She tossed one ball in the air, then added a second and a third.

... the faithful friend of mysteries, Hecate ...

Entranced by the flow of the balls, she marvelled at the way they skimmed across her hands and into the air; their alignment, symmetry and balance were so perfect the thought of adding more balls, of creating a giant spinning wheel of colour was suddenly exciting. She decided juggling was not unlike the cloud swing – any moment she might take off.

... to walk with the eminence ...

Tallulah gasped. The ball she was about to gently ease back into the air jerked forwards from her hand with no control. 'No,' she cried. She lunged forwards for the lost ball. But it was all over. She felt the thud of each ball on the wet cement. She came back to the pool and found herself face to chest with ... Sasha.

She stepped back.

'Out,' he said. And moved on.

She made her way to the stands, trying not to stagger or show her relief too obviously.

By then everyone was watching Mai. Not only could she juggle, she didn't falter when Sasha added more balls – only when it came to throwing to the student opposite her.

'Saskia is waiting, Mai,' he told her.

But it was as if she was deaf to Sasha's directions.

'Mai,' Sasha said sharply, 'if you can't throw it to Saskia then throw to Hui.'

Which Mai did, perfectly.

Sasha gestured to the air, as if to say how hard was that, and moved on. Tallulah wasn't joined by many others in the stand until Sasha began replacing the balls with other items: clubs, hats, small wooden bats, knives and swords. As the random objects clattered to the ground and more students sat down, Sasha's frustration grew.

'You're not much use to me next week, when I introduce the real thing: you'll chop your hand off with the blade of your own weapon.'

A choked silence overcame the group. 'Why do we need real swords at all?' called one of the local students from where he sat in the stand below Tallulah.

Sasha stopped walking on the deck, looked up at the student. 'C'mon, Ollie, you know me better than that! Circus is not pretty performers making pretty moves. It's the anarchy of the street: it's meant to represent the people it entertains; and it's meant to be unpredictable – life heightened to the pitch we would all like to experience. What if, I don't know, a baddie, charged at someone important to you brandishing a weapon, and all you had time to do was toss whatever was in your hand to defend her?'

The idea was so preposterous that Ollie and everyone else laughed.

Except Tallulah. She kept her expression blank – and her mind empty. Sweat beaded her lip as she worked desperately to suppress the image of an impossibly tall masked woman saved from a dog-man by a well-aimed knife. That dream was *haunting* her. It had to be a coincidence, but that didn't make her any less uncomfortable.

The remaining students moved into a circle and the items were thrown this way and that on Sasha's call. Tallulah thought that Tom was the most physically impressive. He was taller than Sasha and his easy athleticism was accompanied by a sparky energy that made him fun to watch. He seemed to always have a big grin on his face as he offered encouragement to any of the group who needed it.

Mai was the most graceful creature Tallulah had ever seen. Small and strong but loose – very loose. Her body seemed to undulate from one extraordinary position to another. When Sasha called for the jugglers to change direction, Mai spun and threw without a care in the world. The good humour that had infected the group was broken as a scream tore through the air and rebounded on the cement walls around the pool.

The clubs and other items were dropped or caught as Saskia doubled over, wrapping her hands around her body and clutching them to her ribs. For a moment no one said anything. Then Sasha said in a bored voice, 'You're out, Saskia.'

When Saskia stood up her face was contorted – although from pain or anger or sheer dramatics it was hard to say. The girl looked to where Tallulah and the others sat in the stands, then took her hands from where they were wrapped around her ribs and looked at them. She shook them, clutched them, made a fist of each and crossed them in front of her chest. It was a dramatic performance. When she lifted her head she spoke to her brother through gritted teeth.

'She hurt me,' she said, nodding towards Mai.

Mai snuck a look to the top of the grandstand; but immediately turned back to Saskia, defiant. Tallulah swivelled to see that Brigitta and Marie were gone.

'Mai hurt you with a plastic club?' Sasha looked at his feet where the implement lay.

'You know what I mean,' Saskia insisted. She glanced at the students in the stands then back to her brother. 'It was like an electric shock.' The last words were spoken slowly, deliberately, as if willing him to understand the meaning in the gaps.

'Because plastic is known to be such a spirited conductor of electricity, Saskia.' He turned to the boy beside Mai. 'Hui, any electric shocks from Mai, so far?'

Hui grinned. 'Ready and waiting, Sash.'

Mai gave an exaggerated groan; Hui responded with a friendly punch on her shoulder.

Sasha grinned at them both. But when he turned back to his sister, she was seething. 'So it's OK for us practise on each other now – or is it just me?'

'Pot calling the kettle black, isn't it?' Mai challenged.

'So you admit it?' Saskia replied.

'What if I did?' Mai took a step towards the other girl.

'Enough, both of you!' Sasha considered the two girls. 'We'll call that even.' He gestured with his thumb to where Tallulah and the others sat. 'Both of you, out.'

'What!' they chorused. But further protests fell on deaf ears.

Eventually, the last juggler left on stage was Adelaide Banks. She was magnificent and never more than when Sasha joined her – it was as if both of them had been waiting all day for the chance to perform together. Two examples of human perfection, long and sinewy and strong, moving with rhythm and grace, the perfect complement to the effortless tumble of ocean onto the shore that had been their backdrop all morning.

'It's embarrassing,' said the guy in front of Tallulah, Ollie. 'She's got no chance with him.'

His mate sighed heavily. 'We're all wasting our time here.'

Ollie turned to his mate. 'What? We're just tired. It was a tough workout.'

'I'm never tired,' his mate countered. He put his head in his hands. 'It's this whole set up. It all feels … weird.'

Ollie shook his head then shivered. 'But Sash invited us. If we weren't meant to be here …'

'We're not. Everything about it is wrong. It's too intense. My head weighs a ton. Like a hangover or something. Can't you feel it?'

Ollie didn't answer.

'It's all wrong, I'm telling you.'

A shout of joy from Adelaide brought Tallulah's attention back to the jugglers. Sasha called in the whirling objects until Adelaide was left with three plastic knives. He dragged a target board, the bullseye made of soft clay, into her eye line. When it was set he gave her the command and she threw the three knives in quick succession. Two of the three flew to the centre and stuck. The students in the stand cheered and clapped; Sasha stood to one side and grinned and applauded as well. Adelaide, who wore a bemused look as she checked and re-checked the target board, eventually shrugged, giggled and took a deep bow.

Saskia clicked her tongue and gave an exasperated sigh. When Tallulah glanced her way, the older girl shrugged. 'It's his obsession: recruiting the plebs, my father calls it.' The only thing Tallulah understood about the statement was that Saskia disapproved.

'See, people,' Sasha called. 'We have to give up this idea that circus is comfortable and easy and controllable. Do you think the performers in Nefertiti's Egypt had it easy, when they had to wrap reeds to make the hoops they twirled? Do you think the tumblers in Ancient Greece had it easy in the rain on uneven cobblestones? Do you think the Romans had it easy walking into a stadium to entertain the seething thousands, as the blood from the gladiators' battle was being washed away from under them?

'That's what's meant when they say entertainment on the edge of your seat. That's why people want to run away with the circus.'

Tallulah found herself clapping like everyone else, inspired by his words. The immediate relief she'd felt when she'd been relegated to the stands had been replaced by deep regret that she had not been able to keep up. She didn't want to be singled out and alone. It was no fun – the fun was being part of the group. All her dreams to be part of a travelling circus seemed certain to disintegrate in one day. She wasn't good enough to be part of this group. Sitting there, she made a determined resolve to at least try. She just had to get better – fast.

'Let's get back to the warehouse. There's a rooftop with a great view and tables groaning with delicious food. You all deserve it.'

But as Tallulah and Saskia began to follow the other students out of the pool Sasha called out to them. 'Where do you two think you are going?

'Lunch,' Saskia retorted. 'Where else?'

He shook his head. 'Not so fast. You can do it all again, just like everyone else had to. Ilya and Marnie will stay here to take you through it.'

'You can't be serious!' Saskia said. 'There is just no way.'

Tallulah could feel the other girl's eyes on her, looking for some support in her protest, but she kept her gaze down. She couldn't remember disliking anyone as intensely as she disliked this pair at that moment. But the waves were crashing into the pool – it was only going to get worse. Ignoring Saskia's continued protests, Tallulah walked out to the pool deck, stood in front of Ilya to be sprayed with sunscreen again, pulled on her swimming cap and jumped in to start her eight laps.

CHAPTER FIVE

Tuesday 14 January

It took Tallulah a few moments to work out where she was when she woke up the next morning: she'd dreamed she was trapped in a twisted, overgrown forest, being bullied by a trainer who seemed to transform back and forth from Sasha to a snarling dog-man. Relieved to find she was lying on her own lovely bed, she sat up, trying not to whimper as each muscle detonated in a series of painful explosions. She froze for a moment, breathless, and debated falling back onto her bed and staying there.

But the grim realisation that lying down wasn't an option made her take a breath as deep as her aching intercostal muscles would allow, inch towards the edge of the bed and slide her body out as gently she could. She landed on her bum on the floorboards with all the grace of a beached whale. Tallulah did more than enough sport at school to know the feeling of overworked muscles – but this was a different kind of weight, a low moan from deep within that made no sense.

She crawled to the centre of her circular room; staying on all fours, she slowly arched and flexed her torso like a cat and then pushed into the yoga position known as downward dog. After holding the pose long enough to get the blood circulating, she moved her body in a series of stretches that would help prepare her for another day at the circus.

Except that fifteen minutes later the heaviness had not shifted. She laid her upper body over her outstretched legs, wrapped her hands around her feet, put her head down on her shins and told herself that the dream meant nothing; it was just her mind playing tricks on her.

'My mind,' she said, sitting up suddenly.

Whenever the world was all awry for her, Irena would sit her down and make her check the protective boundaries around her mind. Whenever she did, she'd find a chink, a small hole through which her strength was seeping. After the day before, the strangest day of her life, it was only natural that there would be a hole big enough to drive a semi-trailer through.

So she crossed her legs, closed her eyes and slowly began her house-keeping. The first barrier, a wrought-iron fence through which a mesh of white climbing roses twisted and turned the moment anyone tried to enter, was bent; the heavy blooms, designed to burst from tiny buds in the presence of a foreign consciousness, indicated that her mind had been entered. The second barrier, a rendered brick wall and oak door that she needed to activate the correct memory to enter, was definitely cracked, as if a shift in the foundations had moved it from underneath.

But it was the final, innermost barrier that was the most damaged. The pretty mosaic tiles hid a reinforced concrete wall that surrounded her well of strength. Only the steel reinforcements remained, a rusted skeleton that mocked her attempt to protect herself, and the well was empty but for the dark sludge way down at the bottom.

Tallulah's heart raced as she took in the destruction. No wonder she felt drained.

Resolving to take better care of herself from now on, Tallulah got to work. She started by filling the well with the incantation that she and Irena had created; when she again saw a pool of strength glittering in the morning sunshine, she began rebuilding the wall around it, reinforcing the concrete with crushed diamonds as well – Irena would roll her eyes at that bit of bling but Irena was not here to help her. Then she fixed the mosaics with the image that, combined with the right thought, was the key to her innermost soul.

When Tallulah was satisfied that she was as ready as she could be for whatever was thrown at her that day, she dressed and went downstairs.

'You're going back,' her father said from the breakfast bar when he saw her wearing her Cirque d'Avenir T-shirt. Her mother was standing by the toaster.

Tallulah nodded. 'Wouldn't want anyone to think I was *beaten* yesterday.'

Her parents exchanged a loaded glance.

'No one said—'

'Not in exactly those words …'

Her father held his hand palm up to halt Tallulah's interruption, '— or even *thought* you were beaten, Tallulah. You didn't turn up for lunch,' he reminded her, 'which worried Marie, who did the right thing and called us.'

A move Tallulah had not anticipated. She'd returned to the warehouse with Ilya, Marnie and Saskia after the session but all she could think of was getting away. When Saskia went to shower, Tallulah took her chance; she didn't want to eat lunch with the other girl; she didn't care if she ever saw Cirque d'Avenir again. But she was so hungry by the time she got to Main Beach that she thought she'd faint if she didn't stop and eat. After a burger-with-the-lot, she felt revived enough for a swim and, in no hurry, pedalled home. By then, Marie had called the house.

'I didn't mean to worry anyone,' she said. 'But surely Marie wouldn't expect me to sit down and eat lunch with one of her bullies.'

'No one knew you felt like that. You must have put on a good show.' Her father poured muesli into a bowl and pushed it towards Tallulah as her mother placed a tub of her favourite passionfruit yoghurt on the bar. 'You know Marie's not expecting you to keep up with the more experienced students straight away. You mustn't put that pressure on yourself today.'

'But are you sure you want to go back, Tallulah?' her mother asked. 'We can—'

'Gemma,' her father said, gently. She dropped her gaze from her husband to the floor. 'We went through this.' He turned to Tallulah. 'Do you want to leave the circus Irena recommended you go to?'

Tallulah thought the tension between her parents had reached its zenith when they'd packed up their city life to move back Seacliff. The collapse of her father's business seemed to have driven a wedge between the childhood sweethearts so wide that Tallulah wondered if things would ever return to the way they had been. Once in Seacliff, her parents had begun to speak to one another again. But going 'missing' yesterday seemed to have rekindled the tension.

'Irena wouldn't want me to drop out after one day, Mum.' How could Tallulah tell her that it was a dream-vision from Irena's cuff and the bizarre events that followed that were intriguing enough to brave the duelling siblings today. 'And what would you think of me after all those years of pestering you to go to circus school?'

'I'd think you must be tougher than me.'

'Nonsense, she's her mother's daughter,' her father said, proudly.

Relieved, Tallulah ate the muesli quickly, farewelled her parents, jumped on her bike and coasted down the drive, joining the main road into Seacliff. A kilometre on, she veered left, opting for the safer and more scenic bike track that took her along the northern Seacliff beaches.

Half an hour later she was on her haunches locking her bike to the black metal rack. She put the key to the lock and, ignoring the shadow that had decided to hover over her and block the sun, pushed it home.

'I didn't think you'd come back today.'

Tallulah started, then glanced up to see the boy who'd tried to reason with Sasha at the pool standing over her. His hair sat in tight blond curls when it was dry; his expression was friendly if concerned.

'Wow, some impression I must have made,' Tallulah replied.

'We didn't see you after the pool.'

'I didn't miss anything, did I?' She pulled the key from the lock, unzipped the front pocket of her backpack and put it away safely.

'Just lunch.'

Tallulah stood. 'I wasn't hungry.'

'That's not the point.'

She stopped, intrigued by his approach. 'Then what is the point?'

'The point is you deprived you and me of the perfect bonding opportunity yesterday,' he replied.

'Deprived *you* of?' she spluttered. 'I didn't deprive anyone of anything. In case you didn't notice—'

'In case *you* didn't notice,' Tom interjected, 'it was happening to us too.'

She shook her head, defiantly. 'No – not to Adelaide and the other Seacliff students.'

He rolled his eyes. 'That's a completely different situation; you're not one of Sasha's local recruits. But the rest of us were copping it too.'

Tallulah's bluster stopped short. She didn't understand the difference. Surely she would have noticed if others were the focus of Sasha's wrath as well. It would have been reassuring to know that it wasn't just her.

She realised Tom was still waiting for a response; Tallulah opened her mouth, but he held up the open palm of his hand. She thought she caught a twinkle behind his brilliant eyes. Was he teasing? Quickly deciding that it might be wisest to stay mute for the moment, she gestured for him to continue.

'We could have had a great lunch together, raged collectively, but particularly at Sasha's treatment of you, which we *might* have conceded – *if* you were there – was a *little* bit more focused than the way he was with the rest of us.

'We could then, with complete vindication, have butchered and assassinated Sasha's character till it was in tatters, given a bit of advice about Saskia and left for home sated, mentally and physically, ready for today's session, resolved to be an even more tightly knit unit, utterly impervious to his taunts and insults.'

Tallulah was at once disarmed and impressed.

'Instead,' Tom said, with a shrug, 'that opportunity, as I said, was squandered. Now, I don't know what it's like in your family but in mine, brothers and sisters reserve the right to argue with one another to the death – well, almost to the death – unless faced with an authority figure who's a complete nutter. That's when we band together.'

Tallulah was genuinely touched. In that moment she had to allow that, for all her so-called desire to be part of a circus family, she had let Sasha blind her to the help and support that had been, possibly, all around her. Feeling a little foolish, she took a deep breath and nodded. 'You're right.'

The boy tilted his head to one side. Under his gaze, Tallulah's ability to form words had apparently disappeared.

She tried again. 'No, I mean, I get it now.' But the more she spoke the more monosyllabic she sounded. She threw up her hands in a gesture of surrender and began to move off, but he blocked her path; he seemed much taller, his shoulders much broader. She'd thought he was fifteen or so like her, but standing this close to him, she realised he was a couple of years older. He smelled of patchouli. She looked up to find him smiling.

'So, have lunch with me today?'

Tallulah felt her whole body break out in goosebumps. She stepped back. 'With everyone, you mean?'

Tom laughed. 'Sure,' he said. 'If you prefer escorts.'

She scanned the street but no one was paying them any attention. Which seemed impossible, since her insides were all fizzy, like a bottle of lemonade that had been tumbled and shaken and was ready to burst.

'So, what do you reckon?'

She looked back at him and narrowed her eyes. 'I reckon you talk a lot. And you're very pushy ...' She tried to hide the fact that she was searching for his name. 'Tom?'

'That's right!' he exclaimed, as though she'd just passed a test. He held out his hand. 'I'm Tom, *Tallulah*.'

Wary, after what touching Sasha had done the day before, she nevertheless offered her own hand. His large callused palm was dry, a working hand, but it was warm and his grip was firm; as his fingers closed around Tallulah's, she felt her insides still. No visions. No voices. She gave a relieved sigh.

'Lu,' she corrected him. 'Please call me Lu.'

'Done. *Lu.*' He released her hand and it felt as though a spell had been broken. 'Shall we go in?'

With a flourish of his hand, Tom gestured for her to pass. She began a slow walk up the hill towards the old theatre. Tom's companionship immediately made her feel better.

'So, besides Sasha, what else would we have talked about at lunch yesterday?' Tallulah stole a sideways glance and found Tom doing the same.

'Well,' he said, as if needing to think about it, 'I don't know.' He looked towards the escarpment. 'We could've talked about our super-powers, for instance.'

'Oh, of course,' Tallulah replied. 'Our *super*-powers! Why didn't I think of that?'

He shrugged. 'OK, our gifts. If that's what *you* prefer to call them.'

Tallulah giggled. 'I'm fine with either term.'

'Or, if you prefer, you could've told me how it is that you've come to Cirque d'Avenir when we've never heard of you. Where did you come from?' He stopped walking and looked at her.

'I'm not the only one. Mai—'

'Mai's grandmother is well known to the Cirku—Cirque d'Avenir.'

'Quite a few of you know each other, don't you?'

'I've worked with Hui for ages. His family found my mum and dad when they emigrated here in, like, the seventies. We've got a little school in Broken Hill. The Robinsons have a travelling family circus but they …' He hesitated. 'We knew them from occasional get-togethers when Marie visited but they kept pretty much to themselves until Sasha left home a few years ago – big bust-up with his dad. He disappeared, but then re-surfaced teaching in a local school here – nothing to do with Cirque d'Avenir but in Seacliff the "family" is never too far away. So he appeared at more events. He just wanted to be seen as his own man, which was cool with us. But some health problems with his mum took him back to the family. He was in a great position to be scouting for Cirque when the time came but it means we're stuck with the two of them now.

'Who else? Guido, Chiara and Luca I've known forever. They live up north. When we were younger we'd alternate holidays – we'd get the tropics one year, they'd get the outback the next. Marie has been the glue between here and what's going on in Europe. She's, like, a super-successful choreographer in France; her grandmother was a member of the Ballets Russes, I think. When she's not working she travels here, New Zealand, South America – that's why Estella and Javier and those guys are here. She teaches, inspires; she's the reason Cirque d'Avenir's up and running. And she brought Brigitta out of retirement.'

Before Tallulah could respond, Tom's name rang out. They both looked towards the theatre to find a small woman marching their way.

'Elen, our trainer from home,' he informed Tallulah.

'Is she angry?' Despite her small stature and the colourful braids wound into a long plait, Elen looked formidable. The woman was shaking her head at them both, as though she had always been in charge of Tallulah too.

'She's never angry,' Tom said. 'She's very cool.' There was no missing the admiration in his voice. Then Tom raised his voice. 'No need to panic, *Mother*,' he told her. 'We'll get there.'

'You're determined to provoke him,' the trainer observed, while holding out her hand to Tallulah. 'Hi, Tallulah, I'm Elen. Don't let this one lead you astray.'

With mock indignation, Tom held a hand to his chest. 'I was just asking Tallulah how she ended up here.'

'He's a busy-body too.'

'Don't tell me you didn't want to ask.'

'Maybe, but I have better manners.'

'My nanny,' Tallulah blurted. She liked these two immediately – and wanted them to know it. 'Irena Stanton. She's a friend of Marie's.'

Elen stared at her. 'Irena Stanton? Was that always her name, do you know? Could she have been married?'

Tallulah wracked her brain. 'She was married. Her maiden name was ... Balkota? Blatkova?' She blushed. 'Something like that.'

'Blatiskova?' Elen offered.

Tallulah considered the suggestion. 'I think that might be right.'

Elen went a bit pale. Tallulah looked to Tom, who was watching his trainer as well, then back to Elen. 'Is that bad?'

The trainer shook her head. 'No. Just interesting. I did not know Ms Blatiskova had returned to ... ah ... being a nanny, that's all.'

'So you know her?'

'Only by reputation,' Elen admitted. 'But she doesn't work with just anyone, so you are very …' She searched for the right word. '… lucky.'

Tallulah smiled as a bell rang from the theatre. 'I really was.'

'Did she die?' Tom asked.

Tallulah shook her head. 'No. She's in Europe, visiting family. I don't know when she'll get back but I get a postcard every now and then.'

'Well, you never know what's in the future,' Elen said. She smiled then ushered them inside. 'You don't want to give Sasha any extra reason to go after you today.'

'Don't I?' countered Tom.

Elen's brow furrowed. 'He's family,' she said firmly.

'Not my family.'

'For a few months last year, you were willing to forget that. Come on.'

Tom turned and walked, but his cheeks were more crimson than they had been.

'We agreed to give him a chance, Tom,' Elen continued, gently, 'because only by forgiving and moving on can we ever get anything achieved. Anchoring ourselves to the past does not allow us to sail into the future.' She gave Tallulah a fleeting look, adding, 'And Tallulah certainly doesn't need things to be any worse today.'

'It's not gunna be worse,' Tom said, brightening. He gave Elen a reassuring pat on the shoulder. 'Lu knows she's not alone today.'

Tallulah had barely walked through the door when her name rang out through the warehouse and Saskia came striding towards her.

'You came back,' she declared.

'You didn't think I would?'

Saskia's answer was to wrap her in a bear hug. On releasing Tallulah, she grabbed her hand and led her further into the warehouse. Once clear of the doorway she turned and was about to speak when she was distracted from behind. Tallulah glanced back to see Tom.

'Oh, Tommy,' Saskia said, 'you're here.'

'Funny about that.'

Tallulah stood aside to include Tom in their conversation but it was quickly obvious that a great crevice could have just split the theatre and sucked the whole world into it and these two would not have noticed. They were lost in a staring competition; the space between them was so thick it was like trying to breathe smoky air.

'Hello, Saskia,' Elen said politely as she emerged from behind her lanky student. 'Tom, I need you over here.' Elen hooked her arm around his elbow and firmly moved him on. Tom didn't resist, but he turned back to Tallulah and gave a wave.

'See you at lunch,' he said.

'And me,' Saskia called after him, but he'd already turned away.

'So you've known Tom for a while?' Tallulah asked.

'A story for another time.' Saskia took a deep breath and smiled. 'I still can't believe you came back.'

'Exhausted, but never beat.'

Saskia nodded. 'Well, good for you. I thought when you weren't at lunch you'd be like the others.' She waved her hand behind her. Tallulah looked: perhaps there were fewer students than the previous day but she couldn't be sure. 'Look, I was really nervous yesterday,' Saskia continued. 'And Sash was at his wits' end trying to rein me in, and I was hostile to everything.' She sighed. 'My family is very intense about all this.'

Tallulah thought of the tension in her own family this morning. 'About Cirque d'Avenir?'

'Yeah, sort of. Look, Sasha and I ... well, he left home a long time ago. A bad argument with our father; reckoned Dad was force-feeding us "generations of hate". But he came back when he realised Dad had transferred his expectations to me. So he's a good brother. I guess I just get annoyed when he gets all high and mighty.' She shook her head. 'What a day, huh? You must have wondered what you'd got yourself caught up in.'

The only thing Tallulah wondered, after her glimpse of the twisted vines strapped around Sasha's mind, is what she'd find in Saskia's. But she put a smile on her face and shrugged. 'I went home and went to bed; I was too tired to wonder about anything.'

'Well, Marie was really worried about you. And angry that we might be the cause. It was wrong that you got caught up in our tension.'

It wasn't an apology but Tallulah suspected it was as close as Saskia got to one. 'We were all nervous yesterday.'

'Yes, we were. But today will be better. We're on the roof, have you heard?'

'The roof?' Tallulah felt a tap on her shoulder. Marnie, one of the trainers from the pool, was beside her.

'You need a reiki session after yesterday. You were supposed to come and see me after lunch.'

'Oh, sorry. Thanks.' Tallulah let herself be led away.

★

Fifteen minutes later, Tallulah re-joined the others, stunned at how easily she could move now. Compared with the massages she'd had that were supposed to do the same thing, Marnie's method was like waving a magic wand – or hand – over sore muscles and making the lactic acid disappear. Talk about performance-enhancing; Tallulah was a little giddy with the idea that she could push herself as hard as she liked and recover in time for the next session.

When she returned to the main theatre, Sasha was on the stage addressing the group. 'Since there were so many complaints yesterday about the pool,' he said with a wry grin, 'I thought we should stay here today. And it will be a little more comfortable for our spectators to see what an impressive group we've gathered.'

He gestured towards the balcony, where Marie and Brigitta sat looking down at the group.

Tallulah waved to Mai, who was laughing with Tom and Hui. But just as she did, Saskia appeared at her side.

'We've got to go up the ropes, out through the manholes and onto the roof for our session,' she whispered as Sasha stepped down from the stage.

'Hecate's torches,' Tallulah said weakly. 'I was hoping you were joking before.'

When she brought her eyes from the roof she found Saskia looking shocked. 'We use that saying, Tallulah. I thought it was just, you know, our family.'

'It's one of my nanny's silly—'

'Get out of here,' Saskia said, giving her a light slap on the shoulder. 'You *are* family! And here I was thinking you were a *local*.' She whispered the last word with such disdain Tallulah could only laugh.

'Saskia, Tallulah,' Sasha called. They turned to see him pushing Adelaide Banks in their direction. 'You can't be in a group alone,' he told her.

'I won't be alone for long. Something must have delayed them. They would never deliberately miss a circus class.'

Sasha did not reply. Instead he spoke to Saskia and Tallulah. 'Not all of my Seacliff students have returned today, so we need to spread those who are here among the groups. Saskia, Tallulah, this is Adelaide Banks.'

'Sasha,' Adelaide pleaded, 'you know my friends—'

He turned on her. 'They're not coming back, all right?' But almost immediately he rubbed his hands through his dark hair and his shoulders dropped. 'I'm sorry. I thought … we'd have a bit more time. But that's not the way it's panned out.' All business again, he added, 'You're working with Saskia and Tallulah today.'

Adelaide's face hardened as she looked at him for a long moment. She coughed, straightened, then looked at the girls and held out her hand out to Saskia. 'Della.'

'Pleasure to meet you, Della,' Saskia said formally. 'Sasha has told me a lot about you.'

'Lu,' Tallulah said, taking a small step towards Adelaide with the hint of an offered hand. But when Adelaide barely met her eye and offered no more than a tight nod, Tallulah turned what might have been a handshake into a half wave.

Sasha dispersed the three remaining locals, Ollie, Wilson and Sara, among the troupe. Tallulah counted; twenty students still remained – it seemed they'd lost about ten students in one day.

'I'll get them,' Adelaide said, as Sasha brought the box of warm-up straps from the stage.

As she walked away, Saskia turned to Tallulah and rolled her eyes. 'We're popular then.' She laughed. 'What did *you* do to her?' She waved her hand dismissively. 'Oh, don't worry, she'll be gone tomorrow. Sasha and his charity projects.'

The opening stretches and floor exercises warmed up not just muscles, but tongues as well. Adelaide might have preferred to work out with her friends but she was happy enough to ask a lot of questions while waiting to climb the ropes to the roof.

'So where are you from?'

Tallulah was about to answer when Saskia jumped in. 'French and Spanish on my mother's side, Russian and Swiss on my dad's.'

Adelaide looked confused. 'So you are … from where? Europe?'

'No, here.'

'Then why didn't you just say that?'

'You didn't ask that, did you?'

'So, "here" as in Seacliff?'

Saskia looked bored. 'We're circus people, Adelaide. From everywhere and nowhere. My parents got to the fork in the road, followed the trail to the left, and then there was me.'

Adelaide didn't bother to hide her expression of disdain.

'Sydney,' Tallulah offered, quickly. 'My parents grew up in Seacliff. Mum couldn't wait to get out. They moved to the city long before they had me.'

Adelaide nodded. 'And that's where you auditioned?'

'Auditioned?'

'To come to Cirque d'Avenir. Seacliff people had to audition.'

It was as much an accusation as a question and Tallulah knew she'd been snookered. 'No. I didn't audition. A friend recommended I come here.'

'Very cosy.'

'Don't make it sound so underhanded, Della,' Saskia chided. 'Cirque d'Avenir has scouts on the lookout always, everywhere. You might have tried out but Sasha handpicked the group who got to audition for Marie. It wasn't just any old cattle call, was it?'

Adelaide gave a shrug of concession.

'Where are the other Seacliff students, by the way?' Saskia asked.

'I don't know. But I'm sure they—'

'Well, there you go,' Saskia declared, 'you have to be tough to cope with one of Sasha's sessions. *You* obviously are. While your friends ...' Saskia shrugged. 'But Tallulah's here. Sasha threw everything he had at her yesterday and she's back for more.'

'I debated not coming back,' Tallulah said, trying to avoid any further confrontation.

'But you did. And that's what makes the difference. But I'm curious, Tallulah,' Saskia said, as if there was a great conspiracy afoot. 'Who recommended you to Cirque d'Avenir?'

'Saskia!' Sasha thundered down from above. 'Don't let today be a repeat of yesterday.'

'Sorry,' Saskia called back. 'Coming.'

All three girls ran to a rope.

'Last one up buys lunch,' Saskia called as they grabbed the ropes with feet and hands and began the long haul to the manhole at the top.

Tallulah was last to clamber onto the roof. She caught her breath as she stood up; the view was amazing. On one side the rooftops of Port Melba vanished into the ocean; on the other side the massive escarpment felt so close Tallulah was sure if she stretched just a little she could touch it.

She saw Marie and Brigitta sitting on a terrace under the shade of canvas awnings that stretched the length of the long picnic tables – clearly the lunch venue Tallulah had avoided yesterday. She turned back from the terrace scene to see Sasha watching her.

'When you're ready,' he said to Tallulah.

'We'll go out on strike if you start harassing Lu again.'

Tallulah cringed.

'Then stop delaying her with your chit-chat, Saskia, or we'll be here all day.' Sasha's voice was like a kid glove over sharp claws.

Tallulah put her head down as her cheeks flushed with embarrassment, and concentrated hard on the undulation of the roof under her feet.

'Now, can we get on with it?'

'Sure,' Saskia said quietly.

'So, as I told you yesterday, the Cirque d'Avenir family has been very generous, helping secure unique training venues, and this,' he swept his arms about him to encompass the warehouse roofs that circled the Cirque terrace, 'is one of them.'

'What?' challenged the boy Tallulah now knew as Guido. 'The rooftops are a training venue?'

A murmur went around the group – of both excitement and fear.

'Yes, of course,' Sasha answered. 'We have permission from all the owners involved. Not just for their roofs but for the padding, bounce boards, safety nets and ropes and everything else that has been added to ensure your safety. We're walking.'

They toured the circuit to get a feel for it: running across rooftops, jumping the gaps between – a flying fox had been erected for the one longer stretch – tumbles across flat spaces, a running jump and wall bounce to a ledge on a slightly higher level, a barrier with parallel horizontal rails to tumble through, slides down slanted roofs, a descent on an exterior ladder to a narrow lane that had to be 'walked' with hands and feet on the walls of the two buildings that created the lane, then running through a maze of lanes, before returning back into the Cirque d'Avenir theatre and climbing the rope to the roof to do it all over again.

Back on the rooftop, Sasha said, 'Like yesterday, we're working on promoting nimble acts in unusual circumstances. But today the exercises are fairly basic for two reasons. First and most obvious, your equilibrium will be challenged by the height unless you regularly do parkour. Look out for one another. There are nets and safety rails everywhere and trainers all around you, but the circuit requires you to take a leap – literally and figuratively. You will know the moment that you succeed, because you'll feel the thrill of true exhilaration and you won't be satisfied until you can do it all over again.'

Saskia tut-tutted, then leaned closer to Tallulah until their shoulders touched. 'He's such a tease; look at him reeling them all in.'

Tallulah nodded knowingly, acknowledging Saskia's observation as if she'd been immune to the reeling.

'The second reason the exercises are moderate is because I need you to make an imprint of the territory in your mind and body. Like a racing-car driver who walks around the racetrack before he drives it, so that he knows every crack and bump in the asphalt before his car does, I want you to know this circuit the same way. You'll need the knowledge next week when we add a twist to your training. So take your time today. Use all your senses to know the space.'

The students looked willing if puzzled. Sasha clapped his hands. 'Let's walk it one more time, this time taking in the kind of detail I was talking about, and then we'll do it for real.'

Sasha turned and walked, Tom followed and everyone else fell into line. Tallulah looked around for Adelaide. She was at the back, looking a bit uncomfortable as she took in the rooftop. She ran her hands through her hair and Tallulah watched her shoulders rise and fall as if she was trying to suck in as much air as possible but couldn't work out how.

Saskia followed Tallulah's gaze and made a quick assessment. 'Scared of heights.'

Tallulah couldn't think of any other reason. She let others pass to wait for Adelaide, despite Saskia's impatience. 'We need to keep you up the front, Lu, otherwise you'll fall behind and Sasha will have you for dinner.'

'He also said to look out for one another.'

Saskia sighed. 'Just don't say I didn't warn you.'

As Adelaide approached them, Tallulah said, 'You all right, Della?'

'Why shouldn't I be?'

'Some people get freaked out by heights,' Saskia said.

Tallulah spun her head to glare at Saskia.

'What?' she asked innocently.

'I don't have a problem with heights,' Adelaide declared.

She locked eyes with Tallulah, who took in her pale face and the sweat beading her top lip, but said only, 'OK. Just checking. Let's go.'

The third time the girls climbed the ropes to take them up to the rooftop from the theatre space, Adelaide was slower than Tallulah to get to the top – and breathing much harder than everyone else as she pulled herself through the manhole.

Sasha noticed Adelaide's predicament and moved through the group of students to try to help her onto the roof. 'I'm all right,' she said as she refused his hand.

'Keep hydrated, people,' he said. He stepped back to give Adelaide some space, pivoted on the spot and tapped the shoulder of the trainer behind him, who was pouring a sport drink into a plastic cup for Mai. 'Can I please have one of those?'

He took the full cup and handed it to Adelaide.

'I've just got a headache,' she said quietly.

'Sit for a moment.' Sasha pulled the rope through the manhole closest to him, then lashed it around his right arm and said, 'Drink up, people. We'll go again in a few minutes.' He dropped through the manhole.

'See?' a voice whispered beside Tallulah as she sipped and waited.

Tallulah turned to find Mai at her shoulder wearing an 'I told you so' look on her face.

'See what?'

'She has to win.'

It took Tallulah a moment to recall their conversation from the day before. Before answering she looked around the rooftop to see Saskia chatting animatedly on the other side of the group.

'Adelaide's headache is Saskia's fault?'

'You know what she's capable of.'

Tallulah swallowed, remembering her sudden attack of self-loathing when she first met Saskia, and the sight of her breached defences and drained well that morning. 'Except there's no competition yet,' she whispered to Mai.

'Every moment is a competition for her.'

'She apologised to me first thing this morning ...' Tallulah paused. 'Sort of.'

'Well, she hasn't apologised to me – even sort of – for trying to freak me out when I first got here.'

Tallulah bit her lip; she hadn't admitted to Mai that she was also partially responsible. 'She will. She was just nervous. Like we all were. I seem to remember you had me up against a pylon yesterday.'

'That came out of her game-playing, don't forget.'

'Don't you think you're a touch too paranoid?'

'Don't you think you're a touch too nice?'

Mai glanced back towards the lunch terrace and Tallulah did too. Sasha had returned to the rooftop via the stairs. After a brief word with Marie and Brigitta he ran through the lunch tables and leaped onto the section of the roof where the students waited. Tallulah and Mai watched Adelaide take the painkillers he offered, with a grateful smile.

'Saskia,' Sasha called, once Adelaide gave the nod that she was ready to continue, 'I want your team to go up front, behind Tom, Mai and Hui, where I can keep an eye on you.'

Adelaide joined Saskia and Tallulah.

'Feeling better?' whispered Tallulah.

Adelaide's brow furrowed, then she nodded. 'I am, actually.' She wouldn't look at Tallulah, but she casually turned her rigid back to Saskia.

She still looked pale when the circuit began but it didn't stop her from leading the other two off in the run across the Cirque d'Avenir roof. She didn't confer with them as to who should go first and the affront to Saskia's pride flashed in her golden eyes. She rocked back and forth on the spot as she stood, waiting impatiently for Sasha to give her the nod to go;

she had barely begun before he jerked his head for Tallulah to follow.

Despite her intention to go steadily, Tallulah felt pressure from all sides. In trying to fulfil the requirements that Sasha had stipulated – do the exercise as well as imprinting in her mind and body the detail of her surroundings – she quickly fell behind. She kept her rising sense of inferiority at bay by concentrating on the myriad details: the number of steps across one roof; the number of tumbles along the next; the feel of the tarred surface underneath her feet; the thickness of her rope.

But when she was confronted by the sprint across the roof, straight at the vertical wall, which she was supposed to leap on at the last minute with one foot, using the bounce to propel her onto a higher ledge, Tallulah had no tactics to overcome the overwhelming fear that she could not do it – at least not without breaking something. Including her pride.

No matter how many times she ran at the wall, no matter how much encouragement from Ilya, she couldn't let herself go. Estella and Javier caught up and offered help.

'Sasha is crazy,' Estella told Tallulah.

Javier said something to her in Spanish but Estella shook her head. 'So what if there's a net to fall into; if you have never done it before it's foolish to start like this …'

'We help,' Javier said, but a series of quick claps from a central roof interrupted the plan.

'Over here, Tallulah,' Sasha called. Estella gave Tallulah an apologetic roll of her eyes and took off – she moved like Marie, liquid bones – followed by Javier. The two of them performed the right-left-right series of hops, Javier including an aerial somersault in between the walls with complete ease.

When Tallulah joined Sasha he showed her a smaller ledge, wall and raised plinth and demonstrated the required hops on a smaller scale. 'Practise here.'

Tallulah stifled her embarrassment and began to practise under his uncompromising eye. When he decided she'd performed it often enough he took her back to the original wall. 'Away you go.'

She baulked on the first attempt, fell into the net on the second. Sasha said nothing. As she climbed out of the net, Ilya gave her a hand up.

'See yourself do it first,' he said, almost under his breath.

Tallulah nodded. She walked back to the start position, closed her eyes and saw it happen perfectly. When she opened her eyes, before she could think, she took off and leaped, bounced, spun and …

She was sure she flew for a moment before landing perfectly on the higher roof. 'Ha!' she cried as she punched the air, then stumbled back two steps before regaining her balance. She shook her head in an effort to combat the overwhelming weariness she felt.

Sasha landed next to her. 'Go! You're a long way behind.'

When Tallulah caught up with Adelaide and Saskia, Sasha was already there, checking on Adelaide and praising her toughness. Adelaide claimed to be feeling fine, but she looked unnaturally pale and, despite the warm summer day, she shivered as though she had a chill – or was fighting an unknown presence. Tallulah could not understand why Sasha was letting her continue.

Back at the start of the circuit, as they rested before the final round, Mai said to Tallulah, 'You've been given a reprieve.' She nodded towards Adelaide, who sat separate to the group, crouched on her haunches, holding her head in her hands. The pain was obviously back. Saskia stood on the opposite side of the rooftop, hands on her hips, recovering her breath as she looked out to sea.

Tallulah grabbed an extra drink for Adelaide as a trainer went past. 'I don't know why he lets her keep going,' she said to Mai, who grabbed her wrist before she could go.

'Stay out of it.'

'Out of what? I'm not going to let her faint.'

'She's the one insisting on going on,' Mai said, 'no one else. It's part of their game. You were in the sandwich yesterday – let her deal with it today.'

Before Tallulah could shake off Mai's grip, Ilya had sat down on the roof next to Adelaide, put an ice cube in her mouth, and a tea-towel-wrapped ice pack on her forehead.

'Good work, people,' Sasha called. 'Be careful on the final round.' When he got to Adelaide he crouched down and consulted with Ilya. Adelaide looked up and shook her head. 'No, I'm all right.'

She pushed herself up as if determined to make her point, and walked away from them.

But within a few steps she stumbled towards the wire safety fence edging the flat part of their roof. Then she righted herself.

'Adelaide,' Sasha called. 'Come back this way.'

Adelaide turned warily, as if unsure of where she was. Then her eyes rolled back in her head. She took three steps backwards, evading the late-reacting Ilya, and toppled into the safety fence.

Cries rang out from everywhere as Adelaide pitched over the safety fence, slipped down the outer slope of the roof and disappeared.

CHAPTER SIX

In a whir of movement almost too fast for Tallulah to see, the wire railing was unclipped and hooked to Sasha's belt. He ran down the steep roof and slid, just in time to catch Adelaide as she reached the edge. As they teetered on the brink, he cried, 'Got her.'

The two of them were pulled up the slope. Back on the safe side of the fence, lying panting on the floor, Adelaide rolled on her side and threw up. Ignoring her protests, Ilya picked her up and helped her away from the group.

'Poor thing,' Saskia said as she stood beside Tallulah and watched Ilya and Adelaide walk to the shaded tables, where Adelaide sat down and pillowed her head on her arms. 'It is so hot.'

Marnie appeared from the stairs and strode across the terrace. As Ilya lifted Adelaide's head to make her drink, Marnie stood behind her, closed her eyes and moved her hands across the girl's shoulders and over her head.

'Still, we have to perform, whatever the conditions,' Saskia said. 'The show must go on and all that. Adelaide knows that; it's why she's so angry with herself. You could see it as Ilya walked her away. I would be too. So embarrassing, especially in front of everyone.'

Tallulah checked Saskia's expression for any hint of superiority and could find none. Nor was there any satisfaction, which she would expect to see if Mai was right and it had been the older girl inside Adelaide's head causing the problem.

And Saskia had a point – a circus professional did have to perform under adverse conditions. It was the first helpful insight she'd had into the Robinsons: raise a tent, perform, move on and do it again. Don't let the show down.

Tallulah had never worked in her life; never had to get back up the next day and perform the same thing over and over again.

After a spirited confrontation with Marie, Sasha returned to the group.

'OK, we're going to leave it for now,' he said. 'It's been an intense morning. At least you've got an idea of what we'll be up to next week. Let's do a cool-down stretch together and then head to the tables for lunch.'

There was no sign of Adelaide when Tallulah returned to the rooftop after a shower – she hadn't been in the change rooms either.

Coloured lanterns hung from the marquees, red-and-white checked cloths covered the tables and delicious smells wafted from the barbecue. But a long line for food had already formed and, since she was in no hurry, she opted for a bottle of water and a seat at the ocean end of one table, from which she had a view of Seacliff roofs all the way to the escarpment.

Tinkling laughter at the other end of the long table drew Tallulah's attention; the Chilean students were already eating and being entertained by the old woman, Brigitta. With a few graceful gestures, Brigitta finished her story, said her goodbyes, and walked towards Tallulah.

Brigitta arrived at the same time as a plate laden with three types of salad and several marinated lamb cutlets was put in front of Tallulah, along with a bottle of ginger beer. Tom climbed in to sit on the bench next to her.

'You didn't have to … You shouldn't have …' Tallulah stammered. 'I was just waiting …'

'She protests a lot, Tommy,' Brigitta said with a grin. 'The famous Tallulah is more worried about the implications of the gift than accepting it with gratitude. Very interesting.'

Tallulah didn't know what Brigitta meant but felt heat rise to her cheeks. 'I just didn't want you to think I was so useless I couldn't get my own food.'

Tom smiled. 'Didn't cross my mind. It just seemed like the right thing to do. I asked you to lunch, after all.'

'Oh!' Tallulah grinned. 'Yeah.'

'Don't tell me you forgot?'

'No! There's just been a lot to think about, to concentrate on, since we … well … I'm not a natural at—'

'Tallulah, you're being modest,' Brigitta interrupted.

'Not about performing on roofs, I'm not.'

'Stop underplaying your ability,' Brigitta admonished. 'Your determination has been exemplary. That exercise you learned on the roof today, changing height and direction at once, was excellent.'

Tallulah sat a little higher on the bench; it was the praise she'd been desperate to hear. 'Thank you.'

'This is new to all of us, Lu,' Tom said. 'A Cirque d'Avenir camp including recruits beyond the same old families? It's never been done. But some of us are better prepared, I'll give you that. For anyone who's new to this – well,' he waved his fork, 'look around, we've lost a few already. But, I'm not about to let another Robinson get the better of me.'

'No one's got the better of you, Tommy,' Brigitta said crisply. 'But you're the one who has to believe it.'

There was silence. Tallulah could feel Brigitta's penetrating gaze; she tried to act naturally but could not stop the tremor in her hands as she pushed potato salad onto her fork and began to eat. When she finally turned back to Brigitta, the old woman was still watching her.

'We haven't been properly introduced, have we?'

Tallulah shook her head, quickly swallowing a lump of potato salad, as Tom said, 'Oh, excuse me!' He put his knife and fork down on either side of his plate. But before he could make the introduction, it was done.

'Brigitta, this is Tallulah,' Saskia said. 'Tallulah, Brigitta.' She stood beside them wearing a huge grin. Tom put his head down and went back to his food. Brigitta held out her hand to Tallulah.

But rather than shake Tallulah's hand, she took hold of it, encasing it firmly between both of her own. She turned the hand gently and surveyed Tallulah's palm. Taking her time, Brigitta traced the long line through the centre of Tallulah's palm with the long fingernail of her own middle finger. Tallulah suppressed a shiver as the woman murmured an 'ahh' loaded with new and deeper wisdom.

Both Tallulah and Saskia leaned forward.

'You have been searching, I see, but now you have found the family you have been looking for.'

Tallulah looked at her palm and then back at Brigitta. Before she could respond, Brigitta continued. 'And when you overcome the need to apologise for yourself, you will truly fly.'

Saskia gasped. Brigitta glanced at her, then back to Tallulah, before scrunching her nose and eyes like a little girl might and chuckling. Saskia started laughing as though she shared the joke with Brigitta, while Tallulah looked to Tom, bewildered. He gave her a wry smile. When Brigitta had recovered she gave a loud satisfied sigh.

'I always thought palm-reading was a load of old codswallop,' she said. 'But I got you both.' She pointed at Saskia. 'Don't pretend I didn't, my dear.'

Returning to Tallulah, she patted her palm gently but held onto the hand as she stared deeply into her eyes. Tallulah felt she was in a kind of staring contest, only way more comfortable; a delicious warmth spread from the hand Brigitta was holding, along her arm and then through her body, settling her nerves and counterbalancing the feelings of awkwardness and insecurity that had plagued her since before her first session at Cirque d'Avenir.

Somewhere in her head a voice reminded her to check her boundaries. But she dismissed it because Brigitta was not trying to get into her mind: she was merely wrapping her in a gorgeous blanket of reassurance.

Finally, Brigitta blinked and Tallulah was released. She took her first deep breath in two days.

'Gorgeous girl,' Brigitta said. 'No wonder Marie was so excited for you to join us. And Irena Blatiskova – why did she not come as well?'

Irena's maiden name already sounded more real than Stanton. 'She's visiting family in Europe,' Tallulah replied. She had a curious sensation that she had said something she shouldn't. But when she checked Brigitta for a reaction the woman merely nodded with polite interest.

'Pity. I would like to have seen her again; it's been many,

many years.' Brigitta stood and put a hand each on Saskia's and Tallulah's shoulders. 'Well, my two gorgeous girls, we're going to have such fun together.' Then she looked at Tom and winked. 'Good luck with your date. I approve, by the way.'

'Date?' Saskia asked, looking from Brigitta to Tom to Tallulah. 'Who's on a date?'

Tallulah noticed Tom's rueful expression as he gazed at Saskia.

'Never you mind,' Brigitta said. 'It's time for Tom to mend his broken heart.'

Saskia mouth dropped into a perfect O. 'Oh, that's right,' she scoffed, 'he broke up with me, but worry about *his* broken heart.'

'Maybe if you had a heart we would worry about it, Saskia,' Hui said as he walked past them with a large plate of food.

'Cut it out, Hui,' said Tom.

'Always the comedian,' Saskia said drolly.

'Spare us the melodrama, young woman.' Brigitta looked around. A grin played on her lips. 'I'm very interested to see just what we shall find here in Seacliff.'

'But where are you going?' Saskia asked as the old woman backed away.

'I've got to share myself around; it would do no good to show favouritism. But don't worry; we begin our training next week, so we'll have lots of time together.'

'Training,' Saskia squeaked. 'It's been approved?'

Brigitta nodded then put a finger to her lips. She turned to the students at the table next to them.

'Well,' Saskia said to Tallulah, 'I've never seen Brigitta so friendly with someone she's just met. Have you, Tom? She's usually very cautious. Takes a while to size people up.'

'Who is she?'

They gave Tallulah twin incredulous looks.

'She's one of the Gazers, silly,' Saskia told her.

Tom said, 'Since when? She's an Elder, yes. But she doesn't predict.'

'Have it your own way; you just want to argue with me and I won't give you the satisfaction.' She turned to Tallulah. 'She's amazing, that's all I care about, and she's going to teach us.' She put her hands together and made fast tiny claps. Then both hands went to her stomach and she groaned. 'But now I've got to eat. I'm starving.'

Tallulah watched her go. She wanted to ask Tom about his history with Saskia but opted instead for a more tactful question. 'Tom, who are the Gazers?'

He glanced at her sideways. 'Hasn't this Irena explained it all to you?'

Tallulah shook her head.

'Your parents?'

She choked back a laugh. 'Hardly!'

Confusion came across Tom's sunny features. His eyes narrowed as he tried to understand. 'But, don't your parents know about, you know …?' He raised his eyebrows and rolled his hand through the air as though she should know what he wanted to say next.

Tallulah grinned. 'You're shy all of a sudden.'

He pushed his hand through his sandy curls and looked down the long tables to where Marie sat with Sasha and a few other trainers, then back to Tallulah. 'I just don't know it's my place to tell you. This camp is about scouting for talent but Elen, for one, worries they've cast their net too wide and risk exposing, well, Cirque d'Avenir, to too many eyes. Maybe this

Irena of yours is not sure of your …' He sighed, and rolled his hand again.

Tallulah made an impulsive decision – she dropped her protective walls and communicated.

… isn't sure of my super-power?

Tom jumped with such force that he bumped the trestle; his plate and what remained of his lunch flew off the table.

'I'm so sorry!' Tallulah jumped up, grabbing a stack of loose napkins, and dived down to clean up the accident. She put the plate and its towering bundle of soiled napkins on the table and sat again.

'I shouldn't have done that.'

'Some super-power,' he said in a constricted whisper.

'Irena would kill me,' Tallulah said. 'She's really strict. But you'd been so, well, brazen about it earlier, and you seem to know a lot and I thought you'd be used to …' she imitated his earlier gesture and rolled her hand through the air '… stuff like that.'

Tom's eyes grew even wider and he leaned forwards. 'You have got to keep *stuff like that* to yourself, Tallulah. For now, anyway. I mean, I'm OK, but you don't know who …' He paused, at a loss once more.

'You sound as paranoid as Irena.'

'She's not paranoid.' He stopped; his eyes lit up in understanding. 'Wait, does Sasha know?'

'Know what?'

'About *stuff like that*.'

'Tom, this is silly.'

'Does he?'

She shook her head, then stopped herself. 'Maybe. My guard was down yesterday and he grabbed my wrist and—'

She sighed. 'I don't know what happened but he accused me of being in his head.'

Tom frowned. 'Can you do that?'

'Do what?'

'Read minds?'

'No!' Tallulah exclaimed. 'Irena taught me to thought-cast and to protect my own mind. But reading someone else's would not sit well with her concept of manners.'

Tom shook his head, a combination of pity and bewilderment on his face. He reached across the table and laid his warm hand over hers. 'Irena taught you to protect your mind for a reason. You *have* to stick to it — until you get further instruction from Brigitta, I guess, or Marie.'

'I'm not stupid. My guard was down *yesterday* but not today. And I don't go practising on just anyone. It would clearly freak people out.'

'I didn't say you were stupid.'

'I just don't get why I have to protect myself at Cirque d'Avenir, if this is where I've been sent for further training.'

'Firstly, because not everyone here is … um … "super". Outstanding local students were invited because those who settled here after the war had relationships beyond the "family"; but no one is sure of who can do what yet. And secondly, because just as in any training squad, there are highly competitive individuals who are not what you might call team players. If they suspect you are a threat to their position they will do what they have to do to sabotage you. Even if you're *not* a threat they'll sabotage you. That's just the way it goes.'

Tallulah had the distinct impression that he was speaking from experience. 'I thought we were meant to be a team — a family?'

'Families aren't competitive? Family members won't exploit their positions? Look after their own interests? You can't be that naive.'

She had no experience to contradict his assessment, so she left it. But a thought crossed her mind. 'Tom, what is your ...?' She rolled her hand through the air again.

He laughed. 'Well, in the spirit of remaining positive,' he paused, then said quietly, 'I'm a firethrower.'

'In the spirit of remaining positive?'

'Can we leave it at that for now?'

He looked genuinely pained and she didn't want to press him. Nevertheless she sensed an advantage.

'On one condition.'

Tom laughed, but his eyes narrowed. 'What?'

'Tell me who the Gazers are.' When he didn't immediately respond she added, 'Come on, you owe me.'

'I *owe* you?'

'Yes,' Tallulah said with as much sass as she could muster. 'I'm sure you must.'

'The Gazers make all the decisions about, well, about Cirque d'Avenir.'

'What do you mean?'

'Well, they gaze, you know, they predict. Like they've decided it's time to go scouting again and re-form.'

'I don't get it. The Gazers are seers?' Tallulah thought of all the conversations she'd had with Irena about seers and fortune-tellers: they were charlatans, according to her nanny. 'Irena wouldn't send me to a circus whose decisions were made by seers.'

'Why not?'

She realised that this might not be the best conversation to have with someone from the Cirque d'Avenir 'family'. But he certainly seemed open enough to other points of view. 'Well, because she doesn't believe in fortune-telling. She believes in paying attention to what's all around us, to looking for the signs and acting instinctively. Seers are ... are ... well, seers are fakes.'

'Go on,' he said, placing a warm hand over hers, 'but quietly.'

'Irena reckons they fudge the truth – because they have to. Think about it. No client really wants to pay money to hear that life is going to be hell. The seer would go broke and the clients would be depressed. So truth is compromised. Then, in trying to make the seer's prediction come true, the clients don't live their lives acting and reacting instinctively, but in the way they think will bring about the prediction. So instinct is compromised.'

'But the Gazers don't have clients. They have been members of Cirque d'Avenir for a long time; they have people with gifts – like you, like me – relying on them. We aren't normal. They wouldn't risk exposing us if they didn't believe in their own predictions.'

Tallulah nodded. He made sense, but she decided nevertheless that until she knew more about the Gazers she would take her cues from her dearest guide. 'You're probably right,' she said. Then she laughed. 'Probably no more than an old woman's paranoia. Just don't tell me there's some mysterious prophecy, OK?'

Tom gave her a bemused look as music swelled from the stage. At the other end of the rooftop, Marie stepped onto the platform and posed, hands held gracefully above her head, face turned down to the ground. As a violin began to weep a quiet lament, Marie's hands and hips marked the beat of the story.

A classical guitar and drums joined in and Marie's hands began to weave a story.

The first movements struck Tallulah in the centre of her heart. She knew this; she sat on the table so she could see better. Tom followed.

The story was about a young woman of exquisite beauty whose performance in a travelling circus troupe was so mesmerising that people travelled from far and wide to watch her weave her wordless tales as she strode the arena on stilts. At least, there seemed to be no words. Yet, on reflection, everyone agreed that her stories were so articulate that it was as if she'd been sitting directly behind them, whispering in their ear, until the words had been woven into their very bones.

Rulers and holy men heard about the girl; naturally they coveted her phenomenal gift. She fell in love with a king, who took not just the circus girl for his queen, but her whole troupe as entertainment for the court.

For a time everything was golden: the kingdom grew vast and, while there were rumours that the queen and her circus troupe worked a strange magic on the battlefield as well as at court, no one complained, because life in the cities and towns of the empire was good. The people began to worship their queen as a goddess; the king honoured his wife and his subjects' beliefs by building beautiful hanging gardens in her name.

But slowly the king became jealous of the queen's power. His envy was fuelled by treacherous advisors, themselves frustrated by the queen's influence. After a loss on a far-off battlefield, the king was convinced that it was not the fault of his generals but that of the queen, whose powers must be on the wane. On the king's orders his advisors began scouring the kingdom for a girl with the same gift – who they could better control.

Whispers of his treachery grew until the queen herself learned of it. Heartbroken, she made an extraordinary decision: she used her magic to encourage the army to turn against their king. When he was dead and his advisors scattered, she became the first ruling queen of the kingdom.

But grief consumed her, and her son, who had been born with no special gifts, played the advantage. Despite the king's intention to do away with his mother, he gathered the court's former advisors and together they spread the story of the queen's treachery throughout the land. She realised too late what was happening. She'd lost the people's respect, and her gift, along with those of her circus troupe, was treated with suspicion and fear. She had no support – nor the will to live – when her son raised his hand against her. With the queen dead, her circus troupe was banished, cursed to walk the land forever.

When the show ended, Tallulah was surprised to find she was in tears on a table on a rooftop in Seacliff, not surrounded by hanging gardens and stepped pyramids. She quickly wiped her eyes with the back of her hands, felt a nudge, and realised Tom was holding a bunch of clean napkins for her. She had a mental flash of herself at seven, mirroring the movements of a clown. She knew the story; she always had. She just didn't know how.

'What … was it a language? Why did I understand it? She was just dancing,' Hui said hoarsely to Tom from the next table.

Saskia spun around from her own seat and gave a victorious laugh. 'Not so smart now, Hui, for someone who calls himself Cirkulatti. It was the choreography of the Ancients – The Dance of the King's Eminence.'

CHAPTER SEVEN

Tallulah barely kept her composure when Saskia spoke after Marie's dance on the rooftop; goosebumps rolled across her skin when she heard the word *Cirkulatti* closely followed by *King's Eminence*. The story of the dance was not the same as the cuff's vision but instinct told her the words were keys to understanding what it was all about: the woman on stilts who led her troupe, the Cirkulatti, into the hippodrome in that riot was called Eminence – Tallulah was almost sure of it – acting not for a king, but an emperor.

Tallulah's impatience during Marnie's post-lunch reiki session was only checked by the knowledge that she'd be completely revived and could ride like the wind all the way home.

Sweaty and breathless when she finally pushed to the summit of her driveway, she was relieved her parents weren't home and she wouldn't have to answer their inevitable questions about the day; she left her bike propped against the back verandah, unlocked the door and took the stairs two at a time to her room. Throwing her helmet on the bed, she crossed the floor to her desk and turned her computer on.

When the words *eminence* and *hippodrome* together yielded nothing of note in the search engine, she tried *emperor* and *hippodrome*.

As the list of options appeared on the screen her breath caught in her throat; she sat forward to read about a famous hippodrome in the city once known as Constantinople, an Emperor Justinian, his powerful and influential wife, Theodora – who'd risen from a lowly circus performer to become empress – and a famous uprising in 532 known as the Nika riots.

'No,' Tallulah whispered. There was no mention of magical powers or battle-trained circus performers but as she clicked on one website after another and learned about events that happened some fifteen hundred years ago, another voice inside her said, 'Yes.'

Eventually, she stopped reading and considered all that she knew. Tallulah had suspected the physical skills she'd witnessed in training the last two days were not normal, not to mention Mai and her ribbons. And didn't Tom considered his firethrowing – when he was being positive – a super-power? Then there was Marie's dance, as well as Tallulah's own ability to thought-cast like Theodora … Whoa. She wasn't ready to look at what sharing a talent with a former eminence might mean.

Then Tallulah laughed; surely she was going mad. Even if there was a skerrick of truth in what she was thinking, what would a mighty, magical circus troupe like the Cirkulatti be doing recruiting in a regional Australian town? Who was the eminence now? And what about the cuff?

The details of that first vision were so hazy she would have thought it was all a dream – except for the moment she met Mai. The memory of the dog-men attacking the acrobats had returned with such frightening clarity that she only *wished* it had been a dream. But hadn't it helped her understand her new friend?

By the time she'd arrived at that thought she was standing in front of her wardrobe. She opened the door, reached up to the top shelf and plunged her hand in behind the sweaters. Bringing the carved box from its hiding place, she closed the door and made her way back to the desk.

'Hecate's torches,' she whispered as she ran her fingers over the embedded amber stones that illustrated the flames. She dropped the boxed cuff on her lap, pulled her chair closer to the desk and quickly typed into the search engine: *silver cuff with thumb piece, eminence, Hecate's torches, owls.*

As the list of suggested websites appeared she clicked on the first: 'Lost Treasures of the Ancient World'. It offered a list of lost or missing items including 'Curios of the Eminence'. 'No way,' she muttered as she clicked again. Included in a group of jewellery and other adornments was a sketch of a cuff that could well have been Irena's – and Theodora's. According to the website, '*the Curios most recently belonged to Carl Lenter, noted collector of Roman antiquities. But when his collection was bequeathed to New York's Metropolitan Museum of Art, late last century, the Curios were not part of the collection.*'

Tallulah read on with a mixture of excitement and incredulity. Included in the Curios was a picture of Nefertiti and her headdress, which further jogged her memory: it was almost certainly the one Theodora had worn for the battle in the hippodrome. But it was inconceivable that her honest, honourable Irena would have given her an artefact to keep safe that, according to the website, had always been '*traded on the black market*'.

'Lu.'

Tallulah jumped in her chair; the carved box and its treasure fell forward in her lap but she caught it between her knees. She turned to her bedroom door.

'Hi Dad.'

'We've been calling for ten minutes. I thought you might be asleep.'

She gave her best impersonation of a weary smile. 'Oh, not yet. I came up to send an email and got a distracted.'

'I'm about to throw salmon steaks on the barbecue.'

'OK. I'll have a quick shower and come down.'

If she hadn't been so distracted by her discovery, Tallulah might have felt guilty about leaving the dinner table so quickly. But all she could think about was the cuff; there'd been that moment before she began juggling when she'd wished for some assistance – and it had been forthcoming. The more she thought about it the more convinced she became that it was an echo from the cuff's vision. And if that were true then what other help might she be able to access if she were to put it on deliberately – when she wasn't asleep.

The cuff was waiting but her trembling hands thwarted all attempts to move quickly; she couldn't get it out of the box and onto her wrist fast enough. As it settled into place she became anxious, and overwhelmed by feelings of guilt, even betrayal. Disoriented, she heard a carriage leave behind her and checked her boundaries. Finding herself in the long corridor of a palace, she walked to where he was waiting in their sitting room.

Justinian crossed the room and took her in his arms. She held her arms at her side, resisting his attempts to soothe her. But it was impossible. She took a deep breath and put her forehead on his shoulder. To rest, even for just this moment, was such a relief.

Justinian led her to an embroidered velvet chaise longue on the edge of the room.

'With your defeat of Hypatius and the Cirknero in the hippodrome we have nothing left to fear, yet you worry more than before. We will unite the west and the east; the empire will be complete. It was my promise to you, and to the Cirkulatti for sharing with me its eminence.'

'Then it is a promise the eminence and the Cirkulatti release you from. The Cirknero is never defeated, Justinian. Just as night follows day, as light creates shade, it waits in the shadows for its moment to strike. And it is prepared to go to places with its magic that the Cirkulatti wouldn't contemplate. You saw the dog-men. They were an abomination – as much an attempt to strike fear into the hearts of your people as to assassinate me. We are vulnerable. Every instinct in my body is telling me so. Your armies are spread too thin.'

'Theodora, you have read the minds of my generals; I know you have. Is there one that you have found disloyal? One whose mind is barred to you?'

Reluctantly, she shook her head.

'Then you must protect your own mind from these thoughts. Perhaps you are seeking faults in my judgement because you are conflicted by your own.'

She did not respond.

'This is about your daughter,' he said.

'We have tested every girl from every gifted family from here to Persia. We must find my true successor, Justinian.' She knew that to talk of her eventual death did not please him but she could not afford to be so sentimental. 'One who cannot be owned by the Cirknero, one who can be certain to act in your interests.'

'You have a successor, Theodora,' he said gently. 'Your daughter has the gift.'

'Birthright does not guarantee succession to the role of eminence. There was no thought-caster powerful enough to lead the Cirkulatti for centuries. And then me. Why?'

'Hecate bestows her gifts on mortals who deserve them. That is what you tell me, isn't it? Your daughter is a thought-caster, yet you resist her succession.'

'I know, I know.' Theodora strode to the other side of the room and looked out the window to where her Cirkulatti practised in the courtyard below. She felt the warmth of Justinian's body as he stood behind her.

'The hoop throwers are new,' he observed.

'From Antioch; they fled here after it was sacked. And they bring fresh skills to my team.'

'They can be trusted?'

'The strongmen, the clowns and the magicians trust them, and they are my most loyal factions.' She paused, her next words caught in the back of her throat – but who could she speak to if not her husband? 'I do not trust Dora.'

When he didn't respond she turned her body and sought his eyes with some trepidation. 'She's arrogant, she's manipulative. She's deeply disgusted that she is the daughter of some nameless man from my youth rather than of you, the emperor. Yet, despite this shame, she has a ferocious sense of entitlement. She wishes to disavow me with one hand and yet emulate me with the other.' She took a deep breath. 'I cannot recommend her to succeed me. Since the battle in the hippodrome, I'm even less inclined to do so. Suddenly she is obsessed by the Curios.'

'But you have always worried about her lack of respect for the many mysteries of your position. "She won't train her mind and win the confidence of the Curios."' He imitated her so well that he earned a smile.

'Precisely. How many hours have you listened to me recount my battles with Dora? How many hours have I spent urging her to hone her gift in the hope that her own power may combine with the Curios and connect her with the eminences of the past, and their wisdom, through the goddess Hecate? But the Curios have never responded to her. She dismisses this as some sort of trickery on my part, claiming that I, embarrassed by *my* past, *her* illegitimacy, am determined to undermine her confidence and sap her power. But now—'

'Perhaps she is maturing. Perhaps after the hippodrome—'

'You think I am punishing her for my own complacency in the hippodrome?'

'Theodora, no ...'

'It was not a lack of respect for the goddess or the Curios that sent me into the hippodrome unprepared. It was a belief that after centuries of wandering and persecution, the safety the Cirkulatti enjoys in Constantinople would be enough. But not for some – including my daughter, it would seem.'

She shook her head and took a deep breath, in an attempt to slow her beating heart, but hurt and disappointment were overwhelming her now. She let Justinian guide her to the stone plinth and sit her down.

'Tell me your fears.'

'Although Dora claims interest in all the Curios and their history,' Theodora gave a sharp laugh, 'she is interested in only one.'

'Fulvia's cuff,' Justinian said.

'The Cirknero know that the cuff warned me of their presence in the hippodrome.'

'But how? Who would have told them?'

'I let Antonina confide in an acrobat we suspect had been disloyal. Within days Dora was at my side, at her sweetest, promising everything, if I would only forgive her arrogance and teach her about the Curios. And her questions always return to Fulvia's cuff.' She mustered the bravest smile she could. 'Only she doesn't call it Fulvia's cuff. It is the cuff made for the Lioness of Rome.' She grunted. 'My own daughter calling another woman "the lioness of Rome". Fulvia achieved nothing for the Cirkulatti – or women – not like I have.'

'My darling,' Justinian cooed. 'You must calm down or you risk making a rash decision. You play a dangerous game. Where is Fulvia's cuff now?'

'It is hidden.'

'Not simply handing your daughter the role of eminence has thrown her, in her fury, straight into the arms of those you wish to keep her from.'

'The Cirkulatti are vulnerable to those same people if she succeeds me. We need to find an eminence who can take her on and play the Cirknero at their own game. If the Cirknero take hold, the danger for you and for the people of Constantinople will be immense. The devil-dogs will be just the beginning. I can't let the Cirkulatti fall into the disarray they were in before I became eminence.'

Justinian kissed her lightly. 'You take on too much, my love, without enjoying all that you have achieved.' His hands went gently to each cheek. 'All *we* have achieved,' he said, before kissing her deeply.

Pleasure rippled through her body and for a moment she wondered if she could stay like this, lips pressed to her lover's, forever.

Too quickly, Justinian pulled away. 'What if we promise her access to the Curios only when she has trained with Antonina, in earnest?'

'She hates to train.'

'Precisely!' he cried. 'But if she wants the cuff then that is the compromise she must make. In the meantime, my armies are close to Ravenna. We will establish a seat there and search for a successor who will be worthy of you.'

She smiled. 'I knew I married you for a reason.'

'We are the greatest couple the world will ever know,' Justinian said.

CHAPTER EIGHT

Saturday 18 January

'What is happening?' Tallulah growled. She'd given up relying on the Favourites file and instead, very carefully, typed in the URL for 'Lost Treasures of the Ancient World' that she'd copied down on Tuesday evening as a backup. But every time she tried it today she got the same result: a plain white page appeared with stark black letters that read: 'Website could not be found'.

If only she hadn't waited so long to open it up again. But as the week went on and students failed to return, the Cirque d'Avenir sessions had got harder. The only thing Tallulah thought of each night after dinner was sleep.

'Tallulah,' her father called from downstairs, 'have you got a minute?'

With a frustrated sigh she closed down the page – or lack of – and pushed back from her desk. 'On my way.'

Her father was waiting at the bottom of the stairs looking very pleased. Without saying a word he turned and beckoned her to follow.

'Where are we going?'

'You'll see.'

They left the house through the back door and crossed the large yard until they reached the bush perimeter. When Tallulah didn't think they could go any further her father pushed back a giant elephant's-ear leaf and revealed a very well-established track into the bush beyond their home. Tallulah hesitated. Her father raised his eyebrows, clearly enjoying the mystery as he held the plant for her to pass.

'Come on.'

'Where?'

'You'll see.'

So Tallulah slipped past the plant then squished back into the undergrowth to let him pass. They walked for five minutes in silence, following the path as it rose gradually. Steps were cut into any rocks that made the path difficult. Finally they emerged into a small clearing, in the centre of which stood a two-storey brick building.

'Is it a stable?' Tallulah asked.

'It was once. And gatehouse for a company road that passed by here and up into the bush where the timber cutters worked.' Her father waved up the hill as he walked over to the building's white wooden double-doors and pulled each one open.

Tallulah entered after her father and looked around. They were in a room on the northern side of the building; it was whitewashed and empty except for a lawn mower, rake and other gardening implements neatly arranged in the back corner. In another corner was a circular staircase to the floor above, but before she could go that way her father beckoned her through the doorway to the room on the southern side of the building. She followed him – and couldn't stop a wide grin splitting her face. The ceiling had been removed to make one tall space. A cloud swing hung from the centre of the room and not too far from that was a tissu: a brilliant red streak against a bright yellow wall.

'Wow, Dad,' she exclaimed softly as tears pricked her eyes. 'But …?'

'You were so distressed after your first day; you needed to find a way to get better fast. Your mum and I thought this might help.'

Tallulah turned a full circle to take the room in. Each wall was a different colour – yellow, red, purple and apple green. And there was enough equipment for a small circus company – unicycles, juggling batons and hoops. Tallulah walked to the red tissu hanging from the highest point in the ceiling and climbed up it before looping her feet into it and performing a backward layout. It was such a relief to be using her body just for the joy of it and not to pass some inexplicable test. When she untwisted herself she called down to her father. 'This is so great.' Then another thought occurred to her. 'But I thought we had no money?'

'Well, we found a lot of it second-hand, online – many, it seems, have dreams of running away with the circus that are never actually realised. And, as it happens, this week we aren't so broke – I've been brought in to consult on a project in the city, which will keep us going for a while.'

She wasn't sure it was the complete truth but for the moment she'd give him the benefit of the doubt – and enjoy her new space. 'I'm going further up.'

From where she hung, Tallulah could see through a window into the upper level of the other half of the building.

'What's that in there?' she asked her father.

'My workshop.'

She slid down the tissu. 'Workshop? Can I see?'

He seemed to debate the request for a moment and then shrugged. 'Why not?'

With a wave of his hand he signalled for her to go into the lawn-mower room. When she reached the top of the stairs she found herself in a workroom. There were posters on the walls featuring the pantheon of ancient gods, another of gems and their spiritual properties, and stacks of books on the same topics. There were shelves of richly coloured wood as well as a small line-up of stones and gems like the one the Isis intaglio had been carved from.

'I didn't realise you were getting so serious about this,' Tallulah said.

'Keeps me busy rather than fretting about …' For a moment he looked lost for words. 'Well, my lost business, among other things.'

Tallulah walked to the poster and scanned the pantheon of gods on display. 'Where's Hecate?' she asked.

'Hecate,' he muttered, scanning the poster again, then crossed the room to a bookshelf. He brought a thick hardback titled *Encyclopaedia of the Ancient World* to where Tallulah waited at the bench. He went straight to the index then to the double-page spread that detailed the goddess.

'She got a bit lost it seems,' he said as his finger ran swiftly along the lines of text. 'Popular early on, she became associated with the underworld and evil in later stories even though she helped Demeter rescue Persephone from Hades. Maybe that's why she's not on the poster.' He looked back at the book, tapping it absent-mindedly as he spoke. 'Hmm, the triple-headed goddess of magic and crossroads. Torches.' He looked at Tallulah. 'Hecate's torches. Irena used to say that, didn't she?'

'Yeah,' Tallulah said.

'Hell-oo,' a familiar but unlikely voice called up from downstairs.

When Tallulah reached the open window, she saw Marie de Clevjard standing in the shady clearing outside the building. Tallulah turned back to her father, who wore a sheepish expression.

'She advised us on the set-up, and when she asked if she could visit today and work with you away from Cirque d'Avenir, I thought it might be a good idea.' He closed the book and returned it to the shelf and together they descended the stairs.

Marie was inside the building by the time they reached ground level.

'What do you think?' she asked Tallulah.

'I love it.'

'And on your time off – you don't mind me coming over for extra tuition?'

'Well,' she looked to her father and then back to Marie, 'I feel a bit embarrassed but I'm happy to get some extra help.'

'There is nothing to be embarrassed about,' Marie assured her.

'Does anyone else know about this?'

'Of course not. It's between us.'

'I'll leave you to it, then,' Peter said quickly. At the edge of the clearing he turned back. 'There's plenty of water in the fridge upstairs.'

Marie gestured to a long wooden picnic bench by the entrance doors. Walking towards it she said, 'This is a beautiful spot.'

For a few minutes they sat in silence, listening to the music of the bush: the warble of a currawong, the screech of a cockatoo. A faint breeze stirred the gum leaves. 'It's been a hard week but not one without achievement, Tallulah,' Marie said.

'You have grown in strength – physical *and* mental, I believe – from the first day, and the work we will do today will further aid that growth. Although, I am not Irena,' Marie admitted. 'That needs to be said from the beginning. I do not pretend to have her skill levels.'

'Since I don't really know what "skill levels" Irena has, I couldn't really compare you to her, Marie.' Tallulah regretted the sarcasm in her voice but it seemed impossible to disentangle the words from the emotion once she opened her mouth. 'This *has* been a hard week – made even harder by the fact there have been so many surprises. I knew nothing about …'

Tallulah hesitated; she did not want to ask questions that might force her to reveal Irena's cuff.

'Cirque d'Avenir?' Marie suggested.

Tallulah nodded. 'Let alone the mixture of people involved when I arrived.'

Marie took her time digesting Tallulah's words. 'Irena is very …'

'Secretive?' Tallulah suggested. She herself was certainly getting a lot more forthright in her nanny's absence, she noticed.

'"Careful" is the word I would use, Tallulah. She has always been careful and for good reason. It's a trait that has not always made her popular but makes her just right for you.'

Tallulah glanced sideways at Marie. '*Made* her just right, Marie. She's gone now. Never to be heard of again.' Tallulah sighed.

Marie's dark eyebrows lifted. 'What do you mean?'

'Well, have *you* heard from her recently?'

'No.' Marie shook her head. 'But I did not expect to just yet. Tell me what is troubling you, my dear. We won't be able to work until you clear your thoughts.'

Tallulah badly needed a confidante and Marie's green eyes, soft as moss, offered solace. 'I've just got this feeling that something has happened to her. I had regular postcards for the first three weeks and then nothing. Irena is reliable and old-fashioned. She marks important occasions. There is no way she'd let my first week of circus go by – when she knew how much it meant to me after all these years – without marking it with a card of some sort. She just wouldn't.'

Marie's expression was inscrutable but she was still listening, so Tallulah continued. 'I thought you might have an idea of where she was going. She didn't leave an itinerary but Dad said that your families go way back and I thought you might have someone in common that she was going to visit.'

'We do go way back but time and great distance means we share fewer connections than we once did.' Marie seemed to weigh her thoughts carefully before continuing. 'It's not *unlike* Irena to disappear, Tallulah. It was in her interests to be a ghost when she was a young woman.

'But there was one lunch I knew about that was being organised for her on this visit by … a man. An important man and a friend of mine. Irena was the guest of honour. It was on, what day? On Friday the third. A week ago?'

'More than two weeks ago,' Tallulah corrected. 'Today is the eighteenth.'

'More than? You're right,' she said with a slight frown.

'So Irena is an older member of the Cirque d'Avenir community? Like Brigitta?'

'Yes, you could say that. Brigitta is someone we honour within Cirque d'Avenir; she is highly respected for her work.'

Marie regarded Tallulah with a tilted gaze; Tallulah met it with a nod and a smile and was rewarded with a pat on the knee. 'What have your instincts told you about Cirque d'Avenir?'

Tallulah recognised an attempt to change the topic when she heard one. 'That I'm lucky to have survived the first week and that I really shouldn't be there at all.'

'Well, without trying to discredit your instincts, I have to tell you that they are not correct when it comes to Cirque d'Avenir. You are *absolutely* where you are meant to be.'

'But how can you say that?'

'Tallulah, this was always going to be a tough week for you. There are all sorts of shifts in your understanding of the world — you have lived in such isolation. But be assured that Irena did the right thing in the way she looked after you, and in directing you to us.'

'She trained me to protect my mind, and to open my mind to the knowledge of the universe available in all things, not to join the circus.'

'The knowledge of the universe?' Marie's voice was full of doubt. 'How?'

'She selects a tarot card from the deck, reads it and then puts it face down in front of her. I drop my barriers, and discover the identity of the card. Then I reveal it to her by thought-casting.'

'So she reads the card and puts it down. Then presumably her own barriers are dropped and she allows herself to be open to your thoughts.'

Tallulah nodded.

'And vice versa.'

'I'm open to her thoughts?' Tallulah shook her head. 'I don't think so.'

'She asks you to reach for the knowledge of the universe in all things, Tallulah. That's all living things. You can't touch the knowledge of a deck of cards.'

'No! She wouldn't want me to do that. It would be … it would be …'

'Overwhelming?'

'That. As well as incredibly rude.'

'So she taught you how to use your gift while protecting you from the overwhelming nature of it. She's taught you how to hone your skill to the point where you can extract the one piece of information that you need – you did not need to know what she had for breakfast, just the identity of the card – and at the same time taught you respect for others.' Marie laughed softly to herself. 'That's why she is so very good at what she does. The possibilities for you are tremendous.'

Tallulah suddenly felt very light-headed. She closed her eyes and took deep breaths but it didn't help steady the feeling that everything was getting more out of control by the minute. She felt Marie's hand on her shoulder.

'It is because you have been so thoroughly trained by her that I will be able to help you, using techniques from my own work, with the week ahead.'

'But how? Your work is telling story through movement, isn't it?'

Marie nodded. 'My storytelling is a call to action for those of us with Cirque d'Avenir in our bones, in our genetic make-up. It is one way of identifying who might be with us on this journey and who might not.'

'It was an incredibly sad story. You don't think there's a risk of scaring people away?'

Marie laughed. 'Of course. But our life is not for the faint-hearted. Those who don't recognise the story must go. Those who recognise the story but are uncomfortable with it need to be identified as well.'

Tallulah thought about the disappearance of Adelaide's friends after Monday. 'But the students didn't all go after you performed on the terrace.'

'I didn't expect them to. No, we have other methods,' Marie said matter-of-factly.

'Of scaring people off?'

'I wouldn't put it like that. It is hard to know whether to identify gifts then determine mental strength or the other way around. Sasha, in his desire to be egalitarian, sees potential in everyone. He's an enthusiastic recruiter – and he has done very well with one or two students. But it takes time – which is fine when he's working at a circus school on his own and there's no risk of exposing Cirque d'Avenir. Brigitta is old school, has real-world experience and believes mental fortitude is everything. She believes in working on the mind, weeding out the mentally weak first.'

Tallulah thought of the past week; Marie's explanation made sense – but didn't make her feel entirely comfortable. 'So Brigitta has been working on our minds – before she works *with* our minds. Is that right?'

Marie nodded. 'It's necessary, and it's not too invasive. The next phase begins this week but you will have no trouble.'

'I've practised maintaining the barriers this past week but not the telepathy. My walls were smashed after the first day.'

'Smashed?' There was alarm in Marie's voice.

'Yes, but to be honest I hadn't paid any attention to them since Irena left.'

'Too angry.'

Tallulah was taken aback by the observation; it was close to the mark. She nodded.

'Let that be a lesson, then. Anger has all the destructive power of a trained telepath.'

'Scared too. There were some big changes happening in our lives.'

'Understandable.' Marie paused. 'You must not practise the telepathy with anyone else. We will work on that together as I work with Mai on her particular gift—'

'And Saskia. Will you work with her? Is she to inherit the role of eminence?'

Shock rippled across Marie's face. 'Eminence? Goodness, Tallulah.' Marie laughed. 'What makes you say that?'

'Your Dance of the King's Eminence; there's got to be one, right? And the way Saskia talks, she just seems to believe she is the obvious successor.'

'Successor? I'm not sure what Saskia has said but there will be no eminence in Cirque d'Avenir. I will speak more about it on Monday with the entire team to be certain we all understand one another. Now let's get to work.'

'But—'

'We have chatted enough,' Marie said in a tone that brooked no argument. 'We have much to do; I think I can help you use those thought-casting skills to improve your physical prowess. When you transfer thoughts, has Irena taught you to imagine a conduit from your mind to another's? Or do you work on expanding your consciousness to take in all that's around?'

'A conduit. It's a purple ball of energy that fills my mind.'

Marie gave a slow nod then stood, directing Tallulah to the centre of the clearing.

'From my observation, you're working like a person who has built up all the muscles of their body but uses only bones and ligaments to move – which is not just inefficient but debilitating. Now, I want you to relax and close your eyes. When you are settled I would like you to visualise that purple core of energy as you normally would.'

Tallulah closed her eyes and followed Marie's instructions.

'Rather than sending a conduit of thought from your mental core to another's, I would like you to harness that energy within, allowing the conduit to travel down your spine to your coccyx, feeling that tingle of energy all the way down your centre line, letting it form another core there, at the base of your spine.'

Tallulah concentrated on the purple conduit of heat.

'Can you feel that, Tallulah?'

She nodded, too engrossed in what was happening in her body to waste her time speaking.

'Good. See its purple tendrils wrap and weave themselves around your core and extend down into your legs, along your feet to the very tip of your toes so that like the great gum trees you have a strong and stable base, rooted firmly and deeply. Then when you feel well and truly planted, allow the tendrils to wrap around your ribs and shoulders and send them along every nerve to the very tips of your fingers.

'Now, take the time to sit still for a few minutes and really experience that crackle of energy, the power of thought. Trained properly, it is more powerful than your physical self.'

Tallulah shivered. The *crackle of energy* radiated from her core with such intensity that Tallulah was sure she looked like the lighthouse on the point at Seacliff's Main Beach, sending out a purple beam that was so strong Australia's whole east coast would be able to see it. She wanted to squeal with delight, she felt so good. It occurred to her that she didn't know how this was going to help her move; the moment she had that thought, the tendrils that were still thin and wispy and unformed in her wrists and ankles began to withdraw. She groaned and refocused her efforts.

'It is natural as you begin this practice that you will falter,' Marie said quietly. 'It requires focused concentration particularly at the edges of your body where the focus is weakest.'

When Tallulah felt she had stabilised again, and extended the purple conduit of energy until it bumped against her skin, Marie asked her to *talk* her muscles through a basic handstand to walkover, to *think* the exercise rather than feel it. When Tallulah had done that she nodded, only to hear Marie tell her to do it again. And again. When Marie was certain of Tallulah's attention to detail, she whispered, 'Now move your body with thought, Tallulah.'

Tallulah nodded, raised her hands to begin, took a deep breath and performed the exercise. When she was done she felt … surprisingly ordinary. She opened her eyes to find Marie looking at her, eyebrows raised. 'What happened?'

'Nothing. I mean nothing different.'

'You used your body, not your thought,' Marie said gently. 'Trust your own power, Tallulah. Your instinct, as Irena would say. It's all in there,' Marie said, tapping her own forehead. 'Try again.'

Tallulah closed her eyes and found the purple ball of energy still in place and working to the edges of her body. Encouraged that she didn't have to start from the very beginning, she took deep slow breaths and raised her hands – only to lower them. She grinned as she recalled her father's description when watching a game of rugby. 'All brawn, no brain,' he'd say in appreciation of the job the forwards had to do, smashing their way through the opposition. All Tallulah had to do was flip it. 'All brain, no brawn,' she whispered.

She remembered the feeling of her arms rising, but from that moment to the one when she next stood upright her body registered nothing else. Perhaps a subconscious blur of movement as the world had tipped upside down and then righted itself. But mostly she'd travelled through space as if she had not been there.

She opened her eyes. 'Did I do it?' she asked.

Marie clapped her hands and beamed. 'It seems so.'

Tallulah felt a wave of weariness hit her; her knees buckled but immediately the muscles in her thighs and calves tensed and she stood straight. She calmed her rapidly beating heart.

'You will tire quickly, at first.'

'Can I do it again?'

Marie nodded. 'But steadily.'

It didn't take long for Tallulah to trust herself in the way she trusted she could pass a thought into another mind easily – and at that moment her movements were transformed. It felt as if her circus skills went from competent to proficient to expert in a matter of seconds. She was so excited that without thinking she did a round-off to a backflip, then backflipped again and stood with a whoop that bounced off the escarpment and back into her brain – at which point she was overcome with giddiness. She swayed and then felt herself topple to the ground. Marie was by her side in an instant, hauling her up. But the exhaustion could not match the exhilaration Tallulah felt as the exercises she had struggled with all week now came together.

'I told you it would wear you out,' Marie admonished. 'That's enough for today. This does not mean that you can suddenly do very difficult things that you have never attempted before. And you must still learn new moves and practise – wasting your mental energy on something your body should be able to do on its own is a poor use of your gift. But I am very pleased with what we have accomplished today.'

'But it's about confidence too. It's easy here, alone in the bush, without others to compare yourself to.'

Marie drew in a deep breath as she took in her surroundings and Tallulah's observation at once. 'Powerful minds can work as easily in the negative as the positive, it is true. Saskia and Sasha can be intimidating – even I find them so.' The admission was accompanied by a shy grimace. 'But only by working with powerful people can one become powerful. You can learn early in life to build protective barriers in your mind, as you have done, but it is only through time that you will understand the way your mind works, what your weaknesses are, and ways to tweak your barriers accordingly.'

The rustle of leaves on the pathway made them both look that way. Peter emerged. 'I just noticed your car still in the driveway; we thought you would have been long gone.'

'We were achieving so much here I could not leave.'

He winked at his daughter then addressed Marie again. 'We thought we'd go into town for a Mexican meal. Would you care to join us?'

CHAPTER NINE

Later that night, driving back through the entrance gate of their home, Tallulah's dad leaned closer to the front windscreen as if to get a better look at the house. 'Gem, what lights did we leave on when we left?'

In the backseat Tallulah shuffled sideways and leaned towards the gap between the front seats as her mother said, 'Same as always.'

But something was wrong. The upstairs rooms were blazing. And the standing lamps that could normally be seen from the driveway had disappeared.

'Lu, did you put the lights on when you ran back upstairs?'

Instinct had nudged her back into the house before going to the Mexican restaurant; she'd shoved the carved wooden box containing the cuff into the bottom of her bag and run back to the car.

'No, it wasn't dark then.'

'Did you see another car anywhere along the road, Peter?' her mother asked.

He shook his head and pulled to the side of the gravel driveway, cutting the engine. 'Maybe you should both stay in the car.'

'I don't want to stay here in the dark,' Gemma replied.

Tallulah agreed. 'We're coming with you.'

They got out of the car together, slamming the doors loudly. Gemma slipped a soft hand into Tallulah's.

They ascended the stairs and stepped gingerly onto the verandah. The front door was locked as it should be. They stepped through the doorway and got their first look inside. Gemma squeezed Tallulah's hand and gave an anguished moan. Chaos ruled. Tears ran down Gemma's cheeks at the sight of emptied cupboards with contents strewn across the floor, upturned lamps and smashed vases. Glasses and linen from the side cabinet had been tossed aside as the burglars had searched the house.

Peter put his arm around his wife's shoulders and pulled his phone out of his pocket. 'It'll be OK,' he said. 'There's nothing that can't be replaced.'

He called the emergency number, gave their address and described to the person on the other end what had happened.

Advised to leave the house just as it was until the police arrived, they sat on the verandah couches and waited. Her father sat between them, an arm around each shoulder, kissing his wife and crooning, 'It's just shock, Gem; it's all going to be all right.'

'We should have had an alarm installed,' Gemma said.

'Yes,' Peter agreed. 'I just didn't think … I'll get one put in tomorrow.'

The sound of a car approaching stopped their chatter and the flashing lights of the white police car came as a relief. Her dad looked at his phone and said, impressed, 'Not even ten minutes.'

The two policemen introduced themselves and let Peter lead them into the house. Gemma wiped tears from her eyes as the police asked her to try to identify anything that was missing – without touching anything just yet. Fingerprinting experts were on their way.

But as they walked around, nothing seemed to be stolen. The sound system was still in its cabinet, the laptop still on a side table in the lounge room, the television still on its stand, as usual.

Upstairs they were confronted by more of the same chaos. In their bedroom, Gemma groaned as she saw the drawers that contained her underwear upturned and everything scattered on the floor. Among her bras and underpants was much of her jewellery. She'd built a gorgeous collection over the years and it was not insubstantial. Tallulah kneeled on the floor next to her mother and held her hand as they talked through what they could see and what they couldn't.

They discovered that the only pieces missing were the antiques. Tallulah pressed her bag against her hip to be certain she could still feel the hard edges of the wooden box. A phrase from a computer screen returned: *only ever traded on the black market*. Tallulah clenched her jaw to maintain control.

'I'll have to tell Mr Morton,' her mum whispered. 'He'll be so disappointed, he helped me find so many of these pieces.'

But Tallulah was barely listening. If there was anyone who might be able to help her find out about the cuff it would be Mr Morton. His knowledge of antiques was incredible.

'Lu,' her father called sharply from down the hall.

Tallulah remembered the first day she'd climbed the stairs and walked towards her new bedroom. She'd been distracted from the distress of saying goodbye to the city and all her friends by glimpses of a red-and-white striped ceiling at the end of the hallway. Her own private carnival eyrie: a turret on the first floor of a circular tower. She'd felt as if she was on the threshold of a life she dared not believe possible.

Now she just felt hunted. Could it be that the intruders had turned their house upside down for only one thing: an item of jewellery that was more ancient than anything in her mother's room? An item apparently not traded by any reputable antique dealer. She told herself she was being foolish, and since that item was in the bag slung across her body she had nothing really to fear now.

As she got to the doorway she grasped the frame to steady herself and take in the scene. Her wardrobe doors had been flung open and everything within was spewed all over the floor; same with her chest of drawers, bedside table and desk. She had a desperate need to run around and hide her things, hide herself from the police officers and even her parents. But she wasn't allowed to touch anything yet. Now she began to fully understand her mother's distress; the horror of burglary wasn't about the mess or the broken or missing stuff: it was about the loss of privacy. It was the knowledge that unknown hands had been riffling through everything that was important and private, handling it without respect.

Tallulah stepped into her room and looked around in a daze. She sat on her bed and looked to the windows of her room – more specifically the curtains. She'd pulled them closed before she left; it was all part of the instinct she'd acted on earlier. She'd pulled the curtains closed then taken the cuff from its hiding place.

Except now the curtains weren't closed; there was probably a metre between them. She swallowed hard and looked along the length of the curtain for any bulge that might be there – a foot poking out from underneath that would give away the burglar's position. But there was none. Her heart slowed and her breath caught and she heard herself giggle. She looked back to see the adults all watching her.

'What is it, Tallulah?' asked the constable.

'I didn't leave them like that,' she said, pointing to the curtains. 'I closed them completely. There was no gap. Just then I got the stupid idea that someone might be hiding there and I spooked myself.'

She got up and walked towards the curtains, but stopped when she saw her father's intaglios on the floor, many smashed to smithereens.

'Oh, Dad,' she said, crouching down, overwhelmed by the sight. Peter was quickly beside her, his hand on her back. The gifts she'd so often dismissed, made with such care and love, were now ground into the floor, and Tallulah felt unspeakably sad.

'I can make them again,' he told her.

She nodded, but it wasn't the point. She reached for a piece of Horus's eye.

'Don't touch …' the police officer warned.

'Sorry.' Tallulah pulled her hand back as the constable pulled on gloves, stood beside her and opened the curtains.

'What is this?' Tallulah heard him say.

'Crikey,' his partner said. 'Who's He-kate?'

But it was the fear in Gemma's voice as she said, 'Oh, Peter,' that made Tallulah and her father look up.

'He-ca-tee,' Peter corrected, weakly. Tallulah met his gaze as he added, 'An ancient Greek goddess.'

He gripped her hand as they both stood and stared at the message scrawled on the glass in what looked like blood. Tallulah stepped towards the window.

'HECATE CANNOT SAVE YOU THIS TIME.'

CHAPTER TEN

Monday 20 January

'So, what's the charge this morning?' Tallulah quipped, without looking up, when the shadow moved over her.

It had become their morning ritual. Tom was always there, waiting for her to arrive. He made her insides flutter in all the right ways; when he stood close to her all other thoughts were swept from her mind except how, without being too obvious, she could bridge the gap between them; and she revelled in his praise. He might not have the brooding dark looks of Sasha, but he was always happy, nothing rattled him and he was sweet and attentive. Though ... sometimes a little too attentive. And he'd taken it upon himself to be her self-appointed advisor in Irena's absence. By the end of the first week of classes there had been nothing she did that he didn't notice, which eventually felt a bit ... suffocating. The flipside to Irena's secrecy, Tallulah realised, was a respect for another's personal space! It was why she decided not to confide in him about the events of Saturday night.

But as she stowed her key in the side pocket of her saddle bag, the anticipation of trading flirtatious comments and having those adoring eyes bestowed upon her tickled her insides until a grin tweaked at the corners of her mouth. She stood, turned and gave Tom her best smile.

Except it wasn't Tom standing there. Adelaide Banks shifted her weight from one foot to the other, glancing between Tallulah and the ocean. Tallulah's stomach sank.

Both girls started talking at once.

'Look, I shouldn't have got angry—'

'I'm sorry I intruded—'

Tallulah stopped but Adelaide continued. 'You didn't intrude. I was out of line. I was scrubbing a picnic booth at the beach – it's pretty public. And a pretty odd thing to be doing.' She took a deep breath. 'I just thought I was early enough to avoid any questions.'

'But it was none of my business,' Tallulah replied. She'd given up on getting any sleep early yesterday morning; the message on her bedroom window tipped the attempted robbery into the too-weird-to-stay-in-bed category. So she'd pulled on her swimmers, left a note for her parents, and headed to Main Beach on her bike.

The repetitive boomp-shhhr of waves stilled her troubled thoughts but the sight of a teenager in a halter-neck bikini top and floral board shorts attacking the wall of a picnic booth with a scrubbing brush was too intriguing. When she recognised the girl, Tallulah couldn't resist investigating.

And Adelaide had turned on her. According to Adelaide, Tallulah had been doing her head in from the moment she turned up at Seacliff High, staring at her, making her do freaky things, and it had only got worse when they got to Cirque d'Avenir – wasn't it enough she'd nearly fallen off a roof and crashed off her stilts? Did Ghost-girl have to follow her on weekends as well? Tallulah had been too shocked to reply;

when Adelaide told her to piss off and leave her alone, she had been glad to.

'I didn't mean to embarrass you. I'd be doing the same thing if someone had written insults about me on public walls all over town.'

Adelaide's eyes went skywards. 'I don't think so.' She shook her head. 'You're clearly the kind of person who can "just ignore it" and "rise above it". That's what my mother tells me I should do.'

'There's a lot to be said for acting on impulse,' Tallulah offered. 'Better than swallowing your thoughts and then having them torment you.'

'Well, you're under no illusions about my thoughts.'

It was the obvious remorse in Adelaide's statement that finally cracked Tallulah's façade of diplomacy. She blinked back tears and clenched her jaw.

'I'm sorry,' Adelaide said, as if reading her thoughts.

'Oh, look that's OK.'

'It's not OK. I was out of line,' Adelaide insisted.

'Maybe.' Tallulah's voice was shaky. 'But unlike you, I'm going to have a lot of trouble just keeping up with Sasha's session, so while it might be the right time for you to offer an apology, it's not the right time for me to think about everything I was accused of yesterday.'

Their eyes locked. Then Adelaide nodded. 'Fair enough.'

Tallulah gave a curt nod. 'Thank you.'

They stood for a moment before walking up the hill to Cirque d'Avenir.

'For what it's worth,' Tallulah said quietly, 'a lot of this is doing my head in as well.'

Adelaide looked down to the footpath and for a long moment didn't reply. When she lifted her head she nodded.

'Yeah, well, maybe we could talk about that some time.'

Tallulah and Adelaide split up as they walked into the change room; Adelaide changed quickly and left with an awkward, 'See you out there.'

When Tallulah emerged Mai was waiting. They had become close during their first week at the cirque. Mai waved a piece of paper in one hand. 'I've got the map for today's route.' She showed it to Tallulah. 'We run right past the pool ...' she said.

'And back into Port Melba.' Tallulah took the map from Mai and looked at the address on the back – just a number and street name. 'What are we in for today? Why aren't we going back to the pool? I was ready for it this week.'

'Expect the unexpected,' Mai sung gaily.

Tallulah handed the map back to Mai. 'You're chipper.'

Mai folded the paper and put it in her cap, which she pulled on her head. As the two of them headed to the back entrance across the deserted theatre space Mai leaned closer and whispered, 'I had my first session with Marie yesterday.'

'How did it go?'

'Fantastic, I love her.'

Tallulah giggled. 'How did you go with the ribbons, I mean?'

But Mai shook her head. 'I'm learning to harness my energy first so that I have control over whether I charge an item or not. Then I won't go around randomly electrocuting people – especially people I don't like.' She gave Tallulah a contrite grin. 'I thought I could only do that when I was wearing the ribbons.'

'But not now?'

'Getting there,' Mai said. 'Although not as fast as you.' She bumped Tallulah's shoulder.

Tallulah stopped. 'What do you mean?'

'Just that Marie said that in your session with her you learned fast.'

Tallulah baulked. 'I didn't think she was going to tell anyone about our session; it was just between us.'

'You don't like me knowing?'

'It's just that … I don't know … I guess I just expected Marie to be …' she searched for the word '… more discreet, I guess.'

Tallulah pushed through the back door of the theatre and met the bright sunshine. She put her black Cirque d'Avenir cap on and they both shifted gear to a slow trot.

'Don't be upset,' Mai said. 'It's my fault: I was badmouthing Saskia in my usual way, which meant Marie explained about the first day. She said that, while Sasha should not have interfered, it was you who shared that awful vision of the acrobats and the dog-men – you'll have to tell me where that came from one day – without realising it.' With a quick intake of breath she grabbed Tallulah's forearm and stopped her, eyes wide as saucers. 'Lu, you know what this means, don't you? You're telepathic, probably telekinetic. Even if you aren't completely in control right now you will be eventually and then …' She grinned so tightly that the muscles in her neck flexed. 'My grandmother said there'd never be another eminence, not after the Cirkulatti's demise in the war. And yet …' Mai gestured dramatically at Tallulah.

'Don't be ridiculous,' she whispered. She looked around to see if anyone had overheard their conversation but there were no students behind them yet and the few in front were more than a hundred metres away. 'You know what happened last week when I was late; can we please run?'

'Sure, Eminence,' Mai whispered, then put her hands in the air in mock surrender to Tallulah's glare. They set off at a proper pace.

'The role of eminence no longer exists.'

They heard a call from behind; Tallulah waved to Saskia but did not slow down. Mai groaned.

'She's a telepath too, or had you forgotten?'

Mai slapped her forehead with her hand. 'That's why she's so haughty,' she whispered.

'I thought it was good,' Tallulah said, louder now. 'The chocolate soufflé was to die for.'

'I love chocolate soufflé.'

'Me too,' Saskia said, panting. 'You found a good one in Seacliff?' She gave a quick nod to Mai. 'Hi, Mai. Thanks for letting me catch up. There are others behind us, so we can't be in trouble this week, Tallulah. But Sasha's in a mood.'

'Why?'

'Same thing: his obsession with the locals. Reckons Marie and Brigitta aren't giving them enough of a chance. He dragged me to the most tedious show on Saturday night; Adelaide was performing with her friends and he was beside himself: *if* she was *gifted* there could be a risk that she'd reveal herself in public and make things very difficult. But it's hardly likely. She's such a drama queen. On Saturday night she fell off her stilts in the second act of their show!'

Mai gasped. 'Is she OK?'

'Yeah, I've seen her today,' Tallulah said.

'She's tough,' Saskia continued, 'but he believes she's got something more. I think he's just embarrassed that he got the locals so wrong.' They turned the last corner. 'Just stay out of his way today, Lu, OK?'

'Hecate's torches,' Mai exclaimed, as she came to a sudden halt.

Saskia followed Mai's gaze. 'He wouldn't,' she muttered.

'Wouldn't what?' Tallulah asked.

'You'll see.'

Anne Street was a short cul-de-sac that ended in front of a double-storey warehouse with huge corrugated roller-doors. The three girls joined Adelaide, Hui, Estella and Guido underneath the painted sign, faded and cracked but still legible: ANDREWS ABBATOIR PTY LTD.

Adelaide turned. 'What do you think?'

'Another morning of slaughter,' Tallulah joked. Adelaide and Mai chuckled.

'I can't say what I think,' Hui said. 'He's brought us *to a giant fridge*? What's he doing, Saskia?' He was so enraged Tallulah thought he might incinerate her on the spot. He walked back down the street, but changed his mind and returned. 'This is a little joke between the two of you, is it? Humiliate Tom like you've humiliated them?' He pointed at Adelaide and Tallulah, both of whom shrank from his fury.

'Hui, I had nothing to do with this.'

'Of course you didn't.'

'It doesn't even look like a working factory any more,' Saskia pleaded. 'It's probably just a big empty space for him to put the scaffolding. We did complain about the heat back in the theatre.'

Hui was unmoved.

'And since when does Sasha confer with me on his training program? You know him better than that.' Saskia's defence sounded genuine.

'What's the issue exactly?' Tallulah asked.

Saskia and Hui were too busy glaring at each other. Tallulah turned to Mai, who shrugged. Adelaide pursed her lips and stared off into the distance.

'Finally,' Sasha called from the roof of the warehouse. 'I wondered when someone from my team might get here.'

A rope was thrown over the roof and Sasha glided down. When he was a couple of metres from the ground he jumped lightly from the rope – and ran into Hui's hot wall of indignation. He stepped back. 'Problem, Hui?'

The younger man rolled his shoulders, stood a little straighter. His head tilted to the roof. 'You've got some sort of perverse power trip going on, mate, and I won't have any part of it.'

'Hui, Tom agreed to this—'

'I don't know what's happened to you, mate,' Hui interrupted, 'but—' He looked between Sasha and Saskia, who had moved to stand next to her brother.

'But what, Hui?' Sasha asked in a bored tone.

Disappointment flushed Hui's face. He moved closer as if to get a better look at his old friend. 'Where did you go?'

Sasha laughed and spread his arms wide. 'I'm all here, charged with the duty of training a group of performers to be part of an organisation like no other,' he said as if to a small child who wouldn't understand.

'I get that. What I don't get is what changed you? You used to be inspiring; now you're just like …' He looked between the siblings then shook his head. 'Like her,' he spat. 'A bloody tyrant.'

Tallulah flinched; a glance Mai's way made it clear that she was also surprised by Hui's attack. Sasha edged in front of his sister.

'I'm sorry if you don't approve, but I won't apologise for taking my responsibilities seriously. And you will be thanking me, one day, all of you.'

Saskia put her hand on her brother's shoulder.

'Don't,' he barked. He walked away from them. 'But you don't have to stay, Hui.'

'Yes, he does.'

They turned to see Tom panting hard ahead of Javier and Chiara. Face flushed, Tom moved to where Hui stood, ready to take control of the situation.

'No one is going anywhere.' He clapped Hui on the shoulder. 'I appreciate your defence, mate, but I've agreed to this.' Then he addressed their trainer. 'We know you've got a big job, Sasha, but it wouldn't be the circus it is if we didn't say what we thought. Or if emotions didn't spill over sometimes. Would it?'

Tallulah felt the question was loaded with history; just as it had done at the pool the space – or was it the time? – between the two young men seemed to rumble.

'No,' Sasha said brusquely, 'it wouldn't.'

'So let's go.'

Sasha moved to the base of the thick rope and took hold of it; in four steps he had scaled the wall and performed a somersault to land. Tallulah was not the only one to gasp. It was as though Sasha could defy gravity. And then the penny dropped – and she laughed softly to herself. Duh! The way Sasha walked, leaped, climbed, did just about everything. He was some sort of super-acrobat. If all the locals without gifts had been eliminated there was no longer any need for Sasha to hide his own ability.

So if all the locals without gifts had been eliminated …

She looked around for Adelaide, who was looking up at Sasha, open-mouthed. They all knew she was physically awesome and she had a dead aim. Could it be possible that Adelaide had a gift, but somehow had no comprehension or understanding of it? As stressful as the first week had been for Tallulah, at least she'd had Irena to prepare her – to help her feel normal when she thought she was the only one. If Adelaide had not had any guidance before now, no wonder she was a mess. Tallulah watched Adelaide as she crossed her arms in front of her chest and rubbed her upper arms; her shoulders went to her ears as if she was sucking in a gigantic breath.

'Team exercise,' Sasha said. He hauled the rope he'd used back to the roof and threw it to his left. He held up two lengths of rope. 'Each has a hook on one end.' He dropped them from the roof. 'You'll need them to get your team up here. We enter the abattoir via the roof. No doors today.'

His face brightened as he looked beyond them up the cul-de-sac. They all turned to see Ollie run down the street. When he was in earshot Sasha called, 'Ollie, I thought we'd lost you.'

'Almost,' Ollie said, between gulps of air. He'd obviously run hard to catch up. 'But ... not ... quite.' He glanced at the others. 'G'day, Dell.'

Adelaide returned his nod with a grim smile.

'Good for you,' Sasha said, genuinely happy. 'I'll see you when you get up here. You're scaling a wall. The others will fill you in. You've got thirty minutes, people. Otherwise there's a much longer run this afternoon after Brigitta has finished with you.'

There was silence while they considered the thirty metres of flat wall, followed by a number of excruciatingly clumsy attempts to hook the ropes to two hoops mounted at different heights. Eventually, thanks to Mai's daring and Tallulah's fledgling telekinetic skills, the team got to the top – but not before Saskia had abandoned them to shinny up a nearby drainpipe.

When Tallulah joined the others on the roof, Marie was waiting.

'Congratulations,' Marie said to the group sitting in front of her. 'You have endured and passed a punishing week of tests, both physical and mental. We could not be more thrilled with the team that have made it through to second week of Cirque d'Avenir.

'Many of you I know. Tallulah, Mai, Adelaide and Ollie, I look forward,' she stopped, turned and gestured to Sasha, '*we* look forward, to getting to know you better. You will have questions; I want you to feel free to come to us any time for whatever you need in these next weeks. The most important thing I ask of you is to accept the truth of who you are. Embrace that which has made you feel different for so long; you may have felt pain and anxiety before now. But Cirque d'Avenir is where you can finally release that pain and anxiety because, mes chèris, to us you are very special. You have found your spiritual home.

'When I told you on our very first day that this was a circus with a rich and wonderful history, I was not exaggerating. Together we are now going to build on what came before to create something new and even greater. You see, Cirque d'Avenir has at its centre a group of people who are descendants of a troupe known as the Cirkulatti – there are a few of you who may not have heard of the Cirkulatti, or don't think you know anything about it, but that's not true. Those dances I perform on the terrace every afternoon speak to what you know deep inside. They speak to instincts. To your heart. Trust that. It is good and true.

'The main danger for us, Cirkulatti's lost descendants, is that our unique gifts, if not recognised, nurtured and trained properly, can turn inwards and destroy us, particularly in our teens, when they really start to gain strength. You may have already felt it happening: begun to feel you were some kind of freak who had no place in this increasingly homogenised, desensitised world.

'I wish it could say it will get easier from here.' Her eyes were full of sympathy. 'It won't, but it will be exciting. There is much work to do to bring your gifts to fruition as well as to train you for what lies ahead. But ...' She hesitated and turned to Sasha. 'Shall we tell them?'

He shrugged.

'It was confirmed last night: from Seacliff, a handpicked group of students will travel to Elbe in Europe for advanced training. We'll be leaving early next month.' Her eyes glistened with excitement. 'And so, voila, hard work will be rewarded. I will not waste any more of your time. Sasha, your students.'

Marie gave them a wave goodbye. But she had not taken more than two steps when Estella called her back.

'Marie. Can I ask a question? What about the Cirknero?'

The bright smile on Marie's face disappeared. She took a deep breath but before she could answer, Ollie asked, 'Who is the Cirknero?'

'It's like the mortal enemy of the Cirkulatti,' Estella explained.

'Of humanity,' added Javier, darkly.

'If the Cirkulatti is re-forming it must be because the Cirknero—'

'Estella,' Marie and Sasha said together. Sasha dipped his head to Marie and gestured for her to proceed.

'Estella, you're scaring people,' she said gently. She addressed the group. 'I won't lie to you. The Cirknero has been a dark presence in history. And a nuisance to the Cirkulatti. But it's important for us to be clear on this. We are *not* Cirkulatti. We are Cirque d'Avenir and we have no interest in the political machinations the Cirkulatti and Cirknero got embroiled in in the past. Yes, times are tough around the world, I will not deny it. And the Cirknero may be involved. But my only goal is to create a safe place for our young people. To train you – which will protect you from any threat the Cirknero might make – and if that is successful, to create a circus that will be a little more magical than others. We have no reason to fear the Cirknero.' She smiled. 'I'll see you at lunch.'

Sasha caught the look on Tallulah's face. 'You have something to say, Tallulah?' he said.

'It's just …' She coughed, looked around and gestured to the escarpment, to the ocean. 'It's hard to believe in these undefined dark forces when we're sitting here on a rooftop in the Seacliff sunshine.'

The other students murmured their agreement and Sasha nodded, seeming to agree. 'Yes, well, what I find harder to believe, Tallulah, is how, with so many *talented* students eliminated, you're still here, sitting with us in the Seacliff sunshine.'

Tom jumped to his feet to defend her, but Tallulah smiled. 'I must be tougher than you think, Sasha.'

Before Sasha could respond, Adelaide coughed and stood. 'Be careful, Sash,' she said lightly. 'People might think you're one of these Cirknero people if you keep attacking Tallulah.'

Colour drained from his face. 'I've never been to Europe,' Adelaide continued, 'can we just get going?'

The abattoir was no longer in use, and it was kind of creepy, but its refrigeration system still worked. They abseiled down into the factory, where a circuit of exercises had been set up. There was an added degree of difficulty – the equipment was cold to hold, slippery with condensation or difficult to grip with numb fingers. In the main room, the safety nets under the scaffolding got a workout as one student after the other slipped on the monkey bars on their way to the next exercise rope or tissu.

The mental energy Tallulah already exerted outside the building along with the cold thwarted her further attempts to use the techniques she'd learned with Marie. It was easier just to attempt the exercise – but it was hard going and she soon felt miserable.

Hardly anyone talked – except Sasha, who constantly reminded them that performers had to be ready for any conditions. His encouragement did little more than add to the general grimness.

For the final exercise of the day they were led into a room where an above-ground swimming pool stood. A narrow platform no more than a metre wide was affixed to the wall at the height of the pool and Sasha pulled himself onto it as they all watched.

'Come on,' he said, gesturing to the pool. 'Up you get; we start on the edge of the pool.'

Adelaide walked to the pool. She put her hand on the shoulder-height ledge he was talking about – it was barely as wide as the length of her hand. She looked back up at Sasha with uncertain eyes.

'We're juggling,' he told her, quietly, 'you'll have no problem.' He gave her an enthusiastic smile as she climbed up the ladder. As the others followed he said, 'That's it. Everyone up.'

When the group was on the ledge, Sasha said, 'Same as last week. I'm going to throw various implements your way – and keep adding. When you drop one, you're in the pool.'

The team looked behind them to the waist-deep water and then glanced at one another. 'Which is heated,' Mai deadpanned, 'naturally.'

'Naturally. Whenever it's touched by the sun.'

Tallulah decided to go for Marie's technique one more time – and if she didn't have the energy for it, then, like last week, she'd pray. Closing her eyes, she pictured the purple conduit and sent it down her spine and to the far reach of every part of her body. She pictured herself in the action of juggling, feeling the balance, the rhythm of her shoulders, the pins in the air—

'Tallulah,' Mai hissed beside her.

Tallulah opened her eyes to find three batons fly into her vision, one after the other. She caught the first before it hit her in the mouth and launched it, awkwardly, but somehow successfully; she quickly plucked the others from out of the air as they came at her and sent them into their intended orbit. On their second revolution she managed to settle them further but she was overwhelmed with such feelings of pleasure and triumph that she did not notice she was tipping backwards until she missed the first baton on its third revolution and toppled back into the pool with all the grace of an elephant.

She jumped up immediately, trying to wipe both the water and her embarrassment away from her face. It was cold but not as cold as the air above the pool. Lowering her shoulders under the surface, it wasn't long before she was jogging on the spot in a crouched position, arms punching back and forth in an effort to stay warm.

Sasha ignored her, striding back and forth across the platform, tossing extra implements to the team. Eventually, Mai dropped a top hat and she was in the pool and soon Ollie and Estella joined them.

'You're up, Tommy,' Sasha called, voice echoing around the room.

Tallulah's eyes followed the arc of a hoop that he threw to where Tom caught it, looked at it, then to Sasha, who said, gently, 'I wouldn't ask you to do this if I didn't think you could, Tom.'

Tom nodded; he glanced at the students in the water, then looked down at the upturned palm of his left hand, muttered a word Tallulah didn't hear – and flame appeared from the ends of his fingers. Tom gracefully curled and uncurled his fingers one by one into his palm and a relieved smile broke across his face. He brought the hoop in front of his body and was about to transfer it to his left hand – when the flame disappeared from his fingers.

A sigh went around the room.

'You're just warming up,' Sasha said encouragingly. Tallulah looked to make sure it was the same Sasha. 'This time you'll do it.'

Tom repeated the action, but again as he tried to unite his left hand with the hoop, the flames spluttered and died.

'Getting better. You've got your team around you, Tom, they're willing you on. Those in the water are relying on you. Again.'

Tom repeated the action to no avail. Tallulah realised she'd stopped moving while watching Tom's quest and she began jogging on the spot again – only to stop. The cold seeped deeper into her bones but she must not distract her friend from his efforts. She wrapped her arms more tightly around her and clamped her teeth together.

'I could jump in,' Saskia offered.

Sasha turned narrowed eyes on his sister; every muscle in his neck and face was taut. Saskia looked at Tom, whose head was down, glanced at Hui, then back to her brother; she opened her mouth as if to speak again but Sasha held up one finger and shook his head.

Saskia gave a tiny nod. Attention returned to Tom who stood on the ledge, flicking the hoop back and forth.

'All right.' Sasha paced the walkway and clapped. 'Tallulah, Mai, Estella and Ollie are freezing in the pool.'

'But …' Adelaide said. 'The flame will die as soon as it hits the water. Won't it?'

'We'll see; with practice Tom will have enough control to keep it alight. Come on, Tom.' Sasha was practically growling. 'Your team needs the firethrower's circle of warmth. Show us what you've got.'

Tallulah understood Sasha's reasoning – Tom worked best when looking out for his team. But did he need to be put under this kind of pressure right now? Something had happened to Tom's gift – that much was clear – and somehow Saskia was involved. But the details would have to wait. It was only necessary to know that Tom had lost his confidence. And as he'd done for her all last week, she would do for him now. She would focus all her positive thoughts on him – at least on that spot where the flame and hoop were supposed to meet. Then she and the others would get warm – and they could all get out of here.

Tom took a breath, shook his left hand and looked down at it again before his lips moved and flame came to his fingertips.

Again the flaming hand was brought closer to the hoop ... and closer.

'You've got it, mate,' Hui called, softly. Tallulah felt herself nod. She stayed focused on the space where the hoop and hand would meet and a minute later, Tom's delighted eyes reflected the ring of firelight he held in front of him. Even Sasha whooped.

Tallulah felt a great breath leave her body. Eventually Tom's smile rested on Tallulah and she returned it. But the flames were distracting; the firelight was so beautiful and so warm she was reminded of bonfires at dusk on warm tropical beaches. She shook off the image, telling herself this was about Tom, but the more she tried to ignore the flame the stronger it seemed to get until again she gave into its gorgeous warmth.

Groans echoed around the room and a cold current lapped at Tallulah's reverie. She looked at Tom and saw the ring of fire had died. Sasha threw him another hoop and, as Tom, quickly repeated his ritual, Tallulah focused on the point where hand and hoop would meet; she needed that flame. Seconds later, a ring of flame burst forth again.

'That's it, Tom.'

Tallulah heard the voice from a long way away. She was back in Tom's flickering light, feeding it, being caressed by it or perhaps the soft breezes of a tropical paradise. She felt deliciously sleepy. From her dreamy place she somehow understood that Tom was weakening and she guessed that knowledge came from her own experience; training her gift was tiring. She wished she could help Tom by taking Mai and Ollie and the others in the water with her into the flame, onto her tropical island. As she had that thought she heard the others around her sigh – Mai even moaned – and she knew they were all OK. Tom needn't worry. They were warm. And happy. And relaxed. And sleepy. Incredibly sleepy.

She felt all the tension leave her body. She felt the water creep up her neck, past her chin, her lips, over her eyelids and tickle her scalp as she sank below the surface. The weightlessness was glorious; she revelled in the feeling of floating, free, all worries fell away as she let the water wrap itself softly around her. All was blissful and black.

The cold came back with the rushing force of an avalanche pummelling its way down a mountain. Then Tallulah was conscious of many hands holding her; her chest and stomach convulsed as she retched and then gasped desperately for air; acid and water spewed from her lungs and belly at the same time as she tried to suck air in and the stinging pain in her throat and ears was so bad that tears sprang to her eyes and she cried out. Voices spoke rapidly around her but she couldn't make out what they were saying. For a moment she was draped over the ledge of the pool like a limp rag doll and more water gushed out of her, then she was lifted off the ledge and out of the water and placed on a stretcher of some sort.

'You're OK,' a familiar voice said quietly beside her. It took all the energy she had to roll her head to see Mai walking beside the stretcher. Then she lowered her eyelids as exhaustion overwhelmed her.

CHAPTER ELEVEN

Tallulah was comfy, which made her inclined to go back to sleep, since she was still as heavy as lead with weariness. When she became conscious of the clinking of cutlery and quiet chatter she decided she was too curious to sleep and opened her eyes.

The Seacliff escarpment loomed over her. She was on the Cirque d'Avenir roof terrace, lying on a couch under a marquee. She remembered coming back to the Cirque d'Avenir warehouse after the ambulance officers had given her the all-clear and walking up to the rooftop on what seemed like a never-ending flight of stairs with Marnie. She remembered a conversation about food.

'How are you feeling?'

Tallulah rolled her head to her right. 'Good,' she told Marnie, pushing up off the lounge. But the healer put a hand on her shoulder.

'Not yet.' Her eyes narrowed and Tallulah felt like she was being scanned by a supernatural X-ray. 'What on earth were you doing to yourself in that pool?' She clicked her tongue. 'It wasn't exposure that caused you to faint; more like some sort of mental burnout. You pushed yourself too far. I had to tell

Marie, of course.' The healer hesitated. 'She was as shocked as she was impressed.

'You're winning a lot of respect, Tallulah, but don't kill yourself to get it. I've given you one of my reiki treatments, which should begin to replenish your mind – Marie tells me Brigitta's lesson is preparatory and work you've already done otherwise I would have ruled it out. But until you replenish yourself physically as well, you are not to move. Anything you don't eat?'

'I'll just walk from here to the food tables and back – I promise I won't do anything else.' But Marnie was shaking her head before she finished the sentence. Tallulah acquiesced. 'I eat everything.'

Marnie approaching the barbecue alerted the others to Tallulah's wakeful state. Tom and Mai were at the end of the table closest to her and they immediately pushed back from where they sat. Mai skipped over like a lit firecracker while Tom loped beside her; his slumped shoulders were as downcast as the frown on his face.

Marnie returned with a plate of food moments after Tallulah greeted her friends. 'Don't let her talk before she eats,' she warned, saving her sternest look for Mai, who sat on her hands on the bench beside Tallulah's couch as if that would help keep her mouth shut. But she left the three of them after Tallulah had eaten a few mouthfuls.

Mai watched Marnie disappear down the staircase to the warehouse below before she turned back, her mouth wide in silent astonishment, shoulders squeezed to her ears.

'What?' Tallulah asked.

'That was you,' she whispered, hands now unshackled and flying free. 'Don't tell me it wasn't.'

Tallulah choked on the piece of pork chop she was eating. Tom passed her the bottle of sports drink Marnie had brought with lunch and Tallulah drank it. She shook her head as she recovered, then gestured to the plate of food in front of her. 'You want me to fail Brigitta's session too?'

Chastened, Mai pressed her lips together and slipped her hands between her thighs, squeezing her knees together. But Tallulah was too curious to leave it at that. When she'd successfully swallowed some coleslaw she cleared her throat. 'What are you talking about, anyway?'

Mai leaned forwards and whispered hoarsely, 'The tropical island, the palm trees, the warm water.'

Tallulah couldn't believe what she was hearing – or what she thought Mai meant. 'You felt … it's not … possible. But … how?'

Mai was nodding wildly. 'Hell yes.' She got down on her knees next to the couch and grabbed Tallulah's hands. 'I was *warm*, Lu,' she said. 'And then I wasn't – the moment you lost consciousness I knew it. And so did the others; I overheard Estella and Ollie talking about it but they don't know how it happened.'

Tallulah looked to Tom, who shook his head.

'Only those of us in the pool could feel it,' Mai continued. 'But I had to tell Tom what happened. He thought it was his fault that you collapsed.'

'I'm still not convinced,' Tom admitted. 'I couldn't get it together and it got too cold for everyone.'

'No, not everyone. No one else is strung out on a couch after fainting.'

'See, both riddled with guilt,' Mai declared dramatically. She looked between the two of them and gave Tallulah a wink. 'Quite romantic, really.' But then she got serious. 'We've been through this, Tom. You heard what Sasha said to the ambos: he got advice from sports scientists at Seacliff Uni about the temperature we could train at without doing any damage. We were cold – but not so cold that we'd collapse from exposure or hypothermia. Tom, I know how tired it made you trying to hold your flame; I haven't got the strength to charge my ribbons to their full capacity yet. But Tallulah telepathically heated all of us in the pool. Think about how much energy that must take – enough to cause her to collapse, for sure.'

Tom shrugged. 'I dunno.' His bleak expression told Tallulah that all this talk of her powers was not helping him. He stood. 'What I do know is there is no point being a firethrower who can't throw fire. I'll see you later.'

'Tom!' the girls called in unison. He gave them a backwards wave as he walked away. Tallulah waited till he'd joined Hui and Elen at their table before she said, 'Do you know anything about—'

But Mai was shaking her head and directing her attention to the top of the stairs, where Saskia stood. When she looked in their direction, Mai waved.

'Did you have a lobotomy while I was out?' Tallulah asked, as Saskia walked toward them.

Mai just giggled, but when Saskia was a little closer she called, 'She's OK.'

'I'm so glad,' Saskia said. Then to Tallulah she added, 'I would hate it if you couldn't take part in Brigitta's session just because of …' She surveyed Tallulah with a critical eye. 'You look OK now. But Hecate's torches, Tallulah! You gave us a fright – didn't she, Mai?'

'Oh, when we dragged you out of that water …' Mai put her hand on her chest.

'It was lucky Mai saw you.'

'I got very *cold* all of a sudden,' Mai said, as if it were a premonition rather than a physical sensation.

'She yelped and when I saw you floating lifeless in the water I jumped in to help.'

'We were so worried.'

'You want to sit down?' Tallulah asked Saskia.

Saskia took in a deep breath and sighed, then she nodded and sat down.

'So, the time has come, girlfriend,' Mai said when she was settled. 'What's with the drama between you and Tom?'

Tears welled in Saskia's golden eyes as though the words were an arrow straight to her heart. 'Last year, my mum got really sick and had to go to hospital in Adelaide. Dad couldn't run a travelling circus and help Mum recuperate so, on Sasha's advice, I went to stay with Elen and train at her school in Broken Hill. And there was Tom. He's completely gorgeous – intense but gorgeous. We were together about six months. Then it was over. He gave no real reason for it, just said it wasn't working out and that it wasn't me, it was him.' She took a deep breath as she struggled to control her emotions. 'I couldn't rest until I got a better explanation. A couple of weeks before Cirque d'Avenir started we found out: he'd lost his gift and I was apparently the cause.'

'*We* found out?' Mai prompted.

'Sash. Sash found out for me.' She took a deep breath. 'I know you think he's tough but he's really the bridge-builder in all of this – without him I wouldn't be here.' She waved at the rooftop. 'A relationship between me and Tom was always going to be tough. Our families have hated one another for … since … Oh, it sounds so stupid, but for centuries.'

'Centuries?'

Saskia nodded. 'Constantine doused the flame of the Vestal Virgins, you see.' Sobs wracked her body. 'The firethrowers have never quite forgiven us for that one.'

Tallulah and Mai exchanged glances, not sure if they'd heard Saskia correctly – or if she was being serious. Tallulah's grasp of history came from lessons at school bolstered by visits to museums around the world with her parents, but it wasn't particularly solid. She knew there'd been a battle between Christian emperors like Constantine and the pagan religions.

'You mean in, like, 300 AD or—'

'394,' Saskia answered, automatically.

'Oh.' Tallulah nodded. It was one thing to have started considering herself part of an ancient tradition; it was another to suddenly understand just what 'ancient' meant. 'That does seem silly,' she agreed, recognising her offering as a classic understatement.

'But Tom's determined to right the wrongs of the ages, you know,' Saskia said. 'Sometimes it felt like I was a cause he'd taken on rather than a girl; it was like he had to justify being with me by making it about the greater good rather than just keeping it about our right to be in love. We argued about that, then we'd make up, and for a few weeks he'd relax and everything would be great. But his stuff just overwhelmed us eventually, I guess.'

'How can one person strip another of his gift?' Tallulah asked.

Mai's glance told Tallulah she was being a simpleton. 'It happens in relationships all the time – there doesn't have to be a gift involved.'

Saskia gave Tallulah and Mai a weak smile. 'I suppose it's flattering – to have such a powerful influence on someone. But as I said, why would I strip him of his gift when I adored him? I asked for a meeting and put that question to him. He told me that I shouldn't listen to what others say – which is a bit hard when mates like Hui take up his cause.' She gave a bitter laugh. 'Tom said he didn't blame me; it was his battle alone. He was very sweet, but – he was *emphatic* – there was no chance of us reuniting. We weren't good for one another.'

Sasha's voice rang out across the terrace. 'OK, guys, Brigitta's session begins in ten minutes. Let's get cleaned up and ready to go.'

Mai reached out and put her hand on Saskia's knee. 'No guy's worth crying over, Saskia.'

Fresh tears filled Saskia's eyes. 'Thank you, Mai,' she said. She wiped her eyes then heaved in a breath and stood, wriggling as if she was trying to shake off her mood. 'You're right. And I'm not going to be one of those pathetic girls who spend their day mooning about a broken heart.' She gave them a brave smile. 'I'm going to go wash my face before our session with Brigitta and then I'm going to be so magnificent that he'll rue the day he decided to dump me.'

'Go get 'em,' Mai said.

Saskia squared her shoulders and, with a quick wave, turned away and crossed the terrace. As they watched her join the other students descending the stairs, Mai leaned closer to Tallulah. 'Every so often, when my grandmother opened up about all this, she'd say there is no such thing as the Cirknero. She reckoned it was a name invented by the Cirkulatti to cover the real truth, which is that time and again the Cirkulatti destroys itself from within.'

'Irena never mentioned the Cirkulatti to me, ever.'

'Well, she probably didn't want you bogged down in grudges that lasted for generations – especially since she was training the—'

'Don't say it,' Tallulah warned. 'Her message was always to act on instinct, on gut feeling. I guess that could be interpreted as staying independent, rather than basing actions on centuries of what had come before.'

'I don't think my grandmother would have let me come here except that she got sick and maybe too tired to cope with me any more,' Mai said. 'She's kind of resigned now, I think. And she liked Marie. Better to know what it's all about, she said when I left, although definitely more to convince herself than me. Still, Tom's got that girl worked out. She's not good for anyone.'

Tallulah snorted. 'Says the person who just feigned friendship in order to get information.'

'I didn't exactly *feign* friendship. She was worried when you collapsed. She acts worldly but I don't think she is.'

'You're lucky that the people *you* get off to a bad start with are a bit more forgiving.'

'But I'm not like her,' Mai declared, offended. 'I don't drain people just by standing next to them. You *must* feel it,' she insisted. 'You can't tell me you don't. She's determined to intimidate us. Make us feel bad about ourselves.'

'Yes, I feel it,' Tallulah admitted. 'But I've thought about it and I don't reckon Saskia's doing anything on purpose. They're our own insecurities, Mai, rising within us; yes, in answer to her energies – but she's not conscious of it. I'd feel *that*, I'm sure.'

Sasha, clearly not mollified by Tallulah's near-death

experience, shouted, 'Why are you two still up here? Downstairs, both of you, now.'

As Tallulah pushed herself up off the lounge she muttered, 'I've lost sight of any good in *him*.'

Mai grinned. 'It's a start, I suppose.'

Brigitta stood at one corner of a long carpet of photos on the floor of the warehouse. The laid-out images featured walls and fences, old and new, as well as doors and gates, and locks of all varieties. Next to the pictures was a stack of blank sketchbooks as well as Textas, coloured pencils, scissors and glue.

Tallulah felt relief trickle through her body; she had done all this with Irena years ago – just as Marie had said, she would coast through this session. But the looks on the faces of other Cirque d'Avenir students told her not everyone was as happy.

'I thought,' Saskia said, a hint of derision in her voice, 'you were going to teach us ...'

Brigitta looked amused. 'Yes, Saskia?'

'Well, not collage.'

'Saskia ...' Sasha's quiet admonition carried a hint of embarrassment.

'It's all right, Sasha,' Brigitta assured him. 'I have nothing to fear from your questioning minds; indeed I welcome them. I would say those who don't question are far more susceptible to attack than those who do.'

Saskia's arched eyebrows and grin at her brother said it all.

'Before we continue let me, first, offer my congratulations. You made it through a difficult first week; you are, physically and mentally, eleven tough individuals. Further training at

Cirque d'Avenir will involve not just attention to your physical ability but your mental ability, as well.'

'Why?' Guido asked.

'Because minds are the key to our power as individuals. They are our most precious gift; our magic, if you will. This class will honour that core mental power, build on that strength you have already displayed, and teach how to protect it.'

'From the Cirknero?' Estella asked.

Brigitta chuckled. 'Marie told me you have Cirknero on the brain, Estella.'

'And why not?'

Brigitta raised her hands as if to surrender. 'Forgive me, I did not mean to make light of your question. And,' she glanced at the stairs that led to the roof before addressing them again, 'I am not naive enough to think that news of a group of uniquely talented individuals being trained in a far-off corner of the world will not attract attention. But let me reassure you that I agreed to come out of retirement only if I could train you for *all* possible dangers.' She took each of them in slowly with her gaze. '*Whatever* the threat may be. But,' she held up a bony finger, 'experience has shown me time and time again that the most potent barrier to releasing our potential, is ourselves – or those close to us.'

'Like me,' Ollie blurted, as though he'd been waiting for the chance to speak and now couldn't stop. 'That's what happened to me. It's like I was scared of myself. My mother used to say it: "My Ollie is scared of his own shadow."' He laughed; his enthusiasm was infectious and they all laughed too. Then he got serious. 'Being here I don't have to be.'

'That's what we are here to learn.' Brigitta's voice was deep with reassurance and conviction. 'My classes will make your minds as rock hard as Sasha's vampire curls make your core.'

'But what have the photos got to do with it?' Adelaide asked.

'They are merely a place for us to start, visual aids to help you to begin the process of building protective walls around your minds. Not everyone has an immediate idea of what walls they might build, and even if they do, in my experience it's better to fortify that with a precise visual image. It is just one more way to help you focus.

'So wander around, look at the images on the floor; when you feel a strong connection with something, pick it up. Once you have gathered a couple of ideas, grab a book and a glue stick and begin to build the walls pictorially. Once you have a strong physical image then we will begin to create the mental imprint.

'But take pens and pencils too, and note down words, phrases – any thoughts you have as you create your pictorial account. Your subconscious mind will get busy the moment you begin. Write down everything as it surfaces, because it is a clue to the way you work internally and will help with the next step.

'Once you have built those walls of protection – I suggest you aim for three barriers, each stronger than the one around it – you will need to create keys you can give those you wish to *allow* into your mind. A word key, a favourite phrase, something that resonates strongly with you, can surface as you begin the process of building. It will become clear when we are working why this is important.'

Saskia let out an exasperated sigh. Brigitta inclined her head. 'Saskia, speak, or your frustrations will infect us all this afternoon and we will not get through the work we need to.'

'This is remedial, Brigitta.'

'How so?'

'You're either mentally strong or you're not.' She waved her hand at the floor. 'It's like our gifts – we either have them or we don't. Anyone who doesn't have a gift should not be here; anyone who is not mentally strong should not be here.'

Brigitta laughed softly. 'You make grand assumptions that everyone is like you, Saskia; that everyone has had the same experiences as you. It's a dangerous way to think. You've just heard Ollie speak of a very different life.'

Saskia opened her mouth to speak but seemed to decide against it.

'Many consider one of our great strengths to be the ability to recognise when we are most susceptible, and to guard our mind accordingly. That takes maturity and understanding; age makes us sensitive, so does illness, emotion and, of course, in our line of work, injury.

'Imagine a truly malevolent person wishes you harm. It is my experience that it is often the most talented who must be on guard; malevolence in the form of jealousy and spite and greed is everywhere just trying to bring us down. Training is the best form of protection. Simple as that.'

'Still—'

'Saskia! It is admirable to be mentally strong and you obviously believe you are. But that is different from being consciously trained to withstand a mental attack against someone who wants, at best, to disarm you, or at worst, to control you.'

Saskia's eyes widened. '*Believe* I am?'

Instinctively, Tallulah checked her own boundaries. She was confident that the only problem she would encounter should Brigitta use whatever power she had was fatigue from the mental practice she'd put herself through in the abattoir.

It hit her seconds later: Tallulah folded at the waist as if that physical action might protect her from the force-ten, white-hot hurricane that ripped through her mind, shaking the foundations of the wrought iron, the brick, the rendered steel mosaics that she had painstakingly built, until she didn't think she could stay standing, but if she let go and allowed the barriers to be uprooted and reveal the secrets of her mind, there would be no relief – there would only be the barren dry emptiness of complete and utter desolation.

And then it was over.

The bright block of sunlight shining on the floor in front of Tallulah was the first indication that she was no longer in the grip of Brigitta's gale – as she looked up she decided she had never found so much joy in the sight of dust motes dancing in the sun. She checked her mental boundaries. A few minor chinks but nothing too bad. But as more of the real world came into focus, she was overwhelmed with such disappointment in herself that she wanted to cry. The next thought hurt her even more – Irena's lessons had been like child's play compared to the power she had just encountered.

It wasn't until she'd sat back on her haunches that she realised it wasn't just her; almost the whole class had been affected. Tallulah looked to her left. Tom and Hui were recovering, breathing hard, hands leaning on knees but still standing; Estella was crouched like Tallulah. But many of the others had been felled; they were lying on the floor and Brigitta and the trainers moved around the room helping them up. Mai was stretching out legs that had curled into the foetal position and heaving herself carefully back to her feet. A groan from Tallulah's right came from Adelaide, her whole body bent over her knees, both hands over her head, rocking back and forth. Before Tallulah could get to her, Sasha was there. He got down on the floor next to Adelaide, gently lifted her by the shoulders, whispering, 'You're stronger than that, Della.'

A cough from the centre of the room got everyone's attention. Saskia stood tall and proud, unaffected by the storm.

'You look pleased with yourself, Saskia,' said Brigitta.

Tallulah was surprised at how much more wary she now was of the light and breezy, almost cheeky, voice Brigitta addressed them with; it was another creature entirely from the storm that had cut a vicious swathe through her mind only moments before.

Saskia grinned. 'Shouldn't I be?'

'If you think that's as bad as it gets.' Brigitta turned away without waiting to see Saskia's grin falter. 'But I think I have everyone's attention now. Let's go. We've wasted enough time.'

Brigitta wandered between the students, offering advice, questioning them about the choices they had made. Saskia hadn't moved.

'Are you going to join your teammates, Saskia?' Brigitta asked.

'I don't need pictures and all this nonsense. Just a clean simple thought that I can maintain forever.'

'And can you?'

'If I had to. Easy.'

'Interesting. I don't think any of this is easy. I believe it's as demanding as anything you could do physically. More, even.'

'Have you done it?' Tallulah asked her.

Brigitta turned her face to the shafts of sunlight while she considered her answer. 'It has been many years now. But, yes, a variety of opponents and a variety of barriers. I assure you the hardest minds to break are the simplest because you cannot distract them from their tasks. Distraction is your only real chance to invade a trained mind. All you need is a tiny crack to force you way in and from there you must seize on it and take advantage. You have to, I'm afraid to say, be ruthless.'

She checked her watch. 'But that is all we have time for today. Think more about this tonight. Tomorrow when you arrive we will sit and I will guide you through a meditation to set those barriers into your mental state.

'Just remember, it is important that what we do in this room goes no further. It is for your own safety.'

CHAPTER TWELVE

Tuesday 21 January

Tallulah was trapped in a bind that wound from her ankles, through her legs and around her body. She grunted as she twisted her shoulders back and forth in an effort to free herself – and was surprised to find less resistance than she expected. A streak of red from above distracted her and she looked up to see the striped roof of her own bedroom. It wasn't until she was almost unravelled that she worked it out: her sheet was damp with sweat.

'Gross!' she muttered as she jumped up, pulled the sheets off the bed and onto the floor, and shook her pillow from its case.

'Hey, I only changed them yesterday.'

Tallulah started at the sound of her father's voice – even though it wasn't much more than a hoarse whisper coming from the doorway.

'You all right?' he asked immediately.

She nodded. 'You gave me a fright, though.' Crouching, she gathered the sheets in a bundle. 'Hot night, I guess. But I'll wash them, don't worry.' She stood and faced him with a smile, but his expression was concerned. 'What?'

'Your mum's still sleeping. She was up very early this morning. You were having a bad dream.'

'Me?' Tallulah was surprised but at the same time she wasn't.

'She even woke you up. Made you sit up and gave you a glass of water. Don't you remember?'

Tallulah shook her head.

'You were talking ten to the dozen about a circus in a twisted forest, about men who became snakes and some who became bears, and gifts being tested.'

She did feel it was on the edge of her memory. As she made a mental lunge for the dream another, much clearer image came forth from earlier in the night, just as she had drifted off to sleep: a cloud swing and flight of lorikeets. It was a key to her mind that only one other person knew.

'Well, it took Mum a while to get back to sleep after that.'

'Sorry.'

'She's OK now.' He gave a nod to the window. 'I'd better get on to replacing your intaglios. Irena would be upset at the thought of you being unprotected.'

'Unprotected?' A weak laugh escaped Tallulah's body.

'She believed they warded off bad dreams, didn't she?'

'Oh, yeah, she did. No word from her, I suppose?'

'Now don't start that again.'

And her father turned and disappeared from the doorway.

Tallulah stood up from locking her bike to see Tom wearing a worried expression.

'How are you?' he asked.

'I'm fine.' She was determined to be fine. Tallulah had taken the coast road to Cirque d'Avenir thinking that the fresh salty air and the beauty of the morning might help her

161

subconscious bring forth more detail of the dream that had woken her mother. But except for the oppressive weight of the dark forest and its unusual inhabitants there was little detail. Normally, she wasn't the kind of girl who'd want to wallow in the specifics of a nightmare but the preceding image of a cloud swing and the lorikeets bothered her. It was the mental key that she and Irena had devised together. Tallulah had the distinct if bizarre impression that her missing nanny was trying to communicate with her now.

For his part, Tom did not look convinced about the state of her health.

'I am, Tom. Much better than yesterday. What about you?' Without waiting for him to respond she continued, 'Please don't tell me you are the kind of person to hold a grudge for centuries.'

Which at least made him laugh.

'Got a problem with Constantine's dousing of the flame of the Vestal Virgins?' she said, keeping her voice light.

'You've been talking to Saskia.'

Tallulah set off for the theatre. 'She talked. Mai and I listened. But it's none of my business, Tom. You don't have to explain anything to me.' She stopped when she noticed he was not walking with her. She turned; he was frozen.

'The Robinson Family Circus came to town at the beginning of last year,' he said quickly.

'I don't need to know.'

'I'm going to tell you anyway. My family, Elen, Hui and my mates, no one was happy when Saskia and I got together. But I thought we'd win them over; and I was obsessed with the idea that together we could break down all that crap from the past. She was ...'

'Rebellious? Gorgeous? Irresistible?'

Tom sighed. '*Keen*, I was going to say: keen to overcome our family's history, just like me. But we'd barely got going when our troubles began. She reckoned I was more in love with the cause than with her. I wasn't, although I admit that I probably felt I had to justify being in love with her since so many people close to me disapproved, which only made me hate myself for being so weak. I got myself twisted in knots. Nothing I did was good enough for Saskia; nothing I did was good enough for my family.

'With every argument I felt a bit of myself disappear until eventually … I lost my fire. I didn't want to believe it was Saskia. I *don't* believe it was her. But everyone convinced me it was. I broke it off for good … but now …'

He stopped and looked down at his open hand, whispered as he'd done yesterday and his fingers seemed to ripple with flame.

'And you're the one who gives me the "be careful" lecture.' Tallulah looked around. 'Why are you doing that out here?'

'It's not exactly coming back like a giant comet from the sky, but …'

'Maybe you're still in love with her.'

Tom glanced at her quickly, gave an almost imperceptible shake of his head and looked back at the tiny flame in his hand. He closed his palm and the light was gone.

'No, I'm not. Until last week I couldn't bring forth the flame at all. Now, I have no problem. In the abattoir when I managed to transfer the flame to the hoop momentarily, I felt strong, much stronger than I'd felt for a long time. And then the strength was gone.'

'Gone?' she said. Her heart was pounding when she met his gaze again; his eyes were definitely sparking with an intensity that made Tallulah uncomfortable.

'What do you make of that?' he asked softly.

Her first answer she couldn't voice; her confused emotions about this boy – this *man* – were making her feel ill. Tallulah shook her head then began to walk. 'That your you-know-what is coming back, surely. And that it wasn't a person that caused you to lose it at all. It was just a growth spurt or something. I mean, if a person affected you that much then you'd be too vulnerable to your emotions, right? Every time you fell in love you'd be losing your you-know-what, and you wouldn't want that, would you?'

'But, you see, no one knows if it disappeared from falling in love – or falling in love with the wrong girl,' he countered. 'Whereas if I fell in love with the *right* girl and that girl loved me back then it could make me stronger than ever before, couldn't it?'

'No.' She knew what he was implying and it made her unpleasantly dizzy to think she could have so much power. 'No, that couldn't work because it's all too dependent on whether the girl loved you back – and you've got no control over that. If she doesn't love you back then where are you?

'Tom, there is nothing smart about what you are saying. Staking your strength on a girl, risking your own personal potential for love – especially when you're, like, *seventeen* – is just dumb. It would make you weak and you mustn't do it.'

'Weak,' he said, dumbfounded, and looked away from her to the pavement. 'Wow. That's some interpretation of love.'

'Don't put words in my mouth, please. I'm not talking about love; I'm talking about you controlling your gift. Isn't that what Brigitta was talking about yesterday?' Tallulah put her hand on his shoulder. 'How about a deal?'

Tom lifted his head, although she merely glimpsed his eyes before he looked out to sea.

'If you promise to work on building your you-know-what,' she said, 'without the aid of falling in love, without the aid of a girl, then I will take your good advice and do my best not to reveal *my* you-know-what to anyone else.'

He shrugged then nodded but with little conviction. 'If that's what you want.'

Tallulah tried a joke. 'I'm fifteen. I have no idea what I want. Except what's best for you. I know I want that.'

Tom walked past her, opened the door to the warehouse and waited for her to enter. As Tallulah walked past him he whispered, 'Well, I'm glad we got that clear.'

The students gathered quietly after climbing the ropes to the roof, not sure what to expect. Brigitta arrived on the terrace from the stairs and conferred with Marie.

Tallulah stood with Mai, watching everyone as they limbered up. It was good to stand and stretch after an hour of sitting downstairs, eyes closed, following Brigitta's meditation to help them set the boundaries of their minds.

Brigitta's final words had been as reassuring as they could be. 'I do not want you to worry unnecessarily. I am not going to do anything that will harm you. The aim of the day is about experiencing confusion and setting your mind against thoughts that can distract you from your goal. As long as you concentrate on the exercise completely, your barriers will stay intact and you will be able to hold me off.'

'"Crocodile Rock",' Mai said in a subdued voice behind Tallulah from where they watched Marie, Brigitta and the others.

'What's Crocodile Rock?'

'It was my mum's favourite song. If something happens and I'm not making it, I want you to help me. "Crocodile Rock" is the key; it's how I'll know it's you.'

Tallulah opened her mouth to speak but Mai stopped her. 'Don't offend me by saying you don't know how you could be any help to me, please.'

Tallulah didn't dare. Instead, she watched Adelaide walk towards them. She didn't look good.

'Della, you all right?'

Adelaide nodded.

'You don't look it,' Mai told her.

Tallulah glared at her.

'Sorry, but I'd be a bit freaked out after last week, if I were you.'

'You really need to stop talking, Mai,' Tallulah told her.

But Adelaide laughed. 'No, that's OK. I am a bit freaked out.'

'It'll be different this week,' Tallulah said.

'You reckon? Someone was in my head last week but after yesterday I don't think it was Brig—'

'Oh, don't worry about that,' Tallulah interrupted. 'They were testing us local recruits last week to sort out who should be here and who shouldn't.'

'How do you know that?' Adelaide snapped.

Tallulah tried to backpedal. 'Just something I heard. But it's good, isn't it? I mean, we survived it.'

'My friends were all freaked out after last week; now you

tell me you knew there was some secret test going on that we weren't told about?'

'I didn't know either; I just heard about it later.'

'I thought I was going mad but I guess you think this is all normal.'

'No.' Tallulah shook her head. 'I don't think any of this is normal. But then I'm not normal and neither is Mai.' Out of the corner of her eye, Tallulah could see Mai shaking her head. 'What about you, Della, are you normal?'

'I want to be,' she said, longingly.

'OK, people. Same groups as last week. If your buddies didn't make it, find some new ones,' Sasha called. 'Let's get going.'

'We're walking the course first, like last week?' Tom asked.

Sasha put a hand above his eyes to shade them from the sun. 'I was thinking that we knew it well enough not to bother with the walk-through. Nothing has changed.'

Tom looked back to the group of students, his eyes resting on Tallulah for a moment longer than she really thought was necessary. Her insides flared; he still felt the need to protect her.

Tom turned back to Sasha. 'It was just a big day yesterday; I thought it would be a good idea—'

'I don't need to walk the course, Tom,' Tallulah interjected. She turned to Sasha. 'I don't,' she insisted. 'I'm fine.'

'I wasn't talking about just you, Lu,' Tom said, quietly.

'That's the way only way Tallulah thinks, Tom,' Sasha said.

'No, it isn't,' Tom said. 'What exactly have you got against her, because we'd all like to know? She hasn't had a chance with you from the day Cirque d'Avenir began.'

'And that's how quickly it can happen.' Brigitta's voice rang clearly across the rooftops. Everyone turned to see her being assisted onto the rooftop by Ilya and Marie.

'Resentment, bitterness and anger are so easy to set loose in the mind. Without your team you are nothing; bickering among yourselves is the first hint that something isn't right – unless these tensions are with you on a day-to-day basis. If that is so then you need to deal with them quickly for disharmony plays into your enemies' hands and makes you even easier to exploit. I expect more – and that includes you, Sasha.'

For a few moments everyone was silent as Brigitta's censure filled them. Tallulah had not been conscious of malevolence in her mind, but as she had been repeatedly told, Brigitta was a master; she was without doubt a new kind of force. Tallulah checked her boundaries; the roses that should have wrapped their way around the wrought iron gates had not even begun to climb.

'You'd better watch out, my friend,' Saskia whispered over Tallulah's shoulder. 'He'll say all the right things and then just when you're hooked he'll decide *you're* no good for him either.'

Tallulah turned slowly as she took in Saskia's implication. 'There is nothing going on between me and Tom, if that's what you mean.'

Saskia shrugged. 'It's none of my business, Tallulah.'

'You're still in love with him. It seems like he's still in love with you. Do you think I'd make a play for him and get caught up in all that?'

Saskia laughed.

'What's so funny?'

'You're just so upright, Tallulah, so *sweet*, I'm scared for you.'

'You too? And why is that?'

'Because one day you'll let yourself down; you're going to have to be mean to someone if you're going to get anywhere in life, and I think it's going to destroy you.'

Tallulah's breath constricted in her chest as the insecurity that always accompanied her confrontations with Saskia began to overwhelm her. But almost immediately, her boundaries repelled the sensation. Her breathing dropped to her tummy, her head cleared and she smiled. 'Tom's just embarrassed after yesterday.'

'Saskia, Tallulah, can we have your attention any time soon?' Sasha called to them.

'He's embarrassed *every* day,' Saskia insisted. 'He was expected to be one of the stars of Cirque d'Avenir. Everyone wants to go to Elbe but he'll be left behind if he doesn't get it together soon.'

The interference began as a buzzing throughout her body as Tallulah cartwheeled across the second roof from where they had begun.

It made her feel blurry – like there was no separation between her body and the air that surrounded it – but it wasn't too bad. She came to a stand at the end of the second cartwheel and steadied herself. She wasn't giddy; her vision was fine; there was only the low hum of static all around her and that sense that everything immediately surrounding her was merged. She checked her boundaries even though she knew what she would find – they were intact. At least she'd noticed Brigitta's presence this time. Bit hard to miss it.

'Just concentrate on form, pure and simple,' she muttered. Fleetingly, she thought of Marie's technique, then put it aside. 'Simple,' she repeated. Cartwheels. Tallulah made the first rotation: four. Then the next: three. Two. One. And she was done.

When Tallulah reached the end of the section and her teammates, Hui was leaving. He was third in his group, behind Tom and Mai.

'Everyone OK?' Tallulah asked.

'Oh yeah,' Saskia told her. 'Easy.'

Tallulah looked at Adelaide, who gave her a thumbs-up. 'Not as bad as last week.'

'All you need to do is concentrate on the exercise,' Saskia said. 'As much as I respect Brigitta, this nonsense about creating boundaries is a waste of time. Uh-oh,' she said, pointing into the distance.

Tallulah and Adelaide looked ahead some fifty metres to see Tom reach the top of the wall he was scaling. But rather than taking up the rope Tom had finished with, Mai was at the bottom of the building – dancing. It was such a mish-mash of styles, part hip-hop, part ballet, that for a moment Tallulah wondered whether it was Mai being deliberately kooky but as it continued and Mai's moves became more frantic, Saskia began to giggle and Tallulah realised her friend was trapped. Hui arrived at the spot where Mai was busting her moves, tried to engage her by dancing with her, around her, in front of her, but she was in her own world. He tried to interest her in the rope but she kept popping and crimping. She didn't seem unhappy, just useless to anyone in her team.

'Can't you do something?' Tallulah asked Saskia.

Saskia looked at her as though she was mad. 'Me?'

'Like the first day,' Tallulah said, trying not to give too much away. 'She said you were in her mind that day.'

'And you saw how she acted – violently. She would have attacked me if Marie hadn't intervened. Then she tried to electrocute me at the pool. Don't get me wrong,' Saskia said, proudly, 'I could touch her mind. But anything could happen.' Saskia looked behind her. 'And Sasha will have us for dinner if we don't get going.'

She took off. Tallulah looked at Adelaide.

'Can't you?' Adelaide asked.

'Can't I what?'

'Do something.'

Tallulah wondered if admitting she could help Mai might sound like a confession that she had trespassed in Adelaide's mind. But there was no alternative. 'I could – Mai … well, she gave me the key to her mind should something like this happen. But I've been taught never to trespass on another's mind. If I do something to you, believe me, it isn't deliberate.'

Adelaide gave a grim laugh. 'I think I know that now, despite what I said to you on Sunday.'

'We need to speak to Marie or someone about it.'

'It's not important right now – just don't leave her like that.' Adelaide gestured to Mai.

'I don't know what will happen with Brigitta around in our heads, though, if I interfere. It might be the end of whatever chance I have of going to Elbe.'

'Well then, I won't go either – we're both making this decision to help Mai.'

Tallulah nodded.

She focused her mind on her own core, created the conduit, dropped the boundaries and silently whispered to Mai, *Crocodile Rock*.

The words had no effect. Tallulah breathed deep, checked their connection and said the words again. Mai seemed to hesitate – or did Tallulah imagine it?

'Keep going,' Adelaide said.

Tallulah glanced behind them. The next group should have caught them by now. 'You should get going.'

But Adelaide did not divert her attention from Mai. 'Don't worry about them. Just do what you have to do.'

'But—'

'You said it—' her eyes turned on Tallulah, 'we don't know what will happen if Brigitta senses someone else in Mai's mind. If she mounts an attack against you then I should be here – two of us against Brigitta are better than one.'

Tallulah didn't argue again; she focused again on Mai. *Crocodile Rock.*

And then, since she knew the words, and since Mai was dancing, she began singing the song. The longer she sang the song the slower Mai's dancing got. And as her dancing slowed, Tallulah got a glimpse of the place where Mai was stuck. Mai was barely more than toddler, running around a room, gleefully following a trail of pink ribbon twirled by a rhythmic gymnast. When the woman stopped and turned around the mini-Mai ran straight into the woman's arms; the woman lifted Mai effortlessly to her hip and then with her free hand kept twirling the ribbon all around them so quickly it was as if they were in their own private world of twirling colour.

Tallulah felt tears prick her eyes. If she kept singing the song then she would bring her friend out of this beautiful memory. It was Mai's mother, and she had died since this day with the ribbons. Mai loved this memory of them together. It felt cruel to tear her away but Tallulah had no choice: Brigitta was using the memory to trap her. Tallulah had to do something quickly. Ah! She'd stopped singing; she ignored her tears and began singing the words that she knew. Trying to maintain her connection with Mai while searching subconsciously for another presence was too hard so she kept her focus solely on her friend until eventually the buzzing interference that she recognised from earlier began to intrude, draining the words from her mind. But rather than panic, Tallulah knew instinctively that all she had to do was keep using whatever words she could recall. She felt strengthened – she must be winning or their enemy would not be trying so hard to stop her. Finally all she could remember was the name of the song, which she kept repeating over and over to the tune until finally Mai stopped dancing.

Beside her, Adelaide bounced up and down and whispered, 'Yes!'

Tallulah and Adelaide watched Mai check her surroundings as if she was coming out of a trance. She found Hui, who had not left her side; the girls watched him talking and Mai nodding. She looked back towards where Tallulah and Adelaide stood.

Don't look for me. Don't acknowledge anything. You brought yourself out of the trap. Are you OK?

Mai froze; Tallulah realised it was the first time they'd communicated telepathically. She waited. Then Mai nodded, ever so slightly.

Great. Follow Hui.

Mai gave another barely perceptible nod, then she put her foot on the hand that Hui offered, climbed up his body, put her hands on his head and lifted her body into a handstand, before looping her feet around the rope and vampire-curling to hang the right way up.

Tallulah became conscious of Adelaide's hand on her shoulder.

'Are you all right?'

She yawned and nodded at the same time. 'Fine. You still reckon Brigitta's a different presence to last week?'

Adelaide's brow furrowed. 'I did. But now …' She shook her head. 'I wasn't even the one trying to free Mai yet she was draining the words from my mind.'

'Really? In case you helped me, I suppose.'

'She could have been the one giving me headaches last week.'

'I thought that was me.'

Adelaide actually laughed. 'You're scary in a different way.'

'Scary?'

'Another time.' Adelaide checked behind them. 'I reckon we'd better get going.'

All Tallulah really wanted was to sit down for a moment to recover. 'After you.'

But before Adelaide took off she turned back to Tallulah. 'You know with Mai … same for me … if anything happens …'

Tallulah feigned shock. 'You're actually giving me permission to *do your head in*?'

Adelaide laughed. 'Just don't get carried away, all right?'

As everyone gathered for lunch on the terrace there was a general sense of achievement – most of the squad had survived Brigitta's test. Tallulah was glad that she'd been concentrating so hard on everyone in front of her that she hadn't considered those behind her – she would have felt the need to help them as well.

Mai did not share the group's relief. She sat beside Tallulah, pushing her food around on her plate, eating little, and saying even less. Tallulah had tried to get her to chat but gave up when it was obvious that nothing she said would make things better.

'You don't understand,' Mai had muttered, 'she distracted me with something really obvious.'

Brigitta had been making her way slowly down the aisle between the tables, encouraging the students on their good work. When she reached Tallulah's table, Saskia also arrived with a plate of food.

'I thought you were going to make it tough for us, Brigitta,' Saskia declared in a teasing tone.

Brigitta laughed. 'It was tough enough for some. I couldn't really test everyone at the same time. But don't worry, I'll get to each and every one of you.' She chuckled. 'And while you managed to free Mai, Saskia, you took your time. Your team would be captured while you were busy with Mai's key. What about everyone behind you? Did you even look to see how the other students were coping?'

Saskia shook her head while pushing pumpkin salad onto her fork.

'We were supposed to be fending you off, not looking out for others,' she said. 'That was your instruction, wasn't it?'

Brigitta chuckled again. 'That was the instruction. But you didn't doubt, did you, that I might wield my powers a little more forcefully with some just to see how others would respond? What might you do if you saw a friend in trouble, for instance?'

'Well, I follow instructions,' Saskia said. 'And Mai and I have a history. I couldn't risk her reacting badly again to my presence her in mind. I wasn't the one using her key.'

It was as if at that very moment Saskia finally understood what Brigitta had first said. She stopped stabbing at her food and looked up. 'Someone was communicating with Mai telepathically, and you could hear it?'

'Oh, not only could I hear it, I counter-attacked, because it was working very well to bring Mai out of the trap I'd laid for her. But I was repelled and Mai escaped. The telepath was very strong; that's why I was sure it was you, Saskia.'

There was silence at the table; everyone turned to Saskia, who was staring at Brigitta with a look of complete bewilderment. 'I don't understand.'

Brigitta smiled. 'Don't you?' Then she turned and walked away.

CHAPTER THIRTEEN

Wednesday 22 January

'Brigitta has asked that we stick to more familiar routines as you get used to her influence on your minds and train yourselves to resist her, so, voila!' Sasha, looking very pleased with himself, gestured around the room. 'Just as you have repeatedly requested: a more traditional workout.'

Cheers and applause filled the room, before there came a rapping on the stage door so insistent that the northern side of the theatre shook.

The door opened and five people walked into the warehouse: two adult men followed by a teenage girl and boy – twins, Tallulah was certain – and then a woman who could only be the mother of the teenagers. They were all extremely uniform in looks, in height, in the way they dressed. The seams of their chinos and short-sleeved shirts seemed ready to burst from the pressure of their enormous muscles.

Tallulah was sure that five people had never exuded so much power. And as she had that thought, the great wooden pole that held the doors of the hippodrome in place was lifted, the doors were parted and the screams of battle hovered on the edge of her barriers, threatening to overwhelm her.

'You all right?' Tom asked over her shoulder.

Tallulah was conscious enough of the question to clutch behind her for something of him to hold on to as she kept the vision from breaking through and leaking into the minds of others. She felt the sure grip of his callused hands on her elbows as another, softer, hand took hold of hers and she heard Mai's voice: 'What is it?'

Tallulah felt breath fall back into her body and the hippodrome gradually disintegrated to nothing. 'Nothing, just a bit hot,' she told Mai.

Tom let go of her elbows and Tallulah returned to the warehouse as Sasha approached the men who had entered first.

'Stellan,' he said, holding out his hand to the man on the right. 'Hello.'

Stellan's hands remained steadfastly on his hips. The man beside him put a hand on his back. 'Brother, we have no issue with Sasha.'

His voice rumbled and echoed in the warehouse. He held his hand out for Sasha to shake.

'We did not have an issue with Sasha until the Herodians were included in Cirque d'Avenir at the expense of the strongmen.' Stellan's voice was as impressive as the other man's.

'Robinson is our name,' Sasha said quietly. 'We do not recognise any other.'

Stellan huffed. He looked around the group. He nodded at Tom and Hui. 'The firemen, the acrobats are here, the aerialists, the contortionists, as they should be. But where are the strongmen? The clowns? The magicians?'

'You know the answer to that,' Marie said. They all turned towards her. 'We are only in the early stages of re-grouping,

Stellan. We could not include everyone this time but the next time we come to Seacliff, the strongmen—'

Stellan stamped his foot and again the building shook. 'You treat me like a fool, Marie.'

'No, I don't,' she said softly.

'We have been excluded because we are not beholden to the Gazers' every word – just like the clowns and the magicians. We have made no secret of the fact that we believe Cirque d'Avenir should re-form the Council, with a representative of every faction, led by a new eminence – just like the clowns and the magicians. We have questioned the decision to include the Herodians – just like the clowns and the magicians. But it seems you are not allowed to have independent thought and opinion in Cirque d'Avenir.'

Marie sighed. 'Stellan, my friend, we have been through this many times. We are only starting up, only scouting—'

'Starting up?' he thundered. 'We have now been told that Elbe is being prepared – that's not scouting, Marie. The next stage is upon us.'

Marie opened her mouth to protest but then shook her head and looked at the floor.

Stellan nodded his head surely. 'Yes, the next stage is upon us. From what I can see, the Cirkulatti's children are being trained. What about my children, Marie? Their gifts are developing faster than we can teach them. They need friends their own age who are like them – different, but all charged with purpose and the same goals. These two young people are more talented than anyone in our family has been before. They are ready to stand loyal for the eminence. And yet you reject them.'

'I do not reject anyone. I'm merely saying the time has not yet come.'

Stellan's face was red, his fury barely contained. Nonetheless, he spoke quietly. 'We are here to see Irena Blatiskova. We want to hear for ourselves what she has to say about this.'

Tallulah's heart started to race.

'Irena Blatiskova is not here.'

Brigitta's voice rang out clearly through the warehouse; everyone turned to see her walking straight and unsupported to join Marie at the front of the stage. Stellan's eyes widened but he was not cowed. He walked towards her.

'Brigitta Sabbas? I understood you to be too frail to travel. Yet you have come all the way from your home in France to be part of this *scouting* mission. When Irena Blatiskova could have—' A new thought crossed his mind, serious enough to funnel his anger in a new direction. 'You're not saying ... You would surely tell us if ...'

Stellan shook his head at Marie and Brigitta as if he couldn't believe what he was thinking. He turned back to his companions with an expression so grave that Tallulah did not have to be a mindreader to know that this enormous man was on the verge of falling apart simply at the thought that something might have happened to Irena.

'She's visiting family in Europe,' Tallulah blurted, as much to reassure herself as him.

Stellan looked at her and then back to Marie, who confirmed the statement with a nod of her head.

'And she will meet you in Elbe afterwards,' the strongman said.

'No,' Tallulah blurted again. Irena would come back to Seacliff after visiting her family. She looked towards the stage. Marie and Brigitta exchanged a glance then Marie looked at Stellan and nodded.

'So our information was correct,' the man next to Stellan cried. 'You would dare re-form the Cirkulatti without us.'

'Irena has not been to Europe in fifty years,' Marie continued. 'We owe her the chance to see her family before she is called on to work for us again.'

But Stellan had turned back to Tallulah. 'And how do you know Irena?'

'She's my nanny,' Tallulah answered.

Tom groaned quietly behind her. Stellan baulked at Tallulah's confession, then blinked slowly, as if he'd just glimpsed a rare artefact and wanted to clear his vision before he took another look. He turned to his companions, who were surveying her in the way Tom's trainer, Elen, had done. Stellan again turned to Marie and Brigitta, a shocked look on his face, and regarded the two women.

'Irena Blatiskova left this girl here knowing that Brigitta Sabbas as well as the Herodians were in the scouting team?' he asked, incredulous.

'You overreach, Stellan,' Marie called.

'And I'm not sure what you are insinuating with your question,' Brigitta added, 'but I'm trying hard *not* to be insulted. Let us state right here and now, in front of Tallulah, that Irena and I have always had deep respect for each other and the roles we have been required to play at times of great stress within the Cirkulatti.

'And may we also deal with your blustering about Sasha and Saskia Robinson? Their parents have done everything required by the Gazers to prove that they should not be burdened by the actions of their forebears. You put unnecessary suspicion and mistrust into the minds of our students.'

Stellan said nothing. He looked around the room, then, to Tallulah's surprise, he dipped his head. 'I'm sorry,' he said sadly to the Robinsons. He turned back to the stage. 'And I'm sorry to you, Brigitta Sabbas. I have overstepped my mark. If you feel insulted then I beg your forgiveness.' He looked back to his family. 'But perhaps you can understand how we feel. We, the original members of the Cirkulatti, the strongmen, the clowns and the magicians, feel insulted by not being included in this initial scouting mission of Cirque d'Avenir.'

'Because it is not the Cirkulatti,' Marie said gently. 'Things cannot be the same as they have been for centuries, Stellan.'

The man nodded and there was silence in the warehouse. 'More's the pity,' he said finally.

'But if we want to take the best—' Tallulah heard the words but it wasn't until everyone turned to look at her again that she realised she'd been the one to say them.

'You want to take the best to Europe. What would Irena have said about their exclusion?' Tallulah looked at Stellan and his companions. 'I assumed that the camp included all possible candidates for Cirque d'Avenir. I didn't know anyone had been left out. But I'm new to all this.' She looked around to the other students for some confirmation. 'Did anyone else know?'

The eruption as everyone in the warehouse spoke at once was not the result of the tension of the last few minutes, but of the tension of past months, or years, or perhaps, as she was beginning to understand, even beyond.

Stellan and his family were not unhappy with the eruption they'd caused. Stellan gave Tallulah an approving smile, which she did not return. She was merely trying to work things out for herself.

You will listen to me now.

The words blew through their minds like a cool breeze. Without hesitation everyone turned to the stage and faced Brigitta.

'The Gazers have decided who should be included in Cirque d'Avenir's first year of operation,' she told them, 'but that does not mean others won't be included later – if they can prove they are willing to move forwards rather than live in the past.'

Tallulah was bothered by the answer, and not just because of Irena's opinion of the Gazers. Stellan's mention of the Council echoed inside her. Despite her resolve not to put the cuff on again until she knew more about it, Tallulah had an undeniable urge wear it.

But Stellan accepted Brigitta's words better than Tallulah had expected. He nodded curtly and then turned back to his companions. With everyone in the warehouse watching, the strongmen walked proudly to the door. Stellan held the door open for his family but they hesitated, conferring quietly before turning back.

The teenage girl spoke in a clear strong voice. 'We will stage our own gathering in Europe and we will train, Madame Brigitta, even if you will not have us – the strongmen, the clowns and the magicians – and we will be ready. We are Cirkulatti, loyal servants to the goddess of magic and the night, the faithful friend of mysteries, Hecate. And we stand ready to walk with the eminence, wherever she may be, whenever she may need us.'

The girl gave a slight bow of her head. The five strongmen kissed their bunched fingertips and drew a circle on their forehead.

'The eminence,' they chorused.

And then they were gone.

★

Sasha drove them so hard there was little time or inclination to speak about Stellan's visit for the next couple of hours. There was a method in his madness; Tallulah had to give him that.

At the end of the session, Marie instructed the trainers to fill their plates as quickly as possible and meet in her office. Hui and Guido suggested they all cool off with a swim in the ocean before lunch and most of the team agreed. Tallulah, preferring to be alone with her thoughts, headed to the rooftop. But Mai and Adelaide weren't about to leave her alone. A set of physically exhausting exercises could distract a couple of fit, curious teenagers only for as long as it took them to recover. They filled their plates with salad and barbecued chicken then headed along the row of empty tables and took seats at the far end.

'Now you can tell us why you nearly fainted when Stellan walked in the door,' Mai said. 'Your presence certainly interested him and his family.'

'You're being dramatic, Mai. I didn't faint.'

'Angling for Tom to catch a damsel in distress?'

'As if.' Tallulah laughed. She did not want to discuss the strongmen's interest in her here. 'This chicken smells good.' She attacked it with gusto. But Mai's stare was white hot – and Adelaide was no less interested. She finished the mouthful and shrugged.

'You didn't see yourself,' said Mai. 'You looked like you'd seen a ghost.'

'And that's saying something,' Adelaide said with a laugh, then immediately checked herself. 'Sorry, I didn't mean ...'

Tallulah waved away the apology then brought a puzzled Mai up to date. 'In the couple of months I had at Seacliff High before school broke up I was, apparently, known as Ghost-girl.'

Mai laughed. 'It's a good name,' she said apologetically, 'you've got to admit.'

'Gee, thanks,' Tallulah said.

'You haven't answered my question,' Mai challenged.

'How are you going with your ribbons?' Tallulah countered.

'Ha!' Mai exclaimed, pointing her finger at Tallulah. She leaned forwards and whispered across the table. 'The question is: how did you know about the ribbons? Another ghostly vision? Where did that come from?'

'What vision?' Adelaide asked.

'Humph,' Mai exclaimed with mock indignation. 'You saved that freaky scene just for me, did you?'

'Yeah, I save my visions for the most annoying people I know,' she deadpanned.

'Annoying? You don't know how annoying I can be.' Mai grinned as she stood and looked around. Tallulah followed her gaze; Saskia and Tom must have taken their lunch downstairs because only four of the Cirque caterers remained on the terrace, playing cards, while a fifth had picked up one of the guitars and was playing a light flamenco-style tune.

Mai ran quickly to the edge of the terrace, where various coils of rope were lined up. She chose a small coil no longer than the span of her arms; she walked back towards them, smiling, all the while running her hands along the rope. When she was a couple of metres from them she stopped and began to twirl the rope as if drawing circles with it on the floor.

'What's she doing?' Adelaide asked.

'Charging it, I think,' Tallulah answered, not knowing whether to feel excited or nervous. But rather than becoming taut, Mai's rope became a hoop that was suddenly spinning on her wrist. Her momentary surprise at the unexpected development was quickly replaced with the thrill of what she'd just achieved. Tallulah pressed her hands together in a series of quiet claps before checking Adelaide, who, she was relieved to discover, seemed more fascinated than freaked out.

But when Tallulah turned back to Mai, her expression had changed.

She looked at Tallulah, then beyond to where the cooks were sitting, then back to Tallulah and shook her head. *What? What are you doing?*

Tallulah wondered if their shared experience from the day before had created a permanent telepathic path between them – or just one for times of stress. Mai looked uncomfortable.

I'm not doing anything.

I'm not that strong, Lu. I can't take that – is it boosting? I'm losing it.

Tallulah gestured helplessly. *Mai, you're in control. I don't know what you mean.*

But Mai shook her head. *It goes faster when you look at it – or me. Can't you see? An electrically charged Frisbee is going to fly off my hand any minute if you don't stop.*

Tallulah turned to Adelaide. 'Could you go and get Marie? Quietly.'

'No,' Mai whispered. 'She'll be angry with me for doing this before time.'

'Then Ilya. Or even Tom,' she told Adelaide, as she moved away from the tables so that only the roofs where they worked out were between Mai and her and the sea.

But despite her intention not to look at the hoop, Tallulah was drawn to the sparking, crackling, spitting wheel of energy. 'It is amazing,' she heard herself say. As she watched, the hooded cobra that had reared at her when Mai had her up against the pylon on their first morning disengaged from the wheel.

'Tallulah!' Mai shrieked.

Tallulah dropped her gaze, but it was too late. The rope uncoiled and straightened into one of the deadly javelins she was all too familiar with. 'Drop it!'

And Mai did, but the action launched the javelin with enough force and energy to fly like a heat-seeking missile.

Tallulah heard Mai cry, 'Duck!' and she knew she should. But she was rooted to the spot, paralysed by the sight of the thing. All she could do was close her eyes, tense her body, and hope the pain would not be too bad.

But instead of pain, she felt nothing.

'Hecate's torches,' Mai whispered.

Tallulah opened her eyes to see the javelin hovering centimetres from her heart; she wasn't sure if it was going to spear her or give her a jolt of electricity so forceful she'd be thrown right off the roof. It juddered as if it had absorbed the electricity itself then undulated like a demented snake and fell to the ground, returning to its regular slack state. She was conscious of the presence of others beside her.

'What happened?' Tallulah heard Ilya ask Mai.

Mai was shaking her head, looking from the rope to Adelaide and back. 'She ... she ...' Mai looked at Tallulah. 'It stopped.'

Tallulah turned to see Adelaide standing on the other side of the lunch table, her face drained of colour, her arms and outstretched hands rigid. When her eyes met Tallulah's they were squeezed into narrow slits, spilling over with tears. 'I just ... I couldn't let it ...' She let out a groan of tremendous pain and gave Tallulah a desperate look. 'This can't be happening.'

Then she ran from the rooftop and disappeared down the stairs.

CHAPTER FOURTEEN

Friday 24 January

On Friday night, Tallulah sat on her bed with the cuff on her lap. She'd resisted the urge to retrieve it from the gatehouse – its home after the break-in – since the upheavals of Wednesday.

Stellan's visit as well as Adelaide's dash from the rooftop – and subsequent failure to return – had disrupted the team. But the arrival, on Thursday, of Marie's friend Avril, a combat coach who specialised in combining acrobatics with karate and kick-boxing, had distracted and exhausted Tallulah sufficiently to leave the cuff where it was.

But having arranged to meet Mr Morton the following morning at his antique shop in the city, the time had come to bring the cuff out from its hiding place. She ran her finger over the amber inlay of Hecate's torches, traced the filigree engravings that covered much of the cuff until she reached the onyx eyes of the owls that flew along the side of the cuff. 'Symbols of wisdom,' Tallulah muttered. Coming up with no good reason not to, she slipped her thumb in and rolled the bracelet over her wrist. It felt good. She closed her eyes and felt her heart skip a beat then pump hard, as though extra blood had just charged into her system.

She opened her eyes and felt relieved: she was not dreaming; she was in their beautiful bedchamber. The enormous proportions comforted her — the rich fabrics, velvets and silks, and the colour on the wall she'd chosen with love and care so long ago. She wished she could look for longer but she was weak now. Soon the goddess would appear, and the other eminences, and they would help her with the last act on earth.

She turned her head until her eyes focused on the younger woman barely a metre away, who was pouring liquid into a goblet inlaid with gems. She was wearing velvet robes of a green so deep the fabric seemed to shimmer in the lamplight. She reached into a pocket of her robe and retrieved a vial, shook it once, twice, then checked the contents were mixed through before adding them to the goblet. The woman turned towards the bed and smiled.

Equal parts blood and regret pumped through Theodora's veins. 'I didn't think I would see you again. The plague … the first dose was supposed to make me immune. I am so sorry.'

The younger woman nodded, but when she sat down on the bed, Theodora's heart constricted. Close up the younger woman's mutinous thoughts were barely concealed. Theodora's instinct was for another attempt at reconciliation but before she could speak her body was again rent by a shriek of pain. Exhausted, she gave into it.

'This will help,' the younger woman purred.

But before the cup even got to her lips, Theodora smelled the bitter contents and turned away.

'It's a draught for the pain.'

'This will only bring you pain, my child. Ancient laws will come into play if you use your gifts against your mother, against Hecate. Don't succumb to evil, child. The goddess bestows her gifts on those who deserve them.'

'And you think you deserve them? You, who sold out your pagan goddess for the bed of a Christian emperor?'

'Love was my motive – for the Cirkulatti and the emperor. What is your motive, Dora?'

The younger woman stood, as if stung. 'Don't call me that. I'm tired of your prattle. There is only what is due to me. The time has come for me to take what is rightfully mine.'

'I asked only that you train your gift so you would not be the puppet of others. Do you think they will give you what is due? They will destroy what you so desperately covet. Will that atone for your mother's sins against you?'

'You have no right to call yourself my mother.'

Pain ripped through Theodora again; when it receded the purple aura that had waited on the horizon of her mind was much closer. She waved for the cup. 'If you think you will find it any easier with me gone, so be it.'

With her daughter's hungry eyes upon her she took the cup, brought the acidic brew to her cracked lips and sipped. There was no emotion on Dora's face; no regret for the act she had just performed.

As the toxin coursed through Theodora's veins, the purple aura drew nearer. Shimmering within the light were the goddesses who had always sustained eminences through time; Hecate stepped forwards.

Eminence, you must call for the Cirkulatti.

Theodora shook her head. *Help my girl.*

She is not fit for the role of the eminence. Call for the Cirkulatti. They will help you now.

Theodora sobbed in spite of herself. She could not die and

let her daughter deal with the Cirkulatti Council alone; she would be shamed.

'Justinian,' she whispered. The goddesses faded back into the purple haze as her husband, her glorious emperor, came into her vision. 'Theodora,' a voice called, as if in answer. And she forced herself to look away from the purple hue, and open her eyes, in the hope of seeing her beloved one more time.

But instead she was confronted by the sight of her daughter furiously searching the room, making no attempt to conceal what she was doing. Theodora felt no shock or outrage; only deep, deep pity. When she found the right drawer, her daughter's head went back with a shout of victory.

The eminence, the empress, the mother heaved a painful breath and with her last reserve of energy began to dissolve the walls around her thoughts and send them across the room. *Trinkets are no substitute, Theodora.*

The woman turned, glowering. Her eyes rested on her mother's arm. With a triumphant, 'Huh!' she marched to her mother's side and grabbed her roughly by the wrist. But when she tried to yank the cuff away, it would not give; Theodora felt a tightening on her flesh as though the ornament had grafted itself to her skin.

Her face awash in confusion and panic, the younger woman wrenched her mother's arm harder and Theodora was certain she cried out. She called for the goddesses.

Please, help her.

But they faded further into the purple. Dora gave up tugging and looked closer at the cuff, turning her mother's wrist over as she tried to find a solution. 'What have you done?'

The purple light burned stronger now. But Theodora forced herself to stay in the room. *Goddesses of magic and wisdom, ancient foes rise up against the Cirkulatti …*

'Stop it,' the younger woman cried.

But there was no stopping Theodora's silent chant: *Bring to this world an eminence who will find a rightful place for us.*

Theodora could hear someone calling out in the corridor.

'I am the rightful eminence,' Dora wailed. 'Give it to me.'

But the purple light was so beautiful and the eminence longed for the suffering to end. 'Oh night, faithful friend of mysteries; and you, golden stars and moon, who follow the fiery start of day; and you, Hecate—'

Theodora felt a solid whack across the face. But the sting on her skin was not nearly as dreadful as the loss of a daughter.

'You keep it. It means nothing,' the daughter said defiantly. 'I have the others.' And then she was gone.

The taste of her own salty tears was the last earthly thing Theodora knew.

CHAPTER FIFTEEN

Saturday 25 January

Tallulah got off the train thinking of all the warnings she'd ever heard about jostling crowds and their potential for hiding pickpockets. She slung one strap of her backpack over her right shoulder and squeezed the rest of it protectively between her arm and her body so she could be certain the wooden box and its unusual cargo stayed where it should.

Emerging from the station on a strip mall she saw a farmer's market at the western end and a large group gathered around a performance at the eastern end. The audience laughed then oohed-and-ahhed as one juggling baton after another was tossed high above them, falling and disappearing momentarily, only to reappear seconds later. A couple of Saturday morning clowns, Tallulah thought, to keep that many items aloft; of course she knew one juggler whose skills might make it possible but Adelaide had not been seen at Cirque d'Avenir since Mai's misfired hoop incident. Seemed she was staying well away from the circus and Tallulah resolved to do the same – especially on her day off.

She checked the GPS on her phone. Mr Morton had relocated his shop to the other end of the suburb in the months since they'd moved to Seacliff but it meant she had to walk past the clowns, before turning left and heading down the hill. She stared at the map to be sure she'd read it right. 'You can do this,' she whispered, in an attempt to still the flutters in her tummy. There was a time when she thought that he and Irena might become a couple but it hadn't worked out that way.

Tallulah stored her phone in the front pocket of her bag and hooked the backpack onto both shoulders. But she'd taken only a few steps when the show ended and the large numbers around the jugglers dispersed; she stopped, caught in another crowd of people. She unslung the backpack and again planted it firmly between her right arm and her body. With new resolve she looked ahead toward her destination – and felt her mouth drop open.

There had only been one juggler after all. But it couldn't be. After days of hunting for her, what were the chances of finding Adelaide busking on a windy shopping mall in the city?

She was wearing a red tutu, striped red-and-white singlet and Doc Marten boots, and was frantically chucking her batons and other juggling implements into a duffle bag. She was in such a hurry she didn't even realise that a little girl, standing knee-high to her mother, was beside her, holding out a five-dollar note. When Adelaide finally noticed the girl, she smiled and thanked her, but it was clear she really wanted to get going.

Despite the risk of being late for her appointment, Tallulah had to speak to her. But Adelaide looked up, saw her, and held her hand up for Tallulah to halt. Adelaide hoisted her duffel bag over her shoulder and instead of coming over, gave her a brief wave, then turned her back and walked to the eastern end of the mall.

'Della, wait!'

Adelaide ignored the call. Tallulah ran after her. She'd almost caught her when the other girl glanced back and said without stopping, 'I stopped my show because I felt my juggling change and I knew you were around. You have to leave me alone.'

'Adelaide, stop and talk, please.'

'Why are you following me?'

'I'm not. I'm meeting my neighbour … I mean from when we lived here … and it was just a coincidence that you—'

'You've ridden past my house every day since Wednesday,' she said, in a tone full of outrage.

'I didn't know that. I don't know where you live. Although I wish I did – I was looking for you. I just want to talk about what happened.'

'*Nothing* happened.' Adelaide's eyes were suddenly shiny. 'Nothing I want to talk about, anyway.' She turned and walked away.

Tallulah followed for a few steps before Adelaide stopped and spun around. 'Get away from me!' she cried.

Tallulah held her hands up in a gesture of surrender. 'I'm visiting Morton Antiques,' Tallulah said quickly. 'Six Ambley Street, just down the hill, if you change your mind. Then I'll get the 2.20 train back to Seacliff from Central station.'

Adelaide gave her a small wave then continued along the mall.

Tallulah found her old neighbour standing behind a glass counter examining a small item from a black velvet tray in front of him. Just the sight of him, magnifying glass pressed close to his eye as he marvelled over some minute detail, was reassuring.

'I see you finally convinced Ganesh that her treasures would be safe with you?'

'Ah, Ganesh.' He put the piece he'd been examining back on the tray and arranged the others around it. 'The remover of obstacles. Yes.' He looked up and chuckled. 'You listened to my many frustrations on the way to mounting this collection, Tallulah. But I didn't think you'd remember.'

She smiled and nodded. He came around from behind the counter to where she stood and held his arms out wide. She stepped in for a hug.

'It's good to see you, my dear.'

'You too.'

In those first months of his grief after his wife's sudden death, Tallulah's mother had insisted Mr Morton – who had no children of his own – join them for dinner every night. She told Tallulah: 'If something happened to your father, I would have you to keep me going. Mr Morton isn't so lucky.'

It was Tallulah's introduction to the fragility of adults, as well as a vivid example of her mother's way of dealing with a problem.

'My new neighbours are not as much fun as my old ones,' Mr Morton said, interrupting Tallulah's thoughts.

'Oh,' she said. 'I'm sorry to hear that. Well, I'm not really,' she admitted with a laugh, 'but I *am* sorry it took so long for me to visit. I forgot how much I love the city.'

'It can't be easy moving away from all your friends when you're a teenager,' he offered. 'You've probably been flat out trying to settle into Seacliff.'

'A bit of that.'

'And your parents?'

'Well, Mum has taken on the local art scene as her special

project. And Dad spends a lot of his time on the highway between Seacliff and the city. Working.'

'And Irena?' he asked, almost shyly.

'You know she went to Europe to visit family?'

He nodded.

'I haven't heard from her for a few weeks. Mum and Dad reckon I shouldn't worry but,' she shrugged in an attempt to be casual, 'I can't help it. You haven't heard from her either?'

He shook his head vehemently. 'But I wouldn't expect to. Catching up would keep her very busy.'

'Yes, I suppose so.' She hesitated, then decided to plough on. No guts, no glory. 'Actually, Irena is sort of the reason I'm here. Apart from wanting to see you, I mean. She left a piece of jewellery with me for safekeeping.'

'Indeed?'

'It seems very old and I wanted to know a bit more about it and I was sure Irena wouldn't mind if I spoke to you.'

Tallulah was rewarded with one of Mr Morton's best smiles. 'I'd love to help if I can.' He waited expectantly at the counter where they stood.

'Could we go to your office perhaps?'

His brow furrowed and his eyes took on a mischievous light. 'Now you are intriguing me, my dear. OK, come.' He nipped out to lock the front door then made his way back to the office.

Tallulah followed him along a path between cabinets of jewellery and furniture laden with vases and lamps into the office, where she sat on the visitor side of his desk and unslung her backpack. Despite the chaos it had brought into her own life, Tallulah couldn't ignore the shiver of anticipation that rippled through her as she retrieved the box, put it on the desk in front of her and opened it. The silver cuff sat quietly in its velvet nest. Although she had to admit that, amid the heavy decor of Mr Morton's shop, the cuff and its gems seemed to shine brighter than they had before.

She looked at Mr Morton – and immediately understood the satisfaction he must have felt in bringing the treasures to show her, her mother, and his many trusted clients. In fact the cuff seemed to have astonished him; he sat still as a statue. For a long moment he stayed like that. Then very quietly, not taking his eyes off the cuff, he said:

'*Before the end, friends make amends;*
A swirling cuff, a mask of gold,
demented ring, a headpiece old;
Chant ancient rites and sacrifice
then cast them off in dead of night;
And should the world survive the heat,
they'll find a way again to meet;
Uniting trinkets bring a peace,
if one will rise up now and speak.'

'What is that?' Tallulah asked.

Only then did Mr Morton look at her – as if he'd forgotten that she was actually there. 'Sorry?'

'The verse you just recited: what is it?'

'I recited a verse?'

Tallulah nodded. 'About friends and a swirling cuff, a mask of gold—'

'*Demented ring, a headpiece old*? Good Lord. Are you sure? How odd.'

Tallulah nodded; odd was the word.

'They always said the headdress was Nefertiti's,' Mr Morton continued.

'Yes.' Tallulah had felt the silken thread of the Egyptian queen's strength and determination weave its way through her. *'And should the world survive the heat?'*

'The war,' Mr Morton clarified. 'But Tallulah, it's just a rhyme. At least,' he looked back at the cuff, frowning vaguely, 'I always thought it was. Something my grandfather always chanted; then, when he died, my father used to repeat it whenever a new collector came along determined to find things that no one had ever found before.' He smiled. 'Early in their career, just about every collector is convinced they will be the one to find the Curios of the Eminence – the Curios are like the Holy Grail. They have, unfortunately, driven more than one collector mad.

'The verse is a story of the most recent splitting of the Curios – no more useful than a child's fairy tale, in my estimation. And yet ...' He laughed and shook his head. 'Irena once told me that one day she would show me something that would make my toes curl. I had no idea—'

'But Mr Morton, I've looked the cuff up on the internet; I typed in a few words, *silver cuff with thumb piece, torches and owls,* and I got a website about lost artefacts of the ancient world. They're always traded on the black market – Irena couldn't have something that's illegal.'

'You found information about the Curios of the Eminence on the internet?'

She nodded. 'I mean, the sketches looked the same. I couldn't be sure, though. That's why I came to you. Plus when I went to look at it again the website had been shut down.'

'Shut down?' He sounded alarmed.

'Building a new site – it happens all the time,' she added quickly. Although the alarm in his voice suddenly made her nervous – could there have been some sort of trace on her computer that led the robbers to her house? 'How do you know it's the real thing? And how did Irena get it?'

'May I?'

She pushed the box towards him. Gently he lifted the cuff from its box. 'Good weight,' he said, turning it over. His fingers ran up and down its length, without touching it, as if they were scanning every detail – seen and unseen. He patted his chest pocket, without shifting his gaze from the cuff, then pulled out his magnifying loupe.

'I think it belonged to an empress from the Byzantium called Theodora,' Tallulah told him as he examined it more closely. She was desperate to break the silence and to hear his thoughts.

Mr Morton shook his head. 'She was a lover of fine jewellery, by all accounts.' He did not take his eyes from the cuff as she spoke. 'But Justinian did not cast this for Theodora. It's too plain, for a start. Her style was far more ornate.' He leaned over. 'Here, you see these engravings?'

'The Roman numerals?' Tallulah nodded. 'Justinian and Theodora ruled the Holy Roman Empire.'

'The Holy Roman *Eastern* Empire. And for centuries the emperors of the Holy Roman Eastern Empire preserved many Ancient Greek and Roman traditions; it's one of the reasons we know so much about the classic cultures. Justinian's dream, it is said, was to unite the two vast kingdoms, east and west, and return the empire to its glory days. He exhausted the empire in the attempt. But this,' he said, tapping the box, 'was made centuries before. When Rome herself was mighty.'

He handed Tallulah the magnifying glass and the cuff. 'Can you read the letters?'

'C-A-E.'

'Precisely.' Mr Morton could barely hide the rising intensity in his voice. 'This was commissioned by Julius Caesar.'

'*The* Julius Caesar?'

Mr Morton giggled almost deliriously as he nodded. 'I believe so; which, according to the legend, means it was cast for the eminence of his day.'

'Fulvia of Rome,' Tallulah said weakly.

'Well,' Mr Morton said, 'yes, she was a famous Roman woman. If you believe the way some people talk, every famous woman of ancient times had to be an eminence. Of course, perhaps a woman needed some sort of super-power to have any effect back then. Some say your Theodora was a circus performer. Like you, my dear! What made you think it was Theodora's?'

Tallulah had to think quickly. 'I looked up ancient jewellery too and she was mentioned as a collector. But couldn't this be just a good copy?'

'Yes, it could, but ...' He took a deep breath and turned the cuff over and over, looked it up and down and then met her eye directly. 'The weight, the colour of the silver, the style of the engravings – Tallulah, I never in my life thought that I would be in the position to say this, but I'd be willing to put money on your cuff being one of the missing Curios of the Eminence. Take this straight home and as Irena instructed, put it in a safe place until she returns. When she does, please come and visit me together so we can hear the story of this trinket.'

'But if it's real doesn't that mean that Irena is a thief?'

'Heavens, no, Tallulah!' Mr Morton exclaimed. He shook his head. 'I'm sorry; you haven't lived with the verse as long as I have. If we take it as our guide—'

'But it's a fairy story; you said so.'

'And then my old neighbour showed me the swirling cuff,' he said. 'The most popular interpretation of the verse involves a famous collector of Roman antiquities, Carl Lenter, whose family owned paper mills in Europe. The story goes that before the First World War he gathered his four most trusted friends in the basement of his castle and gave each a Curio. Europe was in turmoil and it would not do for the wrong side to get hold of the Curios – together they are rumoured to hold immense power. Apparently they came back to Lenter after the First World War, but not after the Second, when he took the same precautions. This is why they were not included in his bequest to the Metropolitan Museum of Art on his passing.'

'Do you think Irena was one of the trusted friends – or knew one of them? And doesn't that mean she or someone she knew stole them from Lenter – if they didn't give them back, I mean?'

'They are highly coveted pieces, Tallulah. People kill for objects such as these.'

Tallulah remembered her vision from the night before and nodded, though violence and dishonour were the last things she could imagine Irena being responsible for.

'If the story is true,' he continued, 'then each of the friends took a huge risk by accepting responsibility for the Curios for a second time, especially as Lenter had already successfully protected them in this way once – and rumours had circulated to that effect. Can you imagine the search the Third Reich was conducting? Anything could have happened to the bearers.' Mr Morton shook his head. 'Maybe two weeks ago a middleman I know very well, very reputable, always does things by the letter, called to tell me that a European collector is on the hunt for the Curios and if I had anything to show him then he would be keen to talk to me. I laughed out loud. But my friend assured me that the collector was certain the Curios would show themselves – something about a new prophecy predicting the rise of an eminence.'

'A new—'

'I know, such a preposterous notion that I didn't think any more of it, Tallulah.' Mr Morton lifted his head. 'That's strange. I thought I heard the door open, but I locked it—'

Tallulah looked down at the cuff – and grabbed Mr Morton's wrist.

'Can't see anyone,' he said. Then he looked at her. 'What is it, my dear?'

She nodded to the cuff. 'They say the gems in Hecate's torches glow when the goddess is present to aid the eminence against the forces of darkness.'

'Tallulah!' He laughed and pointed to the wall on the other side of the room. 'The light is bouncing off the red wall and illuminating the gems. All this talk of the war and hiding the trinkets has spooked you—'

An explosion of cracking glass, followed by something large hurtling into the office, stopped all conversation; Tallulah's arms went protectively around her head and she dropped to the floor for cover as the missile thudded into the desk she'd been sitting at. One after another vases, lamp shades and ceramic items were fired into the office, crashing and bashing into walls and cabinets, nicking her arms with glass.

At the first moment of reprieve, she called for Mr Morton. He groaned a reply; she crawled to the other side of the desk and saw him on the ground, propped against a cabinet, one hand pressing his hip; a vase of thick glass lay undamaged next to him. But before she could check on him she had to get the cuff. She peeked over the top of the desk – and gasped. The surface was a crater. The cuff was nowhere to be seen. Tallulah felt ill. She crawled around the desk, careful to avoid the debris, searching frantically. She found the wooden box in pieces. It was only when she cut her hand on a piece of glass and the stab of pain forced her to stop, pull the shard from her hand and suck at the cut that she heard a crash in the shop and a man exclaim in a language she didn't understand.

His crash reminded Tallulah of her priorities – get out of the shop and get help. The cuff was precious, but so were her life and Mr Morton's. She looked at the damage around her – and the 'weapons' used against them. The vase next to Mr Morton would do; it was like a heavy glass globe. She stretched her right leg out from where she sat and, with her foot, rolled it back towards her. When it was close enough to reach with her hand she grabbed the rim. 'Where are you now, Della?' she muttered, moving into a crouched position.

There was another crash; with her spare hand she lunged for her bag as more glass shattered and an enormous lamp came through the office window. Her fingers just touched the strap of her bag and she seized it, and without another thought she ran from the office, into the corridor.

She almost ran into the cabinet that blocked her way; she spun, searching for the best way now to the door, but she'd taken no more than three steps when a presence came at her from her right. 'No!' She punched with the vase but it was deflected and she was spun around as a man, long and strong and musty, pinned his scaly arms around her.

'Urgh,' she cried, when breath rattled in her ear. She let the vase drop from her arms onto his foot but it might have been a feather for all the good it did.

Tallulah tried to shake him off; she elbowed him in the ribs to no effect; she dug the small heel of her shoe into his shins and he grunted but rather than let go he squeezed her tighter and pulled on her bag until she thought her shoulder would pop if she didn't let him have it. The strap was hardly wrenched from her arm before he'd ripped the buckle from her backpack and, hissing, plunged his hand into it.

Tallulah looked around, saw the vase that she'd dropped and stepped towards it but the man saw her move and swung her backpack; she felt the solid whack of her latest book as it hit her on the back of the head. She landed on the floor with a thud. The intruder planted his foot on her back. Ignoring the pain in her head and her shoulder she tried to push herself up but he put all his weight on her back and she was crushed into the floor.

Pinned in an impossible position she came face to face with an idea. A stuffed eagle stood on the floor in front of her. Not knowing if it would work, but so desperate it was worth the try, Tallulah reached for her attacker's mind with her own conduit of energy and on touching a scramble of incoherent thoughts that included an image of her cuff, she spiked his attention with a new threat … and set soar with the eagle.

As imagined wings spread out and her perspective shot unfathomably high into the sky, she was overcome by a whoop of joy; she could feel the freedom of the bird as it glided and swooped on the wind gusts above the city until, spotting the hissing snake-man, it dropped back to earth in a fast dive. Tallulah dropped the barriers to her mind and used the eagle's trajectory as it plunged along the conduit to send an attack, an assault with illusory beak and claws, at her attacker. He yelped and shifted his foot. She rolled over and saw him cowering, his great scaly arms over his head as though he was being attacked from behind. If she could just get the vase she could whack him on the head while he wasn't watching. She saw the eagle circling and diving, circling and diving and reached over her head for the vase – but it wasn't there. She did a half roll and sighted it a little beyond her reach. She slid her body closer, but as she touched the cool glass she heard a throaty growl, and turned to find the man was no longer cowering from the imaginary eagle but looking straight at her – she'd forgotten to maintain the attack.

Her attacker dived; her hands made contact, she pulled the vase over her head like it was a medicine ball in a set of sit-ups at Cirque d'Avenir and hurled it in the direction of the intruder – but from the moment it left her hands she knew she'd thrown it too high. Then she noticed the vase and the snake-man were slowing down; both froze as if caught in an invisible web, the glass orb suspended like a raindrop above a face of scaly rage. From beyond that strange sight, another came. A long dark bottle – one more at home in a kitchen than an antique store – performed a series of aerial cartwheels as it flew towards them. Base-over-neck, base-over-neck it turned until it hit the intruder square on the back of the head. On impact the invisible web collapsed: Tallulah rolled out of the way and instinctively protected her head as the dark bottle exploded and sprayed its contents around as the intruder fell to the floor. The glass vase dropped from where it had been suspended and dealt him another blow.

When all was still, Tallulah unhooked her arms and found them splattered with brown spots that smelled familiar. She put her tongue to one of the spots on her arm.

'Balsamic vinegar?'

'Are you all right?'

Tallulah looked over her shoulder to see Adelaide stepping over the unconscious man.

'What are you doing here?'

'You called me. In my mind,' Adelaide said, trembling, but offering a hand to help her up.

When Tallulah was on her feet she voiced her first thought. 'Mr Morton.'

'Tallulah!' Adelaide shouted as Tallulah ran to the office. 'Who is this guy? What are you doing? We need to get out of here!'

'In a minute.' Tallulah looked around the office; she went to the desk and spotted the cuff in the crater.

The cuff safely in her hand, Tallulah ran to Mr Morton, who was at least conscious.

'Are you all right?' she asked. 'Where are you hurt?'

Mr Morton groaned. 'I think it's my hip.' Tallulah crouched down. He shook his head as if that would clear the pain and gripped her hand. 'Dear girl, forget that. Where is the intruder?'

'We knocked him out,' she told him.

'We?'

'I told a friend I saw on the mall where I was going and luckily she arrived at the right time.'

'Tallulah,' Mr Morton said, gripping her hand tighter and using it to pull himself closer to her. 'Be careful who you call "friend" now. Do you understand? Where is the cuff?'

She showed it to him; he sighed and lowered himself back to the floor.

'It might have been a coincidence,' she said. 'We don't know that's what he was after.'

'Can't take any chances,' he said in a weak voice. 'Get the phone,' he said, pointing to a corner of the room behind the desk.

Tallulah ran to the portable and brought it to him.

'Dial triple-0 and then leave it with me. You've got to go; you must hide the cuff well and you must find Irena. Do you hear? It's essential she knows people are looking for it. She will know what to do.'

She nodded. 'I'm so sorry.'

But the old man shook his head. 'Don't be. A broken hip is a small price to pay for having seen for myself so great a treasure. You've given an old man one of the best moments of his life.' He waved at the phone, signalling her to get on with it. She dialled the emergency number and handed him the phone. 'Now go,' he commanded.

She found Adelaide in the shop. Her head was thrown back against the wall she was leaning on, her arms hugged her body and she was shaking.

'What is it?' Tallulah asked.

'I went to take his pulse.' Her eyes rolled back. 'Urgh! Look at him,' she croaked. 'He's covered in scales, Tallulah – scales should not be on a man.' She started to moan, and slipped down the wall.

'Della, no.' Tallulah moved to the wall and with her uninjured hand tried to keep Adelaide from the floor.

'Why did I even come? It's not *normal* you can call me in your mind. It's not *normal* that I can … that I …' Tears ran down her face; she jabbed her finger in the air as she pointed at the man on the floor. 'It's not normal for a man to be a snake!' she yelled. 'None of this is *normal*.'

'Della, please.' But the life had gone out of the other girl. Tallulah crouched in front of her. 'Please, I'll explain it all when we are well out of here.'

'Tallulah, are you still here?' Mr Morton called.

'How can anyone explain any of this?' Adelaide asked in a vague whisper. She didn't move. The wail of a siren in the distance reverberated through Tallulah.

'You must go,' Mr Morton urged.

His voice was drowned out by a car horn blasting frantically outside the shop; then it revved its engine and accelerated, tyres screeching as it turned a corner and sped off. The siren wailed closer. She'd take Della to the park at the bottom of the hill where they could talk. She stood but when she moved to hook her hands under Della's armpits she realised the cuff was still clenched in her fist. The light from the stones had faded – the danger had truly gone – but it wasn't the best time.

'Tallulah!' Mr Morton called. 'The sirens!'

'I'm going.' She slipped the cuff onto her injured arm and with sudden preternatural strength, hauled Adelaide onto her feet. 'Listen to me,' she said, half-walking, half-dragging her to the door, not even sure if she was aware of what was happening. 'Outside we're turning right; there's a park at the bottom of the hill.' She pulled the heavy door of the antique shop and squinted with the sudden light; she checked the street. No one. As they hit the footpath, Della started to support herself; relieved, Tallulah continued. 'There's a pergola about fifty metres to the left with ...' The air was thick with the heat and something she couldn't define; she breathed deeply, concentrated, and then she had it – despair.

CHAPTER SIXTEEN

So much had been lost. They weren't prepared. And yet they must be.

Regaining her composure, Antonina touched the Curio in the folds of her dress and took heart. 'I cannot stay long,' she told the members of the Cirkulatti Council. 'Fulvia's cuff was on Theodora's arm when she died but her daughter stole the rest—'

The room erupted as the Council reacted to the news of Dora's theft.

Antonina waited for the hubbub to subside. 'The emperor is grief-stricken. He believes the pursuit of the Curios contributed to his wife's death. He wishes she be buried with them and so end the fighting. Though the others have disappeared, he has insisted I hand over the cuff.'

'The Curios are the property of the Cirkulatti,' the Elder said. 'They must be found and kept safe for the eminence's successor.'

'There will be no successor if the emperor has his way,' Antonina said flatly.

The leader of the acrobats found his voice. 'Who would keep the Curios safe?'

'The one who always has,' a voice from the corner said. Antonina could barely make him out in the shadows but she knew him well; she and Theodora had met the magicians of Alexandria long before. Their lineage went back to the days of the pharaohs.

The Elder rose and his voice thundered down the long stone room. 'Are you saying I cannot be trusted?'

'It is not a matter of trust,' said another in the room. To Antonina his rubbery features were those of a clown's, with or without his makeup. The jugglers and clowns were a powerful faction: as original members of the Cirkulatti, their opinion held more weight than any other in the room. 'It's a matter of stability. History has shown that those in pursuit of the Curios will stop at nothing. The cuff is just the latest to be coveted. I'm presuming that no one in the room thinks a Christian emperor should hold the collection?'

The room erupted with unanimous agreement.

'Then the eminence's most trusted confidante and guide, protected by the magicians, is the traditional holder of the Curios.' He nodded his head to Antonina.

'When there is no obvious successor that is the way it should be,' agreed the leader of the strongmen.

'There is no obvious successor because our eminence rejected every candidate,' the Elder said.

'Their lack of commitment, dedication and respect for the position disqualified them,' the strongman declared.

'A few hours after her passing and already you dishonour her,' the clown added.

'Why did Dora not take the cuff, Antonina?' The magician's tone suggested he knew the answer.

'The cuff welded itself to the eminence's arm; it would not yield for Dora.'

'Proof!' cried a number of the Council.

The magician held up his hand. 'And it lies with Theodora still.'

Antonina shook her head. 'I did not have the same problem. But it is well protected.'

The magician came forward and faced the Elder. 'The cuff works for the rightful eminence and those loyal to her. That is what the legend says; that is why Antonina must be in charge of it.'

The room erupted again. So much grief. So many emotions. The esteemed members of the Cirkulatti Council were nothing more than an angry mob. But as the noise grew, Antonina had the sensation she was being separated from the throng; the longer she stood still, the calmer she felt, until she was sure she was in the eye of the maelstrom that raged around her. No sooner had she had that thought than she realised she was not alone. She turned and faced the magician standing beside her.

'Are you prepared?' he asked.

'I did not believe Dora would do it. But ... I must be.'

'We who are devoted to the eminence and the Cirkulatti respect tradition. Only time will bring an eminence to this world with the strength to unite the factions again.'

'Thank you. Where can I find you? I will ...'

But the magician shook his head and gave her a sad smile. 'We will find you. The Cirkulatti has lost its glue. Many resented Theodora, but they needed her as well. They will not understand that until they discover that without her, Constantinople is no longer home. For now you must go.'

Antonina felt giddy. She nodded to the magician and backed out of the room.

Back in the entrance hall, she slipped on her robe, opened the door and stepped into the murky lane.

Tallulah felt like she had been grabbed by the scruff of her neck and pulled from the oppressive heat of Constantinople through the ages; she landed on her back with a thud and found herself on the grass looking up at a small cream-and-green pavilion.

The cuff. She grabbed her wrist. There was nothing there. She jumped up, trying to get her bearings. The deep loss coupled with the quick degeneration into chaos that she'd seen in the vision only further confused her. Tallulah looked around: she was in a narrow space between the pavilion and a high green hedge. Without the cuff. Grabbing her wrist again to be certain it wasn't there, she looked to her feet, then searched the ground around her until light glinted on something in the grass to her left. Relief flooded her body. The beady eye of Minerva's owl winked at Tallulah and she fell to her knees beside it. 'Thank goodness.' She'd wrap it in the cardigan she always carried in her backpack. But where was her backpack? Again she cast her eyes around – and caught sight of a pair of black lace-up Doc Martens. Further up the long, tanned legs was a red tutu and …

'Della!'

Adelaide did not reply. Her face was streaked with tears, her breath was laboured and she was shaking. She held a bottle of olive oil upside down by the neck as a weapon – aimed right at her.

'Della,' Tallulah whispered. 'Are you all right?'

Adelaide laughed and Tallulah thought she might choke. Then she pulled it together.

'Of course I'm all right. I am absolutely and completely and totally all right. As long as you stay far away from me. Do you hear me?' She waved the bottle.

Tallulah checked their surroundings: the park was empty. 'Della, the bottle … put it down—'

'I've had enough of you. Everyone said you were trouble and they were right.'

'I know how you feel—'

Again that hysterical laugh. 'Know how I feel? How could you know how I feel?' Her chest heaved. 'I just spent one hundred dollars on olive oil and balsamic vinegar and other special things for my dear, lovely, *normal* mother! But then I was stupid enough to feel sorry for a nutcase from circus school. And what have I got to show for my money now? Nothing.' Her mouth twisted bitterly. 'I thought you might be trapped in a hideous cult – but it's me who's trapped. You're part of it.'

Tallulah was more terrified facing a hysterical Adelaide than she had been in the snake-man's grip. Maybe she could ease the other girl's panic. 'I can give you the money—'

'I don't want your money!' Adelaide yelled.

'What then? What do you want? Please just put the bottle down.'

The tears began running down Adelaide's face again. 'Don't you be nice to me,' she growled. 'You can't just drag someone down a road into a lonely park ranting in some weird language and then behave normally. You can't!'

'You're right,' Tallulah said. 'I didn't know I was ranting. Adelaide, I didn't know. It's the cuff; it – did I drop it?'

They both looked at the silver wrist piece, so delicate and harmless in the grass.

'No, I flicked it off your wrist. I couldn't tell if it was hurting you or not. I didn't know what else to do.'

Words came to Tallulah from the vision: the cuff worked for the rightful eminence *and those loyal to her*. She understood enough to know that somehow she and Adelaide were linked. She felt so much gratitude for the brave, frightened, exhausted girl in front of her. But as tears welled again in Adelaide's eyes, Tallulah knew that trying to explain a bizarre tale that she barely understood herself would be no help right now.

'Thank you.' Tallulah said quietly. 'What do you want to do now?'

'I want to go home.' The fight had gone out of her – almost. 'And forget about you and that circus forever.' She looked at the bottle in her hand, and back to Tallulah. 'The next time you come near me, I will use it,' she promised.

Tallulah nodded.

Adelaide lowered the bottle, turned and walked along the narrow path that wound through the park, towards the street. Tallulah wanted to say something, at least to reassure Adelaide that she wasn't mad. For a split second she considered dropping something comforting into Adelaide's thoughts as she walked away. But this was no longer a game. So she let Adelaide turn the corner and disappear from sight.

CHAPTER SEVENTEEN

Sunday 26 January

Sunlight skated across the feathers of the lorikeets, throwing hues of green and red and blue until the girl on the swing felt as if she were inside a rainbow, as light and as free as the birds fluttering around her. She closed her eyes and swung her legs out and then back, until she was surely swinging as high as the bough of the tree that her father had attached the swing to.

The glow behind her eyelids dimmed.

'Now. We have to go now.'

Tallulah opened her eyes to find the sun had disappeared. She was no longer in the rainbow of dappled light in the bush behind her home but in a dark forest of dense trees trapped by vines strangling the boughs. As she peered closer at the vines, one knotted mass became the head of a snake; it lifted its head, bared its fangs and lunged at her. She quickly slid into the corner of the swing as far from the snake as she could get. But rather than following her, the snake slithered away down the tree. Her eyes followed it until it reached the bottom of the tree, where it stood and walked like a man.

'I know about the snake-man,' Tallulah said to the voice.

'You do?'

'He was at Mr Morton's.'

'There is more,' the voice replied. A woman's voice. Tallulah would have been scared but the voice was friendly; she was certain she knew it well.

Tallulah's feet touched solid ground; she stepped off the swing and turned. A wide, tree-lined path had been cleared through the middle of a forest. It stretched between a wall of reflective glass at one end and a bank of lights at the other and candles flickered at regular intervals on the ground at the edges of the forest.

'This way,' the voice said.

Music came from the brightly lit end of the processional route and Tallulah got a glimpse of clowns and acrobats.

She went to the closest window and peered in. A row of girls waited in line to meet a small woman, round and grey-haired, sitting with her back to Tallulah. She looked familiar. The woman had a deck of cards in front of her and Tallulah stretched as high as she could to see them; they had a gold embossed back and … she heard herself gasp. The woman turned a card: the Fool.

The grey-haired woman shook her head at the young girl sitting in front of her. As Tallulah watched from outside, the rejected child stood and shook her head as the older woman nodded to the far corner of the room. An enormous person wearing a shaggy coat that made him look like a bear walked towards the child; she appealed to the grey-haired woman, tears making thick tracks down her grimy cheeks and a wail coming from her open mouth. The bear-man picked the child up and carried her from the room as she kicked and screamed.

Tallulah moved from peering through the window to follow the bear-man and his prisoner as he strode across the snowy ground; his prisoner pleaded with him in a language Tallulah did not understand. They trudged on until an enormous building loomed in front of them. The bear-man stopped at a heavy door in the side of the building and dropped the girl in the snow, holding onto one of her arms effortlessly as she struggled, and searched the pockets of his pants for a moment before taking out a ring of keys. He inserted a key, opened the door, threw the girl in as if she were a sack of rubbish and closed the door on her; and somehow Tallulah knew that there was worse to come.

'It will keep happening until you come,' the voice said sadly.

'Me?'

'Only you can stop it.'

'NO!' Another woman's voice called from the direction of the hut. She was sure she could make out the stout figure of the old woman. 'Go,' the stout woman said. 'Get away.'

Suddenly the lorikeets were around Tallulah's head again but this time they began attacking her. She put her hands over her head, but the birds kept attacking; the forest was fading from her reach. 'But the girls ...'

'They need you, Tallulah,' said the guide's voice.

She was confused. 'They're being hurt.'

'Not hurt, merely emptied. And then they are free.'

'Emptied?' But the lorikeets attacked harder; she closed her eyes.

'Forget all this. Forget me!' the woman cried from the hut.

The birds stopped pecking and Tallulah's eyes opened. She was still in the dark but the birds had gone, which was a relief, because her shoulders were hurting from holding her arms over her head. She let them drop – and saw the stripes on the ceiling of her bedroom. 'Oh, thank goodness,' she whispered, closing her eyes.

When she opened them again her mother was standing over her, looking worried.

'You had another dream.'

Tallulah nodded.

'Are you all right?'

'I think so.' She pushed her body up onto her elbows and discovered her father on the other side of the room, also wearing a concerned look. 'Hi Dad.' She looked at them both. 'You'll be selling tickets next.'

They didn't laugh. Her mother sat on her bed; her father gave her a wan smile. He pushed her desk chair over close to them and sat on it. 'Well, it's quite a performance,' he said.

It wasn't until her father held out his hand to Tallulah that she realised there was something in it. She sat up in bed and took the offering.

'Hecate's torches,' she said as she looked at the amber disc engraved with the goddess. It hung from a long, ochre-brown leather strap that would fit around her neck.

'Well, Irena used the expression so often that I thought it would be a good place to start as I replaced the intaglios.'

Tallulah reacted with alarm. 'Has something happened to her?'

'To who?' her mother asked.

'Irena – Dad said she "*used* the expression so often" as if it wouldn't happen again. And you two are so solemn you're scaring me. Was I saying something in the dream?'

'Let me put it on you,' her mum said. She took the piece of jewellery from Tallulah's hand and put it around her neck. 'It should help with the dreams.'

The disc sat just below the depression at the base of her neck. It felt good. 'It's warm.'

'And will light the dark nights as you sleep. Supposedly,' her dad said with a shrug. 'Although I haven't made one without Irena being around so ...'

'Something *has* happened to her,' Tallulah said.

But her father shook his head. 'I don't think so, unless ... Is that what you dream about?'

It was Tallulah's turn to shake her head. 'But I need to see her,' she added.

'Don't we all?' her father said.

Tallulah's mother glanced at her father as he ran his hand through his hair. It wasn't until he was there sitting in front of her that Tallulah realised he wasn't looking well – he'd lost weight and was pale. The moment of shared need galvanised Tallulah. She'd gone through the events in her mind on the way home in the train and it all seemed obvious.

'I think I know why we were robbed.' Her parents looked at her with new interest. 'Irena gave me a piece of jewellery to look after. I was supposed to keep it secret – I thought I *was* keeping it secret. But I couldn't resist looking it up on the net—'

'Oh, Tallulah,' her mother said.

'I found a description of something like it on a website. The next time I went to look at the site it was gone. Then we were robbed.'

'It might be a coincidence,' her father said. 'Go on, Lu.'

'Yesterday, I went to see Mr Morton. I knew he'd be discreet and I needed to talk to someone, an expert, about the piece and ask his advice and ...'

Her dad was looking at her in horror. 'Yesterday? Harry was robbed yesterday – violently. Lu, did you see anything? The hospital called. His hip is broken. Is *that* where you hurt yourself?'

'No. Gosh. How awful. It must have been after.' Tallulah thought the less she said about that the better. 'No – like I said, I was being clumsy. I broke a glass down in my circus room. It's fine.' And it was. The cut in her hand was only superficial, and her aching shoulder had responded well to ice and anti-inflammatories. No way was she going to let them see the boot-shaped bruise on her back, though.

'At least he's going to be all right. So you went to ask his advice about Irena's stolen piece? Was he also robbed because of—'

'No, it wasn't stolen. I had it in my bag when we went to dinner with Marie. I had a feeling I shouldn't leave it.'

Her mother raised her eyebrows. 'And what did Harry say?'

'That it was a very important piece and there had been people asking questions about it recently. He said that I *must* find Irena and ask her what to do; she would know. And I know this sounds stupid,' she glanced at her mother, 'but I think Irena's trying to contact me in my dreams.'

'What makes you say that?' her dad said.

Tallulah looked at them both, watching her intently. Not even her mother seemed particularly shocked. 'It's going to sound stupid.'

'Try us,' her father said.

Tallulah sighed. 'Irena and I can communicate … well, telepathically. We have secret keys into each other's thoughts – an image, a line of a poem, private things. My dreams have all started with the key she uses to tell me it's her. But they're scary dreams.'

Rather than dismissing the notion, her parents looked at each other in silence.

'Do you think Cirque d'Avenir is a cult?' Tallulah said.

'What on earth makes you say that?' her father asked.

'There are just so many secrets. You don't know what's going on at that circus. I'm not … normal. And neither are the other students there. Irena and I have been keeping a secret from you; she's been keeping secrets from me.' She stopped long enough to take in her parents' calm reaction. 'And now you guys are reacting weirdly. I just told you that we have keys to each other's minds and you didn't even blink. I can do other weird things – I can communicate with another person *without* talking. Do you want me to show you?'

'Tallulah—' her father interjected.

'I saw one of the Cirque students – Adelaide – in the city yesterday, by chance,' Tallulah continued, knowing she was talking fast and sounding more and more hysterical but having begun she was unable to control herself. 'She stopped going to Cirque d'Avenir this week because she's freaked out. She reckons it's a cult. Which seems to me the *right* reaction of a *normal* person. I don't want to go back to Cirque d'Avenir. I just want to find Irena and give her this thing back and then get away from Seacliff and Cirque d'Avenir and all of it. It's driving me mad.'

Her mother leaned over and drew Tallulah close. She rocked her back and forth and kissed her on the top of the head as if she were a baby. 'I'm sorry, sweetheart,' she whispered, as Tallulah sobbed. 'This was all going to catch up with us one of these days.'

'What?' She pulled back and wiped tears from her eyes.

Gemma's eyes held a mixture of pity and remorse. She turned to her husband. 'It was never my idea to keep it from her,' she said, 'but I'm going to get the blame if you don't explain yourself right now.'

Tallulah had never heard her mother speak so forcefully to her father. He put his head down and sighed. When he lifted his head, he asked, 'Do you remember when that circus came to town when you were seven?' Tallulah nodded and Peter continued. 'You walked from the audience and stood opposite the clown and mirrored the mime as he performed it.'

Tallulah remembered the day like it was yesterday; the sun glinting off the harbour had been bright but the clown standing in the middle of the spacious green lawn was an even brighter magnet, drawing him to her. 'Marie did the same mime on the rooftop of Cirque d'Avenir at the beginning of the camp.'

'It's a type of lightning rod for descendants of the Cirkulatti.'

Tallulah stared at him. 'You know about the Cirkulatti?'

'We didn't,' he said. 'We had muddled along on our own for a couple of years by then. *I'd* been muddling along—'

'From the time you could talk,' her mother added quickly, 'you would occasionally speak to us telepathically or show us an image of the day you'd had at preschool – subconsciously, of course: you had no idea.' She gave a half-hearted laugh. 'Many times I had to bite my tongue when some other mother went into raptures about the special schooling her child would need to cater for her particular *gifts*.'

'But about a week after you revealed yourself to the clown we received a visit from a woman – Irena Stanton.'

'You not only mirrored the mime,' her mother added, 'you'd communicated the words that went with the mime, telepathically, to the clown, who had then contacted Irena. And so your training began.'

'You've known all along that I'm ...' She didn't want to say 'weird', but 'gifted' seemed wrong too. She looked at her parents and shook her head. 'But why did we have to be so secretive? I mean sure, with everyone else, but with each other?' Tallulah thought of Irena's reasons for insisting on secrecy. 'Unless you thought you might get rid of me.'

Her mother gasped. 'Never, Tallulah. That was never a thought in our heads.'

'Irena believed,' her father continued, 'and we agreed, that secrecy was necessary for your safety because there is a very big difference between possessing a gift and realising the potential of that gift.'

'And given that yours is a highly sought-after gift, one that could put you in danger, we agreed that it was important to train you, to ensure that you don't feel weird, without making it a really big deal, and the centre of our whole family life. If you and Irena could take care of it between you, perhaps you could have the choice of whether to accept the consequences of the gift and realise its potential.'

Gemma's hopeful tone made it clear which choice she wanted Tallulah to make – and that none of this had been easy.

'Why did you go along with all this if you were so against it?' Tallulah asked.

'I knew what I was getting into a long time ago, Tallulah, even if I didn't quite envisage this particular path.'

Tallulah watched her parents exchange a glance; the admiration her father felt for her mother was written all over his face and she understood in that moment that there were secrets between them that were yet to be revealed.

Her mother continued, 'But what would you have preferred I do, Tallulah? Deny this gift that you obviously have in order to protect you and keep you safe? The advice that we were given was that would only make it worse; the possibility that you would resent me later for catering to my fears rather than your potential was too great. The best option seemed to be to protect you as much as we could while bringing you to this point, where you can make the choice for yourself.'

Tallulah reached for her mother's hand and squeezed it. They exchanged a smile.

'Where's the cuff now?' Peter asked.

Tallulah's smile faded from her lips. 'You know about that too?'

'Irena told us she was going to leave it with you.'

Tallulah's mouth fell open. 'Why?'

'She felt it was right.'

'It's an ancient treasure, Mum. Was she mad?'

'Tallulah, your interest in jewellery has always been,' her mother searched for the right word, 'polite. It's not something you've ever coveted; we thought you'd put it in your wardrobe and forget about it and Irena would have to remind you to bring it to Elbe.'

Tallulah accepted the truth of the statement. It was only her insecurities the night before Cirque d'Avenir began that had made her unearth the cuff from the wardrobe. If she hadn't fallen asleep as she was looking at the cuff it wouldn't have ended up on her wrist and she wouldn't have been seduced by the first vision. 'I've completely stuffed up.'

'Tallulah, Irena thought it was *right* to leave it with you,' her father said. 'And you know as well as I do that she believes in acting on instinct. You haven't *stuffed up*. You've taken a certain course, that's all. Perhaps it was always meant to happen like this.'

His voice was reassuring; even if she didn't quite believe his words she had to admit they were in keeping with her nanny's way of looking at the world. 'It's in my bag,' she said, pointing to the backpack. 'But I've been hiding it in the gatehouse since the night of the robbery.'

He smiled. 'Well, we can put it in the safe out there with my more precious stones until you go to Elbe.'

'I might not be selected—'

'Tallulah, it's not whether you're selected,' her mum informed her, 'it's whether you want to go. Irena will be there – but the choice is and will always be yours. You must promise me to remember that. I haven't been engaged in this exercise all this time for you to suddenly let everyone else make decisions for you.'

Her mother gave such a steely glare that Tallulah could do little but nod in agreement.

'In the meantime, when you go back to Cirque d'Avenir tomorrow I think you should tell Marie everything.'

'What?' Tallulah asked. She checked her dad's reaction but unlike her he was quietly considering his wife's suggestion.

'Irena sent us to Marie,' her mother said. 'We wouldn't be in Seacliff otherwise. Even though it was not Irena's intention, recent events would suggest that someone knows that a Curio is in circulation. For all we know, Marie may have a contingency plan already in place for that very circumstance. We should hear her ideas on how to protect it – and you.' She stood. 'I'm hungry. What about Beachbreak Café for breakfast? I'll have a quick shower.'

Tallulah watched her mother leave the room. Peter waited till she was out of earshot before he spoke.

'There are gifts and there are *gifts,* Lu. And your mother is ours. Never forget that.'

CHAPTER EIGHTEEN

But Tallulah did not plan to go back to Cirque d'Avenir alone. Her mum had a number for Kate Banks, Adelaide's mother, who told Tallulah where she could find Adelaide. After breakfast she jumped on her bike.

When she arrived, she heard Adelaide before she saw her. As she pushed up the slight hill just before Stony Reef Beach, the occasional clang of a heavy object on metal was like the tolling of a dull, dysfunctional bell.

Once on the rise she rolled to a stop. Adelaide was throwing a scrubbing brush at a green metal sign that leaned against a wooden post.

Tallulah coasted down the hill and locked her bike to the rack while rehearsing an opening line. 'I know you told me to stay away but ...' Or maybe she should just forget about Adelaide's instruction and say, 'Hi, we need to talk.' The more Tallulah thought about it, the more right it seemed to start the conversation with strength and surety.

But for all her conviction, it was Adelaide who spoke first. 'I thought you must have been around,' she called as she picked up the scrubbing brush from the grass in front of the target.

'Oh. And you're still here?'

Adelaide kept her head down as she walked back to the throwing mark. She turned to line up the shot. 'I was still emotional and all over the place when I first got here. Then I started to settle down – I realised why.' She glanced at Tallulah. 'You force a person to face up to their potential; like shining a spotlight so they can't avoid it.'

'And that's scary?'

'Torturous – when that person is trying to ignore who they are. If not ...' She launched the missile at the target. The metal thrummed as it hit the sweet spot. 'The last five throws have been spot on.'

'All the better to clock me with, I guess,' Tallulah suggested. For which she won a tentative grin from Della.

'Most def,' Adelaide agreed. 'But at some stage you're going to have to work out how you do that, and if you do it to everyone. Won't be much help if you make the snake-guy stronger as well.'

'I think to become what they've become, their minds are in another place.'

Adelaide hesitated as she considered the thought. 'Maybe.' Then she nodded, walked to her bag by the park bench, fished a black drink bottle from it and sat down.

'Look, Della, a lot of stuff has been happening lately that I have no explanation for. I've known that I can communicate without speaking since I was little. But recently I've been thought- *and* image-casting, which is very freaky. It was involuntary at first but at the antique place yesterday I managed to do it consciously to distract the snake-guy in time for you to get there.' Tallulah sat on the grass, cross-legged, neither obstructing Adelaide's view nor forcing her to make eye contact. It was a lot easier to voice the strange tale of her life without having to watch Adelaide's reaction. And it was a great relief to finally have someone listen. She knew she'd chosen the right confidante. When Tallulah finished the story Adelaide sat very still.

'That is so bizarre,' she said finally.

'Which bit?'

Adelaide smiled. 'I've had a recurring dream all my life that I'm following a woman in robes on stilts, but I can never see where we've come from or where we're going.'

Tallulah was too shocked to speak.

'I haven't had it since Cirque d'Avenir began.'

'Cirque d'Avenir hasn't been going that long.'

'Every week at least for as long as I can remember; but for the last two weeks, nothing. I wish I'd had an Irena in my life. It would be good to have a few things explained to me.'

'Like what?'

'Well, like what happened on the roof at Cirque d'Avenir this week.'

She paused for such a long time that Tallulah was about to ask if she was OK, but Adelaide continued. 'I've never worn a watch but I always know *precisely* what time it is, and how long it takes to do something or be somewhere. When I do look at a clock and the time is out I have to fix it. Well, I don't have to now but when I was little I was a nightmare. It freaked me out when a clock was the wrong time; all I could hear was out-of-sync ticking in my head. Although it was worse when one had stopped completely – that was like hearing death.

'My mum took me to an endless range of doctors. I was diagnosed as autistic – at the low end of the spectrum. One doctor suggested sport as a joke, I think; you know, "She'll be good on a soccer field with that sense of timing, ha, ha, ha."

'Mum was so desperate she signed me up. I was four. It used up a lot of energy, which helped with the relentless ticking, the feeling I had to be somewhere; keeping up with the woman on the stilts perhaps. Except I had such excellent timing that it became embarrassing. People started to think I was somehow cheating. When we found circus skills it was a relief; no one counting goals. The circus *was* safe. Except now ...' She took a long slow breath before continuing. 'Sometimes, when there is a stressful situation, like on the rooftop, I somehow stop time. I think.' The tears came despite her best efforts. She furiously wiped them from her eyes; she seemed embarrassed by her emotion, so Tallulah stayed where she was despite the urge to give Adelaide a hug.

'Your parents don't know?'

Adelaide shrugged. 'I've always been weird to them. I'm sure my stepfather would prefer that he'd got together with a woman who had a normal daughter, like the kids they've had together. Not that I'm completely useless to them.' A bitter smile twisted her lips. 'A few weeks ago I found my twin brothers in the kitchen. They're three. Jake had picked up a carving knife that must have fallen on the floor and he was brandishing it like a sword; he was only playing but his action was kind of slash, slash, point and drive ...'

Tallulah felt her hand automatically go to her mouth.

Adelaide nodded. 'Jake was in the middle of it again; slash, slash, point and ... when Archie took a step towards him. Either his hand or his belly was going to be hurt very seriously except ...'

'You stopped time,' Tallulah finished.

Adelaide nodded. 'There was a warping sound in my head, the air around them sort of rippled and swirled, catching them as if it was an eddy in a river. They froze like little statues. There was a scream, although I don't know if that was the boys or Mum, who'd come in as it happened. She went straight to Jake and took the knife off him and then I grabbed Archie. But there was a split-second after that when we were there, the boys caught, but Mum and me somehow existing around it. Mum whispered something that I didn't catch. And then, I guess, the danger had passed and I relaxed and the ripples faded. When the boys were released, Jake fell to the ground, much more distressed than Archie.'

'What did your mum say?' Tallulah asked.

'She was grateful. Teary, hugging me, saying, "Thank you, thank you," over and over. But it was all really ...' Adelaide put her head down and shook it. 'She's looked at me ever since as if she's searching for something, some clue as to what part of me is missing. Or wondering what she did wrong during her pregnancy.'

Tallulah couldn't help but laugh. 'What?'

'I read a story about parents of children born with disabilities; they think it's their fault.'

'Della, you don't have a *disability*. Did you hear the story you just told? You stopped time. Ask any kid, no, any adult, any *person* if they'd like the ability to control time—'

'I can't *control* time.'

'Yet.'

'I don't even know *how* I stop it.'

'A mere technicality. Della, you have, like, the über-gift.'

'You think so?'

'What does Sasha say? You guys are so close.'

'Sasha.'

Tallulah didn't know how one word could contain so much heartache. 'We *were* close. I thought we were. Last year, anyway.'

She turned away. 'He's been coming to Seacliff regularly for a couple of years to run school holiday classes and master classes, you know. He's still kind of …' she searched for a word '… caring,' she said sarcastically. 'But Hui nailed it that day at the abattoir. He's not the same guy. I don't feel like I can talk to him any more. Especially with Saskia hovering. It's like she resents his interference in her life but she resents time he spends with anyone else as well. And, look, I was really crap to you from the start because I could feel you in my head, but since class started, even when I was angriest, I knew that the headaches and the *blackness* weren't coming from you. I think it was *her*.

'She's a conundrum, though. I reckon she thinks she is this eminence you talk about from your visions. But,' Adelaide shook her head, 'I don't get the feeling that anyone would follow her. In my dream, I can't see where we're going or where we've been but I've got no doubt I should be following the woman on the stilts.'

Adelaide froze, then grabbed a hat from her bag and slammed it down on her head. She looked up again from underneath the brim. '*No way*,' she said.

Tallulah followed her gaze to a picnic booth, where a teenager was standing with his back to them, writing on the wall. 'Is that him?'

Adelaide was all but panting, holding tightly to the bench as if she was stopping herself from jumping up and thumping him. 'I can't believe *he'd* …'

Tallulah looked back at the booth. The guy was tall, tanned, broad-shouldered, with sun-bleached hair, a bit stringy but in a cool way, and wearing boardies and a singlet. 'Adelaide, let's just—'

But when Tallulah turned back to Adelaide her shoulders had slumped. She looked up and appealed to Tallulah. 'I didn't think it would be … him. I thought it was my stepbrother's sleazy friend. Not …' She gestured again. 'I thought he was … OK.'

'Maybe he's writing something else. Why would he—'

But Adelaide was already shaking her head. 'I just finished cleaning that friggin' booth. But I've got him right where I want him now.'

And with that declaration, she stood and marched back to where the scrubbing brush had fallen after the last throw.

'Wait,' Tallulah said, as she got up and ran after her. But Adelaide paid no attention. 'Della,' she tried again. 'There are other ways to do this.' Tallulah grabbed her arm. 'There are other ways to do this,' she insisted. *Let's think now, shall we?*

Adelaide blanched but recovered quickly; her brow furrowed as she contemplated the suggestion. 'Can you do … something?'

'Can *we* do something, you mean? I don't go around practising for a situation like this, but desperate times and all that. I reckon we could give him a bit of a shock.'

Before Adelaide could answer Tallulah took her hand, looked around and decided on a bench that was behind a few cars and out of direct view of the picnic booth. She led Adelaide to it. 'Sit,' she instructed. 'I'll get our stuff.'

When she'd returned to their new position with both their bags, Tallulah sat next to her. 'Ready?' she whispered.

'I think so,' Adelaide said warily.

'We're just two girls sitting on a park bench. There is no reason for anyone to suspect anything of us.'

'Got it,' Adelaide replied.

'And we're not going to do anything awful. But a few whispered words and the feeling he's been caught in a time warp might just make him think again before he bullies another girl.'

'I've never deliberately stopped time.'

'If you can, you can; if you can't, you can't. Hearing voices in his head will be freaky enough. You don't have to do anything to help. It's not like I'm being attacked by a guy covered in scales.'

Tallulah focused on the boy in the booth; his shoulders hunched as he worked. She took a moment to draw on what was around her by expanding her consciousness beyond the two of them on the bench, beyond the bully, out to the energies of all living things around her. She felt amazing and powerful.

She brought her focus back to the boy in the booth and spoke in a voice full of majesty.

I speak for the spirits of scarp; an ancient race of spirits for an ancient land. For whom do you speak?

He looked up from what he was writing, shook his head and put his pen back to the wall.

I speak for the spirits of the scarp. For whom do you speak – your family, your friends? Who gives you permission to stand at that wall and make your thoughts known?

Tallulah heard a grunt beside her and turned her head to see Adelaide's face beetroot-red from holding her breath; her eyes were all but shut she was squinting so hard; her mouth was a twist of pain. Tallulah touched her leg and the other girl jumped. 'It's never going to happen while you're all contorted.'

Adelaide exhaled heavily and the tension left her body. Tallulah looked back to the booth. He was so rigid that for a split second Tallulah thought Adelaide had managed to stop the time around him. Then his head pivoted so he could look around the booth; when his head had gone as far as it could go his body followed. When he was certain there was no one in the picnic booth he came to the edge of the cement floor and looked out. Both girls automatically put their heads down.

But Tallulah could hear the argument he was having with himself as he stood on the edge of the booth: *This can't be happening ... Pull yourself together ... Be calm ... It's not possible to hear voices.*

And yet somehow you're hearing us ...

Tallulah turned to Adelaide. 'Name?'

'James,' she said.

You're hearing us, James, aren't you? How tough do you feel now, James? Or do you feel like the coward you are?

Tallulah was surprised at how she was warming to the job. The boy started trembling. He tried to put a lid on the permanent marker but his hands shook too violently. He threw the pen on the ground and backed into the picnic booth; his knees hit the bench in the booth and he sat heavily and crossed his hands over his head in surrender.

Pick up the pen.

Leave me alone, he thought, *please.*

Pick up the pen, James. There is something we need you to do for us.

He panted as he considered the statement. He wiped his face with the back of his hand. Then reluctantly he retrieved the pen.

Write out your unhappiest memory on the wall.

He dropped his hand and his shoulders slumped as though he couldn't believe that was the request. He threw the pen down and walked out of the booth – but as he stepped off the concrete slab onto the grass the air shimmered and he stopped mid-stride.

Tallulah heard Adelaide whisper a victorious, 'Yes!'

Not so fast, James. You haven't written your story.

The air around him lost its glow and he fell forward, almost toppling on the grass.

'Can't hold it,' Adelaide whispered, pale and shaky.

'Then don't try again.'

Tallulah's attention went back to James, who was sitting on the grass.

Don't like the idea of being the subject of picnic booth posts?

He shook his head.

An unhappy memory. I won't stop you getting the turps to come and scrub it off, if that helps.

This time when he got up he walked back to the booth and picked up the pen. As he stood at the wall, he dropped his head and retrieved the memory he'd most like to forget. The sunny day, the school hall, the surprisingly timid invitation. And then a girl she knew: 'I have a boyfriend, James,' Adelaide said to him as they made their way to their seats before the end-of-year assembly. She spoke kindly, almost apologetically. But James's reaction was to jeer; he didn't believe her. She insisted. But he would not have it and he would not leave her alone, until finally she was forced to say, 'Believe it or not, James Maloney, we're not all waiting around for you.'

She wounded your pride? She said no, so she's yours to humiliate? How dare you! Write about the day you were rejected by that girl.

The air rippled around him, and beside her, Tallulah heard Adelaide emit a determined 'Huh!' But when Tallulah glanced down at her she did not find the victorious face that she expected.

'What is it?'

But Adelaide's only answer was to look at her with terrified eyes and shake her head. Then she cried like a trapped and wounded animal. 'What have I done?' Adelaide croaked.

'What do you mean?'

'There's heaps of ... choices ... I've ... I shouldn't have ... I'm caught in it ... like ... eddy ...'

'Hecate's torches,' Tallulah muttered when she understood what her friend was saying. 'Della, you've got to ...'

Adelaide's head sagged.

'Della!'

Instinctively Tallulah reached into her mind and found herself in a dimly lit room being battered by a storm with an endless number of openings flapping, bashing and sliding. The combined noise made it impossible to think. No wonder Adelaide was overwhelmed. With no other ideas she seized on their own setting; Tallulah brought the sun that was beating down on her skin into Adelaide's mind and watched as it burned away the storm clouds until the sky was clear. The various openings to the room closed and the room was silent. The only thing that could be seen beyond the windows was a still, sparkling ocean. Tallulah withdrew from Adelaide's mind – and found her friend hanging over the back of the park bench panting as hard as Tallulah was. Tallulah checked the booth – James was in a similar position but flung over the table.

Return to your cowardly ways and you will meet us again. We know you now, James Maloney.

He lifted one arm from where he lay and batted the air. It was a futile gesture but she was relieved to see he was still fighting. Tallulah felt as wasted as Adelaide looked; she grabbed her hand and stood her up, walked her a few steps and let her fall on the soft grass. Tallulah fell to the ground as well.

She was tired. She needed Tom. Just thinking of him made her feel better. She remembered meeting him. She smiled as she remembered the fizz that had begun to bubble that day. She'd been unsure since – she'd even thought that perhaps she wanted dark, and mean, and brooding – but he smelled so good. If only she could tell him where they were. But all she wanted was to put her head down on the soft green grass and close her eyes.

CHAPTER NINETEEN

Tallulah wasn't sure what finally brought her to hover just below the surface of consciousness but she was sure that beyond the warm shallows she was floating in, fiery blue lava was bubbling.

The warmth of the surface she was sitting on distracted her. It was a rigid bench but hot. She rubbed her fingers against the surface and decided it must be a stretch of vinyl or tough leather. The hand resting on top of hers was a furnace pumping energy into her tired body. Occasionally, it was removed and she felt regret.

She blinked as she began to creep closer to the surface. A thought returned from before. Tallulah pushed herself up in the chair.

She glanced at the driver and saw sandy curls framing a big grin.

'Tom?'

His grin faded and he shot her a quick glance, full of concern. 'How are you?'

Tallulah took a deep breath as she considered the question. Her head hurt a little – the remnants of a headache. And her skin stung. She looked at her arms and winced. They were pink. Adelaide's skin, not nearly as sensitive as Tallulah's, would have handled it better.

Tallulah gasped. Adelaide!

She looked into the back of the car and felt a whimper of relief escape her. Della was there, asleep on the back seat, her head resting on a rolled-up jacket, pressed into the corner between the seat and the wall of the car. 'Is she?'

'She's OK,' Tom said. 'She came to quicker than you. Went back to sleep about ten minutes ago.'

Tallulah nodded. 'Good.' Although she still wasn't sure exactly what had happened.

'Not so good for the young guy I found at the beach. He was wandering around a picnic booth near where I found you in a very confused state.'

'Oh?'

'Said he heard voices in his head. The spirits of the scarp, I think he called them. Was it worth it?' he asked quietly.

'I would have done the same for you,' she said defensively.

'I wouldn't want you to.'

'Too noble, I suppose.'

Tom didn't respond, concentrating on the winding road. When they were on a straighter stretch he continued. 'How were you by the end of your game, Lu? Ready to defend yourself if some other danger had come along?'

'It wasn't a game. And I wasn't planning for us to collapse. I don't know what happened exactly. Adelaide was testing her you-know-what, but then it all got out of control.'

'Adelaide's you-know-what?'

'Anyway,' she said, 'we were at the beach. Hardly dangerous.'

He laughed. 'Oh, I'd love to hear Irena's reaction to you guys testing your *you-know-whats* at the beach.'

'Well, you're not Irena,' she spluttered, hot and tired but knowing that he was right, 'so it's none of your business. I suppose that's why you came looking for us – just so you could be disapproving. What were you doing there anyway?'

'Answering a cry for help.'

'Oh. Did I … Did you get that?'

'Loud and clear.'

A million questions rushed into Tallulah's mind – but she checked her boundaries were in place first. Then she recovered her manners. 'Thank you.'

Tom gave her a smile that was a little more enthusiastic. 'My pleasure.'

'But where are we going now?' a voice asked from the back seat.

'To see Marie,' Tom said, looking at Adelaide in the rear-view mirror. Then to Tallulah he said, 'Isn't that who you wanted to speak to?'

Tallulah nodded.

'It seems like you've got a lot to talk about,' Tom added.

'I've barely spoken to Marie,' Adelaide admitted. 'I find her a bit scary.'

Tallulah swivelled around from the front seat to find Adelaide wearing a worried expression. 'She isn't, I promise. She's been very helpful to me. I just thought … after what happened … she seemed like the right person to ask.'

'The guy I found told me that the spirits forced him to recall his unhappiest memory and then beat him with it. "Have the spirits ever done that to you?" he asked. I reassured him it happens all the time.'

'Beat him? Was I doing that?' Adelaide asked.

'Were *we* doing that. We were both in it together. He wasn't being physically beaten. But I don't know what he was seeing because I had to leave him to help you.'

Adelaide gave a long heartfelt sigh. 'I didn't think I was having any effect at all; I was trying everything I could think of to stop time but nothing worked. And then I remember thinking, I'll let Tallulah say a few things and that will be enough. But that burning angry sensation I get whenever I see his handwriting on a wall welled up until it felt like my scalp was on fire and I couldn't let you do it all by yourself. When he tried to run I was incensed and suddenly I was able to hold him there – right as he was stepping onto the grass.' She smiled at Tallulah. 'And it was cool. But it was tiring so I pulled out to conserve my energy. I managed to do it again without meaning to when he yelled at you.' She shivered and wrapped her arms around her body. 'As soon as it happened I knew it was super wrong. It was dark and there was lots of popping and banging as all those doors burst open and it was windy and suddenly I understood.' She looked at Tallulah. 'I understood that when I, you know, stop things, well I'm sort of affecting what should happen next. I realised what we were doing was really dangerous. And that I'd really stuffed up.'

The car was silent for a moment before Tom glanced at Tallulah and then looked at Adelaide in the rear-view mirror. 'When you say you stop things and it affects what happens next – you mean you stop time?' He whistled long and low. 'Aren't you two the A-team.'

'You wouldn't say that if you'd just seen us in action. I didn't think of that either, Dell. And then when you panicked I abandoned him to help you. I wonder if that's what he meant by beat him – the noise in that room was awful. I did the only thing I could think of – forced the sunshine in to burn off the storm, which closed the openings. We were lucky.'

'What was the point of the unhappy memory?'

'I thought if he was forced to write his most unhappy memory on the wall of the booth for everyone to see, he'd understand how humiliated Adelaide is. Seemed like a good idea at the time.'

Tom nodded. 'Most embarrassing moment would have been meaner.' There wasn't exactly forgiveness in the statement but at least there was understanding.

He flicked the indicator on and shortly after pulled the wheel hard and turned into a gravel driveway. 'Here we are.' They were travelling down a driveway surrounded by lush bush. Tallulah shivered involuntarily as she was reminded of her dream.

'Camp Cirque d'Avenir.'

A clearing with a group of huts was revealed. Tallulah breathed easily. She saw Mai outside one hut practising with her ribbons, and Guido running through what looked like an Olympic-level floor routine. To the east of the huts was a group of colourful caravans with long tables and canopies not unlike those adorning the rooftop of their theatre. To the west, a car park, which Tom pulled his Kombi into. He turned off the ignition and the car shuddered to a halt.

Tallulah got out and looked around. She waved to Mai, who let the ribbons wrap themselves around her arm before heading over. The other Camp d'Avenir inhabitants were hanging out at the picnic tables, lingering over the remains of a delicious lunch. Tallulah had just realised she was hungry when Marie got up from the table and waved. She approached with a quizzical look on her face.

'Tallulah, you're sunburned. What happened to your arm? Adelaide,' she exclaimed as the girl emerged, 'goodness, you look dreadful.' She looked at Tom. 'What's happened?'

She didn't wait for an answer, gesturing to a larger hut, set a little way back from the others.

'You don't need me for this,' Tom said.

'We might,' Marie said firmly, and waved him along with the girls.

Tallulah gave Mai a quick backwards glance. *Tell you later. Are you all right?*

Tallulah nodded and waved.

The 'hut' was a quaint little rustic home with cosy living spaces; its furnishings were soft and welcoming. But they had little time to enjoy it – Tallulah decided that a quick admission would work best, so she had barely sat before she began to tell the story.

At first, despite Marie's serious expression, she seemed to listen calmly. But when they recounted the stormy room and how they got out of it she shook her head, covered her mouth with her hand and closed her eyes. She stayed that way for a long moment after Tallulah had finished speaking. When she opened her eyes she inhaled a slow, deep breath, exhaled and addressed Tom. 'Please ask Marnie to come and see me.'

As Tom left, Marie gave the girls a grave look. 'Thank goodness you are OK but I will need healers for you both, and the boy at the beach. Do we know how to find him?'

Adelaide nodded. 'I know where he lives, but—'

'We'll be subtle.' Marie's voice was clipped – with efficiency or restrained anger it was hard to tell. She slapped both hands on her thighs before getting up to pace the room. Tallulah and Adelaide exchanged another look.

Marie halted in front of Tallulah. 'I have to say, what were you thinking, Tallulah? Practising on the general public in the open? I can't believe this was something Irena ever counselled.'

Tallulah felt ashamed and stupid. She shook her head.

'And Adelaide, while I don't expect you to be as well-versed in the need for discretion, I would assume that common sense would tell you that—'

'It was my fault, Marie,' Tallulah insisted. 'Adelaide would never have thought of it—'

'No, but I would have decked him if you hadn't stopped me; I might be at the police station right now being charged with assault.'

'Instead you have done who knows what damage to a young man's mind,' Marie noted.

'He's done plenty of damage to my mind.'

'I'm the telepath, not Adelaide ...'

'Girls!' Marie held up both hands for silence. 'I appreciate that you have been harassed, Adelaide, but please try to understand my concern. You disappear from Cirque d'Avenir after an incident on the terrace, which was understandably confusing, yet refuse all our entreaties to return so we can work through it with you. Then when you do turn up again it is after behaving in this rash and foolish manner—'

'Rash and foolish?' Adelaide charged back. 'Rash and *foolish*. You sound like my mother – but you're *not*. This is what you call creating a safe haven, is it, Marie? This is what you call "showing understanding". Well, I'm sorry I haven't acted more perfectly about being a freak but I'm not as practised at it as you.'

She stopped to catch her breath and Tallulah jumped in. 'Della,' she cautioned gently. 'Marie, this is not Adelaide's fault ...'

'No, Lu, I can do this,' Adelaide said without taking her eyes off Marie. 'You scared all my friends off in the first week – some really talented people – playing with *our* minds. Did you care?'

'We had to work fast,' Marie answered quietly. 'There was no choice. And they were counselled.'

'So it's OK when you do it. But when Lu and I make one mistake you get all high and mighty on us. Well, you've convinced me,' she said, getting up and walking to the door, 'this is not a circus I want to be involved with.'

'Adelaide, no,' Marie said, taking a step towards her. 'Don't go. You're right. I'm sorry. I got carried away.'

Adelaide stopped and turned to Tallulah.

'I apologise to both of you,' Marie continued. 'I should have shown more understanding; I—'

'Marie,' Tallulah interrupted, 'before you say any more, I'd like to put *all* the stupid things I've done on the table.'

Marie nodded for her to proceed.

'There's this cuff that Irena gave me.'

'A cuff?'

'Yes. It's silver; it's an usual piece with engravings of torches and owls. And it's old.'

'How old?'

'Ancient.'

The older woman laughed dismissively – and Tallulah thought she heard a note of relief too. 'But how can you say it's ancient?'

'Well, I looked it up on the internet first, and found a picture of a piece that looked just like it. Then I confirmed some stuff with an antique specialist who's a family friend – he is sure it's one of a group of lost antiques called the Curios of the

Eminence,' Tallulah told her. 'I didn't think Irena's cuff could possibly be the real thing but our house was burgled just after I looked it up and they left a weird message in blood: *Hecate cannot save you this time.* Yesterday, when I took the cuff to show our family friend, an intruder broke into his shop when I was there — but luckily, Adelaide was in town and heard me call telepathically for help and we fought off the intruder, who was *very* weird, with scaly cold skin. I finally told Mum and Dad about everything this morning; they knew more than I realised and said that I should come and tell you.'

The deep colour that anger had brought to Marie's face had drained away and she looked like an alabaster statue. She reached behind her for the arm of the lounge, found it and sat. She opened her mouth to speak and then closed it. A vehicle came down the driveway; the crackle and crunch of the gravel seemed starkly at odds with the silence in the room and Tallulah looked out the window. A large black car rolled into the clearing.

'Irena had the cuff,' Marie muttered, 'all this time?'

'I don't know how long.' Tallulah turned back to her. 'She left it with me to look after, but I haven't done a very good job.'

Marie regained her composure to look at Tallulah. 'Where is the cuff? May I see it?'

'It's at home. I hid it after the house was ransacked. I didn't think I should carry it around with me,' Tallulah explained. 'Mum and Dad, like Irena, thought I would put the cuff in the cupboard and forget about it. But now that I've stuffed up, they assumed you and Irena would have a contingency plan for where it should be now.'

Marie emitted a short, sharp noise that left the air so bitter the girls could taste it. She shook her head as though unable to comprehend this piece of news. 'I *don't* have a contingency plan, Tallulah, because, I'm afraid, Irena did not share all her secrets with any of us.'

A car door slammed outside and Tallulah looked out the window. Sasha had got out from behind the wheel and was now at the passenger side of the car, where he opened the door.

'Brigitta,' Tallulah said as a familiar figure emerged.

Marie stood. 'I wonder what brings her here.'

'Doesn't she stay here too?'

'She has more appropriate accommodation, in town,' Marie replied, crisply, as she headed to the door.

'Should we come?' Tallulah asked.

Marie hesitated. 'No, Tallulah. We will need to discuss all this with Brigitta, in here. For the first time, her arrival is a coincidence in our favour. Please wait.'

The girls went to the window and watched Marie go out to meet Brigitta. Marnie intersected the director's path and they had a brief chat; Marnie nodded several times before putting a reassuring hand on Marie's elbow and returning the way she'd just come.

When Brigitta heard Marie's voice, she turned and greeted her with a kiss on each cheek. Marie leaned in close and whispered in her ear. Brigitta's gaze moved towards the hut where Tallulah and Adelaide stood watching her. Brigitta gave Marie a kind smile, rubbed her upper arm and they stood like that for a few moments. They weren't speaking but Tallulah was certain there was communication between them. Then Brigitta turned from Marie and headed in the direction of the tables, shoulders square, head high. Marie walked back along the path to the hut.

'Maybe it's not such a big deal,' Adelaide suggested.

'Maybe,' Tallulah said, doubtfully.

'Afternoon tea,' Marie said when she poked her head through the doorway a moment later.

'For us, even?' Adelaide asked.

Marie's head poked back around the corner. 'We will discuss it later,' she said firmly. 'But now it's Sunday afternoon and we have guests at our camp. What about your parents? Please let them know you are here with us.'

By the time the girls joined Mai and Hui, they already had plates piled with a selection of savoury and sweet treats.

'I am so hungry,' Adelaide exclaimed and Tallulah had to agree.

Tom sat down. 'Everything OK?'

'Better since Brigitta arrived. Sort of. She's not usually here?'

Tom shook his head. 'I don't think Marie wanted to take the risk of having her so far from town in case anything went wrong. Not that there are any real health issues but she must be ninety years old, at least.'

'Does Sasha live in town with her?' Adelaide asked.

'He's here in a hut with Saskia.'

Hui scoffed. 'But they're never in it.'

'Brigitta prefers Sasha as her driver, and Saskia is often with him,' Tom explained, 'so she spends a little more time at Brigitta's than she admits to.'

'I hear there were some fun and games at the beach today.' Brigitta spoke from behind Tallulah and they all jumped. On the other side of the table, Adelaide looked like an animal caught by the headlights of a car, but she swallowed hard and nodded.

Brigitta chuckled and sighed. 'How I'd love to be your age again and feeling that first flush of excitement and wonder as

I began to understand not just that I had a gift,' she bent to Tallulah's head height and in a loud whisper added, 'but that the gift was getting stronger.'

Tallulah felt her body prickle with goosebumps as her companions looked at one another with both thrill and fear in their eyes.

Brigitta laughed. She stood up straight and moved to the end of the table. 'The comprehension, when it came, that I was going to become *more* powerful as time went on ... ooh!' she exclaimed. 'If only I'd met a man as seductive as that. Things might have been very different.'

'How?' Mai asked.

'Well, I might have had a family and all of those things that make normal people happy.'

'We can't have any of that?' Mai asked, sounding disappointed.

'Of course *you* can,' Brigitta cried. 'I couldn't because I didn't learn the lesson I needed to learn early enough.'

No one said anything for a long moment. Tallulah asked the obvious question. 'What lesson?'

Brigitta lifted her head and her tears were bright. 'That we can be consumed by our gifts; we can be consumed by our desire to see how powerful we can be. And that doesn't leave us much time for anything else.' She took a long slow breath. 'It's a delicate balancing act we must perform – train our gifts, realise our potential or we will be burned away from within. But if we become too enamoured with ourselves, if we abuse our gifts, they can have the same effect as an addictive drug – we forget how to say no and the gift controls us.'

'And that happened to you?'

'Almost. I was pulled out just in time.' Brigitta gave them a warm smile. 'Even so it's a never-ending battle that I must fight. But that's why there is sometimes ...' She paused. There was cheering; music was starting to build in tempo and she cast her gaze towards the stage, where Marie and Ilya and a few other trainers as well as cooks were dancing.

Brigitta turned back to them. '... an overreaction when we see younger people taking unnecessary risks with their gifts.'

Tallulah and Adelaide exchanged glances.

'We've all done it,' Brigitta admitted, 'most of the adults here, anyway, even though we would prefer to forget our moments of weakness entirely.' She smiled knowingly. 'Just be aware of the risks.'

Tallulah and the others watched Brigitta walk to the next table and greet those students who weren't dancing.

Mai leaned in towards the girls. 'What happened at the beach?'

Tallulah checked that no one could overhear and took a deep breath.

'You know what,' Hui said, before Tallulah got a word out, 'my gut feeling is that you've just been given a reprieve and it's best to keep this story for another time. Come and dance with me, Little Miss Busybody.'

Hui and Mai got up to dance. Tom stood up and looked hopefully at Tallulah but she shook her head; she was weary and sunburned and didn't feel as though she could move a muscle.

'Can I take a raincheck?'

'Just this once,' he said. He looked at the table and then back to Tallulah. 'Hey, you know, I nearly burned the house down a few years ago; I got a bit carried away with my own brilliance.' His brow furrowed. 'I was probably a bit high and mighty in the car.'

'You were worried for us.'

Tom smiled and turned towards the stage. Adelaide sighed as he walked away from them. Tallulah followed her gaze to Sasha, who was dancing with another trainer. A bleary-eyed Saskia appeared from nowhere, wearing her trademark up-do and a blue floral dress. She sat down with them and said above the music, 'What brings you here?'

'Tom invited us,' Adelaide said quickly and Tallulah silently thanked her quick-thinking friend. 'He reckons by about the third weekend in camp the party begins.'

Saskia nodded. 'Well, he'd know. He loves a camp – and a party.' She smiled as she watched him jumping up and down on the dance floor. 'But you disappeared,' she said to Adelaide. 'I thought you'd gone the way of the rest of Sasha's recruits.'

'You can't get rid of me that easily,' Adelaide said, not really joking.

'Have you been asleep?' Tallulah asked.

'I was having an afternoon nap. The music woke me up. It was so warm and there was nothing better to do. I hate being up here so far from everything.'

'But you aren't here much, are you,' Adelaide commented.

'What do you mean?'

'Everyone said you and Sasha spend a lot of time with Brigitta in town.'

'Oh, here we go,' Saskia said. 'It was only a matter of time before someone suggested I get preferential treatment.'

'I said you didn't spend much time here,' Adelaide retorted. 'Not that you got preferential treatment. *You* said that.'

Saskia blushed.

'Anyway, you can have it. I wouldn't want to spend too

much time hanging out with Brigitta while she poked around in my brain.'

'Well,' Saskia said, nostrils flared as if she could smell victory, 'as you saw the first day Brigitta tried "poking around" in my mind, Adelaide, it didn't work. I'm not saying she isn't strong, but she is ninety years old. If the next telepaths of Cirque d'Avenir aren't stronger than Brigitta now, then they'll never make it.' Saskia looked directly at Tallulah; it was the first time she'd even acknowledged there might be other telepaths, let alone suggest that Tallulah might be one. She laughed. 'They certainly won't have much hope when we we're tested for who will be the eminence.'

'There is no eminence in Cirque d'Avenir,' Adelaide said.

'Oh, come on,' Saskia said with a roll of her eyes. 'You don't really believe the "we're all equal" nonsense. Marie's got rocks in her head if she thinks she can create Cirque d'Avenir without an eminence. At least Stellan got that right.' She gestured around the clearing. 'This organisation needs clear leadership or it's going nowhere. You wouldn't put yourself through all this for nothing, would you? There can be more than one telepath but two eminences?' She shook her head. 'The cream must rise to the top. And the Gazers have their own way of choosing if this camp doesn't sort us out. The eminence leads the troupe; she tells the story; she orchestrates the whole performance. History has shown what happens when they choose the wrong eminence.'

'What happens?'

A shout from the stage distracted them before Saskia answered. Many students stood aside, mesmerised by the one dancer left on stage – Marie de Clevjard. Marie moved with so much soul that Tallulah ached for her; she could feel her breath being taken from her just with the sweep of her arm or the tilt of her head.

But as Tallulah watched, she began to feel that something wasn't quite right. There were missteps and moments when Marie was off-balance. The harder she tried to tell her story, the faster she moved, until she was in a frenzy.

Tallulah looked away; she couldn't bear to watch. It was either their actions at the beach or Tallulah's clumsy revelation about the cuff that was the cause – she suspected the latter.

Tallulah knew that she had to do something. She stood and moved towards the dance floor, away from Saskia and Adelaide, but others had the same thought. Quickly Marie was enveloped in the helpful arms of the trainers.

Tallulah felt a hand on her own shoulder. She turned to find Brigitta at her side. 'This is my fault,' she said to her.

But Brigitta shook her head. 'We knew the risks we were taking when we started this again. You've just given her a shock – you and Irena and her secrets.'

'But it was Marie who told me that Irena has her reasons for doing what she does.'

'She can still be hurt by Irena's actions,' Brigitta said gently. 'I'm sure in the past weeks you must have wondered about the path that brought you to Cirque d'Avenir. How much did Irena reveal to you along the way?'

Tallulah took in the question as she watched Marie being led to a picnic bench by Marnie. The anguish in Marie's face reminded Tallulah of the first day of Cirque d'Avenir, when she'd cycled home hating the world and wondering what Irena could have been thinking to send her to the new circus. Turning back to Brigitta, she said, 'I can bring the cuff here. Marie can take charge of it. It will be such a relief.'

'No,' the old woman said, gripping her arm tighter.

'You then,' Tallulah said, desperately. 'You were an eminence, weren't you? It's yours, isn't it?'

'I gave it up to Irena long ago,' Brigitta told her, leading her away from where the others were gathered. 'And rightly so. I was too in love with it, with what it was showing me.'

'What did it show you?'

'That's not the point,' Brigitta said. 'The point is, it should have been destroyed over and over again through history, yet, when the time comes, no one can do it. Why, Tallulah? Why do we put so much faith in the cuff and its supposed lore? If it's meant to protect the eminence, if it's supposed to only work for the rightful eminence, then why has the eminence been most vulnerable whenever it surfaces and she wears it? I've turned it over and over in my mind and the only answers I can come up with are that it must have been crafted by the wrong hands, or tampered with somewhere along the way. We don't know the journey the cuff has taken through time but I've come to believe that the moment you succumb to its allure you are doomed.'

'Then what should I do?'

'Irena always acts in the best interests of the Cirkulatti no matter how you, or Marie, or I, feel about that. Irena trusted you with the cuff and I respect that decision. Keep it safe. We leave in a week for Elbe. Irena and the Gazers will join us and then we will act as one.'

CHAPTER TWENTY

The final week of Cirque d'Avenir was a revelation. The students had all taken leaps of strength – both mentally and physically. Under Ilya's gentle guidance, Estella learned that when she connected the trail of her hoop with his they could stifle the noise of anyone having a conversation behind it. Ilya encouraged Mai to join them, and she discovered that the electric charge she infused a hoop with could create a trail that, combined with another hooper's magic, could produce a mid-air screen. Ilya suggested Tallulah try to project a telepathic image upon it.

It was just a few seconds of magic – the length the girls could keep their hoop trails in contact – but seeing the simple image that Tallulah conveyed was so astonishing that it give them all licence to let go of what they knew about themselves. When Javier's acrobatics began to match Sasha's they'd become regular sparring partners – one morning he set the wooden pike they were duelling with on fire. Without hesitation Sasha had waved his hand and a mound of bush dirt folded over the fire and doused it. 'Don't get too excited,' he told the group of stunned faces. 'That's all the telekinetics I've got. Brief and only in extreme situations. Be prepared to experience bits of another's gift at some time.'

By the end of the week, Tom finally – albeit briefly – found the ability to keep a ball of flame alight and separate from himself again. Hui came close to achieving the same for the first time but his juggling and target skills improved to the point where he was second only to Adelaide. She found a way to combine her accuracy with Mai's electric charge, while Ollie was so thrilled with how easily he could summon his shadow that he'd prefer to faint than stop. Tallulah's energy for telepathy had improved so much that she had not fainted for days. And Guido's and Chiara's aerial combat acrobatics were getting more and more daring – until Guido injured himself. They had both returned home with the promise that they would be back next year.

Hui, naturally, put the changes down to Saskia's departure. Her mother's health was again unstable and Saskia had gone to visit her in hospital for a few days before her 'inevitable' departure for Elbe.

The morning after the Cirque d'Avenir wrap-party, Tallulah and Adelaide sat dripping wet on their beach towels, discussing the troupe chosen to travel to Elbe.

'I feel bad for Ollie,' Adelaide said. 'After all we've been through, only for his parents to say no. Mum had a chat to them at the party last night but she said they wouldn't budge. He doesn't have a month to spare for Elbe – HSC year and all that. He was gutted; I didn't feel like I could really celebrate in front of him.'

'Oh.' Tallulah stretched back on her towel. 'That's why we're here at the crack of dawn – all that contained excitement.'

'You answered my six am text.'

Tallulah didn't think she'd ever felt as satisfied as the moment Marie announced that she, Adelaide, Mai, Hui and

Tom would travel with her, Marnie and Sasha. Saskia was going to leave from Adelaide, where her mother was getting treatment, and meet the team in Elbe, as would Estella and Javier, who were going via their home in Santiago, to swap the contents of their suitcases from summer to extreme winter. Brigitta had left before the party; she was taking a slower series of flights with stopovers to preserve her energy and would get there a couple of days after them.

'I can't believe I'm going,' Adelaide said. 'I keep expecting that any moment I'm going to wake up from this strange dream and find myself at home babysitting the twins, surfing the net. This is happening to me, isn't it?'

Tallulah, whose eyes were closed as she listened, smiled. *It is happening to you.*

'Freaky,' Adelaide said, as though she couldn't be more pleased. 'Lu, I've been thinking about it, and I reckon Irena probably realised that you had to learn about and decide upon a few things alone. Has she tried to contact you again?'

'Nothing since I started wearing this.' Tallulah tapped the pendant at her neck.

'Is that a coincidence?'

'Don't know. Probably. Every night I think about taking it, off just to see if I have another dream. But ...' Instinct told her that even if she did manage to get to sleep while waiting for the lorikeets, waking up in the morning without a dream would only bring on further anxiety. 'Sasha asked about it though.'

'What did he say?'

Eventually she'd told Adelaide about the early encounter with Sasha in the hope that it might help convince her she'd not caused the distance between them. 'He asked if it was another of my father's craftwork. I told him I'd found it at a market stall in the city and couldn't resist it.'

'I can't wait to meet Irena,' Adelaide said. 'Do you think I could ask her a few questions of my own?'

'Most def.'

Adelaide's attempt to look shocked by Tallulah's imitation of her was a complete failure. They were still giggling as they walked to their bikes.

Tallulah was closing the door of the shed when her father called out from the back verandah. 'I hear it went well last night.'

She went to him.

'Congratulations,' he said, hugging her tightly. 'I wish I could have been there.'

Of all the revelations of the past month, his reason for not attending the final dinner had been the one that really sideswiped her.

'It's just better that he doesn't come,' her mother had said when the invitation arrived, 'for now anyway.'

'Why won't you come to Cirque d'Avenir? You've met Marie – she helped you put my training room together,' Tallulah said.

Her father sighed and sat forwards in his armchair. 'I was given up for adoption by my birth mother when I was four because of my gift,' he said.

Tallulah was glad that she'd been sitting when her father made that simple admission. She looked to her mum, who confirmed the confession with a nod. 'Are you a telepath?'

He shook his head. 'No; I had what everyone called an "episode" one day at preschool. I predicted the death of

259

another boy – when the accident happened a week later, my mother took me to the adoption agency.' He cleared his throat before continuing. 'I went to a few foster families before landing at your grandparents' place. Most people don't want to adopt a school-age child but your grandmother was happy to bypass the nappy stage.' His eyes glistened as he spoke.

Tallulah's mind was reeling with the information. Her father was a seer? 'So does that mean you're Cirkulatti?'

He shrugged. 'I don't know. My birth mother was a single girl in a country town on the state border where we later discovered a community of former Cirkulatti lived. I never knew my father but there is every chance that he passed on a gift – which has obviously been passed onto you.'

'Why didn't you foresee the collapse of your business?'

Her parents exchanged a reluctant glance.

'My business didn't collapse,' he admitted. 'We moved to Seacliff for Cirque d'Avenir. Your mother and I were always determined that you would not be made to feel a freak. The thing is, I didn't mention anything about my gift to Marie-Irena and your mother and I would prefer we kept that little bit of information to ourselves. I think I'm much more useful to you if I'm independent of Cirque d'Avenir for now.'

'Don't worry,' Tallulah told him. 'There'll be other occasions that you won't get out of so easily.'

'I'm sure of it,' he replied.

She almost asked him if he'd seen something in Elbe that she should know about. But if he had seen anything dangerous surely her parents wouldn't let her go – despite her mother's insistence that it was her decision to make.

'I've got to get something from the gatehouse to pack.'

'Of course,' he said, 'you'd better not leave that behind. Check out the discs I made for Della while you're there – see if they match your specifications. She's coming by with her mother later.'

The metal discs Tallulah found at the gatehouse were larger than anything else her dad had worked. When Adelaide learned about her father's work, she wondered if he could make her a set of juggling discs that were also weapons. Tallulah described the discs she had seen Antonina use in the hippodrome, and her father set to the task.

The snap of a branch outside interrupted Tallulah's thoughts. She looked out the window and thought she saw movement. 'Dad?' she called out. Not hearing any reply, she slipped down the stairs, reached in and grabbed a dumbbell from the small rack of weights in her training room, then went to the entrance.

There, in the middle of the clearing, was Sasha. He was surprisingly casual in cargo shorts and fitted singlet that Tallulah had to admit displayed his honed torso nicely. His dark hair was pulled back in a ponytail.

'Hello,' he said.

'You scared me.'

'Sorry. I needed to speak to you. Your father told me you were up here.'

Tallulah nodded; she was glad she had not yet taken the cuff from the safe.

He began a series of moves. Immediately, images of dark and light, sadness and joy filled her head, and a story that had been buried deep inside her body since she was a little girl, or perhaps since a time before this one, stirred inside her. She went to stand in front of Sasha in the clearing. As Tallulah got closer she realised he was already entirely focused on her.

Tallulah felt the rhythm of his movement and let it settle inside her until it was as strong as her heartbeat, as sure as her breath. Without even questioning what she was doing, she began to mirror his actions. As he pushed his arms away from his body, Tallulah did the same and filled the space with the long journey of a shamed people, falsely accused and banished from their land; in unison, they opened their hands and sliced the air as surely as a blade, finishing each slice with a flourished clench. The wanderers had been cut off from their three great truths: home, state and stage. Their fingers pinched and twisted the air in front of them: internal bickering had nicked at and weakened the once-great troupe until – Tallulah and Sasha dropped their hands to the ground, opened them wide and shook and flicked what they held onto the ground – the people were scattered like empty seed husks onto a barren ground.

Sasha brought his hand to his forehead and looked out across the sparkling harbour and Tallulah spun a chapter of hope for the future; she joined in again by mirroring the shallow undulations of his hand as she told of the land of the hard sun across the waves, where the remnants of seeds lodged and slowly strengthened, taking what they could from the ground that seemed desolate but had its own unique qualities. And when they again cast out their roots, they were stronger than they had been before, and they vowed to bring forth a Cirkulatti that would be greater than ever before and an eminence like no other.

By the time it was over, Tallulah was thrilled and drenched and breathing heavily. She came out of the story, out of the trance, and found that she was standing centimetres from the strong chest and distinct earthy smell of the man who had tormented her for the last four weeks. He was standing so close she could feel the heat from his body, the softness of his breath or maybe the winds of time.

They stood like that for an age, long enough for their chests to rise and fall as one, for their breath to mingle, for her chin to lift and his to tilt, and for their lips to be drawn closer and closer to each other until there was no doubt that when they met they would fit each other perfectly. Tallulah could feel the warm summer rain begin to mingle with the sweat on her skin; she felt an exquisite moment of anticipation before finally everything between them dissolved and Sasha's skin touched hers. She closed her eyes so that nothing would distract her from that moment when she could finally melt into him and he would explain everything: who he was; where he'd come from; how he'd known she was capable of this. The thought interrupted her reverie. She opened her eyes.

'How did you know?' she whispered.

He shook his head. 'The first day I met you on the street. It's not just your eyes. Your presence is so strong; and then you recognised Marie's call on the terrace, the day she danced. The stories are there inside you just waiting for you to give them expression.

'But you saw right into my soul on that first day and I hated you for intruding like that. I thought you were like – others. Spoiled and of little use. I convinced myself that you were hurting people with your gift. And once I'd started down that path it was almost impossible to see how good you really are. I made myself push you harder, though. If you could be trained, then perhaps there was a chance you could be what we all need.'

'I understand.' And she did, for the first time. An eminence had to be strong enough to withstand whatever was thrown at her, or the Cirkulatti were nothing. She felt his hands on her shoulders and the touch of his skin was so delicious it was all Tallulah could do not to moan.

'Get away, Tallulah.' His voice was desperate in its need – but not a need for her.

She took a step back, embarrassed, confused. And hurt.

'While you've got the chance.'

'But—'

'I tried to get away but they found me again.'

'Who?'

'My family, of course. Your family. Our family – the *Cirkulatti*. The family that feeds you entitlement for breakfast, injustice for lunch and a sickening combination of both for dinner – until you want to throw up.'

She shook her head. 'Irena never spoke of it like that.'

'Irena was on the run for years, Tallulah. She didn't tell you that, did she? Then when her husband died, and she had no children of her own, when she was lost and alone, they found her, told her about a little girl who just might give her a chance to redeem herself, give her relevance again. And she was reborn.'

'No.' Tallulah shook her head. She did not want to hear this version of the story. 'You're trying to scare me.'

'You bet I am. I didn't have a choice. But you do. Get away.'

And Sasha turned away from her and walked down the path towards the house. Tallulah stood in the middle of the clearing, alone.

CHAPTER TWENTY-ONE

Elbe

Monday 3 February

'Finally!' Mai exclaimed.

Tallulah sat up, yawned and watched as their driver navigated a gravel driveway and parked under a low overhang of rock. Somewhere in the rock was the entrance to the secret Cirkulatti bunker. With the engine cut, the doors were opened and the blast of cold air shocked them into alertness. Tallulah wrapped her arms around her body as she joined her companions on the other side of the driveway, looking out to the valley below.

'Wow,' Adelaide said quietly. The view down to a river over dark forest looked like a postcard. Tallulah had to admit that, for all the travel she'd done, she hadn't seen much that was this beautiful. The national park below them was all rugged, rocky beauty – patchy snow on sandstone boulders among which great pine trees stretched skywards. At the bottom of the valley a quaint town sat on the far side of a meandering river. Small sailing boats were moored for the winter.

'I forget how beautiful it is here,' Marie said. 'But we need to get inside. Your bodies are going to have enough work to do adapting from thirty-five degrees Celsius to thirty-five degrees Fahrenheit without staying out all day in it.' She gave a disappointed sigh and turned back to where the vehicles were being unloaded. 'I thought Jacek might have come out to meet us. They were due to arrive yesterday.'

'Hopefully, they're making up a thick meaty soup and baking warm crusty bread for lunch,' Hui said. 'I'm starving.'

As if on cue, one of the drivers of the vehicles came to their side of the cars and waved Marie over. They spoke in French.

'What's wrong?' Adelaide asked Tallulah, who had already demonstrated a traveller's command of French at the airport.

'She's asking why our bags are being left outside the entrance rather than taken down to the lift.' Tallulah shook her head as she tried to decipher the reply. 'I'm too tired, I think. It sounds like he's saying there's too much glass on the floor. But that doesn't make sense.'

Marie too seemed not to comprehend what he was saying. She proceeded through a doorway that was more like a gash in the hillside. Marnie, Sasha, Tom and Hui followed. Tom quickly reappeared.

'All the lights have been smashed in the foyer and down the tunnel to the lift; there's a skylight so it's easy enough to see but just be careful. We're going to take the lift down to the next level to the living quarters where Jacek should be. Marie wants you to stay here with the drivers until we get back.'

'No way,' Tallulah said.

'We're coming with you,' Mai declared.

'As if,' said Adelaide.

Tom grimaced. 'I told her you'd say that.'

Tallulah told the driver that they'd be back in a moment and was about to follow Tom inside when Mai stopped.

'Wait,' she said. She headed back to her bag where it sat on the ground, which seemed to give Adelaide an idea too.

Tallulah and Tom watched as Mai pulled her jacket off, shivered, then fossicked about for the pretty purse she kept her ribbons in. They curled around her arms and she pulled her jacket back on. In the meantime Adelaide had retrieved four batons and four colourful discs from her bag.

Tom was impressed. 'You were prepared, Della.'

'You would be too if you'd met the snake-guy,' Adelaide told him.

He nodded.

They followed him into the hideaway; a skylight illuminated the vestibule – but it wasn't a lot of light. The artificial lights set into the walls would have been handy – had they not been smashed. The others were waiting at the lift.

Marie looked unsurprised by the girls' arrival. 'Tallulah, do you think you could try to reach for a mind, a consciousness of any kind?'

Tallulah shook her head. 'I'm not able to touch anything living at the moment.'

Marie nodded. 'It was built to be as impenetrable as possible, particularly to people like you – those protective barriers were checked and reinstated before we arrived – but if they'd been breached you would know.'

'Who checked them?' Tallulah asked. 'Not the magicians; they're not involved in Cirque d'Avenir.'

'Tallulah, the fact that the factions were not all involved in the first wave of training for new recruits does not mean that they abandon their responsibilities in a fit of pique. The magicians are as keen as we are to make this new beginning happen; they have always maintained the security of Elbe and our training grounds.'

'We don't even know if the lift works,' Hui said, pressing the button over and over.

Tom grabbed Hui's hand. 'If you stop banging the button we might be able to hear whether it's coming.'

'Sorry,' Hui said. A few moments later came the unmistakeable sound of a lift whirring into action, albeit slowly.

'Marie,' Sasha said, 'what's the layout? How far down are we going and what can we expect when we get there?'

'We'll go two levels down to the living quarters. We'll arrive on an open space like an enormous lounge room,' she hesitated, 'that would be on our right as we exit the lift. The kitchen is behind that. On our left will be a long corridor that has small dormitory-like rooms.'

'Voila,' Tom whispered, as the lift doors opened. Both he and Sasha looked inside before they got in.

'Could anyone be watching our arrival?' Sasha asked.

Marie shook her head. 'We've got a generator but beyond that it's very rustic. No high-tech surveillance. We've always relied on ourselves.'

'So the lift being called to the entrance is the only thing that would alert anyone below to our presence,' Adelaide said.

'What are those, Della?' Sasha asked, pointing to the discs she held in each hand.

'A friend of my stepfather's is a metal worker.' When she'd picked up the discs from Tallulah's dad, they'd explained the decision to keep him independent of Cirque; Adelaide took a vow of silence and invented a story. 'He made these for me. I needed something light but effective.' She held one on the palm of her hand to show them. 'With a bit of speed, the edge is nasty.'

The lift juddered to a halt. All of them stood prepared for what was on the other side of the doors. Marie, Sasha and Tom stood at the front; Marnie, Adelaide and Mai behind them and Tallulah at the rear. Tallulah checked her own boundaries while opening her mind to whatever might be beyond.

But when the lift doors opened no one was waiting for them – though what they saw was bad enough. Chaos. The lounge room that Marie had described had been overturned. Couches upended, cushions on the floor, sidetables and lamps smashed everywhere.

'Tom, come with me while I check the kitchen,' Marie said.

The others slowly fanned out around the room, getting the layout clear. Tallulah felt another consciousness.

'Someone is asking for help,' she told them.

'Here,' Sasha cried as he stumbled and righted himself. He turned back to an upended armchair: a leg poked out from under it. The girls rushed to help but Sasha quickly had the couch off the man on the ground.

'Jacek?' Sasha said loudly as he bent over him. He looked at the girls. 'I haven't seen him since I was a kid but I'm sure it's him. Can one of you get Marie?'

But Marie and Tom had already returned. Marie rushed over to them. 'Tom, you and Sasha search the bedrooms to be sure no one is going to surprise us from there, please,' she said, then crouched down on the floor next to Marnie, who was already placing her hands on Jacek's legs, arms and head, muttering to herself. After a few moments, the man's eyes opened. He looked around uncertainly, until, finally spotting someone familiar, his eyes filled with tears.

'Marie,' he said. He winced as though it hurt him to speak. 'How long have I …? What time is it?'

'It's lunchtime, Monday.'

'Monday.' He nodded, then he shook his head. 'I'm so sorry.'

'No apologies, just tell us what happened.'

'We were ambushed. This morning.' He looked around. 'Where are my students?'

Sasha and Tom ran back into the lounge room.

'Any students?' Marie asked.

Sasha and Tom looked at one another. Sasha shook his head. 'No, there's no one else here.'

Jacek groaned, then tried to sit up, but pain contorted his face and he gripped his shoulder. 'The men, the snake creatures, they've taken my kids. They're only young – the oldest is fourteen. We have to go after them.' Another thought crossed his face and he looked back at Sasha. 'What about Saskia? Where is Saskia?'

'She got here?'

Jacek nodded. 'She arrived maybe an hour after us, yesterday. We all had a great dinner. It was so good to see her again – both of you.' His face was a study in misery as he spoke. 'But why wasn't she with you?'

'She was determined to travel alone.'

'Jacek, tell us what happened,' Marie said firmly. 'How were you ambushed?'

'I don't know,' he said. 'We have to go after them.' He struggled to get up again.

'Jacek,' Marie said. 'You can't go anywhere until Marnie has finished working on you. Take us through what happened, please.'

For a moment Jacek looked determined to defy her; then he relented. 'I only brought a small group. Six kids. There were not as many as first hoped.'

'Numbers never mattered,' Marie said. 'I tried to tell you that. We had to start small.'

'But they are strongly gifted. We'd hardly started to unpack when Saskia arrived. My kids loved her – she was like a big sister regaling them with her adventures. She told us all about Seacliff, especially how hot it was. But she got no sympathy here – we envied all your weeks in the sun.' He smiled. 'We had a great night. But when I went to bed I couldn't sleep. I tossed and turned all night then I decided early this morning to get up and see the sunrise. Saskia was already in the kitchen; she'd had trouble sleeping too.' He gestured with one hand, as if helpless to explain what happened next. 'We were making porridge when we began to smell something really strange, earthy and quite overpowering, unnatural even underground in a mountainside. Then a hissing noise echoed through the caves until it was so loud we couldn't hear ourselves think. And then these reptilian men or creatures or whatever they are were suddenly upon us. It was like they came through the rocks. Marie, I have never seen anything like them.'

'What happened then?' Marie said.

'We fought. Saskia was strong. She was directing us with her mind, Marie. She was extraordinary. But there were too many of them. She was still fighting when I was knocked out and I know nothing after that. I'm so sorry. They have taken an eminence?'

'Saskia is not the eminence – there is no eminence in Cirque d'Avenir,' Marie assured him. 'She has been training with us though and Brigitta has been very impressed by her.'

'I didn't know,' Jacek groaned.

Tallulah couldn't hold back her question any longer. 'Was Irena here?'

Jacek was confused. 'Irena?'

'Irena Blatiskova was supposed to meet us here,' Marie said.

Jacek's eyes were wide with surprise. 'No. She had not arrived before us. Irena Blatiskova. I can't wait to meet her.'

The sound of the lift beginning its ascent to the top floor made them all jump.

'Hui, help Marnie get Jacek to a bedroom and then get back here as soon as you can. The rest of you spread out and take a hiding spot. It should be Ursula with her trainees but we can't chance being attacked again.'

Tallulah's heart was loud in her ears as she waited in her hiding spot for the lift doors to open.

There was a momentary relief when a woman, around the same age as Marie, emerged from the lift – until Tallulah realised that the smudge around her eye was a bruise and her hair was unruly. When she hobbled out of the lift with a much younger woman, whose arm was draped around her shoulder, Marie jumped up with a cry and rushed over to help, followed by Sasha.

'My children were kidnapped,' the woman said, as soon as she saw Marie. Tom had righted another armchair and Sasha and Adelaide took the younger girl and sat her down. Mai had already gone for Marnie.

'It was like they knew we were coming,' the woman continued. 'But how could they?' She looked around at the trashed lounge room, then her startled eyes were back on Marie. 'What happened?'

'Jacek's team were hit earlier this morning. His students have been taken. One of mine, also. Ursula, please, tell us what happened.'

'I've been going over and over it in my mind; the only explanation I can come up with is that we must have been followed from the airport. We'd been driving for maybe an hour, when the team needed to go to the bathroom. I had laughed at them – this was taking acting in harmony a bit too far. There was a bit of silliness about that. Maybe five minutes later, a small service station appeared and the driver pulled in. It was unplanned. No one could have known we were stopping there.'

'Could someone have been tampering with their minds, from another car, perhaps? Planting the need for the toilet?' Tallulah asked. 'Were they trained to repel an experienced telepath?'

Ursula shook her head. 'Barely. We were coming here to work with Brigitta more thoroughly. I was conscious of another bus pulling into the service station. I felt reassured – a tourist bus on a long stretch of forest road, not many cars about. I didn't think anything more of it. Then a hissing noise began – it echoed through the forest. I could hold off the assault but my kids went down like ninepins. Especially when a swarm of huge men covered in scales began attacking us. I was hit from behind and I blacked out. When I came around, the children were gone – except for Lena, who had been thrown aside in the fight and knocked out. They must have thought she was dead.'

'Wasn't there an attendant in the service station?'

'He didn't stand a chance. He was unconscious when I found him, but alive. We got out of there as quickly as possible; I called the local police as we left to say he'd been assaulted.'

While Ursula was talking, Tom and Sasha had begun to make the lounge room look a little more normal. Marnie returned from seeing to Jacek and gave a pained exclamation when she saw Ursula. They were obviously old friends.

When Ursula and Lena had been helped to their rooms, Tallulah and the Seacliff team gathered around Marie in the lounge.

'We need to go after them,' Sasha said.

'Yes,' Marie said, wearily. 'But right now we have no idea where to begin. It would be foolish to move without a plan. You would expect that is what they are waiting for us to do. *They* – we don't even know who *they* is.'

'The Gazers didn't see this happening?'

'The Gazers are big picture, Tallulah,' Sasha interjected. 'They can't be expected to see every small detail.'

'*Small* detail?' Tallulah countered. 'The kidnapping of twenty kids is small? I mean, the re-opening of Elbe is itself pretty momentous, wouldn't you say? You'd think their minds would be open to everything about it.'

'Guys,' Adelaide intervened. 'Forgive me for being naive, but don't we need to call the police?'

'It would be nice, wouldn't it?' Marie said. 'How can we tell them that men who might also have been snakes attacked a hideaway that few people should know about?'

'And the Cirkulatti has never had any reason to trust authority,' Sasha explained. 'The last time we made that mistake was when the Gazers encouraged everyone to move to Leningrad because the revolutionaries were guaranteeing the Cirkulatti's safety. But Lenin's circus schools were really just a ruse to keep track of any possible eminences who might lead a counter-revolution. We were forced into hiding. In the eighties, when the authorities discovered a group of Cirkulatti hiding out in Belarus ...' Sasha hesitated. 'Well, many think that the disaster at Chernobyl was not an accident.'

'Given up by the Herodians,' Tom added. 'You should tell them that. You should also perhaps clarify that the Herodians, until thirty years ago, were Cirknero.'

Tallulah felt like she'd been kicked in the stomach; Adelaide's healthy colour faded entirely. There was a frigid silence in the room.

'So, the police are out, especially here in Europe.'

'But if the police didn't know we were coming here,' Tallulah said, 'who did know, exactly?'

'Senior members of Cirque d'Avenir. The Gazers, Brigitta, a handful of trainers like me, Jacek and Ursula.'

'And Irena Blatiskova?' Sasha asked.

Marie nodded.

'And she's not here,' he said.

'What is that supposed to mean?' Tallulah said.

'We have to look at all possibilities. Irena isn't here and you've got no idea where she is. Isn't it possible that she has been captured and given up our secrets, perhaps to save you?'

'How does giving up the hideaway save me?'

'She might have made a deal – one golden-eyed eminence for another.'

'What? What have golden eyes got to do—I'm *not*—'

'Sasha,' Marie warned. 'Questioning Irena's loyalty when we are all under stress is not wise.'

'Why? Her loyalty has always been questionable. She walked away for years.'

'So did you,' Tallulah challenged. 'You of all people should understand Irena—'

'I do understand—'

'Which bit, then?' Tallulah demanded. 'Because I'm confused – walking away or giving us up to the Cirknero? How do we know *you* haven't given us up, Sasha? From what I've witnessed you have no great love for either side. Did Saskia arrive a little earlier than you expected and muck up your plan?'

'Spoken by someone who knows nothing—'

'Stop!' Marie's deep voice echoed in the room. 'This is not the time. And it achieves nothing.

'The welcome gathering scheduled for tomorrow evening will not be the celebration we were hoping for. But everyone we need will be here – the Gazers, Brigitta and Irena.' Marie looked to Tallulah with eyes full of sympathy. 'I have no doubt she'll be here. And that is when we will decide on a plan. Jacek, Ursula and Lena will mend. The initial camp was kept small on purpose ...' Marie paused and gathered her thoughts, '... in case of eventualities such as this one.' She stopped again as tears welled. She took a deep breath.

'But the other groups remain hidden and presumably safe while our enemy has exposed itself,' Tallulah said, reading Marie's face. 'So we have some advantage. Particularly if they will join our search for the students.'

Marie nodded. 'But not *our* search, Tallulah. The people who will scout for us and help recover the students have experience. Only adult operatives will go in search of the missing students.'

There was uproar among the Cirque d'Avenir team – especially from Sasha.

Marie held up her hand. 'I am not sending you, Sasha, with a team of students who have not completed their training, out into the open where the Cirknero can attack you. I will not expose you to whatever else may be out there.'

When the main living area was restored and the hungry travellers had devoured lunch, everyone retired to their rooms for an afternoon rest. But despite the overwhelming tiredness she'd felt on the drive to the hideaway, Tallulah's mind was too busy to sleep. She stared at the ceiling and tried to block the angry thoughts Sasha had brought on. She had to find a distraction: her book was in her bag. She sat up and swung her feet to the ground – and found Mai looking at her from her bunk.

She sat up too. 'I can't sleep either. What should we do?'

'Explore the place, I reckon,' Adelaide's voice called. She leaned her head over the bunk above Mai. 'Sleep was always wishful thinking.'

Mai scoffed. 'Shouldn't be for you. You've hardly slept since we left home.'

'I've never needed much,' Adelaide said as she lowered herself slowly to the floor. 'A few hours seems to go a long way.'

'Do you think we're allowed to just go looking around?' Tallulah asked.

'They didn't say we couldn't,' said Adelaide.

'But they didn't say we could. They expected us to sleep.'

Adelaide and Mai exchanged a glance. 'You can stay then,' Mai said. 'Della and I will go exploring and tell you about what we find.'

'I was just asking.' Tallulah pulled on some cargo pants and a long-sleeved T-shirt. She picked up a sweater. 'Do you think the whole complex is heated like this area?'

'Bring it just in case,' Adelaide said, tying a jacket around her waist and stuffing gloves in the pocket of her jeans. She pulled on socks but not shoes, which she held in her hand. 'Ready?'

She moved to the door of their room, opened it and slipped through. Tallulah glanced at Mai.

'Like she's been doing this sort of thing forever,' Mai said, smiling.

Adelaide was waiting for them in the living room. But when Tallulah headed towards the lift a soft whistle stopped her. Mai was already on her way to the kitchen and Adelaide was following her.

Tallulah walked into the kitchen and found Mai near the refrigerator, holding a door open for her. Through it was a stairwell.

'If this is how they came in, shouldn't we check it out?' Mai gave her a gentle shove and closed the door behind them.

Adelaide sat on the top step pulling on her shoes.

'Jacek said he was in the kitchen when the hissing began,' Tallulah corrected. 'He didn't know where they came from.'

'We'll get a better sense of the place if we use the stairs rather than the lift.' Adelaide began walking down the metal stairs.

For the next hour the girls made their way through an impressive, luxurious rabbit-warren of caves and rooms that were part training centre, part accommodation; they even found a room that stored as much weaponry as it did circus equipment – swords, knives, juggling batons as heavy as clubs. Adelaide tried on a vest that had pockets that were perfect for a series of knives – and easy to reach with both hands.

'Do you reckon—' Tallulah began.

'—we should be doing this?' Adelaide and Mai chorused in a bored monotone.

Adelaide filled each pocket with the right-sized knife, stood in front of a target, juggled and threw. Mai did the same with new ribbons; they were charged and ready to go in seconds. 'The weight of these is good.'

'And these.' Adelaide threw her a couple of coloured balls. Mai caught them, rolled them in her hands and threw one at the target. It missed, but it hissed and spat as it rolled along the floor. Adelaide pulled on her gloves and said, 'Throw it to me.' Mai did; Adelaide plucked it from the air and tossed it at the target again. The ball put a hole straight through the centre.

'So the snake-men left this alone,' Tallulah said. 'They kidnapped teenagers, but left everything that would help the Cirkulatti fight back.'

'Weapons are useless to us without our people. Though,' Adelaide looked guilty even as she said it, 'they're welcome to Saskia, I have to say.'

Mai snorted with laughter, then suppressed it when she looked at Tallulah. 'Sheesh, Lu, chill. She'll be back making us all feel like crap before you know it.'

They found other staircases, carved into the stone, which took them between floors, as well as rope ladders and various doors — some they had to bend over double to pass through.

When they reached a small junction of three pathways, there was one path that was not quite as well-trodden as the others. It led to a strange, small door.

'What do you reckon this is?' said Adelaide.

'Maybe it leads to the generator,' Tallulah guessed. 'Or some sort of access to the internals — you know, the pipes and the electrical stuff.'

'It's a bit elaborate for that,' Mai said. 'Look at the carvings.' She held the torch towards the door to help them see it.

All of a sudden, Tallulah began to sense the door throbbing. And then there was the surface — it had a certain familiarity to it. 'Look,' she said, pointing. The carving showed a triple-headed goddess holding a torch, keys and a dagger, a serpent at her feet.

'That's your pendant,' Adelaide said.

'Hecate,' Mai said. 'You weren't wearing it at lunch.'

'It was annoying me on the plane,' Tallulah said. 'I'll put it on when I get back to the room.' She ran her hand over the panel. 'And these owls around the warrior woman – owls are on the cuff, which was made in Caesar's time, so I think that's Rome's Minerva. And there's Isis,' she pointed to the lines and squiggles above it. 'That's her hieroglyph.'

'Your dad has lots of images like these on the walls of his workshop,' Adelaide said.

'Yeah, they were on the intaglios that I told you about – the ones Irena had strung in the windows of my bedroom. There was always a story about what each one was and what protection it was supposed to offer, but I didn't take much notice back then. He always said it was just a hobby.'

Tallulah stood back and looked at the panel of carvings.

'I wonder if this is meant to represent the different deities the Cirkulatti has worshipped.'

They contemplated it in silence for a moment before Adelaide shrugged. 'Could be,' she said as she placed her hands on it. 'Do you think it is an entrance? It seems too small – Stellan and the strongmen would never get through.' She pushed on the panel.

'Careful,' Tallulah said.

'Sometimes in movies someone leans on a panel or some random trigger and it opens,' Mai said. The girls stood aside as she moved forwards, turned her back on the panel and casually leaned against it. Nothing happened. She turned and leaned on it with her shoulder. Again nothing. Mai sighed.

'You try, Lu,' Adelaide suggested.

'Me? Why?'

'A hunch,' Adelaide said. 'Just humour me.'

Tallulah stood before the door. She put her hand out to touch the triple-headed goddess at the carving's centre – but at the last minute, not knowing why, she placed her hand just below Hecate instead, out of respect maybe, and opened her channels.

We call on the goddess of magic and the night, the faithful friend of mysteries, Hecate, to walk with the eminence and give the Cirkulatti strength.

The panel slid open.

'Hecate's torches,' Mai whispered.

'It opens for the eminence,' Adelaide said.

'Or someone who knows the right words to say,' Tallulah said.

'The eminence would know the words to say.'

'So would someone loyal to the Cirkulatti.'

'I'm loyal and I didn't know what to say. How did you?' Mai asked.

Tallulah thought about it. 'From one of the visions, I think.'

'But didn't Brigitta tell you not to trust the visions?' Adelaide warned.

'I didn't tell her about them.'

'But she said the cuff might have been crafted by the wrong hands or tampered with,' Mai said.

'Which means you shouldn't trust the visions,' Adelaide insisted.

'And Irena taught me to act on instinct and that seemed the right thing to do and say.' Tallulah couldn't hide the irritation in her voice. 'And didn't Stellan's daughter say something like that just before they left?'

Mai looked at Adelaide. 'I think she did.'

Adelaide nodded. 'Yeah, maybe.'

But as Tallulah moved to walk through the door, Adelaide grabbed her. 'Wait. There's a draught coming from below.'

Mai shone the torchlight into the room. There was a pit about two metres wide not two steps into the tunnel. On either side the path was solid and wide. The girls made their way forwards gingerly and shone the light into the pit. It had stone walls all the way to the bottom, where there was light enough to illuminate a jumble of boulders.

'Instinct could have got us killed,' Adelaide muttered.

Mai shone the torch around the vestibule and stopped on a rope ladder hitched to the wall nearby. She took the ladder and let it drop into the hole. As she did, the door slid closed behind them. In the torchlight, the back of the door was completely flat, not a carving in sight.

Adelaide groaned. 'Why didn't I jam something in there to stop it shutting?'

'You can't think of everything, Della,' Tallulah said.

'Let's worry about it if we have to,' Mai suggested. 'In the meantime we go forwards. Me first.' She handed the torch to Tallulah and started the climb down.

'The ladder doesn't go all the way,' Mai called.

Tallulah and Adelaide peered over the edge and saw Mai standing on the last rung, with one hand reaching out to long handles that led her to a ledge that jutted out from the wall.

'It's an entrance to a room,' she told them.

'Careful without the torch,' Tallulah called.

'There's light coming from somewhere,' Mai replied.

'Wait for us before you go any further,' Adelaide said. 'They could be waiting for—'

But Mai had already gone.

Adelaide slapped her thighs. 'Why doesn't she listen?'

'Like you're any different,' Tallulah said.

Mai's head popped out again. 'What are you waiting for? You've got to see this.'

'There's no one there? No place for snake-guys or anyone else to hide?'

Mai shook her head. 'It's a big empty room but you've still got to come see.'

Adelaide grabbed the ladder and handed it to Tallulah. 'You're up.'

'You go first.'

'You're not staying up here by yourself.'

'What?'

'I don't think we should leave you anywhere unprotected.'

'What?' Tallulah repeated. She laughed. 'You're not my mother, Della.'

'Lu, no arguing.'

'If you're trying to freak me out you're doing a good job.'

'Whether you are or aren't the eminence, Lu, we can't be too careful.'

'There is no—'

'Stop!' Adelaide held up her hand; her face was set hard. 'Think about it, Lu. The snake-men have taken Saskia. She may be powerful, but if the guy in Mr Morton's shop got any sort of report back of a telepath who can image-cast … When they discover that Saskia is not that girl, they may come back. From now on, Mai is in front of you, and I've got your back. End of discussion.'

'Well said,' Mai's voice called from below.

'And *you've* got to be more careful about running ahead,' Adelaide called to Mai.

'Sorry, didn't think.'

Tallulah handed Adelaide the torch and started the descent. She could hear Mai's exclamations echoing around the mysterious room and she tried to climb down faster but missed a rung and slipped. She managed to regain her footing, but the damp walls of the pit were making her feel claustrophobic.

Eventually, the handles appeared and she breathed a sigh of relief. She grabbed them and made her way from the ladder onto the ledge. Behind her the rope rocked again; she waited for Adelaide. When she arrived, she handed Tallulah the torch and the two girls followed the sound of Mai's voice.

The tunnel in front of them was low-ceilinged – they had to duck their heads for perhaps twenty metres. At the other end they were forced to stop: there was a one-metre drop directly ahead. Both girls carefully moved out onto what was essentially the top level of an amphitheatre. Mai was down on the stage, lit by natural skylights in the rocks above.

'Isn't it gorgeous?' Mai said. She'd raised her voice for them to hear but there was no need. The acoustics were perfect.

'It's like a cathedral,' Adelaide said.

Tallulah nodded. Goosebumps rolled across her skin in waves. The floor of the room was roughly the same size as the warehouse theatre they'd used in Seacliff but it was the high ceiling, with its series of eroded patterns, that gave the space the look of a grand church. The natural forms of the space were complemented by arches, some carved and some decorated with colourful mosaics. The floor was patterned with inlaid stone. Around the walls were many murals that told the story of the Cirkulatti through time – a woman on stilts, flanked by her troupe, among the pyramids of Egypt, the ziggurats and hanging gardens of Mesopotamia, the columns of Ancient Greece, and the chariot races of Ancient Rome.

The Cirkulatti were also there, in armies being led to war, in a crowd of onlookers around a girl at a fiery stake, and in ornate palaces as courtiers to a renaissance queen.

'This is it,' Tallulah whispered, walking towards a mural where a woman on stilts was in the centre of a long stadium with winged horses guarding the stands; armed men were fighting one another and trying to defend themselves from the storm of sand being whipped up by the eminence. She put her hand out to touch the mural and as she did, images began to flicker through her mind. Antonina adjusting Theodora's stilts; the galloping horses and the howls of the dog-men; the lone dog-man barrelling towards the eminence and the world stopping as Antonina held the dog-man in space long enough to send a disc spinning into his skull; and the deciding blow – the eminence gathering the sands of the stadium and bringing the rioters to their knees.

CHAPTER TWENTY-TWO

When Tallulah came back from the vision she was on the floor of the stone cathedral looking into the worried eyes of her friends.

'They'll come for you too, Della,' Tallulah whispered urgently, 'if they find out about you.'

Mai and Adelaide exchanged a glance. 'Are you all right, Lu?' asked Mai.

She nodded and sat up. 'It was the first vision in full – from the morning I woke up with the cuff on my arm. It's come back in dribs and drabs but when I touched that mural it all came back. Did you see it?'

Both nodded.

'That vision means the others make sense. The last one – from the day we ran from Mr Morton's shop – was Antonina, Theodora's guide, deciding not to leave the cuff with the Council. Tradition dictated the guide holds the Curios for the next eminence but the emperor wanted Theodora buried with the cuff, and Dora had stolen the rest.'

'Wait, wait, wait,' Adelaide said. 'I remember every second of that day. I wrenched the cuff away from you. That's how it ended. You don't know what happened to Antonina after that.'

'It doesn't matter what happened next,' Mai exclaimed. 'Tradition says the guide holds the Curios for the next eminence, right? Irena was your guide and she gave you the cuff. Isn't that confirmation that you're it?'

Tallulah hadn't even considered that. It was a relief not to think of Irena as a possible thief – even if she wasn't ready to accept the other half of that equation. She looked around the room again. 'Hey.' She stood up and walked to the furthest end of the room, opposite the semi-circular grandstand. 'The murals on the wall show the room that the Council met in in my visions. And this …' Tallulah pointed to a series of paintings that began with a group of girls in front of a group of men dressed in the same dark clothes, each with an intaglio-like symbol on his jacket. 'It's the ritual to find the eminence,' Tallulah said. 'I'm sure of it. Look, the girls become fewer and fewer as these men, they must be the Council, test their minds. That's what these clouds above the girls must be,' she pointed to the paintings, 'various mental attacks. Until gradually, one girl is strong enough to push back against them and then they are on their knees, bowing their heads to her. And here,' Tallulah pointed to the final frame, where the girl was in flowing robes and wearing the headdress, cuff and ring, as well as many other adornments, 'she's dressed and the goddess Hecate and the previous eminences are present for her. This girl is the rightful heir.'

She looked to Mai and Adelaide, then back at the mural and remembered the moment just before Theodora died, when Hecate and the previous eminences pleaded with her to call for her Cirkulatti to protect her as she pleaded for assistance from them for Dora.

'Check out the jewellery,' Adelaide said. 'If they're all Curios, there are a lot of them.'

'Should an eminence need that much help from a bunch of jewellery?' Mai asked.

They sat silently, taking in the picture and the room. It seemed to Tallulah that everywhere she looked, she found something she hadn't noticed before. The room was beautiful but there was something incredibly sad about it too. The strength of the woman and her Cirkulatti was there. But so was the undeniable potential for darker forces to bring her down.

Mai broke the silence. 'Can you hear someone crying?'

Tallulah and Adelaide looked from the mural of the eminence and tipped their heads, as if it would help them hear further. There was a faint sobbing noise.

Mai got up.

'It could be a trap,' Adelaide reminded her.

She immediately crouched down. After a moment more she said, 'Should we go look?'

'I suppose. But I'm not sure the tunnel we came from will take us in the right direction,' Tallulah said.

'But the door will,' Mai said. She pointed at the mural of the eminence's trial. 'Among the vines.'

Tallulah had not even noticed the border of painted vines around the mural, let alone the door hidden among them. But there it was.

'Is it real?' Adelaide stood and moved towards it, caution in each step.

The door had no handle but a strong push against its substantial weight saw it give way. It opened onto a short tunnel that had an arched opening through which late afternoon sunlight shone. As the girls walked through, the tunnel curved slightly and revealed a woman sitting on a flat boulder, rugged up against the cold, punching numbers vigorously into a mobile phone. She waited for a moment, shoulders squeezed around her ears, then she groaned, shook her head and pressed the face of the phone one more time. Balancing the mobile on her knees, she took tissues from her jacket pocket and used them to mop tears from her eyes, as well as blow her nose.

'Marie,' Mai called.

Marie started and the phone toppled from her knees onto the rock she was sitting on. Marie lunged quickly and retrieved the phone before it had bounced further away on the rocks.

'What are you doing here?' asked Mai.

'Are you all right?' Tallulah asked. She'd had a fleeting thought that they should not interrupt the director.

'All right?' Marie seemed confounded. 'Sure.' She wasn't much of a liar. After a few moments she shrugged. 'Relationship dramas,' she said shyly. 'I've been away for a while and now – with our people being kidnapped – it could be longer. I just wanted to speak to …' She sighed. 'There's no coverage in the complex. I used to come down here when I was little and watch the boats on the river and I thought I might get a signal but … no luck. But you girls – why are you not resting as I instructed? And how did you get here?'

'Too many questions in my head to sleep,' Tallulah admitted. She spoke so forcefully that it sounded, even to her ears, like an accusation.

Marie nodded apologetically. 'I understand and I'm sorry. What must you think of me? I've been going over and over again in my mind how it has happened. If I'm responsible.'

'I didn't mean that it's your fault,' Tallulah said as Marie wiped tears from her eyes.

'How could you be responsible?' Mai spoke with such tender reassurance that it again brought tears.

'Thank you, Mai. But someone must be. The Elbe hideout has always been our most secure. It has to have come from one of us, not necessarily deliberately, but perhaps by making a simple mistake, an indiscretion.' She looked at the rocks at her feet. 'What will Brigitta say, and Irena when she arrives?'

The girls exchanged embarrassed glances. Tears for the missing children, for the broken relationship, were flowing freely. Marie sat down again, brought her knees to her chin and put her head down. Her emotion was so raw that the girls didn't know where to look. Tallulah tilted her head back the way they had come and the others nodded.

In the dungeon, the man stood over the curled-up figure of the girl. 'Is it done?' he asked.

'You tell me.' The woman's voice came from the back corner of the room. She showed him the denuded landscape of the girl's mind.

He closed his eyes. 'Enough.' It took him a moment to shake off the bleak image.

The woman laughed. 'So sensitive, Viktor,' she cooed.

Ignoring her taunt, he strode to a table and picked up two lengths of red ribbons. He walked to where the girl lay on the floor at the centre of the room and dropped them. They landed close to her face, clearly in view if she opened her eyes.

He prodded her with his boot. 'Get up.' When she didn't react he repeated, 'Get up – or we'll start the process all over again.'

Slowly, the girl got up on all fours; she glimpsed the ribbons, fell towards them and hugged them to her.

The man waved to the woman in the corner. 'Again.'

'No, Monsieur,' the girl cried. She was sitting up in an instant, clutching the ribbons to her body. 'Not again. Don't let her into my brain again.'

'Then show me your ribbon tricks,' the man said, his voice pleasant now, 'and I won't let her go near you ever again.'

The girl nodded vigorously, a tremulous smile on her lips, but then her mouth turned down, her eyes rolled back in her head and she let out an anguished cry.

The man pointed to the corner of the room and boomed, 'Enough!'

The girl's wail was stifled.

'Then don't make promises you can't keep,' the woman replied.

'Now,' he said to the girl, voice kind again, 'stand up and show me your ribbon tricks.'

Her attempts to stand were as clumsy as a newborn foal's. When she was finally balanced on her two feet, she hooked one ribbon around her neck, crossed the ends and threw one over each shoulder, as if it were a scarf. But the ends would not stay, slipping from her shoulders to hang limp and lifeless in front of her. She repeated the action again and again but to no avail. She looked at the man and then beyond him to the dark corner. 'What have you done?'

She did not wait for an answer. Abandoning the ribbon at her neck she concentrated on the one in her hand. Letting it hang to the floor, she began to slowly wind her hand as if trying to draw circles on the floor. As she struggled to comprehend what was happening – or what wasn't happening – her movements grew more and more jagged, her expression more and more desperate until, eventually, she threw the ribbon down.

'Please,' she moaned, sinking to her knees. 'It's her. She's evil. She's stolen from me. My ribbons are all I've got. What use am I to anyone now?'

'There, there,' he said, softly. 'It's for the best.' He whistled and an enormous man covered in scales came forwards from the shadows. 'You can take her now.'

The girl screamed and pressed herself into the floor, but it was no use. As the snake-man carried her from the room she cried, 'Please, Monsieur, don't let him hurt me.'

'NO!'

Tallulah threw off the hand gripping her shoulder, sat up and used her legs to push herself backwards out of its reach. 'Ow,' she cried as the back of her head hit the wall.

'Lu, it's me.'

A light went on. As her eyes grew accustomed to it, Adelaide appeared in front of her. Another bed-light flicked on and illuminated the room further.

'What's going on?' a sleepy Mai asked.

'Tallulah was having a dream. Did you forget to put your pendant on?'

'Della, by the time we found our way back I could barely keep my eyes open, my jet lag was so bad. All I could think about was bed.'

'Yeah, me too.' For a moment the only sound was the three girls breathing. 'Sorry. You woke me up with your cries. I didn't know where I was.'

'What was the dream?' Mai asked.

Tallulah looked across the room; in the dim light, Mai was nothing more than a pretty face poking out from under a heap of blankets. Next to her, on the bedside table, her red ribbons lay neatly coiled. Tallulah put her head against the wall and closed her eyes; she'd tell them but she couldn't look at them.

'I dreamed of a dungeon where a man they call "Monsieur" stripped Cirkulatti children of their gifts – and an old woman with a lot of secrets was helping him.'

CHAPTER TWENTY-THREE

Tuesday 4 February

Tallulah watched the door as she took her seat on the wooden bleachers. She hoped with all her might that her instinct – the instinct that had told her Irena was missing and not on some secret mission – would be proved wrong. The rest of the Cirque d'Avenir students along with Marie, Jacek, Ursula and her student Lena arrived and took their seats in the stand. Behind them was another group led by a bulky firethrower from the Ukraine called Miriam, who'd arrived that morning with a full complement of ten students completely untouched.

When Brigitta led three men dressed in business suits – Gazer One, Gazer Two and Gazer Three – into the room, and they took their spot on the stage, Tallulah thought she might faint. There was no Irena; there was never going to be Irena in this room, in Elbe.

'Why are we here in this miserable room when the other one is so much more inspiring?' Adelaide whispered.

The bleachers they sat in were at one end of the room and the high stone ceiling was painted to look like a striped circus tent. The murals were of circus performers with slightly bemused expressions watching another performer, in black, who shadowed them. From the vivid colour on the walls and the smell of the room, this was a newly painted space.

It all felt wrong, but Tallulah was too tired and too sad to think right now.

Brigitta rose from her chair on the stage and addressed the students. *Welcome.*

It was such a simple word and yet it held the strain of the last forty-eight hours. What should have been a joyous get-together was now a council of war.

'As you know, or are coming to understand, Cirque d'Avenir has maintained one key Cirkulatti tradition: we seek the counsel of an esteemed group known as the Gazers. At other times only the Elders met the Gazers but in light of recent sad events we thought you would be keen to hear from them directly. So I am not going to stand here and babble on like an old woman.' She gave her audience a wink. 'Please, kind gentlemen, tell us what you know.'

The man seated in the middle, Gazer Two, stood; he looked older than the others by many years. His eyes rested on Tallulah and bored into her, but just as she began to feel self-conscious he moved on. Before addressing them he gave a small bow of his head.

'If you want me to tell you that I thought we would meet under happier circumstances then you will be disappointed.' His voice was low and melodic – his words were delivered in a haunting rhythm. 'We have always spoken with caution about re-forming this group; we understood the risks.

'Having said that, the swiftness of the attacks and the fact they happened here has shocked us. After conferring with Brigitta, we are concerned that perhaps even our minds have been compromised. How else to account for us not foreseeing this turn of events?

'Our students must go home until we can find a new, secure training centre. We cannot afford to risk any more of you. Since the attacks on our numbers we have had to concede that we should have taken more interest in significant, if random, disappearances of gypsy children across Europe. So we must protect you now by scattering you as you were before this all began. Then the adults will search for our children.'

The uproar in the room was considerable for the small number of people it held. Brigitta was on her feet before Gazer Two had sat down.

'With all due respect, Gazer Two, may I ask you to consider a very important aspect in all this? The training process has begun. Once powers have been given room for expression they cannot be buried. You, of all people, know this – but I wonder if you forget what it was like to be young. These students are in an advanced state of training.

'Our enemies have been exposed. Is it not time to confront them? These are exceptional students. What better way to forge a bond among the next generation than to have them rescue one another? This is an opportunity like no other.'

Jacek stood. 'I beg your pardon, Madame Brigitta, but while they may have had their gifts revealed or even simply taken to another level, through these initial weeks of training, they are not sufficiently competent to face what lies ahead. We will be committing them to dangers they should not be facing. We will take care of this but the youngsters should not be part of it.'

Brigitta regarded his words – and the Gazers' nods of agreement – with disdain. 'Jacek, I wonder how you would have reacted at fifteen or seventeen to being told you were *not sufficiently competent*. Your minds have truly been tampered with if you cannot foresee the actions that proud young teenagers will embark on in response to such pronouncements.'

The Gazers spoke common sense; Tallulah recognised that. Still, she could not let them decide her fate. She didn't know whether she was under the influence of her visions or of the murals in the Council chamber, or of everything her missing nanny had taught her, but she stood.

'May I ask a question?' She felt everyone's eyes on her. 'Without any disrespect to our revered Gazers ...' she didn't know if revered was the right word, '... where is the Council? What happened to it?'

The question took the Gazers completely by surprise; they looked to one another, then Gazer One rose and gave Tallulah a condescending smile.

'The Council that guided the ancient troupe known as the Cirkulatti has not survived to the modern era and has no place in Cirque d'Avenir.'

Once, his tone of authority might have silenced her but the contempt that embroidered his words only steeled her. She thought of the cuff and the murals downstairs. 'The Council is recorded in oral and visual histories of the Cirkulatti: you cannot deny that.' She did not take her eyes from his as she spoke but he would not meet her gaze. 'Given recent events, I'd like to move that in order to guarantee Cirque d'Avenir's successful future – since it's entirely possible that we will find ourselves in a situation like this again – we *create* a Council.

'We need one. I mean, big decisions like this could then be shared among so many more – in our group alone are telepaths, a ribbons acrobat, firethrowers, a juggler and a combat acrobat.

The others will have more skills among them. I'm sure the strongmen, the clowns and the magicians would support such a move. It would be much harder for our enemies to tamper with so many minds – if that is what you really believe happened.'

Around her the twenty students clapped and cheered; the noisy enthusiasm they generated within the stone walls was immense.

'We do not feel it is a burden.' Gazer One's voice was shrill in its disapproval of the row Tallulah had created. 'We have done this for centuries.'

'How many centuries? When did you take over from the Council and why? Some of us are yet to hear the story of Cirque d'Avenir and its links to the Cirkulatti and the eminence; you are making a decision for us that we disagree with. We would like to know on what authority.'

'Tallulah!' Marie was indignant as she jumped up from where she sat in the front row.

'It's all right, Marie,' Gazer One said.

Gazers Two and Three rose to stand alongside Gazer One; they were collectively outraged. Tallulah's heart threatened to explode, it was beating so hard. But she remained standing in the face of their obvious disapproval. Before they could answer, a voice from behind Tallulah did.

'The Council was disbanded when comtesse Du Barry was beheaded.'

Tallulah turned to look at Sasha.

'The comtesse was an eminence and under her, Gazers became part of the Cirkulatti, protected by her lover, Louis XV. The Gazers predicted her death but she wouldn't hear of it; she had the love of the king. But when Louis XV died she lost his protection and the Cirkulatti fled. She refused to go; refused to see how her world had changed forever. I always understood that comtesse Du Barry ignored the advice of both Council *and* the Gazers – she was grieving and paid dearly for being the mistress of the former king. And she was very much in love with her trinkets. But when she died the Council bore the blame and the Gazers, having predicted it, exploited the tragedy.'

'We exploited nothing,' Gazer One protested hotly.

Sasha ignored him. 'In such a climate it was easy for the Gazers to replace the Council. And, as no woman could pass the Gazers' tests and become eminence, their influence remained dominant. Their sure advice, their predictions, were a tonic that was needed for a long time.'

'How can I trust you are speaking the truth, Sasha?' Tallulah asked.

'Yes, how can she?' Gazer One asked.

'It is a history that many families can vouch for. The fact is allegiances have shifted among the Cirk family for centuries – this is just the most recent grouping. Some relationships shifted because it is not always easy to tell good from evil. Some members of the Cirkulatti were ostracised because they didn't agree with the Gazers – not because they were Cirknero. Not everything is black and white. Not everything is easily predicted.' Sasha looked from the stage back to Tallulah – he wanted her to believe his family were not the traitors she imagined. 'You don't have to trust me, Tallulah; you just have to trust your instinct.'

'Well, my instinct,' Maric said as she stood and stepped onto the stage, 'is to follow the Gazers' advice. I am guilty of the crime Gazer Two referred to – I was too optimistic.'

Tallulah sat and Mai squeezed her hand. 'Everyone was with you. You must have felt it.'

She nodded.

Marie continued. 'I am finally ready to err on the side of caution. We have lost members of our party to kidnappers; we were expecting Irena Blatiskova and she is not here. I have mostly minors travelling with me and I have responsibility for them. I will not take any more chances and neither will the Gazers. I will not have children exposed before they are properly trained. I have already acted; the Seacliff team is on a flight back home tomorrow.'

CHAPTER TWENTY-FOUR

Tallulah, Adelaide and Mai were in their room discussing the disappointing meeting, when there was a light tap on the door. 'Come in,' they said together.

Brigitta shuffled in. Tallulah jumped up to help her and Mai found her a chair.

'You look tired,' Adelaide said.

The woman's laughter tinkled. 'Thank you, dear – makes me feel much better.' She patted Adelaide's hand, then sighed as the girls sat back down on their beds. 'All these years preparing. The tension, the fighting, the mistakes that we made and then recovered from. The hope. Only to fold at the moment there is a hiccup. You asked good questions, Tallulah. You mustn't be too disappointed at the lack of confidence shown in there.'

'Is that what it was?' Tallulah asked. 'I thought it was just grown-ups taking the sensible path.'

Brigitta's eyebrows arched as she considered Tallulah's words. 'Yes, I suppose you could interpret it that way.' Her lips pursed together. 'I hope you don't think then that I was not sensible – that I was trying to throw you on the path to danger?'

'Not at all! I liked what you said.'

'Good.' Brigitta nodded. 'Because I believe that you are powerful young women. Three old men, and a woman who's acting far too worn for her age, made a decision on your behalf that I find perplexing. I don't know what is wrong with Marie.'

'She's scared. She feels responsible,' Tallulah said. 'I think it's crushing her.'

'And there's a guy – a relationship problem,' Mai said. 'We found her yesterday in tears. I think she just wants to get home for that.'

'A relationship? With whom?' Brigitta said softly.

The girls shrugged. 'We don't know. But she was very low this afternoon.'

Brigitta considered this information. 'That might account for why she didn't fight harder for you.' She tutted. 'I didn't think we should ignore your instincts – you were the only one thinking, Tallulah, and now they're sending you home.' She cast her gaze to the floor and sighed. 'An outrage. I'm sure I wouldn't be accepting it all so easily.'

'We're not accepting it easily, at all,' Mai said haughtily. 'Just trying to absorb it right now.'

There was a knock on the door and it opened slightly. Tom's voice whispered urgently through the crack, 'Can I come in?'

'Of course,' Brigitta said.

He stuck his head around the corner. 'I didn't expect to see you here, Brigitta.'

'And I did not expect to see you; but I'm glad that you are here. The presence of a handsome man means there's adventure in the air.' She looked at the girls and grinned wickedly. 'And I think I should leave, lest I overhear something I should not.'

She stood and shuffled out the door.

'Do you think she was just trying to tell us we should not take notice of the Gazers and Marie?' Adelaide asked.

Tallulah scoffed. 'She was just being her cheeky old self.'

'I think she was telling us exactly that,' said Mai. 'I think she was saying that if it were her, she'd be looking for the missing students, no matter what anyone said.'

Tallulah appealed to Tom. 'We're all slowly going mad in here. Are you OK?'

'No. I'm furious. I'm not a kid and I hate being told that I have to pack up and go home.'

'Me too,' said Adelaide. Tom's words had given her license to voice her own complaints. 'I finally got out of Seacliff all the way to Europe. My parents aren't expecting me back for two weeks.' She straightened. 'I'm not going back tomorrow. I'll say I want to stay and be a tourist.'

'My grandmother's stories about defecting from China and the dangers they went through are usually finished with "young people these days would never survive". I'd never hear the end of it if I went home now.'

Tallulah could feel all eyes on her. 'What?'

'Do you want to go back to Seacliff?' Adelaide asked.

'Well, that's … I …' she stammered. 'That's what we've been told to do.'

'Oh, Tallulah!' Mai was exasperated. 'What do you *want* to do? What is your gut telling you?'

'I don't see the sense of stealing out into the freezing night, in the middle of nowhere in a country none of us knows – where we don't even speak the language. We aren't trained. I wouldn't know where to start.'

'Rubbish. You knew where to start when the guy attacked you at Mr Morton's. You knew what to do at the door downstairs. Your instincts are good, Tallulah. Start with Irena.'

'We don't even know where she is. Europe is a big place.'

'What about the postcards?' Tom said. 'You told me she sent you one of every town she visited.'

'How can they help? There's not a famous landmark among them. You'd think she didn't go any further than her room because they're all pictures of—' Tallulah stopped. 'They're pictures of the pensiones she stayed in.' She crossed the floor to her suitcase and took the postcards from it. She laid them on the bedspread in chronological order.

As the others crowded around her to get a better look there was another knock on the door. Tallulah pushed the cards back into a pile and sat on them. Everyone crowded on the bed around her, trying to look casual.

'Who is it?' Mai said.

'Me,' said Hui's voice. 'Is Tom still with you?'

'Yeah,' Tom called to the door. To the girls he whispered, 'We've already talked. He's in.'

There was a collective exhalation of breath as Hui opened the door. Once in, he closed it, leaned on it and laughed softly.

'What?' Mai demanded.

'You guys had better lose the guilty look before dinner – you've got half an hour. Everyone at the big table for a roast. Smells good too.'

Tallulah groaned. 'They're going to watch us like hawks.'

'We need to eat,' Tom told her. 'We couldn't go until later anyway.'

'And we know the alternate way out,' Adelaide reminded her.

Tallulah shook her head. 'You don't think they'll be watching that entrance too?'

'An exit to a frozen river? Not even frozen,' Mai reminded her. 'If it were frozen they'd have to guard it because we'd have a chance at least of getting to the other side.'

'Instead we've got to make it to the footbridge,' Adelaide said. 'There's a ten-metre drop to a frozen bank or a rock climb about one hundred metres from the bridge. I checked it out today while you were chatting to Marie.'

'That town we looked down on when we arrived yesterday?' Hui asked. 'There's a train line running through it.'

'Too easy,' Tom said. 'We can catch the first train in the morning.'

'We could just get the ride to the airport and then not get on the plane. Go through customs then turn around,' Tallulah suggested.

'Then there'd be calls through the airport for missing passengers; airport security would be involved. It's too messy.'

'But how do we know there will be a train in the morning?' Tallulah insisted. 'As if they won't be sitting down there waiting for us.'

'Then we hitch a ride out of town,' Tom said. 'We'll think of something. But at least we've given it a go rather than accepting the Gazers' word.'

Tallulah sighed. She was outnumbered. It suddenly occurred to her that perhaps this was the moment Irena had prepared her for: the choice between her instinct and the direction of a seer. For the first time in forever, Tallulah felt Irena's true presence. She faced the bed and laid the postcards out.

'That's the order Irena wrote them in,' she said. 'Sienna. Ravenna. Barcelona. Madrid. Paris. Bretz.' Tallulah tapped the card from Paris. 'That's where she had lunch, a reunion with a group of Cirkulatti Elders. Marie told me the lunch was organised by a very dear friend of hers.' A thought crossed her mind. 'That's the guy, I reckon.'

'The guy?' Tom asked.

'Marie's having relationship problems. She told us yesterday when we found her down on the river bank, trying to call him,' Adelaide said.

'Marie blushed when she spoke of the dear friend organising the lunch for Irena.'

'Even Brigitta knew something.'

'Girls,' Hui said, checking his watch, 'stay on target. Marie's relationship with the mystery man doesn't have anything to do with our mission.'

'Aren't you the romantic?' Tom teased.

Hui ignored him. 'The last postcard is from this town in Bohemia – Bretz. That's where we start.' He looked up. 'Anyone know where it is?'

It was a subdued group that gathered for dinner. In an attempt to lift the mood the trainers had pooled their considerable culinary talents to produce an astonishing table: a spit-roasted pig, apple sauce, roast vegetables, sauerkraut, and a variety of sweet fruit pies with lashings of cream and ice cream for dessert.

Tallulah did not feel like food but Tom had coached her. She must eat; even if they were able to sleep for the couple of hours they'd decided to wait before they slipped out of Elbe at two in the morning, it would still be a long night. So she piled her plate high but did little more than push the contents around; every bite made her feel like throwing up. Her instincts said yes, but she was scared, she had no trouble admitting that. She remembered her mother's words: they hadn't come this far for Tallulah not to have choice – which is exactly what the Gazers and Marie had taken away. Her mother too would agree with the course of action she was taking.

With that resolved, Tallulah focused on the room again. Marie provided some entertainment at the table, keeping the conversation going through the evening. Having been the one to take the lead and book tickets to send them home, she was now doing her best to reassure them that all this was temporary. There were options, she said enigmatically. The conspirators, in an effort to hide their plans, responded politely, but without too much enthusiasm.

When the group retired to the lounge, Marie perched on the armrest of the single seater Tallulah had chosen.

'We will find her,' she said.

Tallulah looked at the woman; her cheekbones seemed even more pronounced. 'Where will you begin, Marie? When was the last time you heard from her? Can't you at least give me some idea of that?'

'And risk you getting to Seacliff, turning around and coming straight back?' Marie laughed. 'What do you take me for, a fool?'

'Never. But you understand my distress. Could you at least tell me what your friend said about her after they met?'

Marie looked puzzled.

'Your friend who organised the reunion lunch in Paris for Irena and the others. Did he say she seemed happy?'

Marie nodded slowly – an affirmation that Tallulah didn't find convincing. 'It was a beautiful day,' Marie said. 'Irena was happy to see so many old faces and to talk about the old days.'

'She was?'

'Why do you find that strange?'

'Irena wasn't really one for reminiscing.'

'You'll come to realise one day that time gives people fresh perspective.'

'And it's the same man, the host of the lunch, you are having troubles with?'

Marie smoothed down her skirt as she considered the question. 'I'm sorry you saw that.' She glanced at Tallulah. 'A day is a long time in love. All is fine now.'

'He'll wait for you, then?'

Marie laughed. 'Perhaps I realised it wasn't worth asking him to wait; that I'm better off without him.'

'He's Cirkulatti, though. He understands the need for secrecy.'

'What a difference a few weeks make, Tallulah,' Marie snapped. 'You were not so thrilled with Irena's obsession with secrecy when we first met.' She closed her eyes and breathed deeply. When she opened them, she reached out and put her hand on Tallulah's thigh. 'Forgive me. I'm so jumpy. My friend is in the Lenter heirs' closed circle. Like Irena; like my own mother. I could not have done all this without his support. He is worried sick about our students; about Irena. But we have resources at our disposal and we will use them.'

One by one the renegades, with bare essentials stuffed into their backpacks, made their way silently to the kitchen. Jacek had obviously been assigned look-out duty – unless he'd simply fallen asleep on the couch after too much wine and been left there to sleep it off.

When the five of them had gathered in the kitchen, Tom opened the door to the stairwell and they filed through. Since the girls had already been this way and they knew the steps to be even and properly built without any surprises, they decided to conserve the light they had – and Tom's and Hui's energy – for when they would need it. Adelaide kept a torchlight shining to the floor, and that served them all. They had only progressed down two flights when her light darted around and she let out a stifled cry.

Immediately torches were flicked on and they found Sasha holding her in a tight grip against his body, with her head buried into his shoulder.

'Let her go,' Mai said as she rushed at him. Hui grabbed her as she passed; at the same time, Sasha let Adelaide go and held his hands up in surrender. The stairwell echoed with heavy breathing.

'I'm not trying to hurt her,' Sasha said in a hoarse whisper. 'Or anyone else. I thought if I waited long enough I might run into a few of you.'

'How did you know we'd come this way?' Mai demanded. Her eyes went to Adelaide, who had been sitting next to him at dinner.

'I didn't tell him.'

'She didn't. Well, not directly.'

Adelaide spun on him, eyes blazing. 'What do you mean? Tell them the truth. I said nothing to you all night.'

He nodded. 'Which isn't like you; it was like you didn't dare speak. And I have noticed that when you're excited your cheeks … Well they get really pink. It didn't go with the disappointment of being sent home.'

Adelaide glanced at him, at Tallulah and the others, then kept her gaze firmly on the floor.

'I've been waiting for a chance to get the four-wheel drive keys, but Marie has kept them on her at all times.' He spoke quickly now. 'I took a chance that you wouldn't bother leaving via the lift. And I overheard a conversation about the lower entrance and whether to guard it. Marie told Brigitta you girls know about it. They're guarding it.'

Some of the group groaned but Tom shrugged. 'We should take it as a compliment. They think we have a chance.'

'Look,' Sasha said, 'I would like to come with you. My guess is that you're looking for Irena. I know Saskia is not anyone's favourite, but she's my sister, and if you find Irena there's a good chance she will be somewhere close by. I just want to get her home. I tried to tell her. I tried to tell you.' Sasha gestured to Tallulah as he spoke. 'I'm only here because I thought I could protect her – and I didn't do much of a job at that. I can't go back to Mum and Dad without her.'

'But you could go with Marie and the trainers, couldn't you?' Tallulah asked. 'They said you couldn't take us on the search. And they know more than us.'

'They're waiting another couple of days – they've called Stellan—'

'About time,' Hui said.

'—and he is bringing a contingent. There are two towns they are considering. One is called Bretz; that's where the most reports of missing gypsy children have been. I've looked it up on the map and it's not far from here.'

The renegades exchanged looks.

'What have I said?' he asked.

Tom looked at Tallulah, who nodded. 'We're heading to Bretz too,' he told Sasha.

Even in the dim torchlight they could see shock followed by respect move across his face. 'How did you—'

'You can come with us, but don't ask us to give up all our secrets,' Tallulah warned. She was still strained by the way he had treated her – the ugly accusations he had thrown around in public; the criticisms and the bullying – but she felt his bereft state was genuine. A quick look around the group told her they approved of the deal she'd struck.

'Got it.'

'Good,' Tom said. 'And we'll help you get Saskia back.'

Tallulah took a breath. 'Sasha, you follow Tom, Adelaide next, and everyone in the same order after that.'

CHAPTER TWENTY-FIVE

The moon wasn't full but it was round enough to lend considerable light to their expedition. The arrived at the ledge where the girls had found Marie; having gone via the weapons room they were sufficiently stocked with practical equipment by the time they got there.

'Whoever's on guard duty will be on the bridge,' Sasha told them. Ten metres below was the icy edge of the river, and about the same distance along that to their right began a narrow bank of pebbles and rock that ran under the footbridge. Once on the bank they would have little difficulty getting across it or climbing the few metres from the bank to the bridge – unless they were spotted.

'And I don't reckon they'll be asleep,' Adelaide said as she zipped her jacket high up under her chin and clenched her chattering teeth.

'They could know we've left by now and be waiting for us when we get there,' Tom suggested.

'Who'd have thought the first person we might be using our skills on would be one of our own?' Adelaide said.

'I'm definitely the one to go,' Mai said, as she surveyed the drop to the ice. 'I'm the smallest and the lightest.'

They all agreed. It was a simple operation with a rope. Mai had one end, and was to drop from the ledge with Sasha, Hui and Tom taking the load from the top.

'Do not put any weight on your feet until you are absolutely sure the ice will hold,' Sasha told her as she looped the rope around her hips. 'You can't risk getting even a toe wet when it's this cold and dry clothes are so limited.'

With everyone ready, Mai disappeared over the ledge. Tallulah and Adelaide leaned over to watch her descent. Mai was on the ice and gave the thumbs-up in no time. But the boys, not as trusting, kept the rope tight, ready to pull her up should the ice let her down. Mai inched her way across the ice, following the natural arc of the rock.

'She's there,' Adelaide finally said. And they all breathed a sigh as Mai untied the rope and took a few more steps onto the pebble beach. She bent forwards from her hips and rested her hands on her knees for a moment, then she turned and gave the thumbs-up sign with both hands. Almost immediately she turned away and held the palm of her hand up, indicating they should wait as she walked towards the rock face in front of her. When she disappeared into the rock, Hui, who was on his knees beside Tallulah, swore softly. 'Does she ever think first?' he muttered.

A few moments later there was a soft knock a little way down the wall beside them.

Hui was up instantly; he walked along the wall, his hand pressed against it, until they couldn't see him. Seconds later, he laughed. 'There's a door,' he whispered back to them. Sasha shone a torch into the blackness in time to see Hui turn a key. It clicked twice before the door opened – and out sprang Mai.

'Or we could take the steps,' she whispered with a flourish.

'How did we miss that?' Adelaide asked as she jumped up and walked to the door.

'It's the colour of the wall, Dell,' Tallulah said. 'Easy to miss with everything else we were discovering yesterday.'

Tom hustled them through the door and closed it behind them.

On the river bank, they bent over and stayed low, moving as smoothly as possible across the river bank. They got to the bridge without incident and took cover under its shadow.

Tom indicated for them to stay put while he scouted the bridge. Waiting for him to come back, Tallulah couldn't help a grin splitting her face. There might be danger but right now, crouching by a moonlit river as they embarked on an adventure, she was having fun.

'This is cool,' Adelaide murmured, as if reading Tallulah's thoughts.

They exchanged a silent low-five with gloved hands.

Moments later Tom was back. He whispered to Tallulah, 'Brigitta and Ursula.'

She was about to tell the others when he shook his head. 'Don't speak,' he said in a barely audible whisper.

It took Tallulah a moment to get what he meant. She shook her head and smiled at her own stupidity. Still, communicating in the open without a telepath as practised as Brigitta hearing her seemed daunting. She hoped they'd all protected their minds; she inhaled deeply and concentrated on her purple conduit, splitting it into five separate branches. But just to be certain, she conjured the image of soundproof glass and wrapped the conduit and her own thought in it, then connected with each of her friends' minds.

Brigitta and Ursula are on the bridge.

There could not have been more of a contrast between Sasha's disappointment and Mai's and Adelaide's relief.

Tallulah communicated to Sasha the conversation they had had earlier with Brigitta, and Tom's impression that Brigitta was challenging them to be daring. Sasha was incredulous. He shook his head; fury and frustration were written all over his face.

His emotion was so obvious that Tallulah's immediate thought was that it made him – and therefore them – vulnerable to a mindreader like Brigitta or whoever else might be around. She placed a hand on his shoulder and he looked at her.

Lock your mind. She looked at them all. *Everyone. We can't take chances.*

But it was as if Sasha didn't hear her. 'She was in Saskia's ear in Seacliff too,' he whispered hoarsely. It was only the sound of other voices moving towards them – or at least from the national park towards the river – that stopped Tallulah from putting her hand over Sasha's mouth. 'She's determined to be mischievous,' he continued. 'I think she wants to live again vicariously through you girls. And look where that's got us so far.'

It's going to get us across the bridge, hopefully.

The team moved further under the bridge as the voices – male – got louder. They weren't speaking English but Tallulah decided that the sound of a drunken conversation was universal. It brought the silent river bank to life: small unseen creatures scurried around the rocks as the disturbance to the quiet night came closer. Tom went to investigate again.

While she was waiting, Tallulah crawled further under the wooden planks that were the only thing that would separate Brigitta's and Ursula's feet from her head. The floor of the bridge was the only part made from wood – the rest, handrails as well as the support structure, was metal. Along each side of the bridge, below foot level and running the full length, was a decorative metal trellis. Tallulah could easily reach the trellis from the bank under the bridge, as it almost reached down to the surface of the water. She put her hand up to it and tested the slats between the lattice – there was enough there for her fingers to grasp. She crouched on the stone in front of the trellis, hooked her fingers into the holes at the top and put her feet onto the small ledge at the bottom – it was wide enough for her toes and the balls of her feet. As she hung in her crouched position she wondered if it was a position she could sustain for fifty metres as she crossed a freezing river. There was a good chance that the metal supports would be damp, possibly icy, all the way. To answer her own question she began to move. It wasn't until she'd made her way across the first section, slipped around the metal supports that split the trellis every ten metres and was halfway along the next section that she heard a whisper: 'What are you doing?'

What does it look like? I'm crossing a river.

'Lu, wait for us.'

Adelaide's whisper might have been loud enough to give them away – but for the noisy boys who were now on the bridge. Tallulah was conscious of the others crawling underneath it to hide themselves and check out her trellis. Her muscles were already beginning to feel the effects – but hadn't this been exactly what they'd trained for?

The trick is to move or we'll get stuck.

It wasn't long before Tallulah began to wonder about the wisdom of her actions. The crossing became a game of how long she could travel towards the town before she had to stop and stretch something. Arms and shoulders hurt first; cramps in her feet and instep became relentless. At one point she could barely resist the urge to cry out as a cramp gripped her calf. She stopped and held her breath. But the party boys were still blundering about above. Tallulah continued. A wooden board creaked over the top of her and she stopped. She heard Ursula ask if it was time to go home. 'The police will be here in no time,' her thickly accented voice said. 'It's one of the problems here – young people with nothing better to do than get drunk and cause havoc.'

'We won't panic yet,' Brigitta said. 'their minds are easy to manipulate. If we hear sirens we'll send them back that way. No one is crossing this bridge tonight if I don't want them to.'

Tallulah swallowed – or tried to. Her mouth was dry. Her body was tiring but they were past the halfway point. Tom, Adelaide and Sasha, who were using the trellis on the other side of the bridge, had caught up to her. Mai and Hui on Tallulah's side were closing the gap. Tallulah switched to using her mental abilities to move her body as Marie had taught her. She could feel heat in her hands that had not been there before; the stickiness as she peeled her fingers from the trellis made her realise she was bleeding – numb from the cold, she had not realised her gloves had shredded and her Seacliff blisters had broken. Icy fingers of air, rising up from the cold river, slipped between her shirt and skin. It wasn't long before her garments, damp from the exertion, froze and were like sheets of ice on her back. She could feel her teeth begin to chatter.

'Just two more sections,' she heard Sasha whisper.

But a moment later there was a splash and a frustrated mental cry. Tallulah looked over her shoulder; Adelaide had slipped and was in the water up to her knees. She was still holding onto the trellis as Tom and Sasha crawled beside her;

each boy put a hand under Adelaide's bottom so she was sitting on a makeshift seat.

'One, two, three,' Sasha counted, and together they hauled Adelaide up, high enough for her to lift her legs, heavier now from fatigue and soaking wet clothes, and put her feet back on the ledge. Tom and Sasha linked an arm each under her backpack, gripping one another's wrists, they huddled on the trellis, sucking in large breaths.

'What have you got in here, Della?' Tallulah heard Sasha ask. 'I could have carried that.' Adelaide didn't answer; Tallulah conjured an image of warmth and soothing hands massaging sore muscles and shared it with everyone until she felt something wrap around her own waist and looked down to see one of Mai's ribbons around her. She looked at her friend in the dark.

'It's just a precaution. I don't want you going in because you're using your energy on us. She's OK.' Mai nodded towards the river bank.

Tallulah looked over and saw Adelaide nearly at the river bank. She felt tears spill down her cheeks. 'I can't move.'

'Yes, you can. One hand at a time.'

Tom had reached land quickly enough to crawl across the bank and make his way to Tallulah.

'Is she all right?' she asked.

'No damage. Sasha's finding a place for her to change now.' He put a hand on Tallulah's back, between her back and backpack; the heat was delicious.

'I'm sorry,' she said, emotion breaking her voice, 'this was stupid idea.'

'There was no other way. We're nearly there. Don't give up now, Lu. Can you smell the bread that's baking somewhere in town?'

'I can,' Hui whispered. 'It's driving me crazy. I can taste the pain au chocolat already!'

'Me too.' The more she concentrated, the more the smell of fresh bread rose above the briny smell of the river and the cold.

'All right. So that's where we're heading. To the bakery. On my count,' Tom whispered. 'Left hand, right hand. Left foot, right foot. Easy as. OK?'

Tallulah nodded. It took three rounds of Tom's call before she could make her left hand move; but once she'd imprinted the sequence it didn't take long for them all to be on the town side of the river. Before anyone could sit, Sasha had shepherded them up the bank, across the road, between some parked trucks and into a grove of trees on the edge of a small clearing. They found Adelaide resting against the trunk of a tree, her arms and legs splayed from her body as if she had no control over them. She opened her eyes as Tallulah and the others arrived.

'Can't wait to do that again.'

CHAPTER TWENTY-SIX

Wednesday 5 February

The sun's rays eventually overcame the rocking rhythm of the train to drag Tallulah out of her sleep. Or perhaps it was the muscle that stretched down the side of her neck, strained by the strange position of her head as she slept, that screamed loud enough to wake her up.

'Hecate's torches,' she muttered. She turned from the window to see her travelling companions in slumped positions, each sleeping on some part of another. Grabbing her backpack, she pulled out her phone. She immediately breathed easier: 9.10 am. There were still thirty minutes before they reached their destination. The first train out of Elbe had been at 5.40 am, and although it was not heading for their destination, a couple of hours in a warm carriage before changing trains for Bretz was a good swap for sitting huddled in the cold among a few trees waiting for dawn to come. They had bought steaming hot coffee and hot chocolate – and Band-Aids – from a small petrol station on the edge of the village. When the bakery opened they'd eaten their fill of croissants and pain au chocolat, and stocked up on bread sticks and rolls for later in the day.

'Guys,' Tallulah said as the train rocked towards the interchange station, 'we're nearly there.'

It took them the next twenty minutes to wake up and get ready. They pulled on beanies and scarfs as the train pulled into the station, as much for anonymity as for protection against the cold.

'Do you think you could be any brighter?' Adelaide asked, gazing up and down at Tallulah's purple, belted ski jacket.

'I didn't think I'd be trying to be incognito when I packed it. And it's a bit more discreet than the other side.' She turned the inside of her sleeve to reveal a floral lining.

'The purple isn't bright – it's regal,' Mai said. 'You look like someone we should be looking at.' She nudged Adelaide. 'Even before she knew, she was buying the right colour.'

'The alabaster skin and cascading black locks might have something to do with it,' Adelaide said dramatically.

Tallulah pulled her beanie down on her head and tucked her long dark plait under it. 'I'll be buying a basic black jacket at the next town and be sure to tie you both up in this one when I do – wrapped especially tight around your mouths.'

'You'd be lost without the delightful sound of our musical voices,' Adelaide said, smiling.

As they got off the train and made their way through the commuters they kept their eyes and ears peeled for any sign of Marie, the other trainers or the Gazers – not to mention snake-men. Without any trouble they found the next platform and boarded their connection.

'Eighty minutes,' Tom said as they boarded. 'It's an express to Prague and local stops after that.'

The train had more of an urban commuter set-up than the one they'd just been on, which had catered for longer-distance travellers. Since it wasn't full, Tallulah and the others followed the lead of other young tourists and found a carriage where they could spread out, stretching out across four seats, rather than leaning on top of one another. This time Sasha set an alarm to wake them before Bretz. Almost immediately, Adelaide, Mai and Hui were asleep. Sasha had settled with a book but he seemed to be struggling to stay awake as he read it.

Tom was in the row behind Tallulah. Eventually he said, 'Can't sleep?'

Tallulah shook her head. 'Tummy ache.'

'Maybe I can distract you.'

She looked back at him with raised eyebrows.

'I mean by talking.'

She smiled. 'I didn't think you meant anything else.'

'Well, in fact, that would be a mistake.' He sat beside her.

She blushed. His presence was warm and reassuring. All she really wanted to do was put her head against the curve of his shoulder – which she knew so well from watching him train. But she resisted the urge. No point confusing things right now.

'Was this a really dumb idea?'

He laughed. 'Probably. I don't know. Is it dumb to follow a dream?'

'What do you mean?'

'I've always dreamed of following a stilt-walker with flowing robes.'

'You have not,' she said.

'I thought it was because I'd heard stories about the Cirkulatti and the eminence since I was a kid and it was natural they'd bubble up from my subconscious somehow. But now I'm not so sure.'

'I've never been on stilts and I don't own a robe.'

He raised his eyebrows. 'It must be me then – always following the wrong girl.'

Tallulah sighed. 'Who's probably leading you into danger.'

'Which we'll get ourselves out of. No, we find Irena first and then we get ourselves out.' He turned in the chair and took her hands. 'I've talked to Elen about this, Lu. She says Irena is powerful in her own right – which is why she's your guide. If she's been caught and you haven't heard from her then there is a good chance she has protected herself, and you, from their telepaths by shutting down somehow – maybe going deep into her mind.'

'Yes, I've been wondering about that since Brigitta began working with us.'

'Elen is worried that Irena's not as young as she was, obviously, and might have sacrificed herself in order to protect you. We might never be able to get her to come back to us.'

'But surely Brigitta will be able to help us with that. We can't leave Irena with the Cirknero.'

'We won't, but I wanted to warn you of what might be ahead.'

'If I can just see her.' Tallulah could feel tears building and she fought to stay in control. 'She'll know what to do about your fire, about the Council, about everything, Tom. She's the wisest person I know.'

For the first time since they'd got to Europe she let herself be overwhelmed by her fear for Irena. Tom lifted his arm and offered a safe haven that she could not refuse. She slipped under his arm, rested her head on his chest and felt the strength of his comforting embrace as it closed around her.

They stayed like that for the next hour; they might have slept, Tallulah couldn't be sure. She'd breathed in the steady beat of his heart until it felt like it was her own.

The alarm that had been set before Bretz was unnecessary. The train filled up in Prague and as more and more people poured into the carriage, Tom sighed and raised his arm. Tallulah slid across and he did the same – in time for Adelaide to arrive at the end of their row and slide in next to him. Mai followed. Tom and Tallulah waited for one of them to speak but they were too busy trying to wake up.

Tom chuckled, then turned his gaze on Tallulah.

What? She could feel the heat in her cheeks.

Nothing. He shrugged. *Everything.*

He turned, as if to check on Mai and Adelaide, then swiftly turned back and kissed her quickly on the lips. Almost as fast he pulled away.

'Sorry.'

Tallulah's heart thumped in her chest. 'Why?'

'I don't know. I'm not really.'

They both laughed.

'Good,' she said. 'I'm not either.'

His shoulders relaxed and he leaned back in the chair, his shoulder resting against Tallulah's. 'We will find Irena, I promise you that.'

'Someone's renovating,' Tallulah said, pointing to the small medieval castle, half covered in scaffolding, on the other side of the river. As they walked down the ramp from the train station, the town of Bretz spread before them – a higgledy-piggledy assortment of coloured buildings and cobblestone streets that followed the gentle rise and fall of the terrain.

'*Built in 1474 by the local landowner as a vantage point from which to keep watch over his workers, Bretz Castle changed hands many times,*' Adelaide read from her guide book of Europe.

'*Seized during the war by the Nazis it was eventually reinstated to the owner ...* blah blah de blah ... *A paper mill was the heart of the town for a century, keeping the local population in employment ...*'

'A paper mill,' Tallulah asked, wondering why it sounded familiar.

'Guys, we need to keep all eyes up,' Hui warned. 'They'll know we're missing from Elbe now. It's possible they've sent someone to look for us – especially since they discussed Bretz with Sasha. We came the long way around, remember.'

'I'll need to check the map to see how we get to the pensione,' Adelaide told him.

'And a coffee would be good,' Tom said, yawning.

Twenty minutes later, a middle-aged waitress arrived at their booth with a tray laden with warm beverages. As she put Tom's coffee on the table she spoke to them in English. 'So you like our market day?'

Tallulah leaned to her left as the woman put her tea in front of her. 'Oh, we just got off the train and thought we'd warm up first.' She gestured to the almost full restaurant. 'But it seems popular; good for your business.'

The woman nodded. 'The Monsieur has been good to the town.'

'The Monsieur?' Tallulah glanced at Adelaide, who looked up from her map at the same time.

'He bought the castle,' she hesitated, 'maybe a year ago. He is a gypsy – and now that he is a wealthy gypsy he tries to help the children. He takes the ones that cause the most trouble, and they live in the castle, like a boarding school. No one else will do anything – the government does nothing, someone has to.'

When the waitress had moved to the next table, Tom leaned toward Sasha. 'Do you reckon they're the children the Gazers were talking about?'

'But what's he doing with them?'

Adelaide pushed the map into the middle of the table. 'So I thought it would be better if we avoided the square but I've been looking at the map and I don't think we can.' She pointed to small double lines on two roads leading to the pensione, which she had asterisked in red pen. 'I reckon that means they're dead ends.'

They all leaned towards the map.

'So we go through the square, maybe split up,' Tom said. 'They're looking for six teenagers, not tourists.'

They considered Tom's words as they finished their drinks. Pulling on their beanies, they left the café, heads down.

One hundred metres on, they turned left and hurried down a narrow lane that approached the square. 'Check your boundaries,' Sasha reminded them. 'Keep your minds open to Tallulah, but guarded against anyone else.'

Tallulah took a deep breath in an effort to slow herself down. It was difficult not to run, with the pensione so close – even though she knew she must prepare herself for nothing to be there.

They progressed through the market – browsing over here, letting themselves be entertained over there – and found enough people to mingle among and enough distractions to be properly seduced by. Tallulah's attention was caught by a puppet vendor selling a witch on a broom – which reminded her of Baba Yaga, the children's story Irena used to tell her about the old woman who lured children to her home so she could eat them. Too quickly she was in the dream from two nights ago and a quagmire of questions. Distracted, Tallulah didn't notice a crowd forming around her for a show. By the time she realised, she was trapped.

Quickly, the two jugglers began their show while another, who looked to be a member of the crowd, had been given the job of throwing extra plates to the jugglers when either called. It didn't matter where the onlooker threw the plate, too high, too low, the jugglers caught them – and added it to the rest of the plates in orbit. It was a masterful performance and the audience was mesmerised. Adelaide had materialised at the edge of the crowd, surveyed the onlookers and noticed Tallulah.

Despite Adelaide's disapproving look, Tallulah was relieved to see her. Two gypsy children had jostled their way to the front and now stood in front of Tallulah. They began taunting the jugglers with words and screeching catcalls, which won them no points with the audience, but the children could not have cared less. Angry emotions and ugly hand gestures need no translation – it was pretty obvious that everyone considered the children a nuisance. Tallulah decided no one would notice her leaving in the chaos but as she turned, a lot of things happened at once.

There was a dull thud, the pained scream of a child and the crash of crockery on the hard ground. The crowd's emotion swung from anger to shock. Tallulah looked back, took in the pieces of plate on the ground, saw a child bleeding from the temple and another spinning plate leaving a juggler's hand aimed for the children. Automatically she swung herself around and pushed the children out of the way. The air warped, the plate slowed and it was plucked from the air and thrown back at the juggler. As the shimmer in the air cleared, Tallulah felt a hand grip her wrist and she heard Adelaide echo her own thought: GO!

Pushing through the crowd, Tallulah heard an English-speaking tourist to her left cry, 'Hey, man, watch it.' She looked and saw a tall man shouldering his way towards them; he was wearing a hooded top, but the sunlight caught the scales that covered his face. He did not see the gypsy children charge at his legs and fell him like a giant oak.

'What are you waiting for?' Adelaide grabbed Tallulah's hand; Tallulah could see Adelaide was holding Tom's hand as he led them to the other side of the square, where the others were waiting. Mai gave a relieved wave when she saw them. 'The snake-men are here,' Tallulah told them.

Sasha swore but there was no time for discussion; they had to get to the pensione and then a hiding place.

Within two blocks they knew they were being followed. Their immediate fear that it was another snake-man – or that Marie or Jacek had tracked them down – was allayed when they saw two of the gypsy children darting from one side of the street to the other.

'What do you reckon they're up to?' Adelaide whispered.

Tallulah shook her head. 'I don't know. They didn't like that juggling act.'

'And they helped us get away in the square,' Tom added.

About ten minutes later, Tallulah stopped. 'That's it.'

If anything the pensione was prettier than on the postcard. The building had been given a fresh coat of paint since the picture was taken and the window boxes had flowers even in the middle of winter. When Tallulah opened the door a bell tinkled somewhere inside.

They walked into a small sitting room with deep armchairs piled with plump cushions. A small middle-aged woman came to greet them from a room behind a reception desk as a young girl, maybe ten, who was the image of her mother, came down the stairs. They didn't speak much English but by way of a broken conversation – a smattering of English, Tallulah's school French and Adelaide's guidebook German – Tallulah managed to convey her questions. Tallulah showed the woman and girl the postcard and then a picture on her phone of Irena and her together. Tallulah asked the woman if she remembered Irena staying with them.

The woman looked at the girl, and then at Tallulah and her friends. She shook her head, apologetically, stood and backed away from the desk. 'I cannot. Polizei. Bitte. No.'

'Police?' Tallulah looked at the others, panicked, and back to the woman. 'Did you tell the police Irena disappeared? I don't understand.'

'Mama?' the girl said. And they exchanged a hurried conversation. The woman paused, sighed. She nodded to the girl and held her hand up to ask Tallulah to wait. They both went up the stairs.

Tallulah turned to the others. 'What do you think?'

'I think she was here,' Sasha said.

Minutes later, the girl came down the stairs with an envelope and a picture. She handed the envelope to Tallulah.

The girl nodded. 'This …' She pointed at the envelope, and then held up a picture of Tallulah with Irena. 'For you.'

Tallulah's hands were shaking as she opened the envelope. She pulled out another postcard, this time of the Bretz castle. On the back, in Irena's handwriting, it said: *Dust on the rose leaves is toxic. Don't open the door.*

Adelaide took the card and read it. 'What does it mean?' She handed the card to Mai.

Tallulah sat down on the edge of one of the armchairs. 'It's from her favourite poem.' To say any more was to expose one of the keys to Irena's mental barriers. But Tallulah didn't like the message she was getting from it. 'The poem is about the futility of wanting to go back in time to change things. The message says to me that she's taken a walk down memory lane that she shouldn't have and she's warning me not to. And it must have something to do with Bretz castle.'

The door to the pensione opened, the bell tinkled and one of the gypsy children from the square entered.

'Schnell, schnell,' he cried. He tried to shepherd them out of the pensione. The little girl of the house yelled at the gypsy; walking towards him she waved her hands and cried 'Shoo' like the child was a stray cat. The gypsy backed out but as he went he kept trying, pointing to Tallulah and then out the door. 'Hissss, sssss.' He pointed down the road. 'Schnell!'

Tom hauled Tallulah off the chair. 'Let's go. If he's saying what I think he's saying then I don't like it. And even if he isn't I don't like the word *toxic* whatever the context might be.'

Sasha was holding the door open and Tallulah let Tom guide her through it. The gypsy child's hissing reminded Tallulah of something else: the dream that she had when she finally told her parents that Irena was trying to contact her, of the hissing snake-men, of the girls being tested for the role of the eminence and the competing voices in the dream: one that wanted her to see what was happening and one that didn't. Tallulah had been confused because the communicator had used the key only Irena knew, but someone was fighting the presence of the communicator in Tallulah's mind. The postcard pointed to another key that suggested it was Irena who was present.

'Hecate's torches,' she whispered. She looked at Adelaide and then Tom. 'What if someone's breached Irena's protective barriers? What if the postcard ...'

But her voice was drowned out by a hissing noise. They turned to flee down a side street but the sound seemed to come from that direction too. It echoed and rebounded on the narrow cobbled streets until it filled the space around them completely.

'Wait, guys,' Sasha said. He stood with his hands held out from his body, trying to discern something in his mind above the hissing.

'Sash, come on,' Tom called. 'Let's move.'

'It's Saskia. She's warning me to get away.'

'Bit late,' Adelaide said. She'd already withdrawn her metal juggling plates from her backpack. The others were grabbing their own weapons when Sasha groaned.

His face, which only a second before had looked so hopeful, had now deflated. 'Stupid girl,' he yelled to the sky and his words punctured the hissing as they echoed from one building to another. 'Give me some,' he said furiously to Adelaide as sudden, unprecedented tears streaked his face. Bewildered, she handed him a stack of plates. 'Read my mind,' he told Tallulah. 'I'll get a look at where they're coming from and let you know.' He put his head down momentarily. When he lifted it he addressed them all: 'I'm so sorry.'

He turned and crossed the cobblestones to the nearest downpipe when Tallulah noticed it move.

Sasha cried out as the pipe he was about to touch grabbed him. In a sickening motion it transformed from tube to snake to snake-man. Adelaide threw a disc and it hit Sasha's assailant between the eyes; it released him and he kneed it in the stomach as it fell towards him. He brought another of Adelaide's metal discs down on its head as final assurance it wouldn't get up. He climbed the wall and was on the roof in no time as Adelaide continued to throw with precision at more downpipes-turned-attackers while Mai's ribbons, now electrically charged javelins, were devastating.

But no sooner had they dispatched the first attack than another wave came; Tallulah turned in time to see the vines on Pensione Bretz come to life. Tallulah repeated the attack she had mounted in Mr Morton's shop, conjuring the image of an eagle dive-bombing the snake men. Their confusion gave Hui and Tom a chance to act. Hui brought his hand to flame and blew it at a would-be attacker, who did not know which way to turn until eventually he ran from the aerial attack straight into the flame.

Tom seemed to decide that it wasn't even worth trying to use his gift – he was in a fight with a snake-man who hissed his forked tongue and grinned as though he was merely playing. From the shadows a series of small rocks peppered the creature – the gypsy children were helping from the shadows.

Tallulah spoke to Tom. *Trust your fire. Have faith.*

He nodded. He brought his palm level with his chest and Tallulah saw the flame burst strong and bright, and she felt Tom's pleasure. But before he could take advantage of it an enormous creature rose beside him and with one hand batted him into the wall of Pensione Bretz; he bounced off it and lay lifeless.

Tom!

Desperate to comprehend what she'd just seen, Tallulah looked back to where Tom had been standing and saw the bear-man from her dream: a hulking presence in middle of the small piazza, staring down at her. She had only one thought for the others.

Run.

'Tallulah, behind you!'

As she spun she caught a glimpse of the stream of blood pouring from one side of Adelaide's face and beyond her, Mai's exhausted attempt to charge a ribbon as a snake-man approached her with a smirk. She could hear Hui grunting somewhere and the crash of plates and rocks from the children in the shadows. But it was not going to be enough. In a frenzied whirl of adrenaline, Tallulah opened her mind and touched the animal minds of their assailants. There was only one thought she could grasp: to overcome and deliver to the castle. In a giant surge of energy, in honour of her friend Tom, in homage to the eminence of her visions, Tallulah conjured lightning bolt after lightning bolt and hit the creatures around her.

For a moment the square was in turmoil. Tallulah heard the shouts of her friends as they gained the upper hand. Time and again she rained down the bolts, forcing into the snake-men's minds the image of their bodies being split in two. She enjoyed feeling their pain until she wasn't sure what was theirs and what was hers, and she collapsed to her knees on the cobblestones. But the shouts of her friends changed; they were no longer in control. There was nothing she could do. She could not get up, she was so exhausted. She heard a vicious laugh ring through her mind.

She felt Saskia's joy and suddenly understood Sasha's furious scream to the heavens—she knew who had betrayed them. Tallulah sought the Mai's and Adelaide's minds. *You were right.* She felt a furious pain in the back of her head, saw the cobblestones rise up to meet her and smelled centuries of blood and betrayal between them as everything went black.

CHAPTER TWENTY-SEVEN

Tallulah did not know how long she faded in and out of consciousness. It wasn't that she wanted to fade out. Irena was sometimes sitting next to the bed at the far end of the white room where she lay; she was sure of it. But her early attempts to stay conscious were met by a furious headache that only eased when she closed her eyes again and slept.

Finally she could open her eyes without pain. She lay still for a long time, making certain that she was really awake and that this white chamber, sterile as a hospital operating room, with high glass windows, was not part of a dream. To be sure she lifted her left arm, saw the sleeve of the shirt she remembered putting on such a long time earlier in Elbe, pushed it back and found her arms looked like her own. She repeated the action on the right side then did the same with her legs. At that point she decided she was awake and herself – rather than turned into one of the hideous animal forms she had fought. She sat up.

She groaned and carefully felt the back of her head; sitting up had reawakened pain she thought had disappeared. The whack that had knocked her unconscious had left a lump the size of a hen's egg. Her hair around the egg was matted and bloody.

The door opened without a knock. A teenage girl dressed in black, with what looked like a whip coiled at her belt, brought in a bag of toiletries, a towel and face cloth.

'You wash. Then I take you to the Monsieur.' She kept her head down and did not look at Tallulah.

'Thank you.' She was definitely ready to freshen her mouth.

Ten minutes later the girl returned. This time Tallulah heard the soft footsteps as the girl approached. They had an uneven rhythm that suggested a limp and she wondered what had caused it. When the door opened, the girl said nothing, but waited for Tallulah to stand before she turned and walked back the way she came. Tallulah followed and was surprised to walk out onto a U-shaped balcony rather than into a corridor. She counted six wooden doors along the side of the building before the girl led her through one of the doors and into a stairwell. On the ground floor they passed under an archway, and walked into a courtyard where Tallulah had to shield her eyes: the cool sunshine shone on white marble columns around the perimeter of the square. She stopped in the centre and took in the building: it had a turret covered in scaffolding – they were in the castle that was visible from the town.

'Come.' The girl's voice was sharp. She marched Tallulah across the courtyard to the very back section of the castle. They passed under a series of arches and columns that ran the length of the building, descended six stairs and crossed another corridor before the girl stood in front of double doors and pushed them open. The girl stayed in the doorway but indicated Tallulah should proceed.

She walked past the girl into a long lavish room and gasped. Floor-to-ceiling glass windows that ran the length of the room revealed a long avenue into a dense forest: this was the landscape of her nightmare of the testing of the eminences. Along the avenue were a variety of circus apparatuses.

'Tallulah, welcome,' a man said behind her. She spun around to see, standing behind a table overflowing with food, a familiar-looking man. He was tall, with dark hair peppered with grey, and a long straight nose. Despite his age and his thin lips, he was not unattractive. Tallulah was immediately reminded of Irena's postcard from Madrid – the one with the red doorway and the door-knock in the shape of a wolf's head.

'Who are you?' She gestured to the forest beyond the windows. 'What is this?'

'Please. You must be hungry.'

She looked at his hooded eyes, his wooden smile that promised so little. 'I know you; I'm certain.'

The man nodded. 'We were destined to meet. Viktor Flores,' he said, with a half bow.

'Viktor Flores.' His name was familiar to her but she couldn't remember why. The lump on her head throbbed as she tried to think. Agh! The last dream! The one in the dungeon ... of this very castle. The tortured girl and the woman—

Tallulah's heart failed her. She knew the woman from her dream too. 'Irena,' she said to Viktor Flores, 'I thought she would be here.'

'She usually naps at this time.'

'Naps? Irena doesn't nap.'

Viktor Flores laughed softly. 'The trip to Europe has been more ... challenging than she thought it would be. But Rica will wake her.' He looked to the girl still standing at the door. 'Bring Irena to us, please.'

The girl's body stiffened.

'It will be all right,' he said gently. 'She can't hurt you now. Tell her we have a guest she would very much like to see.'

Rica closed the doors as she left. Tallulah looked at Viktor Flores, then at the buffet. All the stories said that to eat a kidnapper's food ensnared you with him forever. But she was beyond ravenous, and, she reasoned, if she was going to work out how to get out of the castle, she needed to eat. So, swallowing her pride, she walked to the table and began loading it up with succulent slices of roast lamb and vegetables. Viktor Flores also took a plate and filled it, imitating her choices. When she looked at him curiously he said, 'In case you thought I might drug you or something.'

'You could have done that before now.'

He nodded. 'You are right, of course.'

Tallulah sat at one end of the long table. Viktor sat at the other. A million questions bubbled up inside her, But every instinct told her to bide her time. So she picked up her knife and fork. The aroma of the meat and rosemary rushed her sinuses, suffocating her. Just the hint of the food meeting her stomach was enough to make her retch. She was sure that if she didn't pass out she would throw up. She put down the implements and pushed her chair back and took deep breaths.

'That happens after a bump on the head,' Viktor informed her. 'But our healers checked you when you arrived and declared it not too bad. I can call one of them again if you would like me to.'

'I'm fine.'

She moved her chair back to the table and tried again, this time with more success. But she had only just begun to get used to the feeling of food in her stomach when the doors opened and Rica helped a thin old woman into the room.

If Tallulah did not know that the girl was going to retrieve Irena she would not have recognised her nanny. Tears filled Tallulah's eyes. Her knife and fork clattered to the table; she pushed back her chair and ran to Irena.

'I can do it,' she told Rica. Tallulah placed Irena's arm on her own, leading her to a red velvet lounge chair. 'Irena,' she whispered, stroking the cold hand and trying to control the anger building inside her, 'my darling Bubka, it's me, Tallulah. What have they done to you?'

But Irena did not look up. She was in another place altogether. Tallulah crouched in front of her but the woman continued to stare at the floor. She stuffed cushions all around Irena, making sure she was comfortable, but there was no reaction. Crying hot, frightened tears, Tallulah took both of Irena's hands and clasped them between her own but she could not warm them. 'I'm going to find you a cup of tea.'

She strode to a sideboard of beverages and made a black tea with sugar just as Irena liked it. She returned to her nanny and positioned the cup between the limp hands, closing her own around them. Irena stared blankly at the tea. Tallulah helped her take a sip and then another.

Eventually, the cup was empty and Tallulah placed it on the coffee table. Turning back she put her head on Irena's hands. 'I'm so sorry,' she whispered. Somehow she felt responsible – but Irena had been involved long before Tallulah had known about Cirque d'Avenir or the Cirkulatti, or had ever seen the cuff.

What might have been and what has been point to one end, which is always present.

Tallulah felt her shoulders relax. There was reassurance in the words of the poem Irena loved even if there was little of the woman herself present. She looked into Irena's faded eyes;

she reached up and brushed the thin wisps of hair from her forehead, and kissed the cold hands that rested in the still lap.

'What might have been and what has been point to one end, which is always present,' she repeated.

'What is that? I like it very much.' Viktor Flores was standing beside her.

'A line from a poem that Irena loves.' She looked up at him, emotion overwhelming her. 'Who are you? What have you done to her? And what do you want with us?'

'Come, Tallulah, you are much too bright to ask such dull questions,' Viktor declared.

'Why here though? What have Bretz and this castle got to do with—'

'The Cirkulatti?'

'With a circus troupe that rose from civilisations around the Mediterranean.'

He walked around the coffee table to the couch opposite and sat down. 'That is a better question. But since you have done some research, you would know that the Cirkulatti – in its various manifestations – has been banished and moved on many times through history.'

'Various manifestations?'

'I could not have known that this would all turn out so well,' he admitted. 'I started out looking for a few Cirkulatti children to help me fulfil my vision and end up with Irena, and you, and poetry and …'

A broad smile of pleasure – and victory, Tallulah was certain of it – broke across his face. He shifted his weight slightly and delved into the pocket of his blazer as Tallulah's stomach lurched. Before he had retrieved the object from his pocket she knew what it would be. She turned to Irena to see if she was watching the final nail in Tallulah's coffin of shame, but she had not moved.

Viktor leaned forwards and placed her glittering silver cuff on the coffee table between them. 'I'll have to punish Marie for keeping so much from me.'

'Marie?' You're her "relationship". Do you have all the Cirkulatti Elders from the Paris lunch trapped somewhere in the castle?'

He laughed mightily. 'Only the nosey ones, my dear.'

He pushed the cuff towards Tallulah. Knowing it had been in the hands of another, her enemy, made her suddenly possessive. The low rumble of an approaching storm came from somewhere in the back of her mind – or perhaps from deep in the beginning of time. She noticed what she thought was a sparkle in the amber torches. Tallulah checked the windows to see if the light had changed, but it had not. The snow was reflecting brightly; aerialists had begun rehearsing in the trees; workers were sweeping snow from the main parade lane. She looked back to the cuff and leaned forwards to confirm the light in the gems.

'They say Hecate's torches glow when the goddess is present to aid the eminence.'

'If you believe in that sort of thing, I suppose,' she said.

'And you do not?'

'But what has any of this got to do with Bretz?' she said.

'Ah, yes. A family that I know well owned the mill here for more than a century. It was in a room very much like this one that the Curios of the Eminence were last seen together – before they were divided up among trusted friends for the duration of the war.'

Tallulah drew in a sudden breath as she recalled Mr Morton's verse and the story about Carl Lenter.

'Except the Curios never came back together,' Viktor continued. 'The family was very unhappy about that. Tell me how you came to be in possession of an ancient, priceless, stolen artefact, one of the Curios of the eminence of the Cirkulatti?'

'Stolen? I didn't know it was stolen. It was given to me for safekeeping.'

Viktor clicked his tongue. 'Didn't do much of a job. Really, I should thank you, Tallulah. You gave me such a delicious trail to follow. A computer search locked onto your home, though that was a dead end ...'

'You left the message in blood?'

Distaste crossed Viktor's face. 'Those idiots get carried away with the cult of worship. I did not realise how unstable the Serpenti are in the first year of their transformation until they were required to do some real work. I've had to divert police from that scent ever since. Luckily you were already ensnared in another trap. It was just too much to wish for that it would all be so contained – a curio with one of the very students Marie was training. And not just any curio – the fabled cuff of the Lioness of Rome. And you were so clumsy, knew so little of what you were dealing with, that it was merely a matter of time before you came to me of your own accord.'

Tallulah might have cursed her curiosity except that his taunts helped her remember her father's words: that Irena had given her the cuff in complete faith and that perhaps she'd merely set in train a series of actions that were meant to happen. She forced herself to laugh. 'Didn't you ever wonder about that, Monsieur Flores? About how easily it all happened? I'd say you fell into my trap.' She imitated the clicking of his tongue and found the action gave her more confidence than she felt; she sat up on the lounge next to Irena and gripped her nanny's hand in an effort to still the pounding of her heart, of her head. 'You've exposed yourself, Monsieur Flores. Did you really think that you could steal Cirkulatti children and not bring the power of the Cirkulatti down on you and your castle in Bretz?'

Viktor threw back his head and laughed so heartily, Tallulah felt faint. Feelings of insecurity, of her inability to do anything useful, of complete and utter failure overwhelmed her. She pushed with all her might against them and forced herself to laugh as well.

'The power of the Cirk-cirk-cirk-ulatti,' Viktor stuttered as he laughed, 'down on me?' He slapped his thigh in mirth and declared, 'Oh, Tallulah, I like you. I like your spirit. Even as you sit here with the power of the Cirkulatti,' he gestured to Irena, 'so clearly under our control. Marvellous devotion and loyalty. We could have had such fun.'

Tallulah could barely hear Viktor as she fought the overwhelming impression of her inadequacies, but she kept her eyes trained on him. She had not felt this sort of insecurity for such a long time she'd forgotten how overpowering it was. *What might have been and what has been point to one end, which is always present.* She felt the grip of Irena's hand on hers and her mind cleared long enough to see Viktor sober up.

'But, unfortunately, I have already chosen my eminence.' He gestured behind her.

She remembered the last minutes in the Bretz streets and finally accepted where her insecurities came from – where they had been coming from for weeks.

'Being such a good and loyal girl makes you predictable, Tallulah,' Saskia said in a singsong voice. She stood tall and proud, stance wide, hands on her hips. She was dressed in an all-white ensemble – blazer, hot pants, two-tone striped tights and knee-high boots. She seemed exotic and impeccable and impossibly tall. A full-length fur cape was draped from her shoulders and a fur hat extended from her head; this was not unlike the headdress Tallulah had seen in her visions – a grey fleck in the pelt reminded her of a wolf's tail. Saskia walked towards Tallulah and Viktor, tossing the cape from her shoulders and onto a chair with a flourish. 'I told you it would get you in trouble.'

Tallulah was on her feet in an instant, ignoring the nausea that came with Saskia's mental onslaught. For a moment she wondered where the selfish, stupid girl had found her extra power. From her memory she drew a painful image of the final assault on Tom, and another of Sasha's face as they were about to be attacked by the Serpenti, when he had screamed to the heavens. She'd so far avoided showing Saskia just how different her mental skills were but this seemed the time to do it. She shared the images with Saskia.

'Is Tom all right, do you think? Have you checked? And you've made your brother so proud.'

Saskia's smug expression faltered, momentarily, but she recovered. 'Tom is – nothing to me. And Sasha is fine about everything now.'

'Sure,' Tallulah said, biting back the rage and fear that surged on Tom's behalf. 'He's spent his entire life trying to rise above the shame your family brought upon itself, but he's fine about this.' She kept her eye on the Cirknero's eminence as the girl circled the room. 'How did it happen, Saskia? Were you spying on us all along?'

Saskia glanced at Viktor.

Tallulah turned to where he sat on the couch, legs crossed, arms stretched wide along the back of the couch, looking at Saskia with an amused expression.

'You'd trust him over Marie? Why, Saskia?' Tallulah asked. 'No one else in Cirque d'Avenir wants to be eminence; you could have stuck with us.'

'Marie is incompetent. She's indiscreet. She can't even tell who to—'

'Saskia,' Viktor warned gently.

She pursed her lips and shrugged. 'But she had the good sense to bring Brigitta to Seacliff and from Brigitta there was much to learn.'

'Your deception will be a knife to her heart.'

'You think so?' Saskia laughed. 'She was a rogue in her day: till she chickened out and opted for Cirque d'Avenir – a wishy-washy, we-don't-stand-for-anything group of no-hopers. You get what you settle for. I'm glad to be out of there.'

Tallulah nodded. 'Better to lead a kidnapping band of violent creeps.' She gestured with both her hands to the ceiling. 'You don't need us, then.' Tallulah bent down and gently put her hands under the frail arms of her nanny, who stood obediently. 'I don't know what you're up to,' she said to a bemused Viktor. 'But you've got your eminence and you've got your cuff.' She turned to Saskia. 'Good luck with your new venture. You must be so proud.'

Perhaps Tallulah knew she was going to regret the last taunt before as she said it. She instinctively pushed Irena back down on the couch as thoughts of hopelessness and fear exploded in her brain like icy barbs, blasting away every skerrick of courage and faith and happiness that she'd ever felt until there was no reason to stand up, no reason to live, and she crumpled to the floor.

CHAPTER TWENTY-EIGHT

When Tallulah came to, she felt carpet against her cheek and saw the legs of a small table and a pair of highly polished black men's shoes. She got herself up from the floor where she had fallen. Her cheekbone throbbed; putting her hand to her face she felt the warm sticky ooze of blood. She wiped it on her cargo pants and sat on the couch. Irena was not there.

'Do not do silly things, Tallulah,' Viktor said. 'You force me to behave badly and I don't want to, especially with someone so talented.'

'I'm not talented.' Her face felt thick as she tried to speak. She looked around to see Saskia perched on the arm of the lounge. 'Saskia is talented. My friends are ... Where *are* my friends?' She would not attempt to play games now.

Viktor gestured out the window. Tallulah squinted in the glare of the sun and snow until she realised that three of the workers sweeping snow from the stadium floor, in thin clothes, were Adelaide, Mai and Hui. She groaned. How much time had she wasted talking and eating and getting nowhere while they were out there in the freezing cold?

'Where's Tom?'

'Tom?'

'The firethrower,' Saskia informed Viktor.

Viktor laughed. 'The former firethrower.'

Saskia nodded. Tallulah felt rage and grief again. She had a sudden understanding of Saskia's relationship with Tom. 'Were you trying out your power on him? Did you strip him of his fire *deliberately*?'

'Not at first. But when it became obvious that I was having a particular effect, I can't say I wasn't interested.' Saskia strode to the table of beverages and made herself a cup of tea. 'Who wouldn't be?'

'He wouldn't believe what everyone said of you. He didn't think you would stoop that low. And you let him *die*?'

Saskia concentrated on stirring her tea.

'What use was he was to us?' Viktor asked. He pushed the cuff towards Tallulah. 'Tell me about this.'

'What's there to tell?'

She was ready for the mental attack when it came. Panting with the effort to keep Saskia's debilitating negativity at bay she let herself fall into the couch as if crumpled by the immense pain. But she got through the attack without being knocked out. As the two of them discussed her, she lay on the couch recovering. Eventually, she sat back up, pretending that she was coming to consciousness and found Viktor holding a bulging napkin for her to take. 'Ice, for your face.'

If she was going to get out of the mess, Tallulah decided, she had to take any help offered. She reached for the cold package and pressed it against her cheek.

'Tell me about the cuff. Tell me about the Lioness of Rome.'

'Lioness of Rome?'

'Fulvia of Rome – the cuff was made for her.'

Tallulah knew little of the Lioness of Rome, save the few times she was mentioned by Theodora. The cuff may have been crafted for one eminence but the visions she saw were of another. Brigitta was right; it was a confusing piece of jewellery. But Viktor must not know that. 'Will you release my friends?' she asked. 'Release Irena?'

'I don't have to promise anything, Tallulah. Except more pain if you refuse me.'

'I'm not scared of pain.'

Again he laughed. He walked to the windows, nodded and said, 'Now.'

He stood aside so Tallulah could see the action: two Serpenti walked to where Mai and Adelaide were sweeping, picked them up and walked them to great mounds of snow. They threw her friends into the snow and began to bury them.

'No.' Tallulah leaped off the couch and ran to where Viktor stood at the window. The muffled screams of the girls could be heard. Tallulah built the image of a furnace that throbbed deep within their bellies and could radiate heat all around their bodies.

On the other side of the cleared space, Hui flipped the shovel he was holding so the handle was braced under his arm and ran with the metal blade held in front of him. Even through the glass Tallulah could hear the shouts as Hui charged at the Serpenti who held the girls captive. Tallulah concentrated her mental help on him and felt a satisfied grin tug at the corners of her mouth as his speed shifted up a gear and he batted aside the Serpenti who ran at him. From her raised vantage point she warned him of the next danger. *Above you.*

Hui lifted the shovel and Tallulah watched as it ignited, and a blazing jet of heat forced the enemy aerialist to abandon his plan; he jumped from his cloud swing and grabbed a branch on the next tree as his swing and the boughs he'd been surrounded by went up in flame.

'Saskia,' Viktor said angrily. 'Do something.'

Saskia crossed the room as Hui rammed into one of Adelaide and Mai's tormentors. The burning prod hit home. Tallulah kept her whole body on alert for anything Saskia might attempt – she had not shown a lot of imagination so far: she would either go for Tallulah's insecurities or Hui's. Tallulah kept her concentration on Hui as he turned on the other Serpenti and ran at him. But the Serpenti dived for the ground and slithered out of the way and Hui could not stop his trajectory into the cleft of snow beside where Adelaide and Mai lay. Tallulah watched Hui's head drop as if in resignation and she knew Saskia was having as much effect as the stifling snow on his adrenaline-charged attack.

Saskia's in your mind. Watch out – behind you.

He left his weapon jammed in the snow, but it was a tired Hui who wheeled around to face the Serpenti behind him. Tallulah lashed the approaching Serpenti's mind with his own primitive fears. He screamed and cowered from the imaginary attack.

'Saskia!' Viktor shouted. 'Look after my men.'

Tallulah was about to whip the Serpenti again when she felt Saskia's threat on her own mind. She countered it quickly, but the time taken to repel the assault was time away from Hui and the girls. By the time she was able to concentrate on what was happening outside again, Hui had been taken by another Serpenti and the attempted rebellion was under control. All Tallulah could do was flood Adelaide and Mai with warmth. But she was weakening. Telling Viktor what he needed to know was her only chance. She turned and faced him.

'I don't have anything more to tell you than you already know,' Tallulah said quickly. 'Irena left the cuff with the instruction to keep it safe. But I got curious and you know the rest: I searched the net; you traced it. I visited Mr Morton; we fought off your Serpenti. Irena didn't tell me any more. I don't know anything about the Lioness of Rome. I promise. Please stop hurting my friends. I don't know anything else.'

Viktor gave a nod to an overseer she had not noticed almost directly below the glass window, and walked to the back of the room, where he poured himself a glass of red wine from a decanter. Tallulah watched as the overseer and the remaining Serpenti brought the girls out of the snow. Tallulah's heart broke as she saw them emerge wet and shivering. The only reassurance was that in binding them together, the Serpenti now put the two girls in contact with Hui's warmth; he would restore their body heat. As Viktor turned from the scene Tallulah put her hand on the window in a feeble attempt to reach out and touch them and said the only words that came into her head: *We call on the goddess of magic and the night, the faithful friend of mysteries, Hecate, to give the Cirkulatti strength.*

Mai and Adelaide stopped their shivering and stood straighter as they looked to the window.

Change your locks; Saskia's here in the room.

'Here is my problem, Tallulah,' Viktor said.

The girls exchanged a look and then nodded towards her. She turned back to concentrate on Viktor.

'I have big plans. Great, wonderful plans for a better world. And I have spent a long time searching for a golden-eyed eminence, the one legend decreed, to help me execute these plans. And I found her, and she was on her way to me. But then I found a little old woman snooping around my castle.

A woman with a mysterious past, revered by many, and who, I subsequently discovered, had been secretly training a different golden-eyed girl. And I found that this second girl had a very important item of jewellery, an item that belongs with the fabled eminence, and now I have met her I have to wonder if I've got the right golden-eyed girl.'

'Of course you've got the right girl!' Tallulah said.

'Is this just because I don't deal with your slithering henchmen? Their minds make my skin crawl!' Saskia asked.

'Put it on,' Viktor said to Tallulah.

She backed away, shaking her head, forcing her tired mind to come up with a reason not to obey. She looked to Saskia, who stared at them both with a mixture of confusion and anger. Her eyes rested on the cuff, her nostrils flared and in three long strides she was at the coffee table, scooping it up. 'If this is meant for the eminence then I should be the one to wear it.'

'Saskia!' Viktor shouted. 'Not yet—'

But she took no notice. She pushed past where Tallulah sat and slipped the cuff on. Beyond the coffee table, she stopped. Her arms went to her side, became rigid, then loosened again as the surge of energy Tallulah was so familiar with rippled through her tall body. She turned to face them both with blazing eyes that seemed to grow to the size of saucers. Saskia laughed with euphoric glee.

'Ah! Now we will discover the secrets it keeps,' Viktor said and clapped with delight.

Tallulah was stunned; she put her head down and tried to think. She had bet on nothing happening for Saskia. Hadn't Theodora said the cuff would only work for the rightful heir? Despite never admitting it, Tallulah had always been sure that since she saw the visions, since she had a good heart, she was the one the cuff and the goddess were patiently awaiting. Now it seemed she had gambled badly. Brigitta was right: the lore around the cuff meant little. Saskia, despite her failings, was as much the eminence as she was.

'What can you see, Saskia?' Viktor called, hunger in his growling voice. She turned to him and lifted her arms wide as she quaffed great gulps of air. It seemed it was all the girl could do to stay standing.

'Oh, it's beautiful,' Saskia said. 'Magnificent.' Her body undulated with a new rush of power, she threw her head back and lost her balance a little before righting herself and bringing her gaze back to the two of them. She turned to Viktor. 'What did you say about not having the right eminence?'

'You were always the eminence. You know that; you've been groomed for the job. We all knew. But we needed to see what Tallulah could do.'

Saskia scoffed. 'Tallulah! You wouldn't say that if you saw her in class.'

'She has some power over the mind of the Serpenti and we do need to keep them in line,' Viktor purred. 'That is not a job for you, my lovely.'

'Yes, that's a *perfect* job for little Lu.' She turned and smiled. 'You never stood a chance with me – and now that I have this …'

She held her cuffed wrist in the air and the enhanced mental onslaught began to overpower Tallulah. She dropped to her knees; heard Saskia's piercing laugh as she wrapped her arms around her head and folded at the hips; it was better to use the floor for support than to hit it hard in the effort of resisting the attacks. Tears poured from her eyes as every insecurity was wrought from her – fears that she never knew she had beat her relentlessly until her mind and body felt so bruised and weak that even the protective pose she'd adopted became hard to maintain. She screamed in pain, forcing herself to hold on, to stay in that position, not to give in and collapse into the foetal position and expose her heart to Saskia and the cuff.

She had been so wrong. The gems in Hecate's torch grow bright when the goddess is present to aid the eminence against the forces of darkness. If the goddess was present why was she aiding the Cirknero and *their* anointed eminence? Had the centuries left Hecate deaf and dumb? In pure desperation, Tallulah began chanting her parting reassurance to Mai and Adelaide. *We call on the goddess of magic and the night, the faithful friend of mysteries, Hecate, to give the Cirkulatti strength. We call on the goddess of magic and the night, the faithful friend of mysteries, Hecate, to give the Cirkulatti strength.*

It seemed a feeble reaction to the howling strength of Saskia's onslaught, but faith in something beyond herself kept her going. As she repeated the words, they grew in meaning and Tallulah felt the magic and mystery of her own strength begin to push back against the tumult of doubt. The walls around her inner pool of strength began to re-form until they were fully resurrected and could repel Saskia's attacks. She shuffled backwards so that a sofa was bracing her from behind and a table provided some physical cover.

'Saskia!' Viktor's voice was urgent. 'Enough. Take it off.'

'Why should I take it off now?'

Tallulah could only concentrate on restoring her own power and she repeated the words until she felt the ability to move beyond herself and seek the consciousness of others around her.

Immediately she ran into a place so bleak that she was tempted to retreat — until she understood that it was not her own mind but someone else's memory: she was in a slum, a garbage dump, and a skinny, dirty boy, not yet a teen, was being savagely beaten by a gang of well-dressed youths. Then the image was gone as Viktor's voice boomed, 'No, Saskia!'

His fury at being forced to reveal his own insecurities shocked Saskia and she fought back. 'Don't tell me what to do!' she screamed, before crying out in pain.

Now Tallulah saw Saskia bombarded by images of her own: a little girl pleading with a teenage boy not to leave; the same girl turning somersaults on a tightrope, tears streaming down her face as a grim-faced older man shouted instructions from the ground. It was as if the cuff was using her own power against her.

Saskia growled and the dominant image of their shared consciousness was again the boy in the tip. Tallulah felt his grief; she couldn't bare the pain, she wanted to help, to make things better, to show that good things were possible. Before she could get close enough she was stopped just as surely as if she'd run into a brick wall.

Except the wall was purple and bright. The closer she looked the more clearly she could see the outlines of women emerging from the light. She'd called for help and the faithful friend of mysteries had heard.

Leave them. Seek your own strength. The others need you.

Tallulah nodded and retreated from the battle between Viktor and Saskia. She began the chant again and concentrated on getting beyond the room to her friends, Irena, the kidnapped children and the Cirkulatti further away.

She heard an enormous explosion of shattering glass and a blast of icy air sweep into the hall; she heard Viktor's curse and his cry to Saskia, but dismissed it as she searched for and found the conscious thoughts of Adelaide, Mai and Hui – who she found on the run, taking advantage of the chaos created by the destruction of the wall of windows; they'd managed to untie their bonds and were heading for the dungeon where the Cirque d'Avenir students and the gypsy children were being held. Tallulah kept chanting with all her might; the others joined in – Adelaide and Sasha, Mai and Hui, Irena and Tom.

She stopped. Irena *and* Tom? Did that mean they were together? If Irena was with him, then was she dead too?

No! She would not think about that for now – instead, she lingered on the sound of Tom's voice. She concentrated on the heat and strength of his body and his enthusiasm. She spared a thank you to the goddess for this loan of the powers of Cirkulatti past and present.

Tallulah heard Adelaide wonder where she was. Then she heard shouts and cries beyond the window and felt the cold air wrap around her and invade her thin clothes. She came out of her trance and sat up. *I'm in the main hall. Where are you?*

Dungeons – Serpenti have scattered. Cirknero who were rehearsing in the trees are busy trying to herd them back into the castle. The renovations have created holes that the gypsy children from the square seem to have found a way through. They're helping us now.

I'm going to look for Irena.

Wait for us.

Tallulah got up and fought her light head as she tried to focus on what was around her. She turned two complete revolutions before she saw the doors where she had entered. She ran in that direction as she heard Viktor's strangled voice call, 'Rica! Egor!'

Tallulah pulled open the doors – and ran straight into an enormous hairy mountain: the bear-man they'd met outside the pensione, who had thrown Tom to the wall as if he were no more than a twig. She struggled to breathe as he grabbed her by the neck and dragged her back into the room towards Viktor and Saskia. They had barely moved from where Saskia had first put on the cuff; Viktor held tightly to his eminence's wrists as they stumbled around the room, grunting and occasionally crying out in defiance or exasperation. It was the strangest sight Tallulah had ever seen.

'Viktor,' the bear-man called.

Viktor glanced up but with unfocused eyes. The bear-man lifted Tallulah and slammed her against a wall. 'What's happening to them?'

Before she could say anything she heard a *swoosh* and saw a blur of red to the right. Her eyes slid that way since her head couldn't but Mai's twirling ribbon was merely a distraction. From the other side a flaming wooden pole slammed into the bear-man; the blow did not hurt him but his fur coat burst into flame, immediately burning through to his skin. He yelped, dropped Tallulah and turned to strike at whatever had hit him – which meant he didn't see the spinning disc that slammed into the back of his head and with a solid thump knocked him unconscious on the floor.

'Let's go, Lu,' Adelaide said from the door.

'The cuff,' Tallulah told them.

'What's happening to them?' Mai asked.

'The cuff is having a different effect on Saskia.'

'It shouldn't work for her at all!' Adelaide exclaimed. 'She's no eminence.'

'Well, it does. Not the visions like I get but some other weird stuff. You don't want her turning on you, I promise. I thought my body would explode trying to fight her.'

'Instead you exploded every glass surface in the castle,' Hui said.

'Not me.'

'Something did. We were lucky the Serpenti were in front of us when the windows went. They took the force of it.'

'Viktor can't get it off her though,' Adelaide said as she watched them. 'Not loyal to his eminence?'

'I don't think we can trust anything I saw in those visions.'

'I bet you could take it from her,' Mai said. 'Another eminence.'

'How can there be two?' Tallulah asked.

Adelaide gave Tallulah a push. 'Go get it and then we'll find someone to ask.'

Tallulah began the chant again in case Saskia refocused her efforts on her. She filled herself with it – the room, the castle and beyond. Then she walked to the two of them and pulled Viktor's hand off the cuff. Released, he spun and looked at her with a new focus.

'You didn't tell me the truth!' he cried, grabbing at her.

'I didn't know that would happen,' she said.

He raised his hand to strike her but as his open palm was about to smack into the side of her head, the air warped around him and Saskia and they froze.

'I told you not to do that!' Tallulah cried.

'I can't help it!' Adelaide shouted back. 'When you're threatened it just happens. Get the cuff, Lu, and stop wasting time. I'm exhausted.'

Tallulah did as she was told. The cuff lifted from Saskia's wrist with ease; she stowed it in the zip pocket of her hoodie. She heard Hui call, 'Mai, wrap 'em up. One, two, *three*!' and he pushed Saskia towards Viktor. As they all came back to real time, Viktor finished his attempt to hit Tallulah; instead, his arm ended up wrapped around Saskia's body. They were too disoriented to act before Mai's ribbon had coiled around them as surely as one of the Serpenti might.

Saskia cried out in pain as the ribbon touched her body. She grabbed hold of Viktor in an effort to avoid its electric charge.

Tallulah and the others ran out the door.

'You're all *dead*!' Saskia shrieked at their retreating backs.

CHAPTER TWENTY-NINE

They sprinted from the great hall into the corridor. Instinctively they each chose a column for cover but there was no one up in the courtyard. 'It's clear,' Adelaide said in a loud whisper. 'Where to now?'

'Wait, did you feel that?' Tallulah said. 'Like a tremor.'

A rhythmic pounding, barely perceptible but gaining in force. Whistles and shouts went around the castle. Children's voices could be heard from the balconies that overlooked the courtyard, whispering one word, 'Cirkulatti! Cirkulatti!' Moments later a group of children holding sling shots, juggling balls and batons passed through the courtyard heading for the opposite corner of the castle.

'Hui, take Mai and follow them,' Tallulah said. 'If that noise is Marie and the others, let them know we're here. Adelaide and I will go for Irena and whoever else might be locked in the rooms upstairs where I was held.'

'Sasha might be there,' Adelaide said hopefully. 'Saskia would have done some deal to keep him safe, surely.'

'Who knows? She reckons he's fine with her defection.'

'She's lying,' Adelaide said surely. 'He'd never be OK with it.'

Mai gave Adelaide's shoulder a squeeze. 'Let's hope not.'

They watched Hui and Mai depart, then raced across the sandy square.

'Hecate's torches,' Tallulah said as they reached the stairwell. 'Rica,' she said, dipping her head under the last section of stairs and moving to the girl propped up in the corner, blood oozing from a series of gashes in her calf. 'What happened to your leg?'

'We don't have time, Lu,' begged Adelaide.

'Rica. We're going to get out of here; we'll take you with us but I need to find Irena.'

'The old woman's the devil. The Monsieur protects us from her.'

Tallulah shook her head adamantly. 'No.'

Adelaide's hand settled on her shoulder. 'They all said that in the dungeon when we were locked down there. They were the ones who wouldn't agree to the Monsieur's deal. The Monsieur stops her from stealing their gift completely if they work for him.'

'That'd be right,' Tallulah said angrily. '*He* looks like the good guy.' She wiped her face. 'Irena's not well, Rica. I need to take her away and make her better so she'll never hurt you or anyone else again. And you won't have to work for the Monsieur. You can go home. You'd like that, wouldn't you? To go home?'

Rica hesitated. Her eyes glistened.

'Tell me where she is.'

But as the slave-girl opened her mouth to speak, fear seemed to overtake her intentions.

'You don't have to ask, Lu,' Adelaide said impatiently. 'You're the telepath. We don't have time to be polite.'

'You just told me someone is stripping them of their gift,' Tallulah replied. 'I don't see how that can happen without their minds being invaded. If I do it then I'll never gain her trust.'

'When are you going to *need* her trust?'

'How would I know? Let's call it an investment in whatever the future holds.'

Adelaide gave a resigned nod. 'Those tremors aren't getting any weaker, though. There's no guarantee whoever is responsible is on our side.'

'The room next to yours,' a faint voice interrupted them. Rica put her hand on Tallulah's knee. 'She's been there the whole time.'

Rica led them to the room but Irena was not there. The girls opened every door along the corridor. Tallulah's panic grew as each unlocked door opened to reveal another empty space. 'We must be on the wrong floor.' They went back to the stairs and tried a floor higher but still the result was the same. 'Where is she?'

Adelaide leaned on the brick wall, struggling to get her breath back and her own disappointment under control; she shook her head. 'Maybe the dungeon. Now that I've seen the castle from above I get the feeling we were locked in one small section of it.'

What might have been and what has been point to one end, which is always present.

'What did you say?' Tallulah whispered.

Adelaide looked puzzled. 'That we should try the dungeon?'

Tallulah listened again. 'They're using a line I said to Irena in the dining room.' She clenched her fists and struggled to control the nausea. 'How dare they!'

'*They?* Lu, you said the locks have all been discovered and corrupted. It's not Irena.'

'I know. It's Saskia – but she's not the only voice. They've – they've got a room somewhere.' She looked at Adelaide.

'It's … for ceremonies, or something. It's *awful*, Della. That's where they are.' She ran back down the corridor, Adelaide in pursuit.

'Lu, you don't even know what you're walking into. It's a trap.'

'While they've got Irena, I *am* trapped. You didn't see her, Del. She's fading away to almost nothing. I love my mum and dad but Irena was my best friend, my confidante, even though she knew I was weird. I can't leave her to die alone.'

Tallulah ran quickly into one of the rooms, pulled a sheet off the bed and ripped it down the middle.

'But she told you to go,' Adelaide reminded her as she followed her into the room. 'Dust on the petals is toxic – get away, or whatever she said.'

Tallulah worked furiously, tearing the sheet into strips. 'I've thought about that. I wonder if *she* left that note – deliberately, I mean – or if it was part of the trap. Like breadcrumbs leading us here.' She kept tearing until she had a number of strips that she picked up in a bundle. 'Rica will take us to the room.'

But Rica's eyes were wide with fear as Tallulah bound the cuts on her leg and a gash in her arm they had not noticed before, and told her what they needed. She shook her head and began to whimper. 'You must understand. No one comes out of that room the same.'

The girls did not have the heart to make her go with them, but set off armed with her directions. As they descended the stairs at the rear of the castle they could hear running and thumping, cries of victory and pain. Instead of turning towards the fighting, Tallulah headed them straight along the corridor that opened before them.

'The tremors have stopped,' Adelaide said as they ran.

But Tallulah was being drawn to the chant of voices in her head getting louder and stronger. *What might have been and what has been point to one end, which is always present.* They reached double doors almost directly under the great hall she'd been in earlier. She was about to push the doors open when she felt a hand on her arm; she struggled to break free but Adelaide would not let her.

'Tallulah! Wait.' Della's hands went to her shoulders. 'Fix your barriers; do what you have to do. This is dangerous.'

Tallulah's heart hammered in her chest as she took in her friend's advice. She shivered and clenched her teeth. 'Keep up the call to Hecate,' she replied. 'I felt it rebuild my strength after Saskia had blasted through my barriers.'

'It helped us all. One simple thought, just as Brigitta taught us.'

Ready?

Adelaide nodded. Tallulah pushed open the doors. At first the darkness was a surprise. Tallulah had imagined the room to be like the one above – with a wall of windows and the reflection of winter light on the snow – but here there was a wall where the windows should be. Or, as her eyes adjusted to the dark, perhaps heavy dark curtains. Candlelight flickered from brackets fixed to columns. She took a step into the room. Adelaide was so close to her Tallulah could feel her breath on her neck – until suddenly it was not. Adelaide cried out; her weapons clattered to the ground and Tallulah turned to find her trussed up in Mai's ribbons.

A moment later, a grinning blonde girl stepped from the shadows. In a split second she had another ribbon, a white one, around Adelaide's neck and was dragging her to an altar of sorts that had been created on a raised circular platform.

Tallulah gasped. Behind the altar, candlelight illuminated the mural on the wall. It was a copy of the one Tallulah, Mai and Adelaide had seen in Elbe's Council chamber, with one important change: the Council selecting the eminence had been replaced by one man.

In front of the mural stood Saskia. On either side of her were four young women, also dressed in white – although their simple knee-length dresses were dowdy compared with Saskia's ensemble. Tallulah understood why she'd felt that Saskia was not chanting Irena's mental invocation alone. The girls were all telepaths – though weak – and were working with Saskia. They'd tried to push into Tallulah's mind as soon as she entered the room but with the clear focus of the chant, she had been able to repel them. In that instant Tallulah felt like she grew a metre taller. Despite her predicament, she laughed.

'Not a very polite way to treat your hosts, Tallulah.' Viktor was sitting on the front step of the altar. 'You take your time joining us, you bring extra guests, you make a terrible mess and then you laugh at our hospitality. But now you're here, you can put the cuff on and make it work properly. Dana? Put her up here with the other one.'

The blonde girl dragged Adelaide up the stairs and forced her to lie down behind Viktor. It wasn't until then that Tallulah noticed the tiny feet lying splayed and motionless up on the dais. The little body of Irena. Tallulah willed herself to stay focused.

She took in the room. Lining the perimeter of the long rectangular space were the Serpenti, standing as men but with their hoods on and flared; they looked like an army of cobras. Their eyes were mere slits; their bodies were alert. At the end of the room, opposite where Saskia stood on the podium, was a Serpenti taller than the rest. She could feel his strength; his hiss was a seductive whisper, but she would not give him any more attention.

When she'd found her equilibrium again she lifted her head and continued to move around the circle. Whatever she did she would be attacked, with that came the good chance that Adelaide would halt time and reveal her unique gift. Tallulah could not risk Adelaide's secret again. The problem was she was all out of ideas.

When she'd almost finished her turn of the room the curtains rippled ever so slightly, and a person half revealed himself to her from where he hid. She was careful not to display a reaction at all, and looked back to the Serpenti to check if anyone else had caught the moment – they were all focused on the silent women on the altar. She glanced back to the long lean figure, reached for his mind and found it open to her.

They don't know I'm here.

Tallulah put her head down as though she had completed her visual tour of the room. When she was composed she raised her eyes to Viktor. 'Very impressive,' she said. She looked beyond him to the walls illuminated by candlelight. 'The murals are copies from another place I know – you've been to Elbe?'

As Viktor turned and looked at the murals, Tallulah continued to read Sasha's mind. *The tremors are the strongmen's sign they have arrived; the team from Elbe are being shown the way into the castle. He's very sure of himself, this guy.*

'… Marie is so enthusiastic, such an idealist,' Viktor was saying. 'She thinks she's careful and discreet. But she wants to be loved and it's a weakness. She trusts the wrong people.'

'But why recreate the Council chamber from Elbe when you're changing everything else? There is no Council. Whatever this little ritual you've got going here is, it's nothing to do with the Cirkulatti.'

'Nothing?' Viktor scoffed. 'Between you and Saskia we have an eminence and an eminence's curio.'

While Viktor spoke Tallulah relayed Sasha's information to Adelaide.

'But these,' she said, returning to the conversation with Viktor and gesturing around the room to the Serpenti, 'are abominations of nature. The Cirkulatti does not dabble in such dark schemes as this.'

'When you put on the cuff, Tallulah, we will see what the Cirkulatti do and don't dabble in. The lines between Cirkulatti and Cirknero were always blurred. Fulvia's cuff will reveal all.'

Tallulah looked at the mural again. She had not been able to work out what was missing in Elbe and here but now that her name had been mentioned Tallulah realised it was Fulvia's reign. Nefertiti, Semiramis, Theodora. But the woman whose cuff they all coveted had been left out of their history. 'You don't know anything about Fulvia. Is that what you think the cuff will reveal? You want her power but you don't know what it is. That's why all the muscle. You don't know what you'll need to overpower one girl and a cuff.'

'I have felt it work on me, and on my Saskia,' Viktor replied. 'I want to understand the power of the cuff. And you will explain. Put it on.'

'What if I say no?'

Viktor arched eyebrows mocked her bravery. The Serpenti began to hiss and took a step forwards. 'Some say Hecate had a daughter, Circe, who turned her enemies into animals.' A smile crept slowly across Viktor's face. 'The Cirknero is a group spawned from the Cirkulatti, so I took inspiration from

Circe,' Viktor explained. 'Adelaide will look beautiful with scales, don't you think?'

Tallulah smiled too, despite the disgust she felt. She remembered the howling dog-men of the first vision; could it have been less than four weeks since this all began?

'Ingenious,' she muttered. 'And original.'

'Be careful of your tone, Tallulah. I will not be mocked.'

She unzipped her pocket and retrieved the silver Curio. Sitting it on her palm, she held it out in front of her. She walked to the edge of the altar. 'May I?'

'Please.' He gestured with a bow. 'All my girls on a pedestal. I like that.'

As Tallulah ascended the stairs the glow of the cuff's golden gems seemed to pulse in the dim light and get stronger, casting light across the altar and illuminating her path. Tallulah could feel Adelaide's eyes on her; she glanced sideways and saw her expression blazing with a combination of fear and excitement. When Tallulah had reached the centre of the platform she stopped and turned to Saskia. 'Are you sure?' she asked her, gently. 'There is still time for you to change your mind. Once I put this on you will be revealed to everyone as a traitor.'

Saskia laughed, looked at Viktor and then back to Tallulah. 'Cirque d'Avenir is the traitor, Tallulah – to our history of truly powerful women. We will not be held captive by its restrictions, its fear of strong women. No eminence? Join me, Tallulah, and together we will be more powerful that you can ever imagine.'

'Powerful, how? He just called you *his* Saskia.'

'It's a term of affection.'

'You are only powerful as long as you do what he wants you to do, Saskia.'

'You have no idea.'

'Cirque d'Avenir wishes to protect us, not restrict us. But perhaps there is something in what you say. Perhaps the eminence must unshackle herself; perhaps she is a traitor to herself and to the title until she does.'

'Let the secrets of the cuff be your guide, Tallulah,' Viktor coaxed. 'Show us all the power of the eminence.'

Tallulah ignored him. She stood in the centre of the altar, facing Saskia and her assistants, above two of the people she cared most for. Whatever happened when the cuff went on, at least she would be close to them when she fell. Her mouth was dry; sweat beaded her hairline.

Saskia was hungry for the cuff; her golden eyes glinted with crazed desire for it. Tallulah understood the seductive powers of the Curio, but Saskia's yearning was different. She looked like Theodora's daughter, prepared to dislocate her dying mother's shoulder to get at the cuff she was too hard-hearted to safely wield.

'Did Viktor tell you about the gems in the cuff, Saskia?' Tallulah held her palm out a little further. 'They glow when the goddess Hecate is present to aid the eminence against the forces of darkness. Are you ready to fight the very thing you have spent your life coveting? Because that is what you will have to do. You forget the truth that we live by, Saskia: the eminence is no one's puppet *and* recognises that without the Cirkulatti she is nothing.'

With Saskia's laugh ringing in her ears, Tallulah slipped the cuff on; she felt its familiar grip on her wrist and the surge of energy race through her body. A moment later she felt the warm embrace of purple light and one by one the goddess and all the women who had worshipped her appeared in a line. But before she could communicate with them, the translucent figure of Irena appeared in the space between the goddess and Tallulah. She felt her heart clench. 'Are you dead?' she asked.

Irena shook her head but did not speak.

'Please hold on,' Tallulah begged. 'I'll get us away from here.'

Irena faded but the goddess remained. 'Not unless you claim your inheritance, Tallulah.' She gestured towards the curtains. 'Everyone is waiting.'

But Tallulah shook her head. 'Are you bargaining with me as well? You're no better than him. Irena will die if I don't accept this … this … thing? It's a poisoned chalice, Goddess.'

The goddess shook her head. 'I make no bargains, no guarantees. It is the magic within you that demands you claim your inheritance and realise your potential – and the Cirkulatti's. I don't deny the risks. But are the risks any fewer if you walk away? If you deny your gift, your magic, your power, what are you then?'

Tallulah dropped her head. Safe, she thought, from the madness she'd seen in Viktor's eyes, in Saskia's, and from the chaos the cuff had shown. But was 'safe' the way she wanted to live? Hadn't there always been, on the edge of her dreams, a moment like this? And the answer she wanted to give – if she dared? She lifted her eyes and looked directly at the Goddess. 'I claim it,' she said.

Goosebumps rippled across her skin. She put her hand on the cuff and the ground trembled beneath her, and in that instant Tallulah was in contact with the consciousness of all people all around her, in the room and beyond. The chatter was overwhelming; the noise of it swelled as the purple light grew in intensity until she could not tell if the light and the noise were external or coming from inside her.

'Take only what you need,' a voice reminded her and Tallulah understood. Just as she had taken from Irena's mind only the information she needed to reveal the tarot card, so she should do the same now. She breathed deeply and concentrated; there was chaos all around her but she turned the volume down, muting the channels she didn't need, until all was quiet. And peaceful. And for a moment Tallulah thought she'd made a mistake. She'd been asleep; the danger had passed or perhaps they were all dead. She turned to the goddess, who smiled serenely. *Listen.*

Tallulah did. To a whisper, brought across time on a breath of wind. Gradually the gusts were stronger and the whispers became a voice and then a song and Tallulah felt tears fill her eyes as she heard the word they chanted. So much hope, so much expectation, so much fear, so much joy.

Eminence, Eminence, Eminence.

She replied.

We call on the goddess of magic and the night, the faithful friend of mysteries, Hecate, to walk with the eminence and give the Cirkulatti strength.

The purple light Tallulah had been bathed in burst into a thousand tiny stars that seemed to rain down on them as the cheer of the Cirkulatti and those who followed the eminence reverberated through her. Tallulah opened her eyes …

… to find herself in the middle of a battle. Without knowing how, her mind sprang into action. She flowed with energy; she was able to maintain her own mental attacks on Serpenti and human alike and yet, as if she was at one with the unconscious mind of everyone who followed her, she assisted them too.

The dark room she had been in was now as light as it could be; the curtains had been flung back and the glass behind them shattered. Viktor and 'his' girls stood dazed and the Serpenti were either streaming out through the broken windows to defend the castle, or coming at Tallulah. She spoke calmly into their minds and they stopped, confused, looking from her to Viktor and back.

Tallulah, safe for a moment, saw the strongmen, male and female, coming down the forest arena wielding clubs the size of tree trunks. They whacked their attackers aside like tennis balls. Any threat the strongmen might have faced from above was countered by Sasha and a band of acrobats, who ran right across the top of trees and leaped at the Cirknero or fired off a barrage of missiles.

A battle with ribbons was being fought closer to Tallulah. Mai had been joined by a group of girls no bigger than she was, but they could not be cowed. The ribbons reminded Tallulah of what had to be done inside. She turned to see Adelaide being hauled to her feet by Dana and dragged across the altar and down the steps. Tallulah quickly broke her captor's concentration; the ribbons fell from around Adelaide, who followed through with a spinning kick that tripped the girl and brought her down.

Tallulah raced in to help her, but Adelaide reached for a pair of glass candle holders on the floor around the altar and threw them at the approaching Serpenti, who had finally thrown off the confusion Tallulah had planted.

'Ow,' Adelaide said, holding her burned hands against her body as the Serpenti howled.

Even Tallulah yelped. 'I'll get Irena!'

'Before we burn alive,' Adelaide said.

'Saskia, out,' Viktor called over the crackling flames, 'get the girls, and get out.'

But Saskia was focused on Tallulah in one last attempt to fell her. Boosted by the girls she stood holding hands with, she was a force of misery – but the cuff's purple light burned away any attack she tried to mount.

'You've got no chance with me; save yourself, Saskia,' Tallulah called. She ran onto the dais and picked up Irena. The shock of her nanny's lifeless body in her oddly strong arms was greater than anything Saskia could throw at her. She checked on Adelaide, who was running and tumbling, picking up and throwing whatever she could find around the room. As Tallulah crossed the altar she concentrated her primitive attacks on the Serpenti but the flames were doing a better job than she could of keeping them confused and at bay.

'Rica,' Viktor bellowed.

They heard the crack of a whip from the corridor outside and Rica limped to the doorway and took in the scene.

'The Serpenti,' Viktor said, when he saw Rica, 'set them on her.'

As she descended the altar with Irena cradled in her arms, Tallulah saw Viktor grab Serpenti and point at Adelaide.

Della, run.

But Adelaide did not move; she was transfixed by the enormous creatures. The Serpenti were almost upon her.

'Della!' Tallulah screamed with all her might and was rewarded by Adelaide turning to look at her. But the eyes that met Tallulah were not glazed or hypnotised or even fearful. They were eyes full of sadness and betrayal and heartbreak.

What?

I shouldn't be here. I'm not worthy. Sasha has been laughing at me all along.

Tallulah realised what was happening. *Saskia is in your mind. Don't listen to her. Get away from the Serpenti; from Rica.*

Tallulah's attempts to communicate with Adelaide were thwarted by other voices in Adelaide's head – voices turning her against Tallulah.

'No!' Tallulah yelled. Turning her fury on Saskia and the girls, Tallulah battered them with as much mental anguish as it took to knock them to the ground and put them out of action. Turning back to Adelaide, she saw her friend double over as she was released from Saskia's misery, but in that moment a Serpenti lunged. Before he could get his hands on Adelaide, the whip cracked and wrapped around his arms. He howled in pain, bounded away and wrapped himself around one of the front corner pylons so tightly that the marble cracked and that side of the room began to collapse.

The screams came from everywhere as fire leaped all around them, bricks and stone and dust fell. Tallulah could no longer see Adelaide.

Della?

When Tallulah could not reach Adelaide's mind she called for Sasha: *I've lost Adelaide.*

But the fight Sasha was in was all he could concentrate on. *I think she's run to the courtyard. I hope.*

Tallulah hoisted Irena on her back and headed for open windows. She knew the creature who led the Serpenti was now focused on her. She threw every mental trick she had at him but it did no good. Nothing distracted him from his target. Tallulah felt like she was running into a tidal wave. It got harder and harder to breathe. She looked up and tried to focus on the purple light and the goddess but there was only the battle in the forest of her dreams. A battle the Cirkulatti was losing. She'd lost Adelaide and Rica. The strongmen were facing the giant bear-men – the one in her dream had friends – and it was not going well. She couldn't reach the minds of Mai or Hui and fear struck her heart. The purple light shimmered in front of her and the goddess appeared, but the image was weak and Tallulah had no strength left to bring it forth. Of course, she was not yet the eminence that Theodora had been.

The Serpenti leader grabbed her from behind. Her feet flew from under her, Irena slipped from her shoulder and Tallulah slammed into the ground on her back. The creature picked her up, opened his mouth and she saw his great dripping fangs.

'I don't want her harmed!' Viktor screamed at the Serpenti. The creature closed his mouth reluctantly but did not take his eyes from her throat.

'Let Tallulah go, Viktor!' a woman screamed.

Tallulah struggled under the Serpenti's great hand and saw Marie de Clevjard came towards them in a dance-cum-run, twirling a spear all around her body.

'What do you hope to achieve, Marie?'

But before Marie could reply, a bear-man knocked her to the ground. He plucked the spear from her and drove it straight into her heart.

Tallulah vomited on her captor. There was an image in her head as vivid as any vision: Marie guiding her through handstands and walkovers she created purely with her mind. Her purple conduit was already stretching to the ends of her fingers and toes and, despite the battle and the losses and the fear, her core was a renewed, angry, blazing fire. Taking all that despair and whatever magic she still had left inside her,

Tallulah screamed and drove explosive energy into the mind of the enemies around her. The Serpenti and the bear-man slumped where they stood.

The fight in the forest hippodrome was over. Viktor and Saskia were nowhere to be seen. The castle was in flames and it seemed those who had survived had run. Sirens could be heard in the distance. The eminence was calm, but somewhere on the fringes of her mind, Tallulah was frantic.

She looked for Irena's body and found her nanny crumpled a few metres away. Her heart cracking anew, in the name of her dearest companion she chanted, *Oh night, faithful friend of mysteries; and you, golden stars and moon, who follow the fiery start of day; and you, Hecate* …

'Lu, are you all right?' said a familiar, breathless voice.

She opened her eyes, turning to see Tom's worried face looking into hers. 'Tom? What – You're alive!'

'Yes; barely. But we've got to get out of here now.'

'Where did you—?'

'Time for questions later. Can you walk?'

She nodded and looked back to see the castle engulfed in blue flame. She looked back at Tom. '*Your fire*. You found it?'

'Right on time.' He grinned. 'It's not far down the hill,' Tom told them. He grabbed Tallulah's hand. 'Come on.'

EPILOGUE

It was when Tallulah actually felt warmed by the sunlight streaming in through the train window that she realised they must be getting close to their destination. The previous forty-eight hours had been a blur of mini-vans and trains as they moved through countries, avoiding curious authorities, towards Italy and the woman Brigitta had told them was the best of the Cirkulatti healers.

Tallulah would get Irena the help she needed; the team would recover. Brigitta, Stellan, Jacek and Ursula would gather the best people for the jobs that had to be done. And in a short time, Tallulah would convene the first Cirkulatti Council in centuries.

She opened her eyes – the last thought was too overwhelming to contemplate with them closed – and saw her friends beginning to stir. She wondered how long they had until they arrived in Ravenna, the Italian town by the sea. She looked down to the backpack she'd been leaning on, expecting that it would be hers. But it was Mai's leather bag. She looked to the other side of the seat, but her bag wasn't there. She ignored the twist in her chest and turned to Irena. 'I don't suppose you've seen it?' She stood and patted each side of where Irena sat looking at nothing.

'Seen what?' Tom said, opening one eye.

'My backpack.'

He sat up, yawned and looked beside him and under his seat. 'Mine's here,' he said, pulling it out. 'But no one else's.'

'Maybe I put mine down here,' Tallulah said, crouching. No. By this time Hui, Mai and Adelaide were all awake; if she hadn't felt so sick with the thought of losing her backpack – and its precious cargo – she might be amused by the impromptu game of train-Twister they were playing.

When it was certain that her backpack was not in the carriage Tallulah groaned and sat down and put her head in her hands, trying to think.

'I had it when we got on in Trieste. Sasha asked me if I was OK and if I was …' she lifted her head and looked at the others '… keeping the cuff safe.'

The group looked around the cabin, each coming to the same impossible conclusion as they realised that Sasha was nowhere to be seen.

Tallulah stared out the window, desperately hoping to hear the sound of Sasha's footsteps. But there was nothing to be heard in the compartment but the sound of her own breath and the *clickety-clack* of the train, taking them towards an uncertain future.

ACKNOWLEDGMENTS

I'm lucky to have a wonderful circle of friends and colleagues who helped bring *Inheritance* to life.

I might not have written fiction again if my trusted friend and editor, Belinda Bolliger, had not been in the position to coax a new synopsis from me. With Belinda's departure from HarperCollins, Tegan Morrison took on the story of Tallulah and her friends with great enthusiasm; Tegan's patience and support as I created a fantastical world for the first time was invaluable. Thanks also to Kate O'Donnell, Kylie Mason and Chren Byng for helping to sculpt a big manuscript into the action-adventure I was going for.

For the day-to-day marathon of writing this book I am indebted to Joe and Anna Polifroni at the Crown Street Grocer – as well as their staff and regular morning customers. When I was having trouble with the story I took up a 'desk' at the Groce, every morning at 6am, week after week, month after month, and received endless encouragement – not to mention the best coffee on Crown Street. Thanks to Giuseppe for always anticipating when I would need the next macchiato (balanced by the occasional peppermint tea!).

Thanks to Maria Teresa Rizzo, who organised my visit to the National Institute of Circus Arts when I knew little more about *Inheritance* than it was a story set in the circus, and to Jane Davis, who took time away from her newborn baby to offer her expertise. Jane's Circus Monoxide base, in Fairy Meadow, provided all the inspiration for what a circus space *should* look like and what Cirque d'Avenir did *not* when Tallulah first arrived.

Thanks to my writing gal pals, Catherine Moffat, Sharyn Bennett and Anne Rimer for reading and re-reading many drafts and offering great advice, as well as Mark and Marie Tredinnick (and the Cowshed classes) for getting me started.

Mostly, I wish to thank my husband, Jess, and my son, Dex, for being the best storytelling-partners-in-crime a girl could ever have. *Inheritance* would not be story it is without Jess pushing me to honour the grand scope of the Cirkulatti I'd invented, and Dex's endless conversations about magical powers, baddies, battles and snakes.